CRYSTAL LOPEZ

Silencing Sofia

To my wife, Savannah: For every form of love you have shown me, and for being the one who refused to let go when I didn't believe in myself. You saw the end of this journey before I even took the first step.

To our son, Aspen: Our greatest joy. You are the "why" behind every word.

This is for the two of you. My world, my heart, my home.

Crystal

A note to the reader:

Silencing Sofia is a story that explores profound themes of trauma, survival, and finding your voice. As a lesbian and a survivor of sexual assault, it was important to me to write a sapphic romantic suspense novel that handles these topics with the nuance and respect they require. Please be advised that this book contains sensitive subject matter which are handled with care and are strictly not glorified. For a complete, detailed list of content warnings, please visit my website at **www.authorcrystallopez.com**

Prologue

TRANSCRIPT OF 911 CALL

DISPATCH: Gillespie County 9-1-1, what is the location of your emergency?

CALLER: (Young male voice, hyperventilating) We're… I don't know the exact address! We're on the back road between Fredericksburg and Mason. Uh, Ranch Road 783 I think? We just passed the country club gates a few minutes ago. We saw something on the side of the road and stopped.

DISPATCH: Okay, sir, take a breath. What did you find?

CALLER: It's a girl… it's a lady. She's in the ditch. Oh my god!

(FEMALE VOICE IN BACKGROUND): (Hysterical screaming) Tell them to hurry, Luke! They need to hurry! I think she's dead! (Continued hysterical crying)

DISPATCH: What is your name, sir?

CALLER: Sarah, stop! (To Dispatch) Luke, Luke Allard. She's not moving. I don't think she's breathing.

DISPATCH: Okay, I need you to get close to her. Look at her chest. Is it rising and falling?

CALLER: (Scuffling sounds of gravel, heavy panting) It's… I don't know, it's jerking. It sounds like she's snoring or gurgling. She's so cold ma'am. (Yells to female voice in background) Sarah! Get me the blanket from the back!

DISPATCH: Help is coming, Luke. But I need you to start CPR right now, what you are hearing is agonal breathing. Do you know how?

CALLER: I… yeah. Yeah, I was a lifeguard last summer. I know how.

DISPATCH: Okay. Put the phone on speaker and put it next to you. Get your hands in the center of her chest. Push hard and fast. Start now.

CALLER: (Straining) One, two, three, four. Come on. Come on, wake up! One, two, three, four.

(FEMALE VOICE IN BACKGROUND): (Sobbing uncontrollably) Oh my god. Luke, help her, please help her!

DISPATCH: Keep going. Don't stop. Tell me what you see.

CALLER: (Voice breaking between compressions) She's been beaten… really bad. Her whole face is swollen… her eyes are swollen shut. There's blood everywhere… it's matted in her hair and all over her face.

DISPATCH: Stay focused on the compressions.

CALLER: Her neck… oh god. It's covered in bruises. Dark ones. Like handprints. I think she's been strangled. God, who would do this?

(FEMALE VOICE IN BACKGROUND): Is she breathing yet? Luke!

CALLER: No! She's not waking up! (Grunting with effort) Come on! Stay with us! You can do this!

DISPATCH: You're doing a great job, Luke. Don't stop. Keep that rhythm going.

CALLER: (Crying now) Why isn't this working?! Damn it, come on! Wake up!

(FEMALE VOICE IN BACKGROUND): Oh my god, she moved! Her leg just moved!

CALLER: (Gasping) Whoa… wait. (Silence for three seconds) She just gasped. It sounded wet… like a gurgle.

DISPATCH: Is she taking air in now?

CALLER: Yeah. Yeah, but it's really shallow. It's barely there. But her chest is moving.

DISPATCH: That's good. Stop compressions. Don't move her head. Just stay right there with her.

CALLER: (Voice trembling, soft) I've got you. I'm right here. You're safe now, okay? We're not gonna leave you.

(FEMALE VOICE IN BACKGROUND): (Voice sobbing) Who would do this to her? Who would leave her like this?

(SIRENS WAILING IN THE DISTANCE)

CALLER: Oh, thank god. I see the lights. I see them coming down the road.

DISPATCH: Okay. Wave them down. You saved her life, Luke. Stay on the line until they get to you.

CALLER: (To female voice in background) Sarah, wave them down! Make sure they see us! (Choked whisper) She's messed up so bad… god. I hope she lives. They are pulling up now, thank you for your help.

[CALL DISCONNECTED]

1

Chapter 1

Monday morning was already a disaster.

Sofia was late for the Gunthers' appointment, and the clock was ticking down like a bomb. She had promised to bring coffee from her new favorite spot, The Peach and Bean, but at this rate, she'd be lucky to arrive with her sanity, let alone beverages.

"If I drop my keys again, I'll lose it." She huffed, frustration seeped into her voice as she slid into her favorite cardigan, the mustard-yellow fabric enveloping her like a cozy embrace.

She grabbed her well-worn brown leather tote, a trusted companion that bore the scuffs and stories of countless adventures, and headed out. She fumbled with her keys, finally managing to lock the door behind her.

She hurried down the narrow stairs, pausing only briefly at the landing. Through the glass of *The Floral Frame*, her beloved photography studio, the delicate prints in the window usually made her swell with pride. It had taken years of savings and a leap of faith to bring this dream to life. She remembered the way her father had put her very first camera into her small hands, his weathered hands gently wrapping around hers. "Capture what others can't see," he'd encouraged. That moment was seared into her memory, one of the many stepping stones that had led her here. Today, however, there was no time for pride... or memory lane.

The Gunthers were her biggest booking of the season, and she couldn't mess this up. Jane Gunther was the closest client to a "Socialite" she had booked, and word of mouth alone could really give her the push she needed.

With her calendar filled for months ahead, excitement bubbled within her. "See you soon." She smiled at the room, then pushed out the main door onto the street.

The day was cloaked in gray clouds that pressed down on her like a deadline. A cold breeze whispered around her and coaxed her to snuggle deeper into her cardigan. The wind whistled, blowing her long brown hair into her face. As she turned right onto Main Street, the scent of freshly brewed coffee already drifted through the air. With each step, her dark brown boots echoed in staccato rhythm against the uneven cobblestones.

"Hurry, Sofia." Her breath puffed in the frosty air. "Great first impression. You can do this. You *need* to do this."

She made it the block and a half without falling on the uneven cobblestone, which felt like a feat in itself. She felt a wave of relief, but when she looked up to open the door and saw the line of people already forming, her shoulders slumped.

"Crap."

With her heart still racing, she plunged her hand deep into her tote bag, looking for her phone, fingers brushing against crumpled receipts and makeup she had long forgotten.

Suddenly, her keys slipped from the wide outer pocket, clattering against the white marble floor and drawing the attention of nearby patrons.

She bent down, her cheeks warming with embarrassment. As she bent down to snatch them up, she felt eyes on her. She glanced up, her gaze landing on a few onlookers, mostly men, whose eyes lingered a moment too long. It was a sensation she had mastered ignoring. Yet one particular gaze stopped her.

A woman in a tailored navy suit, with a crisp white shirt peeking from beneath, stood out like a beacon of light. Her curly blonde hair was pulled back into a tight, almost military-like bun and her light olive skin glowed against striking ocean-blue eyes that sparkled with intrigue.

For a heartbeat, their eyes locked, a silent exchange crackling in the air. She stood up quickly, her cheeks burning, and focused intently on the counter, desperate to hide her sudden awkwardness. She opened her phone and pulled up the note with the Gunthers' coffee orders, the screen illuminating her face in the crowded cafe. She sketched each order carefully into her mind, ready to roll off her tongue.

A few minutes went by, and the busy sounds of the coffee shop became louder. When it was her turn to order, she flashed a brief, hurried smile, "Hey there! I need a large Raspberry Cream Cold Brew with extra cream, a large Dirty Chai, a medium White Mocha, and a kids' chocolate almond milk."

The cashier rang her order up, repeating it back at lightning speed, her voice bright and cheerful, almost dizzying as it raced past Sofia's thoughts.

How much coffee do they drink before their shifts?! Sofia mused as she tapped her credit card against the machine and gave her name for the order.

She scooted out of the way, allowing the next person in line to step up to the counter. She promptly pulled up the Gunther family's number and typed out a short message to let them know she was picking up their drink order. She sent the message and then pulled up TikTok, letting the vibrant colors and sounds distract her from the morning rush around her.

Soon after, she heard her name being called for her order. She blindly walked forward to retrieve it, entranced by a video of cats leaping onto crinkling aluminum foil, the peculiar sound and airborne felines making her giggle under her breath as she struggled to pull her focus away. Reaching out instinctively, her fingers wrapped around the cool, plastic cup, but before she could grasp her order firmly, she felt a warm hand slide gently over hers, sending a shiver up her arm.

Startled, she looked up, breath catching slightly as her wide eyes met those mesmerizing ocean-blue eyes that had captivated her earlier. The vividness reminded her of sunlight dancing on tranquil waves. She knew she should pull away or say something… anything… yet it was as if time itself had frozen, leaving her suspended in the moment.

As she fumbled for words, a buttery smooth voice reached her ears. "Are we sharing a coffee this morning?"

Her eyes slowly made their way down to the lips that spoke, taking in the delicate, soft pink curve of the stranger's mouth, which transformed from a teasing smirk into a warm, inviting smile that seemed to pull her in even more.

Sofia shook herself, heart fluttering. "Excuse me?" She

pulled her hand from under the stranger's grasp.

"Well, you grabbed my drink, so I assumed we were sharing." The beautiful blonde's voice was smooth... so smooth.

"Oh, uh," Sofia stammered, completely taken aback by how stunning this woman was up close. "I... I didn't mean to. I heard them call my name and assumed it was mine. I... I was watching cats and foil."

CATS AND FOIL?! she screamed in her head, the absurdity of her own words echoing in her mind, *YOU SERIOUSLY SAID CATS AND FOIL?!*

"Cats and foil, huh?" A playful glimmer danced in the stranger's gaze. "That has to be a first."

"No, uh, I was... ugh. Nevermind." Sofia's fingers nervously brushed against the counter as a warm rush of embarrassment flooded her cheeks.

"I mean, it does sound interesting," the beautiful stranger drawled, her voice slow and smooth as she watched Sofia grab her actual order and whirl around. "It was nice to meet you anyway! And I'm Allie... if it matters!"

Allie's chuckle lingered in the air as Sofia fled toward the door.

She ran back into the cold, the chilly breeze shocking her senses. She turned back to steal one last glimpse of this strange woman, who completely mesmerized her. There was no way she could walk back in there, though... too shy... too embarrassed.

"Cats and foil." She rolled her eyes, quickening her pace toward the studio.

Time to focus, Sofia.

But even as she ran, a blush prickled her cheeks as she

replayed the missed opportunity in her head. *Why hadn't she said something? Anything?* The memory of their almost accidental eye contact, the way the other woman's smile had played seamlessly in her eyes… it all seemed so significant in retrospect, now that the chance was gone.

"Well," she muttered, a pang of regret twisting in her gut. "You're never going to see her again."

2

Chapter 2

Allie watched Sofia leave, feeling a twinge of disappointment in her chest. She had never felt such an immediate spark like the one ignited by this beautiful brown-haired woman. The thought that this electric moment might have just slipped out the door made her heart palpitate. It was a feeling she hadn't allowed herself to indulge in for years, a vulnerability she had carefully guarded against.

She had been dedicated to her career for a long time. She focused on her professional goals and ambitions, leaving little room for distractions. But Sofia... with her nervous laughter and mysterious hazel-green eyes had somehow managed to slip past her guard, reawakening a longing she had suppressed long ago.

She reached for her Pecan Cold Brew and turned to exit, but something small and white caught her eye under her shoe. Curious, she bent down. The quiet buzz of conversations around her receded into background noise as her fingers glided over the smooth surface.

It was a business card.

The front was snow-white, adorned with delicate wildflowers that whispered around the card's edges, as if framing the center. At the heart of the card, elegant lettering proclaimed:

The Floral Frame
  Sofia Flores
  512 Main St
  Fredericksburg, TX
  830.530.3131
  hello@thefloralframe.com

Her fingers moved smoothly over the card as she turned it over, revealing a small square photo of a woman with a beaming smile. Beneath the image, the words read: "Your story deserves a beautiful frame."

It was her. It was the spirited whirlwind who almost stole her coffee.

A smile slowly crept across her face, heat spreading through her core as her mind drifted back to the unexpected encounter that had just transpired.

In that moment, she finally knew her name. Sofia. A beautiful name for a gorgeous woman. She tasted the name, savoring its sweetness upon her tongue, "Sofia."

Her thoughts strayed to the hypnotic beauty of Sofia's almond-shaped hazel eyes, her honey-toned skin and her dark windswept hair that looked effortless even in its disarray. She was utterly captivated, enthralled by the memory, until the shrill ring of her cellphone penetrated the air and pulled her back to reality.

Startled, she clumsily reached to retrieve her phone from her pants pocket. It was her boss, Michael. The sound of his voice buzzed with concern as he checked in to make sure she had arrived in Fredericksburg last night and had everything she needed for the morning meeting.

She let him know that she was completely prepared as she swung open the cafe door. A blast of brisk air grazed her cheeks. She slid the business card into her suit pocket, where it sat like a burning secret against her hip.

* * *

Allie stretched in the stiff leather chair and glanced at her smartwatch. The bright digits shimmered 7:15 p.m.

The conference room was thick with the scent of stale coffee, but she savored the bitter aroma. It stood as a reminder of what a grueling day it was.

She was thankful for her job and the opportunities it presented. She felt a deep sense of accomplishment for the effort she put into her new role as the Head of Operations for Victory Edge. It was a dynamic, rapidly growing sporting goods brand and leading it hadn't been an easy journey.

Decades of hard work, of sacrificing personal time for professional advancement, and of pushing past setbacks had finally led her to this point. There were times when the loneliness had been almost unbearable, despite her attempts to maintain a social life. The extended hours, the missed events, and the constant pressure to succeed had taken a toll.

She stood up and walked to the floor-to-ceiling windows. This was the newest and most modern building in Fredericksburg, and the quaint downtown extended before her. The busy sounds of tourists were muted by the glass, but she chuckled softly as she spotted a couple staggering down the road. Their cheeks were flushed and carefree after indulging in too much of the local wine.

For a second, she felt a hollow ache in her chest. She touched her pocket and felt the sharp edge of the business card through the fabric.

The ambiance shifted as the footsteps of thirteen colleagues resounded through the room. They were returning from their short break. Allie turned to the growing crowd at the table and masked her exhaustion with practiced ease.

"You ready to finish this out?" Her voice was mellow and authoritative. Each word carried a subtle confidence that commanded the room.

Tired responses came from the group as she took her seat and flipped the projector back on. "Alright then. Let's bring this home."

* * *

Fifteen hours and they were finally done.

The doors opened, releasing the group into the dimly lit hallway. A wave of relief poured over them as they each stepped onto the tile. Quiet chatter rose up, a blend of tiredness and the comfort of the day being done.

Allie navigated around the table, gathering empty wrappers and discarded cups. She tossed the refuse into the trash with a gentle thud before retrieving her suit coat. Just then, the last gentleman paused at the doorway, the faint illumination throwing a comforting glow around him.

"Great job, Allie, I'm really impressed." His voice was kind with sincerity.

A smile played across Allie's face. While pride unfurled

slowly within her, a flood of exhaustion engulfed her, and she couldn't muster much enthusiasm. "Thanks. That means a lot."

He returned her smile before heading out the door.

It was almost midnight.

Allie stepped out into the refreshing night air. The subtle sounds of country music drifted from a rooftop nearby. She peered at her phone, where the late hour glowed starkly in the darkness. She started walking toward her hotel, which was just a few short blocks away.

The crisp wind blew against her face as she closed her eyes to soak it in. She was proud of the progress they had made today. She told herself that the hard work and the sacrifices were worth it.

But as she walked underneath the glow of the street lights, her hand slid to her pocket. Her fingers grasped the small card tucked safely inside. She traced the edge of it and let the memory of the morning flood over her.

Usually, she would push a moment like that away. She would file it under distractions and move on to the next task. However, tonight the memory of those hazel eyes didn't feel like a distraction… they felt like an invitation.

A soft hope fluttered inside her chest. It was a feeling she hadn't recognized in a long time. She took a deep breath and let the night air fill her lungs. For the first time, she wondered if all her careful plans had left a quiet emptiness, a yearning for connection she was finally ready to let in.

3

Chapter 3

The alarm broke the morning silence at 7:00 a.m. and ripped Sofia from the best dream she had had in years.

She groaned and buried her face into the coziness of her pillow. The remnants of the dream still held onto her like the heat from a summer night, and she closed her eyes tightly. She was desperate to slip back into that momentary world where a pair of ocean-blue eyes were smiling just for her.

"Noooooo." Frustration rose as she kicked the cool sheets. She rolled onto her back and glared at the textured ceiling. "Why? Why wake me up when I'm finally having a dream I want to stay in?"

"Who are you talking to?"

The voice, laced with amusement, jolted Sofia out of her reverie. She screamed and grabbed her knitted throw to her chest.

"Cami! What are you doing here?" Her heart surged from the sudden collision with reality.

"Um, I'm *always* here?" Camilla stood at the foot of the bed. Her young and carefree spirit was a clear contrast to the sleepy morning light.

The strong aroma of freshly brewed lattes floated from the kitchen. It was Cami's favorite drink, and she made it often. At twenty-one, her little sister was constantly seeking refuge in Sofia's loft to escape the loving but suffocating orbit of their mother.

"Okay, spill." Cami bounced onto the plush bed. "Who were you talking to and why were you saying no?"

"No one. I wasn't talking to anyone. I just… didn't want to wake up." Sofia wiped the sleep from her eyes.

"Ohhhhh, were you having a naughty dream, *cochina?*" Cami giggled and swatted Sofia with a fluffy white pillow.

Sofia laughed. It was a warm sound that filled the room as she grabbed the pillow back. "Maybe. It wasn't sexual exactly." She paused, and the air became heavy with the memory of the woman in the navy suit. "But I'm not sure it has to be. She just does something to me."

Cami straightened up. Her playful pout vanished, replaced by shark-like curiosity. "Who? Are you seeing someone you haven't told me about?"

"No, *hermanita.* I ran into this girl yesterday at the coffee shop, and I can't get her out of my mind." Sofia hid her face behind the pillow to mask the blush rising on her cheeks.

"Does this girl have a name?"

"I… I think she yelled it out as I was running away, but I was so embarrassed I didn't catch it."

Cami stared at her for a moment before she flopped down next to Sofia and burrowed into the knit blankets. "Tell me everything."

Sofia beamed. She glided her fingers tenderly through her little sister's hair and told her about the collision. She talked of the voice that sounded like music and the eyes that looked like the ocean.

When she finished, Cami sat up with a sudden burst of energy and tossed the sheets aside.

"Get up!"

"What? Why?" Sofia searched for her pink slippers.

"Because we," Cami announced as she strode toward the closet with frightening determination, "are going to the coffee shop to find this girl. And you need to dress it up."

"Cami! No!" Sofia's stomach knotted. "Do you know how mortified I was yesterday? She probably thinks I'm a total freak for running away without saying a word."

Cami's head popped out from behind the closet door. "That is exactly why you have to go and show her that you're not. Now get dressed."

Clothes began flying through the air. A blouse landed on the lamp, and a pair of jeans hit the floor.

"By the way, your closet is depressing. It needs an overhaul."

Sofia picked up a black tunic from the pile. "My fashion is fine. It's me, earthy and boho."

"It's mournful," Cami corrected as she flung a handful of black fabric aside. "You dress like you're at a funeral for your social life. We need some color! Some *life*!"

"I wear black to be professional!"

"You need *personality* in here, sis! Here." Cami emerged holding a maroon bodysuit with a sweetheart neckline and a flowing, floral maxi skirt. "This is you. Sweet, colorful, and it'll make your boobs look amazing. Wear the good push-up bra, Sissy. The girls need a lift."

"My boobs do not need a lift."

But Sofia took the clothes. She walked over to her

dresser, which she had refinished herself with delicate floral wallpaper and blush paint. She opened the top drawer and dug to the back until she retrieved a pale pink lace bra she hadn't worn in ages.

She slipped it on and checked the fit. She had to admit that the lace did make her feel different. It made her feel softer and more feminine.

She pulled on the maroon bodysuit and the skirt. She wrapped a brown belt with gold accents around her waist and turned to the floor-length mirror. A content grin spread on her face. She didn't look like the frazzled mess from yesterday. She looked... ready.

Cami appeared behind her in the reflection. "Damn, sis. You look good."

Sofia nodded, feeling a rare burst of confidence. "This is as good as it's getting. Now for the hair."

"And makeup!" Cami sprinted to the bathroom.

Sofia kept it simple. She applied a touch of autumn-hued eyeshadow to make her hazel eyes pop and a muted lip stain that looked inviting without trying too hard. She misted the air with her favorite body spray, Victoria's Secret "Pure Seduction," and stepped into the cloud of plum and vanilla.

"You smell edible," Cami said as she checked her smartwatch. "It's almost 8:30. What time were you there yesterday?"

"I was running late, so probably around 8:45." Sofia grabbed her tote and keys.

"Okay, let's hurry. That gives us a few minutes to find a place to sit and—"

"Hide."

"No... we aren't hiding. We are getting comfortable and

observing."

Sofia rolled her eyes, but she couldn't stop the laugh that escaped her lips. She locked the apartment door behind them. "I can't believe I let you talk me into this. You know I don't date. What if she's married? What if she's straight?"

Cami linked her arm through Sofia's and dragged her down the hall. "You aren't going to know unless you go. And I'm not letting you pass this up, Sofia Elena Flores. Besides," Cami grinned, "I want to see if this girl is actually as hot as you say she is."

"Oh, so this is about you now?" Sofia chuckled as they walked out into the brisk fall air.

"*I'm* just providing quality control," Cami retorted.

Sofia shook her head. Her heart was hammering in a frenzied rhythm. She was terrified of seeing the woman again, but as they walked down the street, she realized she was even more terrified that she wouldn't.

4

Chapter 4

The wind fought them for the door.

Sofia and Camilla pulled against the weight of the large white wood, struggling against the sharp gusts that tangled around them. As they finally walked inside, the warm air encircled them in a soft embrace. The full scent of cinnamon, pumpkin, and roasted coffee hit them instantly, strengthening the feeling that fall had truly arrived.

Camilla giggled. The sound was bright and airy against the cafe noise. "Oh my gosh, that wind is insane!" Her cheeks were flushed pink from the chill outside and the rush of the struggle.

Sofia nodded, but she couldn't speak. Her pulse vibrated a fierce rhythm which drowned out the chatter of the room. Her eyes immediately scanned the shop and searched for Ocean Eyes. A wave of anxiety flowed over her. Just recalling the way those mesmerizing eyes had looked into hers unfurled a tender ache deep within her chest.

Maybe she did want to see her after all.

She slowly absorbed the busy cafe as they walked toward

the counter. Her gaze flitted over the scattered tables and took in each guest. Natural light poured in through the large, ornate windows, casting over the trendy grey velvet couches tucked into the corners. They were cozy and romantic little hideaways where people chatted or tapped away on laptops.

She sought out the face that made her breath falter, but she wasn't here yet.

Okay, good, she thought with a flutter of relief. *I have time to grab a couch in the corner and watch her come in first. It'll allow me a moment to pull it together so I don't come off as a bitchy lunatic again.*

They placed their order. Sofia chose her Raspberry Cream Cold Brew, which had quickly become a favorite, while Camilla ordered a Caramel Latte topped with billowing velvety cream foam. Sofia added a freshly baked raspberry scone and paid for them both.

Nervously, Sofia fidgeted with the edges of her cardigan as they waited for their names to be called. Her eyes flitted to the door in anticipation. She was extremely eager for the moment when the blue-eyed stranger would finally appear.

When her name was called, the sound jolted her. She darted forward to snatch their drinks and the scone, then hurried back to the small couch in the corner. It was a private realm amid the cafe's energetic buzz.

"Geesh, sis." Camilla settled beside Sofia with humor dancing in her expressive eyes. "Calm down. You look like a spazz."

Sofia met her sister's gaze briefly before taking a deep breath. She sank into the plush material of the couch and placed their drinks down. She took a small nibble of the raspberry scone and let the sweet-tart flavor explode with delicious freshness upon her tongue.

"I'm nervous, *hermanita*. I don't know if I'm more nervous for her to show or not to show."

"She'd better show." Cami stole a bite of the buttery scone before settling comfortably into the corner of the small couch.

Sofia glanced down at her smartwatch, where the floral pattern of the silicone strap peeked out from around her wrist. She let out a small sigh.

9:32 a.m.

"It's been almost an hour, Cami. I don't think she's coming."

Cami sat up a bit. She looked away from the shining screen of her phone and paused a message she was typing to their sister Isabella. "Don't give up, sis. Maybe we can wait a little longer. I'm not in a rush since I have zero life right now." She looked back down and hit send.

Sofia's sight rested on her little sister, whose feet were folded beneath her knees on the small couch. Cami's delicate features shone with a gentle radiance that reminded Sofia of their mother's youthful beauty.

Sofia looked away. Her thoughts floated back to the crystalline eyes she hoped to see again. A wave of longing came over her as she wondered whether this chance would slip away too, or if fate might grant them another moment. She kept a constant and hopeful watch on the door while they talked. Her sight flitted over the white wooden furniture and the fresh greenery of potted plants. Her stomach fluttered every time the door handle turned.

She took a sip of her cold brew. The ice had melted slightly, but the deep, tangy notes still played on her tongue and refreshed her as she leaned back within the embrace of the couch. She raised her phone to scroll through emails while the screen's blue light reflected in her nervous eyes.

"Oh." Cami's voice bubbled with enthusiasm. "Isabella said you'd better find this girl. In her words, she said 'Tell our sister that she better plant her ass on that couch until this girl shows up because she needs some damn action!'"

Sofia rolled her eyes as a playful smile blossomed on her lips. "Y'all act like I'm the 40-Year-Old Virgin."

"I mean…" Cami teased. "You don't have that much longer to go, sis."

Sofia jabbed Cami in the ribs, and laughter twirled between them. "Fourteen years is a long time! Don't age me *hermosa!*" She glanced down at her watch again. The digits glowed like tiny stars that mocked her. "It's almost 10 a.m., sis. There's no way. I think it's time to pack it up."

"Can we just give it until 10:30? Please?" Cami's eyes were wide and brimming with sincerity.

Sofia let herself fall back into the cushions and shrugged. "Sure. I don't have any shoots this morning, so I guess it doesn't hurt to relax here a bit longer."

Cami nodded with her fingers racing across her phone again. "And go get another scone… that was really good."

Sofia grinned and stood. *It was delicious,* she thought as she savored the excuse to stay just a little longer.

Another thirty minutes slipped by. They were busy with laughter and the latest gossip from Cami's young life, but the door kept stubbornly closed to the one person Sofia wanted to see.

Suddenly, the sharp ring of Sofia's watch pierced their chatter.

10:30 a.m.

She looked down, and her heart throbbed in her chest while she pressed END to silence the alarm. She lifted her gaze to scan the busy cafe one last time. A trace of hope tried to ignite, but her spirit fell.

Ocean Eyes wasn't here.

The stranger who had aroused such a longing deep down inside her would become just one more fleeting memory and another missed chance.

"Wow." Cami tossed the empty scone wrapper into a nearby bin. "This place is really busy for being this late in the morning."

"Yeah." Sofia's voice was quiet. "Can't blame them. I love this place."

She picked up her cardigan and wrapped it around her shoulders like the gentle embrace she desperately needed. She grasped her keys and moved toward the door. Each step weighed down by the heavy pain of regret.

She reached for the handle when a spark of awareness dawned on her. She had left her phone on the couch.

Turning slightly, she called out over the noise of the espresso maker. "Cami, grab my phone, I—"

Her words wavered as she collided with a warm body entering through the door.

The impact was solid and sudden. Her hand reflexively flew up to steady herself against a firm chest as her breath faltered in surprise. The vivid scent of cedar wood and sea air filled her senses.

She turned quickly with apologies tumbling from her lips. "I'm sorry! I—"

But as her gaze met theirs, the words froze upon her tongue.

She found herself submerged in a calm sea of crystalline blue waters, radiating with golden sunlight. Those eyes were unmistakable.

It was her. It was Ocean Eyes.

5

Chapter 5

Allie rushed down the chilly road. The cold air bit at her cheeks while she hurried to the warmth of the local coffee shop. She was hoping to grab a coffee before heading back home to Austin, and her body moved urgently as she realized she was running late after sleeping in. Her eyes were still heavy from fifteen hours of grueling meetings and a restless night spent in yet another transient hotel room.

As she opened the heavy white wooden door, a rush of heat encompassed her. She paused to hold the door for a woman hurrying out. The lady flashed a grateful smile and said, "Thank you" in a sweet Texas drawl.

Allie turned to step inside, but she was abruptly stopped by a collision. A hand pressed firmly against the middle of her chest, warmth radiating through the fabric of her shirt.

Allie's breath stopped as her hands instinctively grasped the person's waist. As she looked down, her pulse pounded through her body. Glistening in a field of mossy green were those same stunning eyes from yesterday. Flecks of golden light shimmered within them.

It was Sofia. It was the beautiful stranger who had haunted her dreams all night.

A slow and deep smile unfurled on Allie's lips as realization washed over her. Her hands lingered on Sofia's waist, where she felt the plush cashmere of her cardigan. A thrill rippled through her. The simple touch triggered a heat that had nothing to do with the coffee shop. Her fingers clenched slightly and almost possessively as she watched Sofia's lips freeze mid-apology.

The atmosphere between them pulsed with tension. Their eyes were enthralled by the depths of one another, drawing them further into a maze of silent want. They stared into each other's eyes for what seemed like an eternity. The world surrounding them faded before Allie finally broke the silence.

"Hi," she breathed. A tender smile lifted the corners of her mouth.

Sofia stuttered as she searched for her footing in the intensity of Allie's gaze. "Uh, hi. Hi there." She steadied herself but didn't pull away. Her gaze flickered down to her own hand, which was still resting on Allie's chest. "Oh my gosh, I'm so sorry. I wasn't paying attention, I—"

"I'm not," Allie interjected smoothly. Her voice was breathless.

She watched Sofia's chest rise and fall. She watched the way the light from the window caught the honey tones of her skin. She had been beautiful yesterday, but today she was radiant.

Sofia steadied herself. Her gaze never left Allie's as she nervously whispered, "I don't think I am either."

Allie's breath trembled. A sudden flutter ignited in her chest. It was a new and exciting feeling that completely caught her off guard. She stuttered and knew she couldn't let Sofia walk away again. "Would… would you like to have coffee with me? You can make it up to me then."

Sofia beamed softly, and hope sprang up in her expression. "I'd like that."

Suddenly, a high-pitched squeal broke the moment. A young woman rushed up, and her sneakers skidded across the marble floor. She cleared her throat loudly right next to Sofia.

Sofia jumped and turned. The newcomer's wide eyes shone with curiosity as she took in the evident electricity between the two women.

"Oh uh… this is my sister Camilla." Sofia glanced at Camilla; her voice was scarcely audible.

"Little sister," Camilla offered with an impish smile. "And it's nice to meet you…" She paused, her gaze expectantly fixed on Allie.

Allie snickered softly. She appreciated the bright energy that radiated from the girl. "My name is Allie. Allie Mackenzie."

"Nice to meet you, Allie!" Cami beamed, then slowly turned to look at her sister. She gave her a playful nudge with her elbow.

Sofia snapped out of her daze. "Oh! Uh… I'm Sofia. Sofia Flores." A timid smile crept across her face.

"It's really nice to meet you both. Are you joining us for coffee, Camilla?" Allie's eyes were bright with warm friendliness.

"No, no." Camilla's voice was light and airy. "And it's Cami. Everyone calls me Cami."

Allie gave a small nod. "Cami, it is then. What would you

like, Sofia? I can go get it ordered for us."

"Just a Diet Coke, please. I just had a cold brew while I was waiting for you and…" Cami quickly jabbed Sofia in the ribs again.

Sofia jolted from the sudden poke, her cheeks flushed pink.

Allie's eyebrows rose in surprise. *Waiting for me?*

"I mean… I already had too much coffee today, so a Coke would be magical." Sofia's voice sank to a mortified undertone.

"Alright." A knowing smirk formed on Allie's lips as she turned toward the counter. Her mind replayed the slip. *Waiting for you.* Her heart fluttered. *Could she have wanted to see me again as much as I wanted to see her? "And it was nice to meet you, Cami."*

Shaking off the unanswered thoughts, she approached the counter and ordered their drinks. The barista's cheerful voice beeped through her focus as she paid.

She watched as Sofia hugged Cami quickly. The cold air pricked at the door as Cami rushed out and vanished into the brisk morning. Allie picked up the drinks and saw that Sofia had found an empty table bathed in warm light shining through the large cottage-style window.

It was an intimate nook tucked away from the main crowd. A small chandelier sparkled above the table like a constellation. In the center sat a stack of vintage books topped with a ceramic cup blooming with wildflowers. It was the perfect place for their story to begin.

Allie walked toward the table with an effortless confidence she didn't quite feel internally; her heart was still racing from the collision.

Sofia looked up as she put her phone on silent and slid it

into her tote. Her eyes swept over Allie's distressed leather jacket and ripped denim. There was a hunger in Sofia's expression that softened her features. She looked at Allie as if she were the only source of light in the room.

Allie reached the table and set the drinks down with a soft clink. "Here's your Diet Coke," she said as she extended the frosty glass toward Sofia.

She pulled out the mismatched chair opposite her. The soft scrape of wood against the floor hardly registered in the backdrop of her thoughts. While she settled in, Allie smiled brightly. She let the warmth of the moment envelop them. It felt preordained. It felt like a moment she had been waiting for forever, just like time itself had conspired to bring them right here and right now.

6

Chapter 6

Allie set the cold brew and Diet Coke onto the round table, her gaze taking in the quaintness of the space before landing on Sofia. Sofia's long eyelashes fluttered slowly as she gazed back.

A wry smirk pulled at Allie's lips as she slid the Diet Coke across the wood. "One Diet Coke. Since you already had a coffee while waiting for me."

"Oh, um, I…" Sofia looked at Allie's mischievous expression and her heart throbbed. She offered a sheepish grin. "You caught that, huh?"

Allie nodded, her smile deepening, a trace of mischief in her eyes. "I did." She watched Sofia as she fidgeted nervously, her gaze lingering on Sofia's lips. "You're cute, you know that?"

Sofia's cheeks reddened. She fumbled with the straw, suddenly fascinated by the condensation forming on the glass. Why was this woman having such an effect on her?

She mustered up the courage as she cleared her throat and looked up at Allie formally. "Thank you. You aren't so bad yourself."

Allie's laugh was low and warm, causing a shiver down Sofia's spine. "Thank you."

"So, what was this cats and foil thing you were talking about yesterday?" Allie swirled her coffee before taking a drink.

Sofia rolled her eyes teasingly, "You just had to bring that up, huh?" Allie laughed as Sofia smiled. "It was a stupid TikTok I was watching… it was literally cats jumping onto tinfoil. I guess there's something about it they don't like because they were springing into the air and smacking into things." Sofia laughed as she finished explaining herself.

Allie joined in her snicker, "No way, that does sound pretty funny."

Sofia took a long sip, the icy soda a pleasant contrast to the heat spreading through her. "Maybe I'll show you one day."

"Hmm," Allie's voice was playful but serious. "I might hold you to that."

Sofia felt her cheeks flush again. She looked at Allie, noticing the small freckles that danced delicately across her cheeks and nose.

"So you're in town visiting?"

"No," Allie leaned forward a bit. "I'm in town for work. My job is in the process of opening up a large warehouse here, so I have to come in once or twice a month for meetings to get things up and running."

Sofia nodded, listening. "Oh wow, that has to keep you busy. Where do you work?"

Allie told her about her job at *Victory Edge* - the tireless travel, the long hours. Sofia listened intently, watching Allie light up as she talked about the position she had worked so hard for and where she wanted to go in life.

"It sounds like you're pretty amazing." Sofia's voice was genuine and tender. "Your work ethic is something you should be proud of for sure. I don't even know you well, and I'm proud of you."

A gentle feeling, almost like butterflies, stirred in Allie's stomach, a feeling she wasn't used to. She paused, looking into Sofia's warm hazel eyes, seeing truth and gentleness there.

"Thank you," she spoke quietly. "I think we should always work toward being proud of ourselves. But enough about me, tell me about you. Aside from being a drink stealer and clumsy."

Sofia laughed, though she was a bit flustered. "Well, those are my two best traits, but if you must know more…" They both snickered. "I love photography. It's not just a hobby, but my passion. When I'm feeling down or angry or well… anything… I just take my camera, head out to a country road, and snap some pictures of whatever I find beautiful in that small moment."

She paused, engrossed in thought as the sunlight shone through the window, catching her eyes and making them sparkle like mossy green quartz.

Suddenly, Allie's smooth, low voice fractured the silence. "I think *you* are beautiful in this moment."

Sofia slowly turned her eyes to Allie, her breathing speeding up as she took in the seriousness on Allie's face. The gaze held her captive, a wordless command that made her feel like she would follow her anywhere. Somehow, Allie managed to make Sofia feel vulnerable yet strangely excited.

"I… I love flowers. Peonies and wildflowers are my

favorites… and thank you," she breathed.

"So, tell me something someone wouldn't know just by looking at you," Allie challenged, her eyes twinkling with a teasing glint.

Sofia's brow scrunched playfully as she considered the question. "Hmm. Well, every fall I volunteer to help plant over thirty thousand wildflower seeds along the Texas highways," A hint of pride radiated in her voice. "It's one of the reasons Texas is known for its beautiful roads in the spring."

Allie moved in, her gaze roaming over Sofia's face. "Honestly? I think I might have guessed that." A teasing smirk hovered on her lips.

Sofia's laughter echoed through the coffee shop, warming Allie from the inside out. *Yeah,* she thought, *I could definitely get used to this.*

They continued chatting about life, asking questions, their connection becoming stronger with every passing hour. Allie's playful flirtatiousness kept the air light, but there was an intense undercurrent radiating between them. Allie's confidence was a visible force, a magnetic field that drew Sofia in and made her feel like the only person in the room. It was a heady mix of desire and vulnerability; neither wanted the moment to end.

Suddenly, Sofia's watch vibrated on her wrist. The subtle hum pulled her from the intoxicating conversation that had enthralled her for hours. She glanced down - **3:00 p.m.** glared back like a neon sign.

"Oh crap."

"What's up?" Allie inquired.

"Oh, nothing bad," Sofia's breath seized as she remembered

her schedule. "I have a shoot in an hour that I need to start preparing for. It shouldn't last too long, though, maybe an hour, if you'd like to hang out afterward?" Her speech quivered, a hint of nervousness dancing on the edges. She didn't want to look overly eager.

Allie glanced at her own phone, sitting face down on the rustic table. "Oh wow, it's three already? Time really does fly when you're in the right company."

Sofia smiled, warmth spreading through her chest as she locked eyes with Allie. "Yeah, it does. Don't feel obligated, though. I just—"

"I'd really like to keep this going," Allie interjected, her voice a low, sultry croon. "Can I call or message you in a couple of hours to make plans?"

"Yeah, that would be perfect," Sofia said, grabbing her tote, fingers sliding against the distressed leather as she reluctantly stood. A hesitant wave of anticipation coursed through her. "I'm sorry, I have to run. I totally forgot I even had a shoot today."

"You don't have to apologize, Sofia," Allie's voice was soothing. She glided over, pulling Sofia's chair out with a smoothness that brought them achingly close… only inches apart now. The air became heavy, charged with electric energy.

"I'm really glad I saw you today," Allie murmured, the invitation in her tone seizing the essence of the moment.

"Me too," Sofia's heart fluttered as she felt the heat of Allie's body near hers. "I wasn't sure I would."

Allie inhaled deeply, her breath faint as she shifted slightly, regaining her composure. "Wanna know a secret though?"

"What's that?" Sofia cleared her throat, regaining some of

her own composure.

"I was planning on stopping by your studio before I left." A semi-nervous smirk added playful tension to the air.

Sofia's head cocked slightly, interest sparked. "How would you have even known where my studio was?"

Allie chuckled as she retrieved a small floral business card from her pocket and handed it to Sofia. "You dropped this yesterday. I like the name. *The Floral Frame.*"

"Oh!" Sofia laughed, surprise spilling over. "That is crazy! Maybe we would have seen each other regardless then. What a small world."

"Or fate," Allie replied with a lighthearted grin.

"Or fate." Sofia's heart skipped a beat. The possibility of something exceptional lingered around them.

Allie helped Sofia slip her cardigan over her shoulders, then grabbed her own snug leather coat and slipped her phone into her back pocket. With a gentle push, she led Sofia to the door, holding it open as the cool breeze tickled their skin. They paused outside, locked in an intimate moment that danced between lingering and the call of reality.

Allie smiled, catching Sofia's gaze. "I'll see you soon."

Sofia nodded, her eyes shimmering. "See you soon." The silence twirled around them, humming with wordless possibilities that filled the space between their words.

Leaning in, Allie embraced Sofia, breathing in the soft, intoxicating fragrance of her delicate perfume, longing to taste the softness of her full, beautiful lips, but hesitant to cross the fragile boundary that existed.

They held each other for just a second longer, and when they pulled away, the tension hummed, enveloping them like static, igniting small, dancing sparks of anticipation.

"Bye for now," Sofia's voice was permeated with longing as she turned to leave. "I look forward to talking to you again… soon."

Allie watched her walk away, her ivory cardigan swirling against the brisk breeze and her floral maxi skirt fluttering like vibrant petals. Allie drew her leather jacket tighter, fumbling with the zipper, her eyes drawn back to Sofia's brown hair dancing in the wind.

Damn, she thought, a sweet pain of admiration settling in her chest. *She's incredible.*

A sharp gust of wind knocked Allie back into reality. She stood there, each breath filling her lungs with sharp freshness. She had planned to leave today; the appeal of avoiding rush-hour traffic usually tugged her. Yet, her heart hesitated. She didn't want to miss the chance to spend more time with Sofia. She wanted to sit in her presence, feeling the warmth emanate between them, to watch her lips as they danced animatedly while she spoke, the taste of her sweet laughter lingering in the air. Each twinkle of Sofia's eyes drew Allie further in, the accounts of her family and friends building a beautifully rich story of her life.

Home just didn't sound as enticing as it had earlier. The usual comfort of her own space was now diminished by the thought of missing out on this.

With that, Allie pulled up the calendar on her phone, the screen glowing in the early evening light. She scanned through her work and social plans for the evening and tomorrow. She had a work lunch scheduled, and her stomach knotted slightly at the thought. It was a movable commitment, and the rest could be managed from anywhere with a decent connection. She paused as thoughts of Sofia's sweet laughter again lingered in her mind.

She pulled up the hotel's number and listened to the repetitive beeping as the phone rang to the front desk. She was extending her stay tonight, accepting a decision that was nearly foreign to her… she wasn't putting work first.

7

Chapter 7

Sofia finished her session, a contented smile adorning her lips as she thanked the family for their business. She waved goodbye as they exited the studio, the weight of her camera growing heavy around her neck.

She sat on her pastel pink velvet rolling stool, a welcome comfort after the session. She admired how it harmonized with the floral patterns decorating her space. Shifting her focus back to her calendar, she searched for the date two weeks ahead - October 31st .

"Halloween already?!" Her voice had a hint of disbelief as she jotted down *"Emerson family photos due"* with a flourish, before returning her pen to a mason jar bursting with dried petals.

The large front window, embellished with intricately patterned floral glass prints, cast radiant rainbows onto the floor. Above, lush floral arrangements tumbled like vibrant waterfalls, creating a breathtaking frame that fit the studio's name perfectly: *The Floral Frame*. At the far end, pastel-colored frames embraced the walls, resembling a whimsical puzzle.

The walls were a pristine white, with the largest wall holding an array of fabric and paper backdrops, each roll bearing a new adventure.

Sofia's love for rehabbing old furniture allowed her to show her most beloved piece, an intricate, large white dresser that stood prominently against one wall, an array of her best work forming a stunning collage of memories, blended with small vases holding fresh blooms on its top. Above it, a TV quietly played a slideshow of families and couples she had taken, bringing to her mind countless smiles and beloved moments.

As she viewed her little studio, a burst of pride swelled in her chest. It was a beautiful expression of her journey, where every carefully selected piece contributed to a breathtaking vision that was undeniably and beautifully hers.

Her phone played a little bell toll, announcing a text message. She pulled it out of the snug, black, slim-fitting pants that she changed into before her session and tapped the message from an unfamiliar number. As she read the words, a smile lit up her features.

"Heya, Sofia, it's Allie. Still up for hanging out tonight? I'm available whenever you are. Oh, and save this number."

The message ended with a cheeky winky face that made Sofia chuckle under her breath. She leaned forward on the counter, excitement beaming from her. *"I might save it... depends on how this evening goes. I'm just finishing up at the studio. Where did you want to meet?"*

She stood up to switch the wall monitor off, but before she could take a few steps, the bell tolled again, ringing out sweetly, calling her back. She snatched her phone from the cool countertop and read the text:

"I'm actually right down the road at The Peach & Bean, decided to do some work here for good internet. I can walk down and meet you there?"

Her heart fluttered, nerves bubbling up. *Oh my God,* she thought, her thoughts spinning. *She's going to come here.* Frantically, she scanned the studio. Thankfully, it was spotless. She texted back: *"Sure, do you need the address? I'm about a block and a half away to the west."* Hitting send, she dashed around, adjusting decorative items that didn't really need it, her pulse racing.

Her phone sounded again. *"I have it... business card, remember? On my way."*

Inside, she was screaming, nerves sparking like fireworks. *Why am I so nervous?! You're acting like she's coming up to your bedroom!*

Rushing to the full-length mirror in the dressing area, she checked her appearance. She wiped away a tiny speck of mascara and smoothed her messy bun before striding toward the door.

She reached the muted blue wooden door with "The Floral Frame" engraved in the glass. Peering out, her heart skipped a beat at the sight of Allie's intoxicating smile gliding toward her. With a flutter in her chest, she opened the door.

"Hi," Sofia's voice was bright with enthusiasm, "Welcome to my studio!" She swept her arm wide, inviting Allie inside.

Allie paused a few feet into the studio, her eyes wide as she took in the decor. "Wow," Her voice was full of genuine awe. "This is amazing, Sofia. It's beautiful in here."

Sofia felt her chest flutter again at the compliment, a warm feeling spreading through her. "Thank you. I put a lot of love into this place."

"I can tell," Allie's gaze paused fondly around the room. She looked back at Sofia, still standing at the closed door, a mutual smile lighting a spark of connection. "Thank you for letting me see it."

"Thanks for coming to see it," Sofia smiled. "It's always nice to have a fresh look at it." She stepped forward, momentarily pausing in front of Allie. "Would you like to sit at the desk until we figure out what to do?" She led Allie to the counter that doubled as a desk, pulling out a chair with a flourish. Sofia glided behind the counter, settling onto her faithful pink stool, the metal squeaking lightly beneath her.

"Okay," Allie looked at Sofia perched on the stool, "That stool looks like it has a story… you have to tell me about it."

Sofia laughed, the sound bright and contagious as she twirled playfully. "This old thing? Not much of a story, but I can make one up for you." They both laughed, the air around them humming with anticipation as their evening together unfolded.

* * *

They were both totally unaware of the time that had flown by as they sat at the desk talking. It was so easy for both of them to get completely wrapped up in their conversation that time just swept by.

Sofia's stomach rumbled, making her pause. She checked the time. "It's getting kinda late. Did you just want to order something for delivery?"

"Yeah, that sounds good. What's good around here?" Allie felt the first pangs of hunger herself.

Papers were heard rustling as Sofia searched through her

desk drawer, looking for some delivery handouts she had shoved in there some time ago. "There really isn't a whole lot of options around here, but if you like Vietnamese food, there's an amazing fusion restaurant that delivers."

Allie felt her stomach rumble again at the thought. "That sounds delicious. Let's do it."

As the food arrived, Sofia finished setting up a comfortable little spot on the floor for them to eat. A pile of large pillows created a nest, illuminated by the warm radiance of flameless candles nestled around them.

It somehow reminded her of the scene from Sixteen Candles where Jake and Samantha sit on the table, the candlelight casting light on their faces, cozy and intimate.

They sat down, their stomachs in a contest for who would rumble the loudest, as the smell of the food saturated the air.

"Sofia, this looks absolutely amazing," Allie's eyes glazed over as she looked at the pork fried rice, crispy spring rolls, jalapeno cream cheese wontons, and the best-looking orange chicken she'd ever seen.

Sofia took a long breath, inhaling the mixture of smells coming from the food, "Mmmmm, it smells sooooo good," she crooned, taking her first bite.

* * *

As they finished dinner, their jovial banter continued effortlessly. Sofia refilled her cup with more Diet Coke. "So, tell me about your family," she inquired gently.

Allie looked down at her cup, swirling the ice cubes. "It's just my parents and me," her tone was carefully neutral. "No siblings, no huge family gatherings. A pretty quiet childhood, actually."

"And your parents?" Sofia leaned forward slightly, her eyes full of affection and reassurance.

Allie hesitated, a shadow drifting over her face. "They're... good people," she took a slow breath before selecting her words with care. "Hardworking, successful. But not exactly... warm and fuzzy." A wry smile brushed her lips. "We're not the type to have heart-to-hearts, you know?"

Sofia nodded, sensing the unspoken longing in Allie's voice. "I understand. My dad passed away when I was young, so it was just my mom and my two younger sisters. We were... and still are... really close. We had to be, I guess." She shrugged. "It made us who we are."

"I'm really sorry about your dad. It sounds like y'all made the best of it, though. I always wished for that kind of closeness."

"It isn't always easy, but the love and support... I wouldn't change it."

Allie nodded, drawing patterns on the condensation of her glass. "I love my parents, don't get me wrong. But sometimes I wish... I don't know... that we had more. That I could talk to them about things, you know? Like real things. Every conversation we have is based around my career; they are so proud, and they tell me that, but anything else, like... life... it's never a discussion."

Warmth covered Allie's hand as Sofia reached over and placed her hand over hers. A calm silence rested between them, the unsaid understanding hanging in the air.

"So where do you see yourself in like five years?"

Allie's expression lit up. "Career-wise? I'm going to go as far as I possibly can. Work my ass off and not only climb that ladder but break every single ceiling down."

"I love your ambition." Sofia was sincerely impressed. "What about like… personally?"

Allie's expression eased. "Like kids?" Her voice swelled with a longing that surprised even herself. "I definitely want kids. I love them. But…" Her eyebrows knitted a little. "I'm terrified of messing it up. Of being like my parents."

Sofia squeezed her hand reassuringly. "You won't be. You're already so self-aware… so gentle. You'll be an amazing mom one day."

"Thanks." Allie's heart glowed because of Sofia's genuine belief in her. "What about you? Marriage? The whole white picket fence dream?"

Sofia laughed warmly, "That obvious, huh? Yep, I want it all. The falling in love, the proposal, the dream wedding, kids… all of it. I want to build a family filled with love, trust, laughter and understanding. The kind of home where everyone feels safe, supported and that they will always be welcomed home regardless of the reason."

Allie watched Sofia's eyes light up under the candlelight as she talked about her future dreams. "The dream life," she smiled. "You'll have that one day, I can see it."

* * *

As the skies grew dark into a rich indigo and the full moon poured silver beams through the large studio window, they continued to explore each other's hopes and dreams, their fears and vulnerabilities. With each joint moment, their connection intensified.

Allie felt her phone buzz insistently against her thigh,

interrupting their reverie. She pulled it out, the screen alit with the picture of her best friend, Dylann, a familiar female face that delivered comfort even from afar. Holding up a finger to Sofia, she mouthed "one sec" before answering.

"Bro, where *are* you?" Dylann's voice faltered with urgency. "I've been waiting for you for hours now, and you haven't been answering your texts!"

Allie's brow furrowed in confusion. "I'm still in Fredericksburg. I decided to stay another night." She looked at Sofia, who wore a curious expression, fully unaware of the plan that had slipped Allie's mind.

"Why are you still in Fredericksburg? I thought you were supposed to be home this afternoon! I was waiting for you at seven like we planned." Dylann's tone was a mix of irritation and genuine concern.

"What?" Allie exclaimed, her voice climbing as a slow wave of realization started to hit her. "What are you talking about? Waiting for me where?"

"At Trudy's, bro. We said we'd meet up for drinks before hitting up those league players on Sixth Street tonight."

Allie cocked her head back, suddenly remembering their plans with the visiting softball league. "Craaaappp," She pressed a hand to her forehead. "Dude, I'm so sorry! I totally spaced on dinner tonight!"

"You okay, Allie? It's totally not like you to forget things."

Suddenly, Sofia coughed, a soft sound penetrating the mix of emotions surrounding them, and stood up with an apologetic smile. "I'll be right back." She headed towards the fridge tucked into the corner of the back room. "Do you want a drink?"

Allie shook her head, smiling warmly amid the turmoil of

her thoughts.

"Ooohhhh," Dylann said, feigning realization. "You're with a girl!"

Allie snickered nervously, still enveloped in the warmth of the moment. "Yeah, I guess I am."

"Well, dude, why didn't you tell me? Or text me to cancel or something! And when are you coming back? Please tell me you're coming back for the league dinner tomorrow night! I don't want to go alone."

"Yeah, I'll be back tomorrow. Just staying this extra night, it wasn't expected. She's just…she's worth it, Dyl." The softness in Allie's voice evident.

"Oh." Dylann sensed the change in Allie's tone, a hint of awe sliding into her voice. "Damn, bro, you're gonna have to fill me in soon." She knew this side of Allie was rare.

"I will tomorrow. I'll call you on the drive home."

"Alright, bro, see you tomorrow. And you better call me!"

"I will, I will. Bye." Allie ended the call and glanced at the time on her phone, her heart pulsing as she saw the clock ticking toward 11:00 p.m., her notifications blinking like fireflies against the dim light, an overwhelming reminder of existence outside this intimate moment. Sixteen text messages and three missed calls.

Time seemed to have melted away as they sat, lost in each other's company. Their shared laughter and conversation still remained in the air from hours before, filling the cozy studio with gentle warmth.

Sofia returned, carrying a small bottle of water. "Here you go, I didn't want to come back empty-handed," she said. Her smile illuminated the subtle shadows on her face as she sank back onto a plush, beige pillow.

"Thanks, that was my best friend, Dylann. I totally slipped that we had planned to meet up for drinks tonight."

"Oh no, I hope she's not too upset with you. I had no idea you were supposed to leave today."

Allie smiled sheepishly, fingers tucking strands of hair back into a ponytail. "Yeah, I was supposed to head back to Austin today but…" She paused, letting her eyes linger on Sofia. "Something I wanted to do more came up."

As Sofia's heart pulsated in response, her cheeks blushing a soft pink, her next words fell in a whisper, shyness causing her voice to dip. "I'm glad you stayed."

"I am too." Allie's fingers caressed Sofia's hand, sending jolts of electricity between them.

Sofia had the courage to look up, meeting Allie's captivating blue eyes. As their hands entwined, Allie moved in closer, shadows swaying on their faces.

With a heart that thudded like a drum throbbing in the stillness, Sofia felt a burst of emotions, thrill and tension intertwined. Allie hovered only inches away, the candlelight shining on the tension between them.

Allie gently cupped Sofia's chin, tilting her face upward, gaze fixed in a beautiful embrace as she leaned in, her lips brushing tenderly against Sofia's full, inviting lips. The world outside vanished as Allie sensed a flood of longing rise inside her, wrapping them both in an intoxicating warmth. Her arm slipped around Sofia's waist, pulling her close in a tender fusion of fresh passion as their lips came together in a tender yet passionate kiss.

Sofia's desperate fingers explored the contours of Allie's body, tracing the softness of her golden hair, every caress lighting a flame of desire. Allie's moan reverberated softly, laced with longing, as their kiss deepened, her tongue exploring Sofia's mouth with a sweet possessiveness. The atmosphere between them was a blend of innocence and hunger, as the laughter and worries vanished, leaving only the unmistakable air of connection.

Allie nurtured a deep passion running through her veins, a vibrant hunger to grab Sofia and place her beneath her, her hands itching to wander the soft curves and contours of Sofia's body, exploring, needing, craving every inch of her to keep for herself, but she knew that tonight was not that time. Not with her... Sofia deserved more.

Allie kissed Sofia deeply, a rich matrix of soft, velvety warmth mingling within their kiss. She gently pulled away, her gaze deep within Sofia's eyes, where the flame of passion flickered like a small bonfire in the dusk. She smirked lightly, planting another soft kiss upon her lips before nestling back into the plush fold of one of the many large, inviting pillows that cushioned them.

She gently pulled Sofia closer, feeling the silkiness of her hair brush upon her skin as Sofia nestled her head into Allie's chest, the coziness of their closeness wrapping them like a snug blanket. Allie leaned down and kissed her forehead, the soft thump of their heartbeats creating a soothing rhythm. Both of them lay in silence for a moment, their breaths slowing, the world around them fading into repose.

Sofia let out a small sigh, her body melting into Allie's arms, a dizzying heat spreading within her. She had never been kissed like that, never felt such electric passion, and she longed for it to last. "Wow," she uttered softly, her voice shaded with wonder.

Allie laughed, a sultry, low sound that encircled them as

she pulled Sofia in even closer, her fingers caressing Sofia's back, feeling the warmth emanate off her. "Yeah. That was... amazing."

They both chuckled in that moment of glowing light, Sofia gazing up at Allie, her beautiful face glowing from the dancing candlelight. She leaned up, connecting their lips once more, her lips lingering against Allie's, enjoying the tender heat. With a playful bite of Allie's bottom lip, she settled back against her still chest, embraced by her warmth.

Allie's breath faltered, a flood of warmth pooling in her belly, igniting a trace of desire running through her again. "Damn girl," she laughed, her voice suffused with both surprise and longing.

"What?" Sofia giggled, mischief shimmering in her eyes.

"You know what." Allie groaned, her voice a muted whisper. "You know I want you."

Sofia froze momentarily, a thrill pulsing from between her legs, causing her to exhale softly, a mixture of anticipation and new longing.

"I want you so badly," Allie confessed, her eyes tracing the detailed tin tiles on the old ceiling. "But I want this to last. I don't just want something quick with you. I don't know what it is, but everything in me is saying there's more to this. That it's deeper than just this."

Sofia nodded silently, her heart quivering in understanding, though unsure of how to express it. She felt the same sensation within her, a part of her that had suddenly come alive, as if she was being filled with light. She didn't know how to explain it; maybe she was crazy...but it was true.

They both lay entwined in each other's embrace, Sofia's head cradled perfectly against Allie's chest, the steady beat of her heart lulling her into tranquil contentment, while her arm lay draped gently across Allie's waist, both of them secure in each other's presence.

The passion that had found its way into their hearts remained in the air, thoughts of their hidden moments entwined in a tender dance within their minds. Slowly, they each succumbed to the soft pull of sleep, wrapped in a rare safety that neither had ever known before, their hearts beating together within the quiet of the night.

8

Chapter 8

The morning ebbed gently after awakening in the warmth of Sofia's studio. Sunlight shone through the wide front window as Allie pulled her close. Although her back ached from sleeping on the floor, Allie wouldn't have traded that intimate experience for the most luxurious bed in the world.

As Allie drove back to Austin, she finished up the few work calls she needed to make and dialed her best friend, Dylann, whom she imagined was still curled up in the softness of her blankets, the traces of sleep thick in her speech when she finally answered.

"Heeeyy," Allie drawled, her voice brimming with a playful lilt. "You still sleeping?"

"Yeah, but you know you're good." Dylann's voice was slow, full of sleep.

"I'm about halfway back to Austin. I have to stop at the office and sift through some loose ends before the weekend, but I should be home by four."

"Dude, I know you didn't call me to talk about work. Fill me in! Who is this girl? And did you..."

"Whoa, dude, no. We didn't get that far. This one's different."

"Oh yeah? Well, tell me about her then." Dylann leaned in, her inquisitiveness practically buzzing through the line.

"Well, she was in the coffee shop near the hotel. She dropped her keys, and we ended up making eye contact. I noticed her right away. She's gorgeous, bro." Allie kept her eyes on the road, but her mind drifted back to that moment. "I was just kinda watching her. I was feeling shy for some reason, but then she tried to grab my drink from the counter without looking. So I stepped in." A small smirk curved on her lips.

Dylann broke in with a small chuckle. "No way, what did you do?"

Allie laughed. "I put my hand over hers and asked if we were sharing drinks."

Both of them broke into laughter.

"And what did she do?"

Allie continued, her snicker infectious, "She looked at me like I'd just stolen her purse and then mentioned something about watching cats and foil."

"What the hell is cats and foil?"

"I asked her that yesterday. She said it was a TikTok video she was watching." Allie smiled, the memory sparking humor again.

"Man, you sure have a way with the ladies, Al." Dylann teased. "How did you manage to see her again if she ran off?"

"Eh, well, she accidentally dropped her business card." A mischievous smile crept onto her face. "I thought about stopping by her studio like a stalker, but she showed up at the coffee shop the next day, hoping to see me instead."

"No fucking way," Dylann's incredulity was obvious. "You're shitting me, right?"

"Nope, she even confessed it while we talked last night. We both admitted we were totally going to stalk each other." Her laugh rang out, light and playful, knowing that neither of them held an ounce of true stalker tendencies.

For the rest of the drive, they talked about Sofia. Allie recounted the little details, her desire to see Sofia again spilling over in every word.

"When do you plan to see her again?" Dylann asked curiously.

"I don't know. We haven't set up any plans yet."

Dylann paused, enabling the silence to encourage Allie to elaborate. "Well, dude, you better get on it. Don't let this girl pass you by."

"I won't. Not this one."

"Hey! Why don't you invite her to the Halloween party next weekend?" Dylann suggested, sounding hopeful.

Allie considered it, picturing the vibrant costumes and the energy of Sixth Street. "Hey, yeah, that's actually not a bad idea. If you're down, I'll ask her."

"You know I'm down, Al," Dylann affirmed earnestly. "I wanna meet this girl."

Allie felt a smile cross her face. "It's a deal then. I'll let ya know what she says when I see you tonight."

"See you tonight." There was an air of eagerness in her voice as she ended the call.

As Allie slowed for a red light, her mind sped. *Will Sofia want to come? Where will she stay? With me? Is it too soon?* She chuckled. *We are lesbians, but I'm definitely not a U-Haul lesbian.* The light turned green, and she stepped on the gas, focusing on the hope that Sofia would say yes.

* * *

Allie opened the walnut door to her townhome, the rich grain inlaid with striking black trim. A modern frosted window filtered daylight into airy shapes on the floor. The recognizable scent of her home, smelling of grapefruit, sea salt, and cedarwood, drifted out in a gentle welcome. Large windows adorned the twenty-foot back wall, letting bright sunlight spill in across the hardwood.

She looked around, her eyes gliding over the grey L-shaped couch with a crisp white throw folded carefully over one arm. Framed photos glimpsing fleeting moments with friends were artfully displayed on the tables, while verdant plants scattered throughout infused the space with life.

The kitchen was tucked toward the front, lined with gleaming granite countertops that sparkled under the sunlight. The chef's stove stood prominently amidst sleek walnut cabinets. Allie delighted in the contemporary style, softened by the warm wood elements.

Her favorite piece was the long rectangular dining table positioned between the living space and the kitchen island. It was a live-edge walnut table, the raw edges contrasting strikingly with the smooth surface. She loved to run her hands along it, feeling the rough patches, nature's artistry. Four Sungkai wood chairs wrapped in distressed leather straps surrounded it. The warm wood against the deep chocolate leather created a stunning visual. She was proud of that set; it was her first big purchase after her promotion, a representation of her hard work and independence.

She tossed her overnight bag onto the couch before she sank down to remove her shoes. As she stretched back into the sofa, she let her head fall back with a deep, relaxed sigh, the golden sun shining through the windows kissed her face with its warmth. For a moment, she let herself indulge in the blissful silence before the chaos of getting dressed for work.

Her fingers fumbled blindly in her pocket for her phone, reluctant to part from the sun's tender glow just yet. After a second of hesitation, she found Sofia's number and quickly tapped out a message.

"Hey, beautiful, just got home."

She hit send, a rare bubble of nervousness stirring in her stomach. She wrote again:

"A couple of friends and I are getting together this weekend for a Halloween bash. Would you be interested in joining?"

She hit send and held her breath.

Suddenly, the familiar movement of dots appeared. She peered at the screen, her heart racing.

The dots stopped. No message.

Then they started again. Allie waited motionless, her nerves growing every passing second, the silence weighing thickly in the air.

Despite her escalating anxiety, she couldn't look away from her screen... *What could she possibly be thinking?* The stillness persisted. No words appeared.

Just when she was about to put her phone down, it chimed.

"Hey there! Glad you made it home safely! I would love to come this weekend! Should I look for a room? And what are you going as?"

Allie let out a breath she didn't know she was holding, relief pouring over her. She hadn't even considered a costume yet;

her past attempts were so lackluster, she typically settled for something like a simple mask or a last-minute outfit.

Typing furiously, she replied:

"I'm okay with you staying here if you'd like. I have a guest room, or if you're not comfortable, I can get you a nearby room. As for costume.... no idea. I suck at costumes." Send.

With restored energy, she sprang up and climbed the modern stairs. Inside her closet, she selected a pair of heather grey twill suit pants, a black high-cut long-sleeve shirt, and a matching grey suit jacket that accentuated her figure. Slipping into a pair of black leather loafers, she tied her hair into a neat bun at the back of her head.

As she sprayed her cologne, its scent floating around her like confidence, her phone shrilled again.

"Hmm, I think the guest room sounds nice," the text read, followed by a flirty winky face. *"I might have an idea for a costume if you're open to it.... I have a Día de los Muertos dress I didn't get to wear last year, and I'm pretty good at costume makeup... are you down for being my skeleton side piece?"* A playful tongue emoji followed.

Allie grinned. *"Yeah, I think I'd be down for that. Let me know when you'd like to come in, and I'll send the address. Heading to work, so I'll text when done. xoxo."*

She hit send, excitement building. Sofia would be here with her this weekend, and her entire being hummed with anticipation.

9

Chapter 9

Sofia placed her suitcase into the back of her car, a custom blush-pink 2023 Convertible Beetle that sparkled in the golden sunlight. The car's curves projected a playful femininity, much like her own style. It was basically her, in car form.

Camilla helped her heave the garment bag, weighted with the velvets, sequins, and lace of her *Día de los Muertos* dress, into the trunk. "Ugh, you know I've always wanted to go down Sixth Street for Halloween!" she whined, her voice touched with longing.

Sofia closed the trunk with a gentle thud after placing her makeup bag in it as she turned to her sister.

"I know, little sis, but this thing with Allie is new, so I want to give it the space and energy it needs, and *your* crazy young energy around all weekend is not it." She laughed, playfully poking her sister in the ribs.

"Yeah, yeah, I know. I still might go with some friends tomorrow, but I don't know. I'm too poor to get a hotel room, and the prices are *so* high right now." Cami leaned a hip against the car.

Sofia nodded, "Yeah, I checked them out just in case. That's what happens in the city for big events!" she said as she walked to her car door. "Let me know if you decide to go, though. We can meet up or something."

Cami straightened up and walked over to Sofia, wrapping her arms around her in a tender hug. "Be safe, sissy. Have fun, and take lots of pictures… all the things."

Sofia pulled her tight, soaking in the familiar lavender fragrance of Cami's sweater. "I will. I love you."

Cami squeezed tighter before stepping back onto the grass. A calm breeze kissed her cheeks, making her wrap her sweater tighter around herself. "Oh, make sure to miss me and feel really, really bad for not bringing me," she teased, a smile beaming on her face.

Sofia rolled her eyes as she eased into the driver's seat, the leather chilly against her skin. "See you Sunday, *hermanita*."

She started the car, the engine purring to life. She could hardly contain herself at the thought of seeing Allie again. Their daily conversations had been like a tender melody playing on repeat, but now the eagerness to look into her eyes sent delicious shivers throughout her body. She glowed at the thought as she backed out of the driveway, giving Cami a final wave, the sun throwing a warm, gentle shine over the world around her.

* * *

The British accent of her GPS cut through the air. "In half a mile, turn left, and you will be at your destination on the right."

Sofia's stomach flipped with a combination of excitement and nerves at the realization that she was about to pull into Allie's driveway.

She did a quick check of her hair and makeup in the rearview mirror, catching the slight scent of her newly sprayed perfume hovering in the confined space. She checked her teeth for lipstick smudges, as she had reapplied in a hurried frenzy at the gas station, and swiped her tongue nervously across her lips.

Turning left, she spotted the glistening silver numbers on the side of the garage. She pulled into the driveway, carefully staying to the right as Allie had instructed. With a quiet click, the engine fell silent. Sofia fidgeted, gathering her belongings: purse, phone, charger, and a sweating drink in her hand.

"Okay, I'm ready," she exhaled deeply.

Her breath stuck in her throat when she saw Allie walking toward her from the open garage door. Allie's smile shone with warmth, the sunlight shining on her hair. Sofia let out a sigh, a powerful sense of comfort rushing over her as she opened her door.

Allie met her outside her car door, her touch gentle as she helped Sofia up while effortlessly taking her drink and purse. "Hi there," Allie beamed.

"Hey, stranger." Sofia smiled, leaning in to plant a quick kiss on her cheek, perceiving the warmth of Allie's skin against her own.

Allie wrapped an arm around Sofia's waist, pulling her close. She leaned down to capture her lips in a soft kiss, a whisper of sweetness lingering as she withdrew. "Glad you made it," her words cloaked in a welcoming, flirty smile.

"Me too, that traffic was a bitch. I despise I-35."

"I hear that," Allie agreed, pressing a kiss to her forehead. "Are your bags in the trunk?"

"Yep!" Sofia walked to the rear of the car and popped the trunk. "It's all here."

Allie reached in, bringing out the lavender suitcase and the square makeup case, while Sofia grabbed the sleek black garment bag.

"Is this everything?"

"It is," Sofia answered, grinning. "But you can roll that suitcase, you know."

"Well, that makes it easier," Allie laughed as she pulled the handle up and began to roll it up the driveway, the pulsating sound corresponding to the beating of Sofia's heart.

* * *

Later that evening, the restaurant buzzed with vibrant energy.

Dylann stretched, settling back in her chair, laughter streaming into the crowded restaurant like music, while she glanced playfully between Allie and Sofia. "Y'all have a hell of a 'How We Met' story already," she chuckled, her voice combining with the clinking of crystal and energetic conversations around them. "But I'm just happy to see my girl happy. It's pretty rare to see her serious about someone."

"Ohhhh," Sofia teased, the taste of the rich red wine remaining on her tongue, "you think she's *serious* about me??"

Allie beamed, her eyes sparkling like topaz gems inside the dim lights as she took a sip of her cold tap beer, the glass caressing her lips, and then turned her gaze deeply into Sofia's.

"Well, it's honestly still really early, *but* Allie doesn't just jump into relationships. She does quickships," Dylann laughed as she looked at her best friend. "NOT relationships… err… if this is a relationship."

Allie raised one eyebrow, her look unflinching. "I think it could be heading that way." She smirked, her eyes playing into Sofia's.

"Ooohhhhh!" Allie's good friend, Danika, squealed playfully, her mischief spilling out from her full, dark red lips, her glorious, dark halo of hair bobbing with every movement. "Look at that eye contact going on! I cannot wait to have eye contact like that with someone special!"

"They're probably playing footsie under the table," Dylann quipped humorously, her giggle infectious.

Sofia and Allie erupted, their chuckles fusing with the animated atmosphere as they both abruptly pulled their feet from each other under the table, a shared trace of mischief brightening the moment.

"Oh my God," Danika shifted her sight between the two, her speech dancing in the moment. "They totally were."

The entire table dissolved into laughter, a joyful orchestra that seemed to thread through the air, while Allie and Sofia remained lost in each other's eyes, the world around them fading into a warm blur.

* * *

Back at the townhouse, the night quieted down.

Sofia slipped into the ivory pajama set she had brought. The fabric was delicate against her skin, decorated with small ruffled edges and whimsical black eyelashes scattered across the pattern. The spaghetti strap top rested just above her navel, displaying her smooth skin, while the low neckline hugged her breasts. The shorts offered a teasing glimpse of her thighs, just short enough to toe the line between cute and absolutely sexy.

She pulled her hair back into a loose ponytail and brushed her teeth, the minty freshness invigorating her senses. After applying her moisturizer, she cast a critical glance at her image in the large mirror.

Drawing in a deep breath, she exhaled, trying to let the nervousness disappear, as the anticipation remained thick in the air. She wasn't sure what tonight had in store; her heart throbbed with a fusion of excitement and apprehension. She arrived at a crossroads, uncertain if she was ready for something sensual to unfold, yet totally curious with regard to the possibilities that could lie ahead.

She walked into Allie's bedroom and stopped, her breath stalling.

Allie was stretched on the bed, clad in tight-fitting black boxer briefs that hugged her curves and a simple white shirt that contrasted against her bronzed skin. Her hair was caught up in a carefree, messy bun. A chilled beer glistened in her hands while another sat temptingly on the nightstand. It was a simple outfit, but Allie's natural confidence made it incredibly sexy.

Allie turned her sparkling eyes toward Sofia, lips arching into a glowing smile. She extended an arm, beckoning Sofia to the bed.

Sofia's own smile blossomed, a mix of nervousness and excitement rushing through her as she walked forward and climbed up onto the bed. She leaned into Allie's warmth, taking the cold beer from her hand, the frosty bottle sending a refreshing chill up her fingers as she took a long sip.

The evening melted away, flowing into a cadence that felt entirely their own. They moved seamlessly from heavy, hushed confessions that uncovered parts of their pasts to lighthearted banter that had Sofia breathless in bursts of laughter. Allie seemed determined to break the tension with a series of terrible "dad jokes," every one earning a moan that eventually gave way to snickers until their sides burned and tears gathered in their eyes.

But as the laughter waned, the hush that followed wasn't empty… it was charged.

Allie's eyes grew softer into something more intense… something warmer. When their lips finally met, it wasn't just a kiss; it was a dialogue without words. The first press of their mouths was slow, a question asked and answered with intoxicating tenderness. Gentle hands roamed, memorizing the shape of one another through the friction of their clothes.

Soon, the tenderness blazed into something fiercer. The hum of the room was now only uneven breathing as the kisses deepened, becoming desperate and all-consuming. Hands tangled in fabric, pulling each other closer until there was no space left between them. They tasted the sweetness lingering on their lips, drinking it in… needing more.

It was a passion that didn't need to race toward a finish line to feel complete. It simmered in the resonances of their sighs and the worshipful caress of their fingertips, leaving them both deliciously intoxicated in the tender gleam of the moonlit room. They were content just to exist in this frenzy, savoring the overwhelming realization that this… *them*… was real.

Sleep eventually claimed them around three in the morning. Safe in Allie's embrace, Sofia buried her face against her neck, breathing in her intoxicating scent. The soft pressure of Allie's arm around her waist felt like a guard against the world, a wordless promise of protection that grounded Sofia.

10

Chapter 10

It was a beautiful early evening on Saturday as Sofia and Allie finished getting ready for the big Halloween bash down Sixth Street.

Sofia stood facing the mirror, applying the final touch of deep crimson lipstick to her precisely crafted *Día de los Muertos* makeup. She paused, taking in the stark drama of her image. The pale white of her face paint was offset by the deep, dark hollows of her cheekbones, the black eye sockets that extended to her brows, and the shadowed tip of her nose. It was a skull, yes, but a dazzling one.

A wave of pride came over her. She turned her head slowly, catching the sparkle of the jewels bordering her dark eyes. A large, ruby-red gem, like a drop of blood, sat centered on her forehead, surrounded by a constellation of diamonds.

Her beautiful dark brown hair, straightened into sleek perfection, fell down her back, seizing the light and shimmering like liquid silk. She smiled lightly at herself, careful not to smudge her handiwork, and turned to the dress she had waited two years to wear.

Halloween was a sacred ritual in her family, a tradition they prepared for almost half the year. This dress was a true labor of love, consuming nearly five months of her time. But two days before Halloween last year, her mom had suffered a small stroke and was hospitalized. The world had slanted on its axis. Sofia and her sisters had rushed to their mother's side and hadn't left it. Their mom was the heart of their family, and Halloween, like so many other things, had to be put on hold.

Now, finally, the dress was going to have its moment.

She stepped into the gown, the cool satin of the skirt murmuring against her skin. She shimmied it up, the internal black corset doing its job immediately, squeezing her in all the right places, cinching her waist, and accentuating the flare of her hips. Her breasts, full and high, swelled over the top of the corset, an impeccable fit. She carefully slipped her arms into the sheer black fabric of the sleeves.

She took a breath and admired the full effect. The bodice was formed from black velvet, curving into a low sweetheart neckline that dipped to a V in the back. The skirt, a cascade of deep red satin, adhered to her hips before flaring dramatically at the knees in a mermaid cut. Three layers of puffy petticoats created volume, ending in a small train that trailed behind her like a phantom.

Her favorite detail, however, was the cluster of five red roses, each with green leaves, painstakingly made from glass beads and sparkling sequins. They were arranged in a gentle curve on the sheer black mesh, flowing from her shoulder, down over her chest, and sweeping up to the opposite side. It was a masterpiece... *her* masterpiece.

She turned, admiring the way the dress hugged her curves,

making her feel sensual and powerful. She grabbed her floral crown and headed out of the bathroom to enlist Allie's help with the zipper.

She moved into the room, holding the back of the dress closed. "Can you help me with my—"

The words stuck in her throat. Allie was sitting on the bed, pulling on her black socks. Her eyes gazed on Sofia and traveled slowly, appreciatively, over every curve... from the flare of the red satin to the subtle rise and fall of her chest beneath the shimmering roses.

"You look amazing," Allie breathed, her voice laden with awe.

"Thank you." Sofia felt a blush flush her cheeks beneath the paint. "Can you help me with the back?"

She walked over and turned around, sweeping her long hair to the side. Allie's eyes rested on the graceful curve of Sofia's spine. She bent forward, pressing a tender kiss to Sofia's lower back. The unanticipated warmth of Allie's lips caused a shiver to race through Sofia.

Allie's kisses traveled higher, inch by inch, as she slowly pulled the zipper up. She rested at the nape of Sofia's neck, where Sofia angled her head, offering the space to her. Allie slid her hands around Sofia's waist, pulling her flush against her, and kissed her neck, a deeper , hungrier pressure this time.

Sofia let out a quiet moan, her eyelids fluttering closed as Allie's embrace tightened. Allie lingered there for a moment before fastening the delicate clasp at the top. She pulled back slightly. "You're done, gorgeous."

Sofia turned to face her. She noticed that Allie's once-perfect makeup was now smeared near the mouth.

Sofia laughed. "Hold on. I need to fix your lips."

"Crap. You distracted me. I totally forgot about the paint. I'm sorry."

Sofia walked into the bathroom and grabbed the black face paint. "You don't need to apologize; the kiss was worth it." She carefully reapplied the paint to Allie's lips.

She smiled, admiring Allie's haunting look that she finished earlier, which complemented her black suit and shirt perfectly. Her hair was styled back into a low ponytail, soon to be completed with the black fedora and cane they had picked up from the Halloween shop earlier that day.

"I think we are ready!" Sofia exclaimed, her excitement overflowing. "You look great!"

"I am *nothing* compared to you." Allie bowed, winking playfully.

Sofia chuckled and twirled, the full satin skirt rustling about her like a whisper of fire. She *felt* beautiful, confident, and ready to dominate Sixth Street.

* * *

Sofia and Allie loaded into Allie's sleek, black 2024 Jeep. The engine thrummed to life, and they headed toward the vivid chaos of downtown to meet Dylann and Danika.

For Sofia, Sixth Street was a hazy memory, a collage of flashing lights and pounding music. Her 21st birthday and a friend's bachelorette party had both been celebrated there, but her memories were scattered, lost in a sea of tequila shots and an overly sweet mixed drink whose name remained forever forgotten.

The drive was a slow crawl, the bumper-to-bumper traffic

proof of the city's vibrant nightlife. "This is insanity…" Allie said, her voice stiff with frustration as she surveyed the rows of cars on the highway, barely moving. The brake lights extended out before them like a river of red lava.

Sofia nodded, carefully holding her delicate floral crown on her lap. "Yeah, this is crazy. I've never seen traffic like this."

Allie let out a short, sharp laugh. "Traffic in Austin always sucks, but this… this is just stupid. Thankfully, we only have one more exit." She drummed her fingers impatiently on the steering wheel.

Sofia looked out the window, mesmerized by the illuminated buildings of the downtown skyline. Every street they passed pulsed with life. Music spilled out from open doorways, laughter resounded in the cool nighttime air, and costumed figures skittered among the crowds.

Finally, they managed to escape the highway and found a parking spot off Fifth Street in the Warehouse District. The sidewalks were packed with people hurrying toward the main event on Sixth Street.

Allie helped Sofia with her floral crown. It was a magnificent creation: a large wreath of deep blood-red roses that encircled the top of her head. Brilliant, sparkling golden "sun rays," studded with jewels that caught and refracted the street lights, radiated upwards, creating a halo of radiance around her face.

Sofia looked stunning, a celestial beauty that descended from some magnificent realm. A flood of pride swelled inside Allie. She took Sofia's hand, fingers intertwining, and led the way toward Sixth Street, feeling immensely proud to have such a radiant being on her arm. The music grew louder with each step, the bass thumping in their chests, an indication of the night to come.

11

Chapter 11

Sixth Street slammed into Sofia's senses like a roaring wave. She had braced herself for the chaos, but the sheer mass of humanity, a sea of over fifty thousand souls, was staggering. Her nose stung with the cloying sweetness of spilled cocktails, mingling with the pungent tang of cologne and the faint, unmistakable undercurrent of sour vomit that persisted in the air in the denser pockets of the crowd.

As they pushed their way into the throng, a jumble of shouted conversations, booming music from overflowing bars, and drunken laughter pulsated in her chest.

The sidewalks were a solid mass of pushing and pulling bodies, while the streets swarmed with thousands more. A kaleidoscope of ghosts, superheroes, and fantastical robotic beings, and, of course, the predictable hordes of scantily clad revelers, sexy nurses, cops, and a veritable army of Playboy bunnies.

But what Sofia hadn't prepared for was the sheer intensity of the attention. It was like being ensnared in a whirlwind of flashing lights. Every step they took, they were swarmed by people clamoring for photos; their faces were illuminated by the ceaseless bursts of camera flashes like crazed paparazzi at a movie premiere. It was exhilarating... a taste of celebrity... but utterly overwhelming.

Her head swiveled, trying to keep up with the voices calling to them, the constant requests for poses. At one point, they remained trapped for over thirty minutes, a stationary island in the human current, and as soon as one group finished their photo op and moved on, another would rush in to take their place; the cycle was never-ending. Sofia and Allie traded glances, a mixture of laughter, yet a touch of apprehension in their eyes.

Even amid the chaos, Sofia felt secure with Allie at her side. As they threaded through the crowd, the inevitable catcalls and unwanted advances from drunken men rang out around them. But every time a hand reached out to grab her, Allie was there, a protective barrier. Her voice stiffened into a sharp, "Don't touch her," her stare darkening as she pulled Sofia closer, shielding her from harm. Every instance of Allie's protectiveness caused a thrill through Sofia, a comfort spreading through her chest.

She had never felt so safe, so cared for, and the feeling left her a bit breathless. The press of Allie's hand in hers, the fragrance of her cologne, the sound of her voice filtering through the noise... all of it anchored Sofia in the midst of the whirling turmoil.

Allie and Sofia finally worked their way through the horde of costumed party-goers and slipped inside the bar where they were supposed to meet Dylann and Danika. It was a swanky establishment with fancy uplighting, the air dense with expensive perfume and fruity drinks.

Allie spotted Dylann first, dressed as none other than a softball player, complete with her team socks and signature backwards hat. Beside her stood Danika, transformed into a sexy bumblebee, her black-and-yellow stripes clinging to her warm chocolate curves.

Allie and Sofia pushed their way through the crowded room, making hand gestures and shouting above the booming music to get their attention. Danika's mouth dropped open when she saw them, her eyes expanding as she took in their costumes. She let out a high-pitched squeal of excitement.

"OH MY GOD!!!!! Y'ALL LOOK FUCKING AMAZING!!!" she screamed over the bass.

"THANK YOU!" Sofia yelled back, her throat already feeling a little raw.

Dylann grinned, giving them both a thumbs up. She reached next to her on the bar and handed each of them a shot glass filled with a golden liquid floating on top of a clear, flecked liqueur. She gave Allie a questioning look.

Allie downed her shot in one gulp, scrunching up her face. She leaned in close to Sofia's ear and shouted over the music, "It's a Pirate's Treasure! Captain Morgan on top of Goldschlager! It's not too bad, just a little strong on the cinnamon!"

Sofia's stomach jolted again. She'd only had Goldschlager once, and the memory of the fiery cinnamon liqueur and the subsequent nausea wasn't a pleasant one, but she needed something to loosen her up, to take the edge off the night.

She screwed up her face a little and tossed the shot back as quickly as she could, feeling the burn of the rum followed immediately by the intense heat of the Goldschlager. Her stomach did a little somersault, a wave of heat spreading through her chest. *Whew,* she thought, a small bead of sweat forming on her forehead.

Dylann laughed and grabbed another round.

"Oh God," Sofia laughed, accepting the second glass.

Dylann and Danika raised their glasses to the center of their little group, Allie and Sofia following suit. "To tonight being one hell of a night," Dylann shouted. "And to our new friend, Sofia! May Allie not scare her off because we are keeping her!"

"HELL YEAH!" Danika yelled. "She's ours now!"

Sofia laughed, feeling a warmth radiate through her, a feeling of belonging amidst the sheer chaos. They clinked their tiny glasses together and downed their shots. "Here's to tonight!!" Sofia yelled, raising her glass high. The cinnamon fire of the Goldschlager already starting to work its magic.

Four shots and a mixed drink later, the group spilled back onto the pulsating street. The crowd had swelled, a mass of costumed humanity, and keeping up with Allie, even with her hand firmly clasped in Sofia's, was a struggle. The press of bodies, the constant jostling, the smell of sweat… it was sensory overload.

They walked the length of Sixth Street, a slow, meandering journey through a sea of costumes. Between maneuvering the crowds, they were constantly stopped for photos. The flashes of cameras were unrelenting, but the warmth of the shots had loosened Sofia's inhibitions, making her feel carefree and adventurous. She found herself striking playful poses with strangers, throwing her arms around them, and laughing. Allie watched from beside her, shaking her head with a smile full of affection while she watched Sofia completely take in the madness around them.

Hours appeared to fade away as they walked, posed, and chatted with friendly strangers. But eventually, the heat from the alcohol began to wear off, and a more immediate need asserted itself.

Sofia pulled Allie close as they posed for yet another photo, this time with a cute young couple dressed as peanut butter and jelly. "I really have to use the bathroom," she uttered, the urgency in her tone barely masking the slight panic.

Allie nodded, her brow scrunching slightly with concern. She leaned in and whispered back, "Alright, I'll take you." She didn't want Sofia navigating it alone in her slightly inebriated state.

Sofia shook her head playfully. "No, no. It's okay, I'll just run into the club right here and be out soon." The music from the nearby bar pulsed through the open doorway.

Allie pulled back a little, her eyes looking into Sofia's. "No," she replied firmly, though her voice was gentle. "I'd rather go with you, just to make sure you're okay." There was a protectiveness in her inflection, a quiet insistence that Sofia had started to appreciate.

Sofia shook her head again, smiling. "No, I'll take Danika. She said she had to find one a bit ago. Can you and Dylann grab us a drink, though? We can meet at the bar in there." She glanced quickly towards the club as the bass from the music grew louder.

Allie paused, a trace of hesitation flickering over her face. She wanted to say no, to insist on going with Sofia, but she also didn't want to come off as possessive or controlling. She knew Sofia was capable, but a small worry still bothered her. Finally, she nodded, her brow still slightly furrowed.

"Okay, as long as Danika goes with you. What do you want to drink?"

Sofia grinned, leaning in to kiss Allie lightly on the cheek. "We won't be long. And get me one of those Pirate Booty drinks or whatever. They were good!"

Sofia shuffled over to Danika, who was swaying slightly to the music, and took her hand. "We are going to find the bathroom, girl."

"Oh GOOD!" Danika exclaimed, her voice bursting with relief. She grabbed Sofia's hand back, and they plunged back into the whirling mass of the crowd, disappearing into the throng.

Allie watched them go, a small frown still furrowing her forehead. She laughed quietly to herself. "Come on, Dyl. Let's go grab some Pirate Booties."

Dylann looked at Allie, a confused expression on her face as they started to follow the direction the girls had gone. "What the heck is a Pirate Booty??"

* * *

Sofia plunged into the overcrowded bar, the press of bodies a choking wave. She clasped her satin skirt in her hand, holding it up as best she could, while desperately trying not to lose Danika in the spinning mass.

The music was a booming roar, the sound shaking through the floor and rattling her teeth. Her own thoughts were hardly audible, a confused mass of impressions. The bar itself was dark and dingy, a place Sofia would never step in under normal circumstances. It spread across multiple rooms and levels, each pulsating with a different genre of music. There was no space to sit or stand, and simply moving was becoming a Herculean task.

They eventually reached the bathroom line, a queue of at least twenty people. Sofia's bladder felt like it was about to burst. There was no way she could wait that long.

Danika pulled her close, yelling into her ear to be heard over the music, "I think they have a bathroom on the third floor, wanna try there?"

Sofia nodded desperately. Danika turned and pushed through the crowd with increased determination, her small frame surprisingly effective at navigating it. They reached a dark, narrow staircase up to the second floor. The air here pulsed to the rhythm of Latin music, couples twirling and dipping on a crowded dance floor.

Danika spotted the stairs to the third floor and, without a word, pulled Sofia after her. They flew up them as quickly as they could, each step powered by the growing pressure in their bladders.

The third floor was smaller, darker, and moodier. Chopped and Screwed R&B filled the air, mixed with the smell of weed and cigars. Danika spotted a flickering sign for the bathroom and tugged Sofia along, leading her down a narrow, dimly lit, shadowy hallway.

They passed a couple locked in a passionate, drunken embrace, their bodies pressed together against the wall. Sofia and Danika squeezed past them, careful not to disturb them.

The line for the bathroom here was mercifully short, only three people. Sofia prayed she could make it.

They stood in line, each of them shifting their weight from foot to foot, holding themselves tightly. Finally, it was Sofia's turn. She rushed into the tiny bathroom, pulling Danika in after her.

"There's no way I'm going in here alone." She hiked her voluminous skirt up around her waist.

"I can't blame you." Danika faced the wall and continued her frantic dance. "This place is disgusting and scary."

"Ugh, there's pee all over the seat," Sofia complained. "There's no way I'm sitting on that!"

She hovered precariously over the toilet, performing a feat of acrobatic contortion to keep her satin skirt away from the filthy surfaces.

"Gross!" Danika howled. "People are so disgusting!!"

Sofia gasped. "Shit! There's no toilet paper!"

Danika darted to the sink and grabbed a wad of paper towels. "Here, girl. Wipe gently."

Both girls broke into laughter at the absurdity.

Once they were both finished, they washed their hands vigorously. Suddenly, a loud bang on the door made both of them jump.

"Someone's in here!" Danika yelled at the door.

"Hurry the fuck up!" an angry voice yelled from the other side.

Danika and Sofia traded a look. "I hate drunk people," Sofia muttered.

"We're almost done," Sofia called out politely.

Danika hurried, grabbing a paper towel. "Let's get out of here, girl," She pulled the door open as Sofia nodded and slipped through the narrow opening after Danika, leaving the bathroom to the impatient, and presumably large, woman who yelled "Fucking lesbians" after them.

They ran down the dark hallway and the stairs to the second floor, colliding at the bottom in relieved laughter.

"Oh my god, it was scary up there," Sofia said, still giggling.

Suddenly, Danika stopped, patting herself down frantically. "Crap, I forgot my wristlet in the bathroom! Stay here, I'll be right back."

"Okay, but hurry up and don't talk to strangers," Sofia joked as Danika dashed back up the stairs.

Sofia moved out of the way of the stairwell, the salsa music pulsing around her. A long, crowded bar stretched to her right; to her left, the crowded dance floor. Behind her was a dark hallway that appeared to lead to an office or storage area.

She walked over to the hallway entrance, tucking herself into the edge of the shadows so she wouldn't be bumped by the passing crowd. She pulled out her phone to text Allie, letting her know she was waiting for Danika.

"Hey, sexy."

The deep, rough voice came from inches away. The smell of strong liquor and stale cigarettes coming from him assaulted her.

She looked up. A heavyset man in a cheap police costume stood there, blocking her path. His stomach bulged from the ill-fitting shirt, handcuffs dangled from his belt, and aviator sunglasses hid his eyes.

She moved back, clearly creating distance between herself and the man. "Hi there," she kept her voice carefully neutral, "I'm waiting for my boyfriend, and you're probably in his way." She knew better than to say *girlfriend*; some men took that as an invitation to be disgusting, and she wanted to prevent that at all costs.

He swayed as he bent closer, his breath hot and stale against her face, and growled, "I don't give a *fuck* about him. I'm the one that's here right now."

Sofia froze, a cold knot of panic tightening in her stomach. "Well, *I* care about him. Now, can you move out of my way, please? I'd like to leave."

He moved closer, deliberately crushing her small frame against the rough wall. The lights dimmed as a Reggaeton song blared, sending red and green prisms swirling. The crowd howled, drowning out everything else.

He leaned into her ear, his hot breath grazing her cheek. His hand grabbed her waist, the grip painful. "I'm going to make your sexy ass *mine,*" he growled.

Sofia's heart raced in her chest. She pushed against him, a desperate attempt to create space. "GET OFF ME!" she screamed, but the music swallowed her cry. His hand moved higher, groping her breast roughly, the other pulling at her full skirt.

Suddenly, the man was yanked backward. He fell to the ground in a drunk heap.

Sofia's vision clouded, her ears ringing. She saw Allie standing there, her painted skull face glowing within the dim light, eyes narrowed, fists clenched.

Allie glared at the man on the floor before grabbing Sofia's hand and pulling her away from the dark hallway. Sofia's heart slammed in her chest, a combination of fear and adrenaline. Allie's voice sounded distant, muffled.

"Sofia! Sofia!" Allie's voice sounded clearer, more urgent. She shook Sofia gently. "Are you okay??"

Sofia nodded, trembling. "I'm okay."

Allie pulled her close, holding her tightly. Sofia hung onto her, the solid presence of Allie a supporting force in the aftermath of the terrifying encounter. Her breathing slowly began to even out, the racing in her chest gradually subsiding.

"Where's Danika?" Allie asked sharply.

"She went to grab her purse upstairs. She left it in the bathroom."

Allie nodded, her jaw rigid. She pulled Sofia toward the bar, quickly explaining the situation to a bouncer and pointing at the man still sprawled on the floor. Just then, Danika reappeared, seeing Allie's anger.

"What's wrong?" she yelled over the music.

Allie pointed downstairs, motioning for Danika to follow. Keeping a protective arm around Sofia, she led them out of the club and back onto the street.

Dylann was waiting nearby. She noticed the confusion on Danika's face and the brewing anger in Allie's. "What happened, bro?" she asked.

Sofia finally allowed Allie's grip to loosen a bit as she stood straighter. She turned to Allie. "How… how did you find me?"

"I came up looking for you," Allie said, her voice subdued and seething. "You were taking a while, and I thankfully saw the light hit the jewels on your crown."

"What happened??" Danika and Dylann asked.

Both Sofia and Allie were silent, neither wanting to relive the moment. Sofia took a deep breath. "Some dude tried to… attack me," she said, the word lodging in her throat.

"*DID* attack you," Allie corrected.

"Did attack me," Sofia whispered quietly. "He was drunk, pushed me against the wall, and was trying to… feel me up." A shudder ran through her while she spoke, the memory of his touch still vivid and repulsive.

Allie drew in a deep breath, trying to control her own anger.

She gently wrapped her arm around Sofia's waist.

Danika stepped forward, placing a hand on Sofia's arm. "I'm so sorry, girl. I shouldn't have left you."

"This wasn't your fault," Sofia said firmly. "And I'm okay. I promise. I'm shaken up, but I'm okay." She reached up and touched Allie's face gently. "I promise I'm okay," she spoke quietly. "You got there before anything else happened."

Dylann playfully punched Allie on the arm. "Look at you, being the hero and shit."

Sofia laughed weakly, trying to lighten the mood. "She *is* my hero." She leaned in and hugged Allie around the waist.

Allie didn't laugh, but her expression eased, and she returned the smile gently before kissing Sofia on the top of her head.

Danika squeezed Sofia's arm. "Maybe we should wrap the night up. It's almost two in the morning anyway."

"Yeah, I think that's a good idea," Allie agreed.

The group swapped hugs and goodbyes, the earlier tension slowly dissipating. As Allie and Sofia walked away, Allie's arm remained wrapped protectively around Sofia's waist. A deep protectiveness poured through her. Sofia was soft innocence in a harsh world, and Allie knew, with an assurance that rooted deep in her bones, that she would do anything to protect her from the darkness.

12

Chapter 12

Sofia scrubbed her face, the cool water a welcome relief upon her skin. She lathered and rinsed, erasing the layers of her *Día de los Muertos* makeup. With each wash, she tried to cleanse away the residue of the club… of him. His disgusting breath hot against her cheek, his jagged voice in her ear, his rough hands on her body.

"Gross!" she shivered as she dried her face.

A quiet knock sounded on the door. "Did you say something, Sof?" Allie's voice, muffled through the wood, was tinged by concern.

"No, you're good! I'll be out in a minute."

She applied her night moisturizer and headed into the bedroom. Allie was sitting on the edge of the bed, waiting for her. Her hair was ruffled from the night, but pulled back into her regular messy bun.

Sofia's eyes drank in the sight of her. Allie wore a white crew-neck tank top and fitted black boxer briefs that highlighted the curve of her hips. It was such a basic outfit, not something typically deemed "sexy," yet it produced butterflies in every part of her. Allie was captivating in every sense of the word, like no woman had ever been.

"Come here, beautiful," Allie murmured, her voice low and inviting as she patted the space beside her, a playful gleam in her eyes.

Sofia obeyed, a command given that she wished to follow. When she settled beside her, Allie's arm slid around her waist, strong and warm, a calming weight that drove away anything the night may have left.

"How are you doing?" Allie's voice was tender as her eyes searched Sofia's.

Sofia pressed into her touch, "I'm okay, I promise." She leaned forward, pressing a kiss to Allie's lips. "It was scary, and…gross…but I'm okay now."

Allie's arm tightened around her for a moment, a silent expression of concern. "Good," she breathed, kissing Sofia's forehead. "I'm so sorry that happened. I wish I'd been there sooner to—"

Sofia cut her off with another kiss, this one deeper, more forceful. "Nope! This was no one's fault, and you *did* protect me, which I am so, *so* thankful for. So shush your mouth and let's cuddle."

The mattress dipped as Sofia positioned herself under the covers. She smiled at Allie and playfully patted the bed next to her. "Your turn."

Allie grinned, her smile radiating so brightly that it lit the room more effectively than the bedside lamp. As she crawled across the bed, the muted light emphasized the delicate curves of her cheekbones and the fullness of her lips. Sofia's heart was pained by a longing that was sweet, yet terrifying.

As they lay there intertwined, they both shared stories of their childhood and how they grew up, each memory a building block of intimacy and understanding.

"So, how long have you been out?" Allie's fingers drew soothing patterns on Sofia's arm.

"Oh gosh, a while. I came out my senior year of high school."

Allie's brow lifted playfully. "Oh yeah? What's your 'coming out' story?"

Sofia shifted slightly, nestling her head more comfortably on Allie's shoulder. "You sure you want to know?"

"Mmhmm." Allie hummed, her warm breath ghosting over Sofia's hair, eliciting shivers along her back.

"Well," Sofia began, "I was dating my best friend, Jacob. We'd known each other practically our whole lives; he lived right across the street from me. We eventually went from besties to dating in ninth grade. I always knew I was attracted to girls, but never really thought much about it until high school. That's when I started realizing there might be something more, but I was terrified of exploring those feelings, of saying anything. Jacob was amazing, the best friend I could ever ask for. He was kind, loving, compassionate. He never pressured me." Sofia paused, a touch of reservation in her voice. "But, like every teenager, we decided to have a few drinks with some other seniors one night and got a wild hair to... well... you know."

Allie nodded, her chin resting atop Sofia's head, listening intently.

"So we did it." Sofia continued, her voice barely louder than a whisper. "It lasted all of two minutes and was the most awkward moment of my life."

A shared chuckle filled the quiet room.

"And I think the drinks gave me liquid courage or something," Sofia went on, "because suddenly I decided *that* was the perfect moment to tell him I liked girls." She groaned, her hand moving to her face as the memory came back.

Allie's laughter filled the space between them. "Oh no, how did that go?"

"Not well," Sofia admitted, her voice colored with sadness. "It really hurt him. I mean, we had both *just* lost our virginity to each other, and he asked if it was okay, because, well, I'm pretty sure I looked like a deer caught in headlights. The reality of who I was smacked me right in the face, and I blurted out, 'I think so? It was short, but I don't have anything to compare it to. But I think I really, *really* like girls, Jacob. I think I'm gay.' And he just… sat there, staring at me, his heart breaking in his eyes."

Allie's lips found Sofia's temple, pressing a gentle kiss against her skin. "That had to have been really hard for both of you."

Sofia nodded, emotion thick in her voice. "It was the moment I found myself, but it was also the moment I lost my best friend. He could have hated me, been so mean, but he simply said, 'Don't be sorry, Sof. You deserve to be happy, and if this is who you are, then you need to find your happiness, regardless of whether it's with me or not.'"

"Wow," Allie breathed, her fingers slowly trailing up and down Sofia's arm. "He sounds like an amazing guy. And he was right, you do deserve to be happy."

"I know." Sofia sighed, a touch of sadness hovering in the air. "I just wish it didn't have to be at the expense of his happiness."

Allie nodded silently, offering her sympathy and compassion. "Were y'all able to remain friends?"

Sofia shook her head. "He said he still wanted to be in my life, that he just needed some time, but I guess it was too much. He never came around, and shortly after, he changed his plans from going to college here in Austin to going to Oklahoma. Life moved on, and I've never felt right about getting in touch. I figured if he wants to reconnect somewhere down the line, he will."

"Yeah," Allie agreed softly. "Hopefully one day he will."

Sofia's fingers slid into Allie's, their hands resting on her chest. "What about you? What's *your* story?"

Allie chuckled, the sound warm and comforting. "Mine's pretty boring. I had my first girl crush in kindergarten and pretty much knew I was gay as hell after that."

They shared a laugh, the sound light and joyful inside the quiet room.

"How old were you when you came out?"

"I think everyone knew pretty early on," Allie admitted, "but I officially came out to my parents right before I left for college."

"Oh wow. Did you do it then on purpose, or did it just happen that way?"

"Totally on purpose," Allie chuckled dryly. "I'd wanted to come out for years, but I knew my folks weren't going to take it well. So I decided to tell them right before I got in the car to leave for college, that way I wouldn't have to face them for a while."

Sofia's eyes widened. "Yikes, how did they take it?"

"Not well, as expected," Allie answered with a sigh. "They never called to discuss it, but when I called them needing a little financial help one month, they gave me an earful about being financially independent and how they 'knew I was different at an early age', but it wasn't to ever be a discussion again in our home."

"Ouch." Sofia winced, her hand squeezing around Allie's in a silent gesture of empathy.

Allie nodded. "Yeah. I think they've tried to come to terms with it on their own. They've known I've had girlfriends, but every time I've tried to bring it up, it's like they bury their heads in the sand, or pretend I never said anything at all."

"That really sucks, Al." Sofia's voice was full of genuine concern. "I'm sorry they're like that."

Allie shook her head, gently kissing the top of Sofia's head. "Don't be. They're the ones missing out. I'm happy with who I am and where my life is going. If they choose not to be a part of it, that's on them."

Sofia nodded, sympathetic but still hurting for her. "I know. And they truly are missing out on an amazing person. But still… it has to hurt on some level."

A heavy quiet descended between them, the unspoken acknowledgment of Allie's pain hanging in the air.

"Yeah," Allie finally admitted, her voice just a whisper. "On some level… it does."

As the hour grew later and their eyelids grew heavy, their thoughts roamed back to the stories they had shared, the vulnerabilities they had trusted each other with, and the connection they had developed. A sense of tranquility settled over both of them, a feeling of inclusion and acceptance that neither had ever truly experienced before.

13

Chapter 13

Sunlight, warm and golden, spilled through the large, open window in Allie's room, bathing Sofia's face in its warm shimmer. The warmth spread into her skin, chasing away the last traces of sleep. She let out a quiet groan of contentment and rolled over, snuggling against Allie's back.

Allie's hand touched Sofia's, her fingers twining with hers. She brought Sofia's hand to her lips, pressing a kiss to her knuckles before tucking it against her chest. "Good morning, beautiful," she uttered, her speech still thick with sleep.

Sofia smiled against Allie's warm shoulder. "Good morning. What time is it?"

Allie grasped her phone on the nightstand, the screen shining on her face with cool light. "Almost eleven."

Sofia yawned again, the lingering exhaustion evident. "Gosh, already that late?"

Allie nodded, turning to face Sofia. She brushed a single strand of hair from Sofia's forehead. "How are you feeling?" Her voice was soothing and warm.

After a momentary pause, Sofia met Allie's gaze, her

expression sincere. "Aside from the slightest of a headache, I'm good." The memory of the unwanted advances was a quiet resonance in her head, but the rest of the night was a beautiful blur.

She leaned in and kissed Allie, a quick, affectionate kiss that expressed volumes. Then, she hopped out of bed, the 2000-thread-count cotton sheets rustling in her wake.

She walked towards the en suite, then paused, peeking her head back out. "Do you mind if I shower?" She wrinkled her nose. "I'm pretty sure I brought back every single disgusting scent from Sixth Street on my dress last night."

Allie laughed as she sat up on the edge of the bed, watching Sofia. "Of course, I was wondering what that smell was."

Sofia stuck her tongue out playfully before disappearing into the bathroom. She turned on the shower, the water cascading from the large rain shower head like a summer downpour. As the steam rose, she began to undress, slowly removing the ivory pajamas she'd worn to bed.

* * *

As Sofia finished drying her hair, she heard a soft knock at the door. The scent of her shampoo, a subtle mixture of coconut and vanilla, persisted in the humid air.

"Come in," she called out, switching off the blow dryer.

Allie opened the door, a tender smile adorning her lips as she took in Sofia's reflection. "I made you some breakfast. It's ready whenever you are." The odor of freshly brewed coffee and something savory wafted into the bathroom, making Sofia's stomach grumble.

Sofia walked over to Allie, the wool rug plush below her

bare feet. Leaning in close, she whispered, "You're so sweet, thank you," her breath soft against Allie's ear, before kissing her cheek.

Allie winked and closed the door gently to give her privacy.

A few moments later, Sofia emerged from the bathroom. She was dressed in a light blue, fuzzy sweater that draped casually off one shoulder. Her jeans were a light faded wash, clinging snugly to her legs, with a few artfully distressed tears scattered up and down the denim. Light brown ankle boots completed the laid-back yet sleek ensemble. Her hair fell in a natural wave, swept over one shoulder in a classic, effortless style.

On the bed sat a wooden tray with a breakfast spread laid out with care. Two steamy mugs of coffee sat beside plates of cheesy scrambled eggs, crisp bacon, and two slices of multigrain toast, browned and buttered to golden perfection. A small glass vase held one single, exquisite peony.

Sofia's stomach growled gently as she took in the delicious scene, the smoky flavor dwelling in the room.

"I didn't have much here," Allie said, taking a small bite of the eggs, "but I do remember you telling me that you love cheesy scrambled eggs. And I personally think they came out rather good."

With a grin, Sofia walked over and snatched the fork from Allie's hand. "Let me see for myself." She took a generous bite. The texture was light and fluffy, and the cheese melted to perfection.

She raised a single eyebrow at Allie. "I *think* they'll do."

Allie laughed, wrapping her arms around Sofia's waist and pulling her down onto her lap. "They'll do, huh?" she growled playfully, grabbing a piece of bacon. The crisp edges crackled invitingly as she sank her teeth into it.

"What time do you have to take off?" Allie finished her piece of bacon, the smoky flavor lingering upon her tongue.

Sofia paused, swallowing the bite of toast. "Pretty soon, unfortunately. I have to be home in time to do a bit of work and get the studio ready for my sessions tomorrow." The thought of leaving already cast a slight cloud over the cozy morning.

Allie's bottom lip jutted out in a pout. She pulled Sofia closer, her arms tightening around her waist. "I have to be back in Fredericksburg in about two weeks to meet with the new sales team. I'll be there Thursday and Friday, but I was thinking of maybe extending it to Sunday if you're up to spending some time together."

Sofia's face lit up. She twisted around in Allie's lap, wrapping her arms around Allie's neck. Fingers tangling in the hair at Allie's nape, she smiled into those magnetic ocean-blue eyes.

"I would absolutely love to spend every second I can with you."

Allie let out a quiet moan, her hands slipping under Sofia's sweater to trace the skin of her back. She leaned forward and captured Sofia's bottom lip between her teeth, playfully nipping at it. Sofia gasped, sensing the warmth of Allie's touch against her skin.

Sofia leaned her head back, arching her back as she felt Allie's nails trace down her back. She rolled her neck to the side, her hair spilling over her shoulder, as Allie's hands moved around to her front, her fingers drifting lightly up her smooth, flat stomach. Allie cupped Sofia's breast firmly in her hand, giving it a light squeeze as her thumb stroked across Sofia's taut nipple.

A soft gasp escaped Sofia's lips as she leaned forward and found Allie's mouth, her tongue gently exploring, tasting her, drawing her in. They both could have stayed in that very moment forever… intertwined, enraptured, lost in the sensations, the taste, the touch of each other.

A shrill ring shattered the spell.

Sofia reached for her phone. "Ugh, I should probably answer this. It's my mom." She said, reluctantly moving off Allie's lap.

"Hey, Mom!" Sofia answered cheerfully.

"Hi, mija," Blanca said. "I'm just checking to see if you've taken off yet. It's supposed to start storming here soon."

"Ew, gross," Sofia pictured driving in the pouring rain. "I'm taking off soon, Mom. I'll make sure to call you when I'm on the way."

"Okay, mija, be safe, love you."

"Love you too!" Sofia ended the call as she looked at Allie. "I guess I'd better get packed up. It's supposed to start storming soon."

Allie nodded, the lingering heat of their embrace still apparent in her eyes. "What do you need me to help with?"

* * *

Allie lifted the lavender suitcase into the trunk with a thud. The garment bag and makeup case followed.

The silence around them stretched, heavy with unvoiced emotions. Sofia closed the trunk with a click and turned to Allie, her smile more tender now, tinged by melancholy. The gentleness of the morning, the laughter, the shared intimacy of the past few hours, felt like a short-lived dream, already slipping away.

"Thank you for everything," Sofia said quietly. Each word felt inadequate, as if she were unable to fully express the depth of her gratitude for the unexpected connection they had found.

Allie came closer, her eyes looking into Sofia's. "I'll miss you," her voice was husky with emotion. She reached out, her fingers caressing the delicate curve of Sofia's cheekbone. The touch was light, nearly hesitant, but it caused a shiver down Sofia's body.

Sofia leaned into it, closing her eyes for a moment, enjoying the feeling of Allie's skin against hers. She opened her eyes, meeting Allie's gaze. "I'll miss you too," The words were a soft promise but also an admission of the distance between them.

The atmosphere between them sizzled with the burden of the goodbye. The storm clouds gathering on the horizon appeared to echo the silent ache in their hearts.

Allie pulled Sofia into a tight embrace. Sofia wrapped her arms around her, clinging to her, wanting to take in every detail – the scent of her skin, the warmth from her body, the feeling of her heart beating against hers.

Finally, they broke apart, the silence returning, more intense now. Sofia flashed a small, sad smile. "I should go."

Allie nodded, her eyes swimming with a mixture of longing and understanding. She stepped back, giving Sofia the space she needed to leave.

Sofia turned and walked towards her car door, then paused, glancing back at Allie. Their eyes met one last time... a wordless exchange that words couldn't capture. Then, Sofia got into her car, closed the door, and started the engine.

As she pulled out of the driveway, she looked in her rearview mirror. Allie was still standing there, watching her go. Sofia raised a hand in a silent wave, a bittersweet farewell. As she drove away, the image of Allie standing there persisted in her mind, a reminder of the momentary beauty and the ache of knowing it was over.

14

Chapter 14

A week later, Sofia found herself peering at her desk calendar, a date circled in red. Allie would be in Fredericksburg in less than a week. A smile played at the corners of her lips as she thought of their daily phone and video calls. They both felt the same pull, the same undeniable attraction, admitting how strange it was to feel such intensity when relationships had never been a priority for either of them.

They'd talked in depth about their previous relationships – the good, the bad, and the ugly. They'd lived moments that had been hard lessons and moments that made them both belly laugh until tears streamed down their faces.

Sofia had told Allie about her history with Jacob... how much she loved him as a friend and still missed his easy companionship to this day. She shared what an amazing guy he was, how she was sorry she broke his heart, but would never be sorry that she'd found her truth in that moment. The memory of Jacob's kind smile brought a stab of tender nostalgia.

Her mind drifted back to a specific conversation with Allie

from a few nights ago, a shadow crossing her features as she recalled Allie's words.

* * *

"So, there's this one girl who had a hard time letting go," Allie said on FaceTime, her voice slightly hesitant as she ran her fingers through her damp hair.

Sofia plopped onto her bed, tucking a pillow under her chin as she lay on her stomach. "Oh?"

"Yeah, her name is Britney."

Sofia laughed. "It's always a Britney."

Allie joined in her laughter. "We met at a club one night. She was pretty cool, and we hit it off well, so she gave me her number. We hung out the next day, grabbed some coffee, and ended up hooking up."

Sofia's stomach flipped uncomfortably. She tried not to let her expression change, knowing Allie could see her, but a trace of jealousy arose inside. "Wow," she kept her tone light but guarded. "That was fast." She maintained a poker face, her voice still sweet but a little cool, her mind darting to the fact that they hadn't been intimate beyond some hot and heavy makeout sessions.

Allie let out a small, nervous laugh. "Yeah, but that hasn't been uncommon for me. I'm great at quickships, remember?"

A sly smirk darted across Sofia's face. "I think I do remember Dylann or Danika saying something like that."

"Yeah. Not that I sleep around a lot. I don't," Allie clarified quickly. "But I also don't really do relationships, so all they turn out to be is friends with benefits or..."

"Quickships."

Allie nodded, a cheeky smirk forming across her lips. "Quick-

ships."

"Okay, so what happened with this Britney? How did she have a hard time letting go?"

Allie shrugged, holding her phone. "I told her from the beginning that I didn't want a relationship, but I was down to be friends. She knew this when we slept together and seemed okay with it, but she obviously wasn't. We slept together a few times, but I was never affectionate with her outside of that. We didn't hold hands or kiss; it was basically, and obviously, friends with benefits. Well, to everyone but her."

Sofia nodded silently, listening intently.

"After a couple of months, she ended up telling me she was in love with me," Allie continued. "I was honest with her. I said that I didn't have those feelings for her and that I wouldn't. She got really upset, she'd been drinking, and ran out of my apartment. I followed her, not wanting her to get hurt, and drove her home. The ride there was rough." Allie looked away from the phone, as though reliving the unpleasant memory.

"What happened?"

"Nothing much that night," Allie replied. "I brought her home, got her into her apartment, and left. She was crying, begging me to stay, but I didn't. I knew it wouldn't be right to feed into her feelings like that."

Sofia nodded again.

"Then the texts started. Calls every day, leaving unhinged voicemails."

"Like what?"

"Things like, 'Why do you hate me?' 'Why can't you love me?' 'What can I do to get you to love me?'" Allie's brow tightened at the memory.

"Geesh. That's both sad and kinda scary."

A moment of silence passed before Allie nodded. "It just got worse. I tried to be gentle and supportive, but that seemed to make it worse. She started showing up at my apartment, sending flowers all the time. She even showed up at my work."

Sofia's mouth dropped open. "Wow, that's crazy. Did you do anything? What did Dylann say?"

"I was too embarrassed to even say anything to my friends," Allie admitted. "They had no idea. Dylann knew she was no longer around, but she didn't think much of it. But then Britney started messaging Dylann, asking to hang out with her. One night, I was supposed to meet Dylann at RAIN, and when I showed up, Britney was standing right there with her."

"No way!" Sofia 's mouth opened, shocked.

Allie let out a dry laugh. "Yeah, it was wild. Dylann looked so confused when I asked why she was there."

"What did she say?"

"She said that Britney told her that I wanted her to come!" Allie said, the shock still apparent in her voice, even though it had been years ago. "I confronted Britney right there, telling her she was lying and that she was no longer welcome around my friends or me."

Sofia shifted, propping herself up on her elbows. "Oh boy. How did that go?"

"Not good," Allie answered. "She flipped out and had to be removed from the bar. I ended up blocking her on everything that night and changed my number. We stopped going to RAIN for a while because she would show up there and watch us all night from across the room."

"Okay, yeah, so now she was basically your stalker."

Allie answered with a slow, "Mmm-hmm."

"She was still sending flowers, and I would just leave them out

on the street until I saw her across the street one day and yelled to her that I was going to put a restraining order on her if I saw her again or if she sent one more thing to me."

"Did she?" Sofia questioned.

"Nope. That was the last time I saw or heard from her, but the whole thing lasted about a year."

"A year?!" Sofia exclaimed, shocked.

Allie nodded. "I think a little over a year, but yeah, it was not a fun time."

"Oh my gosh, I can't even imagine. I don't even know what I would do if that happened to me."

"You would call me," Allie's voice was instantly protective.

A small smirk formed on the corner of Sofia's mouth. "Unless it was you," she teased.

Allie laughed, a grin lingering on her lips. "Would you really mind if it were me?" she asked, raising a brow.

"Absolutely not," Sofia's smile blossomed. "Send me all the flowers you want!"

They both laughed, the thoughts of Britney already fading into the past.

* * *

But now, sitting at her desk, the memory of that conversation dwelt in Sofia's mind, a small, unsettling whisper.

What if Britney shows back up? The question was a cold prickle against the warmth of her anticipation. The image of Allie, her face furrowed with a weary expression as she told the story, flashed in her mind. *How would that even play out? What if she's psycho or starts stalking her again?*

A tremor went down Sofia's spine, a surge of unease

coursing over her. She could nearly sense the weight of Allie's fear, the lingering anxiety that had latched onto her voice.

She imagined Britney, a murky form, powered by resentment and obsession, hiding in the corners, waiting to attack. The scenario played out in her mind, a series of worst-case scenarios. *What if Britney showed up in Fredericksburg? What if she confronted Allie, causing a scene? What if... what if she was truly dangerous?*

The sound of the front door opening startled her. Her 3:00 p.m. appointment had arrived.

The questions, the worries, the spinning anxieties would have to wait. Sofia plastered a professional smile on her face, pushing the anxiety to the back of her mind as she greeted her client. But the image of Britney, and the reverberation of Allie's story, persisted just below the surface.

15

Chapter 15

Sofia woke up slowly, the heaviness of sleep lifting as the sun shone through the sheer white curtains. The building that housed her apartment and photography studio was over 150 years old, and it held such beautiful history in every room, each creaking floorboard and worn brick telling tales of the past.

She lay there, letting the warm sun spill onto her face, a smile emerging on her lips. It was Friday. She would get to see Allie today. A flutter of anticipation quivered in her stomach as warmth filled her chest.

She recalled the phone call from Allie last night. Her voice had been laden with exhaustion after a full day of meetings. She had explained that she was heading to the hotel to crash, but would see Sofia the following day after work.

Sofia was a little bummed not to be able to see Allie yesterday, but she had a lot to do at the studio herself and knew it would keep her busy. The thought of seeing Allie, just a few hours away, made butterflies dance in her belly.

She rolled over and tossed her legs over the bed, her feet

settling into the plush rug beneath them. She stretched her back, her muscles groaning with satisfying pops as her hair fell around her shoulders, a perfectly chaotic mess.

She suddenly realized that the room was infused with the strong smell of espresso and steamed milk. She looked around the open living space and saw her little sister, Camilla, curled up in her favorite spot – a pale yellow, overstuffed Victorian chair. The velvet cushioned her as she stared out the large window, latte in hand. The high, curved edges of the chair hid Cami's legs, forming a cozy, secretive little nook.

"Hey, little sis," Sofia's voice was still full of sleep.

Cami turned, a warm smile beaming on her face as she took a sip of her drink, steam twirling around her. "Good morning, sissy."

Sofia cocked her head, sensing Cami's quietness. "You okay?" She walked over and sat on the large, drum-shaped wooden coffee table that occupied the center of the living room. It was sturdy yet elegant, with decorative patterns carved into the rounded sides forming beautiful shadows in the sunlight.

"I'm just stressed about school," Cami's smile slightly faded. "It's *so* much to take on, so much to handle. Then you throw trying to work on top of that, and sometimes I wonder if I can do it."

Sofia leaned forward, placing her hand over Cami's. "College is hard, hermanita. But you're doing so well, and it's only a few years of your life. It will be totally worth it when you're done and working at your dream job."

Cami looked at her sister, eyes expressing the admiration she'd always held for Sofia. "Well, my dream job would be me being a famous influencer and making millions off of doing my makeup and showing off my fabulous life."

Both girls chuckled. "So, then be a famous influencer!" Sofia encouraged.

A small scoff escaped Cami's lips as she took another drink of her steaming latte. "I totally would if it were that easy, trust me."

"Well, nothing worth it is ever easy. And being a Child Advocate Attorney is *soooo* admirable, sis. You should be proud of all the work you're doing and the dedication it's taking for that! You're going to help kids who really, really need it in their darkest moments. I'm proud of you."

Cami squeezed Sofia's hand and looked up at her again, her eyes sparkling with gratefulness. "Thank you, sissy. That means a lot."

They leaned toward, wrapping their arms around each other in a genuine embrace. "I love you, *hermanita*."

"I love you too." Cami sensed the burden of her worries lifting. She squeezed her big sister tighter before releasing her, suddenly remembering the day.

"Hey, doesn't Allie come today?"

Sofia nodded, grinning. "Yep! She'll be coming by after she finishes up at work."

Cami bounced playfully in the chair. "Oh my gosh! I'm so excited for you! Do you think you'll bring her to dinner at Mom's tomorrow?"

Sofia's face scrunched up in a confused look. "Oh, I don't know, sis. I want to, but part of me feels it's just too early to introduce her to Mom. It's only been a month."

"I mean," Cami shrugged, "sure, it's still early, but how are you feeling about everything so far? How are you feeling about Allie?"

A genuine smile crossed Sofia's face as she thought about Allie and how she made her feel. "It's unlike anything I've ever experienced. She's amazing."

Cami wrinkled her nose playfully as she smiled. "I think you really like her, sissy. And I think she really likes you, too."

Sofia nodded as her heart fluttered, "I really like her, Cami. I really, really do."

Cami watched her big sister as she spoke about Allie, seeing the truth shine in her eyes. She knew her sister had it bad, and she was here for it.

"Okay, so then YES, we will see you BOTH for dinner tomorrow." Cami chuckled. "I'll let Mom know."

Sofia let out a small groan, but she couldn't hide the smile on her face. "Okayyy, let Mom know then. I have to start getting ready, though, I have a shoot at 10:00 a.m."

She got up, stretching as she stood, then started walking towards the bathroom, ready to take on the day.

* * *

The click of the camera shutter traveled through the studio, a familiar sound to Sofia's workday. The morning had been a frenzy: a family portrait session with three rambunctious toddlers, a maternity shoot with a glowing expectant mother, and a high-school senior eager for the perfect yearbook photo. Each camera click was a little piece of Sofia's passion, freezing fleeting moments and transforming them into lasting memories.

However, beneath the surface of her professional focus, one thought kept repeating... Allie. The thought of seeing her again caused a shiver of joy through Sofia. She peered at the clock on the wall, its hands seeming to slow down as the day passed. Just a few more hours, and then she would be with her.

As she worked, her thoughts drifted back to their conversations, their joint laughter, the easy intimacy that flourished between them. She thought of the way Allie's eyes shone when she smiled, the gentleness of her touch, the way her voice lowered when she spoke Sofia's name. A blush warmed Sofia's cheeks when she recalled the passionate kisses they'd shared and the way their bodies seemed to fit together perfectly.

Sofia paused, drawing in a deep breath and enjoying the momentary quiet of the studio. Soon. Soon she would be with Allie again. The thought filled her with anticipation, making her heart sing.

The small bells above the studio door tinkled, and Sofia looked up with a welcoming smile.

The door opened, and a tall, handsome man stepped into the studio. He was flawlessly dressed in a black tailor-made suit, his blonde hair neatly styled, his smile emitting confidence and charm. This was Josh McCoy, the son of a prominent lawyer and owner of the prestigious law firm, McCoy & Sons. He also happened to be Sofia's client for the afternoon.

"Hey there!" Sofia beamed as she walked towards Josh, "I'm Sofia." She put her hand out to welcome him.

"Sofia, it's a pleasure to finally meet you." He extended his hand with a deep and genuine smile. "I've heard impressive things about your work."

"Oh, that is always good to hear!"

Josh had recently landed a prestigious position at his

father's renowned law firm, and he needed professional portraits for the firm's website and marketing materials. Sofia was excited about the chance to work with such a high-profile client, but she was also a little nervous. She wanted to make sure she captured Josh's personality and professionalism perfectly.

As they began the session, Sofia was struck by Josh's easygoing nature and natural charisma. He was quick to laugh, and he excelled at putting people at ease. They chatted comfortably throughout the shoot, discussing everything from their favorite local restaurants to their travel aspirations. Sofia found herself genuinely enjoying his company, and she could tell that he was relaxing into the session; his initial stiffness was giving way, letting his true personality shine through.

The shoot progressed smoothly, with Sofia capturing a variety of poses and expressions. Josh was a natural in front of the camera, his confidence and charm shining in every shot. Sofia had a surge of creative energy, inspired by his presence and the ease of connection between them.

As the session wound down, the conversation continued to flow. Josh seemed reluctant to leave, and Sofia found herself equally focused on their conversation. He talked passionately about his aspirations for his legal career, his desire to create a positive impact on the world. Sofia was impressed by his intelligence and ambition, but also by his genuine warmth and kindness.

"You know," Josh said, leaning forward in a conspiratorial manner, "The firm really needs some updated headshots for the website, brochures, and all that other crazy social media stuff. Maybe I can put in a good word for you with my dad and have you become our firm's photographer."

Sofia's heart skipped a beat, and she tried to maintain her composure. "Oh, really?"

"Yeah," Josh continued, "he was saying how outdated the current staff photos are, and how they could really use a refresh. I think he could be persuaded your way."

Sofia's mind surged. This could be a huge opportunity for her business, a chance to expand her clientele and gain recognition in an influential circle. But more than that, she was delighted about the prospect of working with Josh again. She enjoyed his company, and she sensed a spark of connection with him that went beyond just the professional... she could truly see him as a friend.

"That would be amazing, Josh! I would love to work with your father and the rest of the firm."

Josh smiled, his eyes beaming. "I'll put in a good word for you," he promised with a wink. "As long as I don't come out looking like a troll in these photos."

The sound of their laughter resounded in the studio as the tinkling chime of the doorbell announced a visitor. Allie walked into the studio, the sound of Sofia's laughter drawing her in. She spotted Sofia behind the counter, her elbows resting on the polished white wood surface, leaning forward in a relaxed pose. A well-dressed man in his upper-twenties stood casually at the counter, mirroring Sofia's posture. A bright smile stretched across his lightly tanned face, his teeth a flash of white against his skin. You could tell he came from money; it was like a thick, invisible aura surrounding him, from the top of his well-groomed hair to his shiny leather dress shoes. His suit was an exemplar of black Italian cotton cashmere, perfectly crafted and made for his tall, slim frame.

His teeth practically gleamed as he laughed, his smile wide and genuine.

"Hi!" Sofia exclaimed with delight upon seeing Allie. She jumped up from her stool and strode across the studio floor, throwing her arms around Allie and bringing her into a tender embrace.

Allie braced herself for Sofia's enthusiastic hug, wrapping her arms around her and kissing her softly on the forehead. "Well, hi there."

Sofia pulled back excitedly, her eyes beaming. "Come meet Josh," her voice bubbled with zeal as she took Allie's hand and led her towards the stranger.

Josh straightened as they approached, his bright smile beaming. He extended his hand towards Allie, his voice smooth and confident, "You must be Allie."

Taking Josh's hand in hers, Allie returned the warm handshake, her smile deepening. "That I am!"

"I've been hearing quite a bit about you today," he glanced at Sofia, a lighthearted shimmer in his eyes.

"Is that right?" Allie's smile turned into a teasing smirk as she looked down at Sofia, who was now clinging to her arm, eyes beaming with amusement.

Josh nodded, a slight pause remaining in the air. "Well, I'd better let you two ladies get to your events of the evening. Thank you again, Sofia, and we will see each other soon. Coffee on Monday?"

Sofia nodded, a friendly smile spreading on her lips. "Yep! I'll meet you at the Peach and Bean at nine."

"It's a date!" Josh declared, turning towards the door.

A playful giggle rose from Sofia as she called after him. "I'll see you then!"

Josh stopped at the door, turning back to them with a smile and a slight bow. He exited, the twinkle of the doorbell ebbing into silence as the old door closed behind him.

Allie turned towards Sofia, one eyebrow raised playfully. She leaned down, her arms enveloping Sofia, pulling her close until their bodies melted together. "A date, huh?" she growled, her voice a mellow, playful rumble against Sofia's ear.

Sofia laughed, her body shaking against Allie's. She leaned forward, capturing Allie's lips in a soft kiss. "Just a friend date," she uttered against Allie's mouth.

They stood there, wrapped in each other's arms, authentic smiles on their faces, happiness overflowing inside. Both enjoyed a sweet release, a feeling of completeness at being together again. Excitement surrounded them, the knowledge that the weekend was now theirs.

16

Chapter 16

The aroma of simmering spices and warm tortillas spread through the air as Sofia and Allie pulled up to the cozy yellow house nestled on a quiet street. A worn welcome mat lay on the porch, its dim lettering proclaiming "Bienvenidos." The house was small, but it expressed a coziness that rose above its painted walls. This was Blanca's home, a harbor of love and happiness, the heart of their close-knit family.

Sofia's stomach shuddered with a fusion of excitement and nerves. She reached for Allie's hand, fingers interlocking. "Ready?" she asked, her voice just a whisper.

Allie squeezed her hand reassuringly. "Ready as I'll ever be."

They walked up the creaking steps. Before they could knock, the front door opened, revealing Blanca, her round face beaming.

Blanca, at fifty, was still a captivating woman. Her Hispanic heritage was visible in her warm, olive complexion and the thick, dark hair that now held an alluring blend of silver and black, framing her face in a stylish bob. Her brown eyes bore a hint of the mischievous twinkle that had undoubtedly entranced audiences during her brief stint as an actress in her younger years. Though time had etched fine lines around her eyes and softened the contours of her face, her beauty remained undeniable. She was a woman who had accepted the passage of time with grace, her faded laughter lines an imprint of a life rich with joy and love.

"Sofia! Allie! Welcome, welcome!" Blanca exclaimed, her voice kind and sincere. She pulled them both into a hug, her embrace a comforting mix of cinnamon and floral honey. "Come in, come in! Dinner is almost ready."

The house was a serenade of familiar sounds and smells for Sofia. The chatter of her sisters, the fragrance of fresh tortillas in the air. Sofia's heart overflowed with a known comfort, a sense of belonging that only this home and her family could give her.

Allie, however, held a complex combination of emotions. Excitement, yes, but also a trace of apprehension as this was her first time meeting Sofia's family. But underneath those feelings, a deeper ache was forming, a longing for the kind of acceptance and love that she witnessed here.

As they entered the dining room, they were greeted by Sofia's sisters, Camilla and Isabella, already seated at the table. Camilla jumped up excitedly as she saw Allie and Sofia enter, a huge grin spreading across her face.

"Allie, you've met Cami already, but this is my sister Isabella. Isabella, this is Allie," Sofia lovingly introduced Allie to her sisters.

Cami pounced over to them, her young energy charging the air of the small dining room.

"It's nice to see you again!" She said earnestly, "Can I give you a hug? We're huggers."

Allie smiled as she answered, "Yeah, of course you can hug me!" She leaned forward and folded Camilla's small frame into a genuine embrace.

Isabella slowly stood. Her curvy frame perfectly sported a black, oversized sweater and leggings, with a forest-green shawl draped gracefully around her neck, an artistic touch suggesting her life as an art student. She had a calm air to her, her dark eyes taking in every detail of Allie's face with the focus of a reserved observer.

"Hi, Allie," Isabella said, her voice composed and kind. "Welcome to our home. It's nice to meet you, and you can call me Izzy."

Allie walked forward and extended her hand to Izzy as she smiled, "It's really nice to meet you as well, Izzy. I'm happy to be here."

The tension in Sofia's chest unspooled into relief, her heart expanding as she watched her sisters pull Allie into their circle with an easy, natural warmth.

The table was laden with a feast: homemade chicken enchiladas, fluffy rice, and savory beans, all prepared according to a secret family recipe carried down through generations.

As they sat down, the conversation developed easily. Blanca, a natural storyteller, told Allie stories of Sofia's childhood, her voice steeped with love and amusement. Camilla and Isabella chimed in, drawing a vivid picture of Sofia's life. While Cami was loud and animated, Isabella's contributions were quieter but sharp, her loyalty to her sister apparent in how she corrected Cami's exaggerations to make Sofia look better.

Allie listened closely, digesting every detail, feeling a

growing fondness for this warm and loving family. She narrated stories of her own, her childhood in an upper-class neighborhood outside the city, her dreams and ambitions. Sofia's family listened with genuine interest, and their questions and comments made her feel welcome and valued.

But as the voices and laughter whirled about them, an ache settled in Allie's chest. She couldn't help but compare this to her own family gatherings, where strained silences and feigned smiles commonly overshadowed everything else. The acceptance she felt in this room, the easy affection between Sofia and her sisters, the open love in Blanca's eyes, was a strong contrast to the guarded interactions and silent judgments of her own family. A wave of sadness came over her, a reminder of the kind of familial love she longed for but couldn't find in her own parents, one of the reasons she felt kept her from forming actual relationships in her life.

The enchiladas were delicious, with flavors that blended into a pleasant spice. Allie savored every bite, appreciating the love and care that had gone into preparing the meal. She knew it was more than simply a meal; it represented a symbol of family, of tradition, of belonging.

Allie felt herself drifting, lost somewhere in the maze of her own thoughts. The heat of Sofia's hand, soft and calming, grasped her own, pulling her back. She looked up, meeting Sofia's gaze. A small smile formed on Sofia's lips as she whispered, "Are you okay?" The tenderness in her voice and the open, honest worry in her eyes rolled over Allie.

A sincere smile spread across Allie's face. "I'm good," she mouthed silently.

Sofia squeezed her hand, a silent gesture that said so much. Then, she turned back to her family, seamlessly rejoining the conversation. Allie watched them, absorbing the effortless affection, the mutual jokes, and the easy silences that showed what family love is. It was a scene she had often dreamt of, a vision of family that had always appeared just out of reach. But here, in this cozy dining room, embraced by the warmth of Sofia's family, she had a trace of hope, a possibility that maybe, perhaps, she could find a place, a belonging, she had never had the courage to believe in.

After the delicious meal, the dishes were cleared, and the family gathered in the living room for a game night. Laughter filtered through the air as they played a couple of board games, the competitive vibe mixed with jovial banter and heartfelt affection. Allie found herself relaxing completely, her earlier apprehension waning into a distant memory.

As the evening advanced, the conversation changed to Allie and Sofia's budding relationship. Isabella, who had been quietly studying the chemistry between them all evening, finally spoke up. She was usually reserved, but when she had something to say, she made it count.

"So," Isabella began, her voice steady as she looked between them. "Are you two officially a couple?"

A blush flushed on Sofia's cheeks as she glanced at Allie. "Well," she began hesitantly, "we haven't really put a label on it yet."

Allie nodded in agreement. "We've been taking things slow, just letting them progress naturally."

Isabella nodded contemplatively. "I get that. I've been with my boyfriend, Mateo, for a few months now, and navigating it while he's away at school in Houston is... a lot. But you know when it's right."

Blanca smiled affectionately at her daughters. "Exactly.

Love doesn't always follow a schedule."

The conversation continued, considering the nuances of their relationships, and the story of how Sofia and Allie met became a source of much laughter.

"Some would call that fate, Mija." Blanca smiled as she extended her hand and squeezed both of their hands.

Allie related stories of their adventures in Austin, her voice alive with laughter as she described Sofia's infectious youthful spirit while being bombarded for pictures down Sixth Street. Sofia then spoke of the safety she felt with Allie, her fondness obvious in every word.

The lighthearted mood shifted as Sofia told them about the incident on Sixth Street, the encounter's details casting a gloom over the room. Allie felt her fists clench slightly, her brow tightening while she listened to Sofia describe the man's actions, the anger building up inside her like a surging wave. The memory of that night, of seeing Sofia cornered and vulnerable, sent a strong wave of protectiveness flooding over her.

A stillness came over the room as Sofia finished the story, ending with a description of Allie flinging the man to the ground and pulling her away from his grasp. The image of Sofia, her eyes staring with fear, her body shaking, was engraved on Allie's memory, like a scab that would not heal.

"I hope you kicked him in the balls," Cami said loudly.

Izzy scoffed as she looked at Cami, "You and your obsession with balls... but I hope you did too."

The atmosphere lightened as they all laughed. Sofia's mom, Blanca, leaned forward, her eyes swelled with concern. She reached out, her hand gently covering Sofia's. "I'm so sorry that happened, Mija."

She then turned to Allie and grasped her hand. "And thank you for getting her out of that situation, Allie. I'm so glad she had you there."

Allie nodded silently, unable to find the words to express the storm of emotions churning within her. The recollection of that night, of the rage and fear which had consumed her, was still raw.

The evening edged to a close after a couple more rounds of laughter-filled games. Allie felt she fit perfectly into the family dynamic, and she basked in their kindness and acceptance. The genuine affection she had observed throughout the evening echoed deeply, making her long for the kind of family love and acceptance she felt here.

Sofia also felt contentment. Seeing Allie interact so easily with her family and witnessing the acceptance they offered her filled her with appreciative joy. It felt natural… right, as if Allie had forever been a part of their lives.

* * *

Back inside the cozy confines of Sofia's studio, the world shrank down to the edges of the mattress. They lay tangled together, the high of the evening settling into a heavy, delicious gravity that pulled them closer.

Allie, her eyes beaming with the warm light of the small lamp, traced the line of Sofia's knuckles with her thumb. The playfulness of earlier had blended into something thicker… heavier.

"Sofia," she began, her voice husky with emotion, "I want you to be mine."

Sofia's breath faltered, the air lodging in her throat. She

looked into Allie's eyes and saw a hunger there… a look that was possessive yet vulnerable.

"I want to be yours," she said in a whisper, the confession quivering on her lips.

"Then be mine," Allie murmured, leaning in until her breath ghosted against Sofia's mouth. "Be my girlfriend. Officially. Completely. Undeniably."

The word *girlfriend* felt small compared to the magnitude of what grew in Sofia's chest… a flooding warmth of belonging. She didn't trust her voice, so she let her eyes do the talking, nodding slowly, surrendering to the pull.

Allie didn't wait. She closed the distance, capturing Sofia's lips not with a question, but with an answer. It was a claiming kiss, deep and slow. Sofia met her with equal enthusiasm, her mouth opening, inviting Allie in. Their tongues tangled, tasting of wine and sweet desperation, a wet, hot friction that shot a jolt of electricity straight to Sofia's core.

The shift was distinct. The soft cuddling evaporated, replaced by a sudden, sharp urgency. Allie's hands, usually so gentle, closed on Sofia's waist, pulling her flush against her. Sofia could feel the solid, athletic strength of Allie's body, the hardness of her defined muscles lying against her own soft curves.

Clothes became obstacles neither wanted there. There was the hiss of a zipper, the soft thud of denim hitting the floor, the swish of cashmere being pulled over heads. When they finally broke apart to look at each other, the hush in the room was deafening.

Allie's gaze was dark, growing as she drank Sofia in. She looked at her not simply with desire, but with an admiration that made Sofia's skin quiver. Inside the quiet wash of moonlight, she was completely exposed, yet under Allie's eyes she felt not naked, but adored.

"You're so beautiful." Allie breathed, the words faintly audible.

She reached out, her fingertips rougher than Sofia's, tracing a line of fire from Sofia's sensitive collarbone, between her breasts, over the soft swell of her stomach. Sofia shivered, arching instinctively into the touch. She reached out in kind, her hands exploring the naked landscape she had merely imagined, the sculpted definition of Allie's shoulders, the smooth, taut ripples of her abs.

Allie kissed her way down, her lips hot against the cooling air. She lingered on the sensitive skin of Sofia's ribs, biting gently, making Sofia gasp and curl her fingers into Allie's thick, golden curls.

"Allie," she breathed, a plea falling from her lips.

Allie didn't stop. She moved lower, her kisses tracing over the soft curve of Sofia's hip, blowing warm air across the skin of her inner thigh. Sofia's legs parted instinctively, her hips lifting off the mattress as a heavy, aching pulse began to throb between her legs.

Allie settled between Sofia's thighs, pausing for a torture-filled second to look up at her. The fierceness in her eyes burned. Then, she lowered her head.

The first brush of Allie's tongue was a shock of pure heat. Sofia's head fell back into the pillows, a ragged moan tearing from her throat. Allie hummed upon her, the vibration traveling through Sofia's body as she began to taste her... slow, deliberate strokes that targeted the most sensitive bundle of nerves she possessed.

It wasn't purely physical; it was an unraveling. With every

wet, rhythmic swirl of Allie's tongue, Sofia felt her control fracturing. She reached down, her hands gripping Allie's hair, not to push her away, but to hold on to the only solid thing in her world as the room began to spin.

Allie responded to the grip, her rhythm deepening, her suction growing more fervent. She tasted Sofia like she was starving, drinking in her sweetness, her tongue teasing the swollen nub with an unrelenting pressure that verged on too much and yet wasn't nearly enough.

"Allie, please!" Sofia cried out, her hips bucking, seeking more friction.

The world closed down to this… the wet sound of Allie's mouth, the perfume of their mingled arousal, and the dazzling white light building behind Sofia's eyelids. Allie felt the inevitable unraveling begin, sensing the moment Sofia was about to come undone. She didn't let up; she drove Sofia toward it, her mouth working faster, harder, drinking down every cry.

When the release came, it shattered Sofia completely. A flood of pure, unadulterated ecstasy crashed over her, bowing her back. She cried out Allie's name, her body shaking violently as the pleasure crested and broke, leaving her gasping, floating in a sea of white noise.

Allie stayed with her, slowing her movements but not stopping, soothing the sensitive flesh until Sofia's tremors subsided into soft, aftershocks of bliss.

Moments later, Allie crawled up the bed, her skin flushed, her lips slick. She pulled a breathless, limp Sofia into her arms, burying her face in the crook of her neck. They lay in the tangled bedding, pulses racing so hard it was impossible to tell where one heartbeat ended, and the other began.

The room was quiet again, but everything had changed. The air was laden with their scent, charged with the intimacy of barriers broken. As Sofia curled into the solid heat of Allie's embrace, listening to their breathing slow in the moonlight, she knew this wasn't just a night of passion. It was a seal. A promise. It was the first terrifying, beautiful page of a story she never wanted to end.

17

Chapter 17

The usual essence of freshly roasted coffee beans filled the studio. Sofia, bundled in a light scarf and a knit sweater, sat across from Josh, their chuckles filling the empty space. These morning coffee rituals had become a welcome routine for both of them.

On mornings when her schedule was packed with photo editing or clients demanding her attention, Josh would appear at her studio door, a piping-hot latte or Raspberry Cream Iced Coffee grasped in his hand, and a smile that could melt the frostiest of mornings.

"Alright, beautiful, what does lunch look like today?" Josh draped his long wool-and-cashmere coat over the counter, steaming beverage in hand.

Warmth coated Sofia's throat as she took another drink of the delicious latte Josh brought her. "Busy," she sighed. "So busy. 'Tis the season for family portraits!" she said with a tired but happy smile.

"Ah, yes," Josh smirked playfully. "The inevitable and dreaded Christmas photos!"

"Hey!" Sofia shot back with a mock pout. "They aren't that bad! I love doing our holiday pics every year!"

Josh chuckled as he shifted, taking another drink of his coffee. "If I had *your* family, I might look forward to them too. But there is nothing enjoyable about the McCoy Christmas Pictures."

They both laughed, enjoying the easy rhythm of their company.

"Okay, so lunch is out." Josh conceded. "You owe me a dinner date then. Where shall we go tonight?"

Sofia ran her fingers through her hair thoughtfully. "Mmmm, I don't know. What are you feeling up for?"

Josh watched her fluff her flowing hair for a moment, the soft perfume of it filling his senses. "Your hair always smells so good," he commented with a small smile. "Okay, dinner. I've kinda been craving some buttery lobster. Are you up for Martini's?"

Sofia leaned forward, her eyes twinkling as she looked into Josh's baby-blue eyes. "Josh, you know I'm always up for any place with you! I love your company... the food is just an added benefit."

A sly smile crept across Josh's face as he leaned back and popped a piece of gum in his mouth. "Then it's a date, babe. Pick you up at six?"

Sofia nodded as she took another drink, enjoying the sweetness of the foam. "Mmhmm, six works."

Josh pushed away from the counter and grabbed his coat. "Alright, beautiful... I gotta fly." He walked to the door, pulling it open, "Don't have too much fun without me!"

"Never!" Sofia yelled after him with a chuckle.

Her mornings always seemed a bit lighter, happier now

that Josh had entered her life. It felt, in some way, that the hole that Jacob's exit left was now filled a bit.

They had become inseparable in a matter of weeks, their connection growing so close that it felt as if they'd been friends for years. Every spare second was spent together, a mutual gravitation toward one another. Josh was a constant anchor and a fantastic listener, lending a patient ear even when Sofia dominated the conversation, endlessly over-talking about Allie and the intensity of their romance.

Sofia found herself anxious to share this trace of happiness with Allie. Every evening, their relationship was anchored by long video chats where Sofia would vividly recount the day, her voice distinctly bubbling with zeal whenever she described Josh's antics and the laughter they had enjoyed. Allie listened thoughtfully, offering nothing but support and encouragement, smiling along with Sofia's stories before trading them for her own accounts from the corporate world.

She was happy for Sofia, reassured that Josh was by her side. In Sofia's eyes, he was the ultimate big brother figure, acting as a protective buffer she hadn't realized she needed. Whenever they were out, and a man tried his luck, Josh's demeanor would shift instantly. He would lean in, his presence heavy and grounding beside her, effectively walling her off from the rest of the room. He dismissed the unwanted advances with a sharpness that felt like safety to Sofia, never noticing that he was guarding her less like a sister and more like a prize.

* * *

With Black Friday looming, Sofia and Allie had hatched a

plan for a weekend of Christmas shopping in Austin. The thought of spending a long weekend with Allie, exploring the thriving city, and indulging in some retail therapy, filled Sofia with happiness.

So, when Josh brought up needing to do Christmas shopping that night, she blurted out that they should meet in Austin and shop together, her excitement obvious as she imagined the fun they could all have.

"Oh, and we could do lunch at *The Lonesome Dove!*" His eyes lit up as he leaned in, the fragrance of his Tom Ford cologne wafting toward Sofia.

"I've heard of that place!" Sofia exclaimed, her own anticipation growing. "But I've also heard that it's almost impossible to get into." The image of the restaurant, with its rustic charm and renowned cuisine, came to mind.

Josh dismissed her concern with a wave of his hand. "No, no. I'll put in a call to Chef Tim's team. My family is well-known there; they'll get us a table." He leaned back in the comfortable booth, a confident smirk resting on his handsome lips.

Sofia, briefly forgetting the extent of Josh's family's influence, blinked in surprise. Sometimes, she still found it hard to reconcile the down-to-earth, coffee-loving Josh with the privileged world he inhabited. "That would be amazing, Josh! I've heard such fantastic things about their food and the whole experience!"

Josh pulled out his phone, its sleek surface shining beneath the restaurant's glow. He searched his contact list effortlessly, his fingers flicking across the screen.

Sofia, mirroring his action, pulled out her own phone, her joy overflowing. "I'm going to text Allie and tell her," her fingers already tapping out a message. "She'll be so excited! She's such a foodie."

A minor change occurred in Josh's demeanor. He froze mid-tap, a trace of something unreadable flitting across his features. He cleared his throat, a slight hesitation in his voice as he lowered his phone.

"Oh, damn. I'm sorry, Sofia." The bold tone from a moment ago vanishing. "I just realized that my dad is going to need me to help with a trial coming up, and jury questionnaires are due by noon. Maybe we can meet up after you get back from Austin."

Sofia's face fell, her early excitement replaced by friendly disappointment. "Well, damn, Josh. That sucks! I was looking forward to shopping and having lunch with you both. Every time I try to get us all together, something pulls you away."

"We'll catch up when you're back in town, babe." He casually slipped his phone back into his pocket. "I'd better get out of here, though. Long day ahead tomorrow!"

Josh picked up his wine glass, draining the last few drops of the subtly sweet wine before grabbing his coat from the booth.

Sofia watched him, a small pout on her lips as she stood up to give him a hug. "Okay," her voice was colored with disappointment, "Martini's when I get back then."

"Sounds like a plan, doll." Josh embraced her with a quick kiss to the top of her head. The scent of her favorite body spray filled his senses, stirring a deep longing inside him. He held her a moment longer than necessary, his fingers clenching slightly around her waist, before reluctantly releasing her.

They went their separate ways as she assembled her things from the table, leaving a few extra dollars for the waitress. Josh refused to ever let her pay for anything, so it was the least she could do.

I'd better call Allie, she thought, her mind already shifting to tomorrow's schedule. Images of clients, poses, and lighting setups flashed through her mind. It would be a long day, especially with Christmas approaching, but this was her favorite season, and she looked forward to the creative challenges and the enjoyment of capturing holiday memories.

Still, a tinge of disappointment lingered; she couldn't figure out why Josh seemed so hesitant to hang out with Allie and her.

18

Chapter 18

Outside, the ticking sweep of the wipers fractured the stillness of the dark morning. The road ahead remained clogged with early risers hunting for Black Friday bargains, turning the highway into a sea of red brake lights. Sofia barely noticed the delay. Her focus was singular, her heart set on a treasure far more valuable than anything in a store. She was driving toward Allie, chasing the memory of her embrace.

The miles melted away, each one drawing her closer to Austin along with the promise of an intimate weekend with the woman who had captured her heart. Sofia smiled, remembering their phone call last night, Allie's voice husky and sensual as she uttered what she wanted to do to her. A shiver went through Sofia as memories of their last weekend together filled her head… a night she thought about often.

As she pulled into the driveway of Allie's modern town-home, the polished lines of the building illuminated by the subtle light of the front light, a figure appeared at the front door. Her figure, framed against the warm light, made Sofia's heart speed up. She parked the car, the engine coming to a stop, and practically flew out of the door, her heart hammering with anticipation.

Allie met her halfway, their bodies colliding in a hug that felt both fierce and tender. Sofia buried her face in Allie's hair, inhaling the recognizable scent of citrus and cedarwood, something distinctively *her*. Allie's arms folded around her, her lips finding Sofia's in a tender, passionate kiss.

They stood there for a moment, lost inside the embrace, the world outside disappearing. The light patter of rain and the hum of the morning traffic blended into the distance as they smiled at each other once again.

Allie pulled back, her eyes brimming with affection as she walked toward the trunk of the car, "Let me get your bags."

"Thank you," Sofia replied, her cheeks glowing with warmth.

They entered the townhome, the door closing behind them with a heavy click that effectively sealed out the rest of the world. The interior was an inviting haven of sleek refinement, with clean lines, warm wood tones, and a few pieces of art by Allie's favorite local artists adorning the walls. A fire already crackled inside the sleek fireplace, its flames glowing over glass stones and casting the room in a golden comfort that chased out the lingering morning chill.

Allie led Sofia to the living room, where her plush couch called to them. They nestled into the deep embrace of the cushions, soaking in the gentle heat emitted by the fire. Sofia snuggled into Allie's side, her head resting firmly on her shoulder as their bodies fit together with an easy familiarity.

"This is perfect." Sofia sighed, the tension of the drive melting out of her shoulders.

Allie wrapped her arms around Sofia, her fingers outlining soothing patterns on her back as she whispered into her hair, "I agree."

They lay there for a long while as the storm settled in, the room growing quiet aside from the unceasing rain rapping against the window. Their breathing synchronized with the sound of the water, becoming the only rhythm in the morning light. Slowly, the calm silence began shifting. The air among them thickened, charged with a sudden and magnetic tension.

Allie shifted first. She sat up slightly, pulling away just enough to look at Sofia. With fluid motion, she grabbed the hem of her shirt and pulled it over her head, tossing it onto the floor. The glowing firelight fluttered across the sleek, black sports bra she wore and the toned muscles of her stomach. She shifted her weight, the rough denim of her jeans scraping softly along Sofia's legs as she moved closer, her gaze darkening.

Without a word, she hooked her fingers into the hem of Sofia's sweater. She peeled the fabric up and over Sofia's head, tossing it aside without ever breaking eye contact. The cool air of the room hit Sofia's skin, but was instantly replaced by the heat of Allie's attention.

Sofia lay back, her chest rising rapidly as Allie lowered herself over her. She didn't rush. She dragged her wet tongue along the delicate lace edge of Sofia's bra, tracing the floral patterns before lifting up to her collarbone. She kissed every inch of the sensitive skin there, dipping into the hollow of her throat and trailing a line of wet heat down to her stomach.

Her fingertips dug into Sofia's waist, the grip both teasingly gentle and possessively forceful as she hauled Sofia's hips flush against her own. Allie moved back up, her teeth grazing the sensitive peak of Sofia's breast through the material, biting down with a pressure that made Sofia gasp and arch off the cushions. Allie's hands roamed everywhere, kneading her skin, grasping her thighs, and pulling her farther into the friction of their bodies.

Allie's voice was a quiet rumble against her ear as she growled, "I've missed you."

Sofia reached up, her hands tangling desperately in Allie's hair as she tried to pull her down for a kiss. She needed the contact, yearning for the wetness of her lips against hers… but Allie denied her. She hovered centimeters away, her lips ghosting over Sofia's but never making contact. Sofia could feel the heat of Allie's breath, could almost taste the passion waiting there, but Allie held back. The teasing was maddening. Sofia whimpered, straining upward to close the gap, but Allie just smirked against her.

"Please, Allie." Sofia gasped as her voice shivered.

Allie's hand slid down Sofia's stomach and slipped beneath the waistband of her panties.

The touch seemed electric. Allie didn't give her what she wanted right away. She cupped Sofia through the wet heat, the palm of her hand pressing firmly against her while her fingers slid along the sensitive crease of her thigh. Sofia bucked up, seeking more friction, but Allie kept her touch light and maddeningly elusive. She brushed her thumb over Sofia's clit, a feather-light stroke that made Sofia's breath stutter in a sharp cry. Allie watched the reaction, a satisfied look in her eyes as she fine-tuned her rhythm. She circled slowly, alternating between a firm pressure that grounded Sofia and barely-there touches that made her whine in frustration. Sofia tried to widen her legs, offering herself up, but Allie used her free hand to grip Sofia's hip to the couch, holding her still as she tormented her.

Sofia threw her head back, her back arching violently as ecstasy began to roll through her limbs. Her nails dragged down Allie's back, scratching lightly over the bare skin of her shoulders as she tried to anchor herself. She tried to chase Allie's mouth again, desperate for the release of a kiss to ground her, but Allie pulled back again. She watched the pleasure wreck Sofia, her eyes focused on the way Sofia's lips parted, and her breath stumbled in broken gasps.

Allie didn't look away. She held Sofia's gaze, her eyes burning with intensity as her hand moved in slow, agonizingly deliberate circles against her clit. She watched the tension build in Sofia's face and felt the trembling start in her thighs. She waited, controlling the pace with maddening precision, pushing Sofia right to the edge and holding her there until the air in the room appeared thick enough to break.

At the very last second, just as Sofia's head fell back and her body began to convulse, Allie advanced forward. She crushed her mouth against Sofia's, swallowing the broken cry that escaped her throat. It was the deepest, most passionate kiss they had ever shared. Allie tasted the sweet sound of Sofia's release, letting the vibration of her moan fill both their mouths as the kiss deepened and Sofia fell apart in her arms.

Sofia collapsed back against the cushions, gasping and quivering in the afterglow. Allie didn't pull away. She pressed soft, lingering kisses to Sofia's neck, her upper chest, and the swell of her breast, soothing the skin she had just set on fire.

The warmth of the fire and the comfort of Allie's embrace wrapped around them once more. The sound of the rain returned to the forefront, lulling them as their breathing finally evened out. Legs tangled together in the dusky light, exhaustion finally pulled them into a deep sleep.

* * *

Refreshed after their morning heat and cat nap, they moved out into the Black Friday madness, equipped with coffee and ready for adventure.

The shopping centers were alive with activity, an overload of sights and sounds. Crowds fought to get to items first, and eager hands reached for discounted merchandise.

Sofia and Allie, making their way through the chaos hand in hand, found themselves immersed in the excitement. They snagged a few good deals, their laughter reverberating through the crowded aisles as they threw the items in their cart and gave each other a high five. But the true highlight of their shopping trip came with an unexpected encounter.

As they rounded a corner, their shopping cart full of treasures, a crazed woman with crazed eyes and a determined expression lunged towards them. Before they were able to react, she snatched a KitchenAid mixer right out of their cart and turned and bolted, disappearing into the crowd.

Sofia and Allie stood there, stunned, their mouths hanging open in disbelief. Then, as the ludicrousness of the situation sank in, they burst out laughing as more crazy people scurried by.

"I can't believe that just happened!" Sofia exclaimed, wiping tears of laughter from her eyes.

"These people are INSANE," Allie shook her head in amusement.

Both decided that Black Friday shopping wasn't for them and abandoned their cart and the crazed crowds. They retreated to a charming little Italian diner, its comfortable vibe a welcome relief from the chaos. They shared a few plates of fresh pasta, the full aromas of garlic and homemade sauce wafting through the air, their chatter flowing easily and intimately.

The rest of the weekend unfolded in a mist of intimate moments. Tender kisses by the fireplace, conversations that stretched late into the night, along with laughter that resounded throughout the room. Every moment deepened their connection as they wrote their story page by page.

They invited Dylann and Danika over for a "Friendsgiving" dinner, the table laden with a delicious array of potluck dishes. The evening was filled with good wine, card games, and easy laughter. Sofia watched with affection in her heart as Allie interacted with her friends, the genuine affection between them evident. It mirrored how Allie felt, as she witnessed the close bond between Sofia and her family. A feeling of belonging, of finding a home in each other's worlds, began to grow.

As the weekend came to a close, the aching pain of parting once again settled in their hearts. The thought of leaving and returning to their separate lives was a shadow cast over their happiness. But through the sadness, a new sense of hope awakened. They had found something special, something definitely worth fighting for. And as they said their goodbyes to each other, a wordless promise hung in the air... a vow of more intimate moments, more laughter, more love.

And that promise was kept. Every weekend was now a promise to each other. Allie would drive to Fredericksburg for the weekend, or Sofia would find her way to Austin, leaving little pieces of her within Allie's home. A toothbrush, her own shampoo and conditioner, a few pairs of pajamas and clothing pieces. Every weekend, something new was left behind, another little piece of her, as Allie did the same. And as Christmas grew nearer, they began to make plans. Allie was going to come and spend Christmas with Sofia and her family.

The decision hadn't been made casually. For years, Allie had followed the customary routine of spending Christmas with her parents and a small circle of extended family. It was a tradition that her parents held her to, a fancy dinner with expensive wine, followed by polite conversation and the exchange of gifts. Though beneath the facade of holiday cheer, an ingrained unease constantly lingered. Her parents, though outwardly polite, had never truly accepted her sexuality, and their disapproval hung heavy over every guarded conversation.

This year, however, things would be different. The kindness and acceptance she experienced with Sofia's family during every get-together, the genuine affection and openhearted love they had shown her, had stimulated a craving for a different kind of Christmas, one brimming with genuine joy and openness.

When she had broached the subject with her parents on her last visit home, their surprise and disappointment had been palpable.

"You're not coming home for Christmas?" her mother had asked, her voice laced with incredulity. *"But it's tradition! We always have Christmas Eve dinner together."*

"I know, Mom," Allie's voice was firm despite the shiver in her chest. "But I'm going to be spending it with Sofia and her family this year."

A solemn silence had filled the room, the implicit disapproval hanging weighty in the air. Her father, ever the stoic figure, had finally spoken, his voice coated with a thinly veiled disdain.

"I see." His vision fixed on a point just beyond her shoulder. "Well, that's certainly...unexpected."

Allie had taken a deep breath, steeling herself for the unavoidable confrontation. "I know it's different, but it's important to me. Sofia's family has welcomed me with open arms, and I feel more at home with them than I ever have here."

Her mother's face had crumpled with a combination of sadness and disapproval. "Allie, honey," her voice was permeated with a pleading tone, "we're your family. We love you."

"I know you do," Allie's voice quieted as she talked to her mother, "but your love comes with conditions. You've never truly accepted me for who I am, and I'm tired of pretending or keeping the people that I love away from my family because I'm afraid of how you'll treat them."

The conversation had continued, a tense back-and-forth filled with veiled accusations and hurt feelings. But Allie had stood firm, her voice unshaken as she explained her decision. The years of pretending, of suppressing who she really was to appease their expectations, were over. She craved the kindness and genuineness of Sofia's family, the kind of love that accepted her fully, without reservation or judgment.

The prospect of spending Christmas with Sofia, surrounded by the mirth and love of her family, filled Allie with a feeling of anticipation she had never felt before. It was a chance to create new traditions, build new memories, and forge a sense of belonging that transcended bloodlines and societal expectations. And as she went over plans for Christmas with Sofia, her heart blossomed with love and gratitude; she knew that this Christmas would be unlike any other, a homage to love, acceptance, and the true meaning of family.

Chapter 19

They nestled into the plush privacy of a cozy, corner booth at The Maverick, surrounded by the low croon of jazz and the ambient din of a busy Friday night. The lighting was low, carving the room into intimate patches of shadow and suggestion. Sofia lifted her glass, the first sip of her martini sending a welcome warmth through her body, instantly unraveling the tension of her workday.

"So," Josh began, his eyes twinkling with playful intent, "I have a proposition for you."

Sofia arched an eyebrow, intrigued. "Oh?"

"Our firm's annual Christmas Gala is coming up soon, and I was wondering if you'd be my date. I know I'm not giving you a lot of time to prepare since it's next weekend, but I want you to be there… with me."

Sofia's eyes grew wide in surprise. "Your date?" she repeated, a mixture of eagerness and anxiety spinning within her.

"Yes," Josh confirmed, leaning forward, his voice sinking to a discreet whisper. "It's a black-tie affair, the whole nine yards. Think tuxedos, floor-length gowns, and *really* expensive champagne."

Sofia's mind envisioned images of glittering chandeliers and flowing ballgowns. She had never been to a formal gala before. Her world usually revolved around leggings, t-shirts, and the comfortable mess of her photography studio. However, the thought of crossing into that world, of experiencing a night of glamour, fanned a spark of delight in her.

"It's at my father's estate," Josh continued, "just outside of town. I'll arrange for a limo to pick us up, and I've already got my eye on some exquisite jewels for you to wear. And don't go worrying about any of this, I've got it."

Sofia's heart skipped a beat. It was like she was being offered a true Cinderella moment... aside from the whole Prince Charming thing. She had always been a practical, down-to-earth person, but who could resist the dream of a fairytale night?

"Josh," she began, her voice uncertain, "I don't know..."

"Come on, Sofia," Josh urged, his smile expanding. "It'll be fun! A chance to dress up, let loose, and experience a different side of life. Besides," he added, his eyes twinkling, "I think you'd look absolutely stunning in a ballgown."

Sofia's resolve folded beneath the strength of his persuasive charm as well as the undeniable appeal of a glamorous night out. "Okay," she agreed, a smile radiating across her face. "I'd love to go with you."

Josh slapped the table, a huge grin spreading over his face, "I'm going to have the prettiest girl on my arm then." He winked and picked up Sofia's hand to place a playful kiss on the top of it. "I'll pick you up tomorrow morning so we can go find you a dress. I know just the shop."

As they clinked glasses, a wave of anticipation rolled over Sofia. The Christmas Gala and all the elegance it brought awaited. For one night, *she* would be Cinderella, stepping into her own fairytale.

* * *

The next morning, she awoke to her phone ringing, the shrill ring breaking the silence. It was Josh, his voice way too awake for the early morning hour.

"Hey, babe, you awake? I'm heading to *The Peach and Bean* to grab some coffee and will be over to get you."

Her speech was full of sleep, her eyes weary after their martinis last night. "No, not awake, but I'm getting up. I can be ready in an hour."

She slid her legs out of bed, shoving her feet into her slippers, and shuffled across the worn floorboards to the bathroom. She took a quick shower, filling the space with warm steam and the smell of her regular body wash, a smell she had grown to look forward to with each shower.

Within the hour, Josh was at her door, hot coffee in hand, a lazy smile greeting her.

"Hey, beautiful," He said as he entered her loft. "You smell amazing!"

Sofia laughed as she threw on her soft brown wool-blend Ralph Lauren coat.

"Ready?" He took a long drink of his steaming coffee.

She nodded, grabbing her trusted old leather tote from its hanger near the door. "I'm ready."

"Let's go find you a dress!" Josh extended his arm for her

to take. His light southern drawl and old-fashioned manners made her giggle inside.

They piled into Josh's sleek black Mercedes GLE 450e. The smooth, expensive leather slid easily against her jeans. She loved his car and all the bells and whistles that came with it; secretly, she made owning one a goal for her future.

The morning found them embarking on an hour-long drive to San Antonio, the anticipation of their shopping trip buzzing between them. Their destination: the renowned Neiman Marcus, a temple of luxury and high fashion that housed designer labels Sofia had only ever dreamed of.

When they entered the store, Sofia was awestruck by the alluring fragrance of expensive perfume. Gleaming marble floors, sparkling chandeliers, and perfectly dressed mannequins created an atmosphere of exclusivity.

Accustomed to the cozy, casual charm of Fredericksburg's boutiques, Sofia felt a trace of intimidation in the midst of the gleaming displays. Josh, however, was entirely in his element. He made his way through the labyrinth of designer labels with confident ease, his hand resting gently on the small of her back to steer her through the crowd. "Don't worry," he whispered, detecting her unease. "You'll fit right in."

He approached a polished counter, a warm smile adorning his lips as he noticed the stylish sales associate. "We're looking for Heather."

"Of course, Mr. McCoy," the associate replied, her voice velvety as silk. "Right this way."

They were led to a private suite, an oasis of plush chairs, soft lighting, and a discreetly placed table with two chilled glasses of champagne awaiting their arrival. Sofia's eyes opened wide in surprise, the luxury of the space both impressive and intimidating.

Heather, a tall, elegant woman with a welcoming smile, greeted them with a natural ease. "Mr. McCoy, it's a pleasure to see you again." Her gaze shifted to Sofia. "And you must be Sofia. Josh has told me so much about you."

Sofia blushed, flustered by the attention. Heather sensed her nervousness and offered a soothing smile. "Don't worry, darling. We'll find the perfect dress for you."

Heather took Sofia's measurements before disappearing into the racks of designer gowns. She returned with an armful of dresses, each dress more gorgeous than the last. Shimmering sequins, delicate lace, and flowing satin made Sofia's head spin.

The large main dressing area held a private dressing room that Sofia was able to get dressed in, with the assistance of Heather, who never left her side unless she was getting more dresses.

She slipped into each gown, the luxurious fabrics rustling over her skin. She slowly whirled about in front of the mirrors in the main dressing area, the champagne adding a sparkle to her eyes as she admired her own reflection. Josh, perched on one of the plush chairs, offered encouraging smiles and honest critiques.

"You look beautiful in that one, Sofia," he'd say, his eyes twinkling. "But I think this one accentuates your curves even better."

Sofia, overwhelmed by the choices, loved them all. She had never experienced such luxury, such attention to detail. It proved a whirlwind of fashion and fantasy, a Cinderella moment come to life.

Josh, perceiving her indecision, turned to Heather. "Do

you have any new Maria Lucia Hohan dresses in?"

Heather nodded. "We just received a new shipment this week. Let me see what we have."

She disappeared into the back room, returning soon after with a dress draped over her arm. It was a vision of pale pink, a whisper of color that shimmered like moonlight on water. Sofia's breath seized in her throat. It was the most beautiful dress she had ever seen.

Heather ushered her into the private dressing space. The dress slipped over Sofia's head, the soft fabric cool and fluid. It was a work of art in draping and pleating, the mermaid silhouette hugging her curves with exquisite precision. A deeply daring sweetheart neckline accentuated her bust, while the back, daringly low and embellished with a thin satin ribbon that weaved across her back in a deliciously low "x" pattern, revealed a tempting glimpse of her smooth skin down to her tailbone. A soft drape flowed from where the ribbon ended, cascading to the floor in a small, elegant train.

Sofia gazed at her own reflection in wonder. The dress was elegant, sophisticated, and indisputably sexy. It was a dress that held attention, and on Sofia, it was simply breathtaking.

When Sofia emerged, Josh gasped.

The pale pink gown glimmered around her, clinging in a way that made his mouth go dry. Josh sensed a jolt go through him, a spike of adrenaline that had nothing to do with brotherhood. It was the visceral response of a man seeing exactly what he desired. A wave of possessiveness engulfed him, fueling a burning need to claim her, to ensure that when the room gasped upon her entrance, everyone knew exactly whose arm she was holding.

He bit back a gulp, pushing down the unforeseen wave

of emotion, his features settling into a guise of friendly admiration. "Sofia," he breathed, his voice in a low husk. "You look… incredible."

Sofia blushed, her cheeks pink with a medley of excitement and self-consciousness. She twirled slowly, the soft fabric swirling her like a cloud. "Do you really think so?" she asked, her eyes seeking his approval.

"I do," Josh confirmed, his glance lingering on the way the dress hugged her curves, the delicate drape accentuating her back. "It's perfect."

And he knew it was. This wasn't just a dress; it was a transformation. It was the Cinderella gown she had not dared to dream of, the one that would make heads turn and hearts race. And as he watched her, a shade of something darker… something possessive, blazed within him.

But he pushed those thoughts aside, reminding himself of her relationship with Allie. He flashed a smile, his voice recovering its usual lightness. "This is definitely the one," he declared. "You're going to be this season's *'Diamond'.*"

Sofia beamed, her eyes shimmering with delight at the nod to her favorite show. She had never felt so beautiful, so confident. This dress, this moment, was a dream come true. And as she looked at Josh, she had a surge of gratitude for his friendship, his support, his constant belief in her.

20

Chapter 20

The memory of Allie's visit the previous weekend persisted in Sofia's mind. They spent the day exploring the quaint shops of Fredericksburg, their laughter reverberating amid the cobblestone streets as they searched for the perfect accessories to complete Sofia's gala ensemble. Allie, with her flawless taste, found a stunning necklace, a delicate gold chain embellished with two small, lab-created diamonds. One was perfectly round, a classic symbol of enduring love, while the other, nestled beside it, was a unique pear shape, a representation of their individual personalities and the beauty they created together.

"This is for you." Allie had said, her eyes full of affection as she fastened the necklace around Sofia's neck. "An early Christmas present. To me, it's a symbol of us. We're beautifully complex individuals, Sofia, but together? Together, we're flawless."

Sofia's heart blossomed with emotion as she gazed at her image in the mirror, the diamonds seizing the light and casting rainbows on her skin. The necklace was more than merely a piece of jewelry; it stood as a symbol of their growing love for each other.

"I'll never take it off." She uttered softly as her hands ran over the smooth, small stones.

Their shopping trip continued as they searched for the right shoes for her dress. Sofia wasn't used to wearing heels, and she was intent on finding a pair that was both stylish and comfortable. After trying on countless pairs, she finally settled on a pair of elegant ivory leather heels with delicate straps and a slender heel, adding a dash of sophistication.

The final hurdle was finding the right undergarments. The daringly low back of the Maria Lucia Hohan gown demanded a solution that wouldn't detract from its elegant lines. After much deliberation, Sofia opted for a nude, seamless thong that sat low on her hips, making sure it remained hidden from view.

The sole hiccup of the weekend was the peculiar encounter with Josh at the new local brewery that evening. Sofia was at the counter, adding their names to the waitlist for a table, while Allie made a quick run to the bathroom. She spotted Josh at the bar and ran up to him to give him a hug.

"Hey, beautiful!" he wrapped his arms around her. "What are you doing here? Pull up a stool, or here, have mine," he offered, hopping off the leather stool.

"No, no, it's okay!" she strained over the loud voices at the bar. "I'm waiting on a booth with Allie. Why don't you come join us?"

Josh hesitated, then settled back onto his stool. "Oh, no, it's okay. I don't want to disturb you."

Sofia laughed. "Josh, you wouldn't be disturbing us! You know I love you more than my luggage, and I really want you to get to know Allie! Every time we've tried to get together, you've had to cancel."

"No, babe, I don't want to intrude. Plus, I'm here with some guys from the firm," Josh insisted, his tone cool and flat. He took a sip of his drink and signaled the bartender for another. "I'll just see you for our Monday morning coffee."

Sofia's brows furrowed, confused by his reluctance. "Okay, coffee on Monday then," she said slowly.

Josh leaned down and gave her a quick kiss on the cheek. "See you then, babe. Love ya."

Sofia walked away, a knot of irritation and confusion clenching in her stomach. But the sight of Allie approaching drew her attention, and her thoughts shifted back to their evening together.

As they sorted through their purchases back at the studio apartment that evening, Allie couldn't help but express a tinge of wistful longing.

"I wish I could be there to see you in that dress," she said, her voice tinged with a trace of playful jealousy. "I know you are going to be absolutely stunning."

Sofia, sensing Allie's mixed emotions, stretched out her hand, their fingers intertwining. "I know… and I wish you could be there too. But I promise to wear it again for you at the New Year's party in Austin."

Allie smiled, wrapping Sofia in her arms, "I'm going to hold you to that, gorgeous. Might even throw in you owing me a dance or two."

Sofia laughed, her heart bursting with affection. "Definitely," she agreed. "A whole night of dancing, just for you."

Allie's eyes looked into Sofia's, adoring the subtle golden flecks in those hazel depths. Her heart fluttered as she gazed at Sofia as if discovering her face for the first time. The smooth, light olive skin, the tiny freckles that somehow stood out even more whenever she laughed, the full, rounded lips that formed a perfect heart shape when she was serious, the impossibly long, dark eyelashes that framed those expressive eyes, every detail was engraved into Allie's memory, a masterpiece she could never tire of admiring.

A warm, profound yearning arose in Allie's chest as she studied the details of Sofia's face. Her gaze followed the familiar geography she adored, the delicate cut of her cheekbones, the soft slope of her nose, the way her hair tumbled effortlessly over her shoulders. But it was Sofia's eyes that captured her most quickly, with a depth and clarity that could captivate every part of her soul.

"Sofia," Allie whispered, her voice husky with emotion, "I love you."

The words left her lips with a soft conviction that seemed to suspend time. It wasn't just a conversation but an intense confession and a vow whispered from the deepest part of her soul.

Sofia's breath faltered, her heart duplicating the wild beat of Allie's. A comfort, a feeling of belonging she had never felt before, spread through her, scattering the shadows of past hurts and insecurities. She stared into Allie's tranquil sea-blue eyes, seeing nothing but truth and acceptance reflected back at her. Allie was safety, she was home, she was the missing piece she had been searching for her entire life.

"I love you too," she breathed, her voice hardly a whisper, her thumb gently caressing Allie's cheek, the skin soft and warm beneath her touch.

They held each other's gaze, caught in a quietness that

spoke more loudly than any voice. The room slipped away, leaving only the synchronized rhythm of their hearts amid the quiet. It seemed as though time had paused just for them, blurring the outside world in the background as they finally said everything they had been waiting to say.

Allie, unable to resist any longer, reached out, her fingers running through Sofia's thick, dark hair, gently tugging her closer. Sofia yielded willingly, her body leaning into Allie's touch, her heart hammering with anticipation.

Their lips met in a kiss that proved both passionately tender, a culmination of all the unspoken longing and the calm moments of intimacy that had brought their hearts together. It was a kiss that expressed vulnerability and trust, of a love that blossomed amid the turmoil of their lives, a love that vowed to be a light in any darkness.

And in that instance, as their lips moved in perfect sync, their bodies pressed together in a silent embrace; they both knew, with certainty that exceeded words, that they were truly, deeply, irrevocably in love. The two small stones of her necklace warmed against her collarbone as they kissed, a gentle oath she wore like a secret.

21

Chapter 21

Sofia woke with a gasp, her eyes flying open as if startled by a dream. But it wasn't a dream that woke her; it was the date. December 21st, her Cinderella day. A thrill of excitement shot throughout her as she launched herself out of bed and into the bathroom.

The first order of business was a long, luxurious shower. The warm water lapping over her skin, she soaked it in and let it wash away any lingering doubts as she welcomed the magic of the day. When she stepped out of the shower, a smile lit up her face. This was it. Her fairytale was about to begin!

Her gaze wandered to the calendar on the fridge, tracing the bright pink scribbles that marked the day's agenda. It began with a nail appointment alongside her sisters, followed by a full hair and makeup session at the city's most exclusive salon—a luxury fully funded by Josh's generosity and insistence. The mere thought of being pampered, of shedding her everyday self to transform into a vision of beauty, made her want to dance in the streets with excitement.

At 5:00 p.m. sharp, her mom and sister, Cami, were going to arrive to help her prepare for the grand evening. She couldn't wait for them to see her in her gown with her hair and makeup complete. She could already hear Cami's excited chatter, her voice brimming with a mixture of envy and admiration.

"Oh my god, Sofia, you're going to be like a real-life princess!" Cami had exclaimed when Sofia first told her about the gala. "Imagine, walking into that massive mansion, surrounded by all the elite of Texas!"

Blanca, ever the devoted mother, had radiated pride, her eyes beaming with affection. "Mija, you're all grown up and going to a fancy gala. You're going to be the most beautiful woman there."

The knowledge that she was about to step inside a world of unbridled luxury, to grace the halls of the grandest mansion in the area, filled Sofia with a breathless, trembling hope. It was a rare chance to experience a different side of life, to shed her insecurities and finally feel divinely beautiful. Tonight, she would be the 'Diamond of the season,' a Cinderella entering a fairytale that felt perfectly real. And she had the perfect Prince Charming to guide her, not a lover, but a devoted friend who made the magic possible. With Josh as her safe harbour, her heart blossomed with a radiant, unsuspecting joy, beating fast with the promise of a night that was supposed to change everything.

* * *

The clock clicked towards 5:00 p.m., a countdown to the

moment Sofia would transform into a princess for the evening. Her mom, Blanca, and sister, Cami, were already there, radiating with eagerness.

Sofia entered her apartment fresh from the salon. Her hair, usually an untamed mane of dark waves, was swept up into a perfect up-do, a work of art made of intricate twists and delicate braids. Soft tendrils, curled with care, encircled her face, bringing a hint of romantic softness to the regal style. The golden hair vine that Josh had surprised her with, a delicate masterpiece of interwoven leaves and shimmering crystals, caught the light upon every movement.

Her makeup was completely flawless. Soft contouring sculpted her cheekbones, while a rosy blush added a trace of warmth and vitality to her complexion. A gentle shimmer dusted the high points of her cheeks, catching the light at every turn of her head, creating an angelic glow that denoted her inner radiance. Her eyes, framed by perfectly applied liner and mascara, sparkled with excitement, their hazel depths reflecting the anticipation of the evening ahead. Her lips, painted a natural pink, were soft and romantic, a subtle enhancement to her natural beauty.

Blanca, her eyes welling up with tears, couldn't contain her pride. "Oh, mija," she murmured, her voice heavy with emotion, "you're absolutely stunning."

Cami, the budding fashion critic, couldn't help but squeal with delight. "Sofia, you look like a real-life princess!" she exclaimed, her eyes wide with admiration.

Sofia was touched by their affection as she smiled shyly. "Thank you, Mom, Cami, I feel like a princess already."

Cami's excitement overflowed as she retrieved the dress from the closet, her bare feet barely making a sound as she crossed the room towards Sofia. She hung the bag on the bathroom door frame; the lightweight black garment bag barely rustled as she unzipped it, revealing the pale pink gown within.

"Oh my gosh!" Cami's eyes widened as she carefully extracted the whisper-pink gown. "You didn't tell me it was a Maria Lucia dress! Do you have any idea how much these cost?" Her mouth remained agape, a combination of awe and amazement tinting her features.

Sofia, taking the dress from its hanger, shrugged nonchalantly. "No, I tried not to look at any price tags," she admitted. "I felt bad enough with Josh paying for it that knowing the cost would just make me feel worse."

Part of Sofia wondered why he was going to such lengths… the dress, the glam squad, the urging. It seemed like an apology for something she hadn't even accused him of yet, but she pushed the thought away. Today wasn't for overthinking.

"Sissy, Maria Lucia Hohan's dresses *don't have* price tags. Okay, I *need* to Google how much this costs." Cami scoffed as she pulled out her phone, her fingers scrolling across the screen while she scrolled to her search engine.

Blanca, ever the caring mother, moved forward to help Sofia into the gown.

"Thanks, Mom."

Sofia carefully stepped into the opening her mother had created.

"Of course, my love," Blanca's eyes filled with a trace of nostalgia. "I'm so glad I get to be here to witness this moment. It brings me back to my days on stage. Every time I put on an evening gown, I felt so beautiful, so grand. It's amazing what a dress can do." A trace of sadness crossed her features as she recalled her past life, a life filled with glamour and momentary fame.

Blanca gently pulled the dress up, turning Sofia so she could secure the delicate satin lacing that crisscrossed her open back.

"Make sure it's tight, Mom." Sofia chuckled. "I don't want the dress falling off in the middle of the gala!"

She turned towards her mother and sister, smoothing the fabric at her sides. Both gasped, their eyes growing in awe. The setting sun, streaming through the window, bathed Sofia in golden light, casting a tender glow on the pale pink fabric. The delicate curls framing her face shimmered like spun gold, and the dress seemed to shine with an ethereal luminescence. Sofia was beyond breathtaking.

Cami, her phone briefly forgotten, stepped next to her mother, her head resting on Blanca's shoulder. "That dress was made for you," she uttered softly, her voice overflowing with sincere admiration.

"Thank you, hermanita."

She turned to her mother, seeking her approval. "Do you like it?"

Blanca, speechless for a moment, finally nodded, her eyes filled with unspilled tears. "You couldn't be any more beautiful. You truly are a princess."

Sofia beamed, twirling playfully, the soft fabric swirling and encircling her like a cloud. "I *feel* like one, mama."

Cami, suddenly remembering her search, gasped. "Um, yeah!" she exclaimed. "That dress is almost $4,000! You're officially wearing my car! That dress is more expensive than my car!"

Sofia laughed, her fingers caressing the delicate pleats of

the fabric. "That's crazy," she shook her head in disbelief. "This is the most expensive thing I've ever put on my body. I'm afraid of moving in case it rips or gets a stain or something!

Blanca chuckled as she came forward to adjust a rogue curl that had escaped its carefully crafted position. "Don't worry about those things, mija. Just go have fun tonight. Take it all in and thank Josh for offering you this experience. He's a kind man."

Sofia nodded, her smile deepening at her mother's touch. "I will, Mama. I'd better call Allie so she can see me before I take off."

She took her phone from her dresser and called Allie on FaceTime. Blanca held the phone, capturing Sofia as she twirled, the dress dancing around her like a dream. The image of Sofia, radiant and beautiful, filled Allie's screen, a picture of true beauty that took her breath away.

22

Chapter 22

The sleek black limousine, crafted solely for elegance and exclusivity, rolled to a stop in front of Sofia's building. Josh emerged from the car, a vision of masculine elegance in his black Tom Ford mohair silk twill suit. The suit was perfectly tailored to his frame, and a crisp white shirt paired with a matching black silk tie completed the ensemble. His golden blonde hair was styled impeccably, and the $11,000 Ludwig gold watch adorning his wrist was just a whisper of the immense wealth he came from.

He strode towards Sofia, his eyes fixed on her as she emerged from the building, her mother and sister trailing behind. Time seemed to slow as he took in the sight of her. The pale pink gown shimmered in the gentle wind, making her look like a dream, its delicate fabric clinging to her curves with exquisite precision. She was breathtaking. He couldn't look away; she was simply perfection.

Josh's heart skipped a beat. He had known she would be beautiful, but the reality of her beauty surpassed his expectations. He felt a tightening in his chest, a yearning to claim her as his own. A swell of pride rose within him… he was the one escorting her into the gala, the one who would witness the envy in the eyes of other men.

"Sofia," he breathed. "You look absolutely exquisite, as I knew you would."

Sofia blushed, her cheeks flushing with a delicate pink that mirrored the hue of her gown. "Thank you, Josh," her voice soft and laced with a hint of nervousness. "You look quite *dashing* yourself."

"Not as dashing as you, though." Josh countered, his eyes twinkling with admiration. "Shall we?"

He extended his arm towards her. Sofia, her heart fluttering with excitement, placed her hand lightly on his arm with a smile.

"We shall."

The chauffeur, impeccably dressed in a black uniform, opened the car doors for them. Sofia and Josh stepped inside, the plush leather seats inviting them into their grandeur. As the limousine pulled away from the curb, Sofia couldn't help but be filled with anticipation. The McCoy Holiday Gala, a world of elegance and extravagance, awaited. And for one night, she would be Cinderella, stepping into a fairytale with someone she had quickly come to call her best friend.

Sofia's excitement bubbled over as the limousine glided through the moonlit streets. "Oh, Josh!" she exclaimed, bouncing playfully on the seat, "This is so…magical! Thank you for talking me into coming with you."

Josh, his own anticipation growing, chuckled at her enthusiasm. "You're welcome, Sofia," he replied, his eyes twinkling with a mixture of admiration and something deeper… something possessive. He reached into his coat pocket, retrieving a long, elegant leather jewelry case.

"Sof," he began, his voice softening, "I would love for you to wear this tonight."

He opened the case, a small light illuminating the interior, revealing a stunning necklace. Rows of sparkling jewels, a symphony of light blues, pinks, and whites, shimmered under the soft glow. It was a masterpiece of design and craftsmanship unlike any she had seen before.

Sofia gasped, her fingers tracing the delicate lines of the jewels. "Josh," she breathed, "this is exquisite."

He reached for the necklace, a smile playing on his lips. "Like you," he murmured, his gaze locking with hers.

But as he went to remove the necklace from its case, Sofia gently stopped him, her hand resting on his. "I can't." Her other hand instinctively rose to touch the small diamond necklace she already wore… the one Allie had given her. "I promised Allie I would wear this necklace. It was her gift to me, and it means a lot. It's the only thing of her I could bring to this magnificent night. I hope you understand."

Josh's smile faltered, a flicker of anger igniting within him. *Why would you want to wear that when I'm offering you luxury?* he thought, his frustration growing. He wanted her to wear *his* gift, to be bathed in the extravagance only *he* could show her. Allie could be left behind for this one night; tonight was his night.

His fingers tightened around the velvet box, the leather creaking audibly in the quiet cabin. For a split second, the air in the car felt heavy, suffocating. Then, just as quickly, his grip loosened, and the dazzling smile returned. "I understand," his voice betrayed a hint of disappointment. "I just thought I would get you something beautiful to wear tonight."

"Oh, Josh, it *is* absolutely stunning, but you've already given me *so* much. You've made this a beautiful and incredible night for me already."

Her words, though innocent, were a sharp reminder of the woman who held Sofia's heart, the woman who stood between them. A flash of hatred, swift and intense, crossed Josh's eyes. He kept his head down, his jaw clenched, fighting to maintain his composure. He wanted no part of *her* here tonight, or any other night.

He shoved the jewelry case back into his pocket, clearing his throat and shaking his head slightly as if to dispel the unwelcome thoughts. "Okay, Sof," he said, his voice regaining its usual lightness, "I'll save it for another time. Another gala."

Sofia, oblivious to the turmoil raging within him, leaned forward and kissed his cheek. "Thank you for understanding, Josh. I really am truly grateful for everything you've done. For making me come, for *totally* spoiling me with everything for the gala, and for being you. Thank you for being an amazing friend."

* * *

The limousine glided through the wrought iron gates, joining a line of gleaming vehicles that curved along the expansive driveway. As they approached the McCoy mansion, Sofia's breath caught in her throat. It was even grander than she had imagined. The driveway, lined with perfectly manicured hedges and vibrant floral patches, stretched into the distance, flanked by ancient trees that formed a majestic canopy overhead. The mansion itself, a sprawling edifice of brick and stone, loomed before them, its facade illuminated by the warm glow of countless windows. A grand staircase, adorned with massive flower-filled urns on each step, led up to the imposing entrance, where light spilled out onto the landscaped grounds.

A balcony on the second floor overlooked the scene, offering a panoramic view of the arriving guests. Christmas lights, intertwined with festive red bows and garlands of greenery, adorned every window and doorway, casting a magical glow over the estate. Even the hedges and trees were draped in twinkling lights, creating a winter wonderland that sparkled beneath the moonlit sky.

The soft strains of music and the murmur of laughter drifted from the open doorway, hinting at the lively scene within. As the limousine came to a stop, the chauffeur sprang to open the door, extending a hand to assist Sofia. She stepped out, her heart pounding with a sense of awe and excitement. Josh offered his arm, and together they ascended the grand staircase, the sound of their footsteps echoing softly in the crisp night air.

Inside, the mansion was a symphony of luxury and grandeur. A massive marble staircase, splitting to the left and right, dominated the foyer. Marble floors stretched out in every direction, their polished surface reflecting the glittering chandeliers overhead. Countless rooms were filled with elegantly dressed guests. The air buzzed with conversation and laughter, the clinking of glasses a constant counterpoint to the music that swirled through the expansive home.

Josh navigated the crowd with practiced ease. He led Sofia through the maze of hallways, his hand gently resting on her back. He stopped often to introduce her to colleagues and acquaintances, his voice smooth and confident as he presented Sofia as his date. Sofia, though initially overwhelmed by the sheer number of people and the opulence of her surroundings, found herself relaxing, her initial nervousness giving way to the sense of magic that seemed to flow around her tonight.

Finally, Josh ushered her into the ballroom, a vast and opulent space that took her breath away. Crystal chandeliers, each one a masterpiece of intricate design, glittered overhead, casting a dazzling light on the scene below. Columns soared towards the vaulted ceiling, and the walls were lined with priceless artwork. But it was the guests, each one dazzling in their shimmering gowns and tailored suits, that truly captivated Sofia's attention. She had never seen such a display of elegance and sophistication, such a concentration of wealth and power. It was a world that had always intrigued her, a realm she'd glimpsed but never truly entered. And yet, here she was, a part of it, if only for tonight.

Josh charmed his way through the crowded ballroom, leading Sofia towards a group of distinguished-looking individuals engaged in conversation. "Sofia," he said, his voice smooth and confident, "I'd like you to meet some important people."

He gestured towards a tall, imposing man with silver hair and a commanding presence. "This is Judge Thompson," Josh introduced, "and his wife, Elizabeth. And this is Sofia Flores." He said as he nodded his head towards Sofia.

Sofia extended her hand, praying her palm wasn't sweating. In her mind, she felt like a child playing dress-up in her mother's closet, terrified that one wrong word would shatter the illusion. She took a breath to steady herself, "It's a pleasure to meet you both."

"The pleasure is ours, Miss Flores," Judge Thompson replied, his voice deep and resonant with his strong Texas drawl. "Josh has told us so much about you."

Elizabeth Thompson, a woman with a warm smile and kind eyes, stepped forward. "He certainly has," she agreed, her voice sweet like honey with its Southern accent. "We've been eager to meet the woman who has captured our godson's attention."

Sofia blushed, a wave of warmth spreading through her cheeks. She glanced at Josh, who offered a reassuring smile. She was confused at the comment, knowing that Josh and she were only friends, but she smiled back at them and Josh.

"And this," Josh continued, gesturing towards a woman with fiery red hair and a confident air, "is Senator Davis. Senator, this is Sofia Flores, a talented photographer and a dear friend."

Senator Marlene Davis, her eyes sharp and intelligent, extended her hand. "Miss Flores," she said, her voice firm and authoritative, "it's a pleasure. Josh, you've been keeping your friend a secret."

Sofia somehow managed a smile, even with her insides turning with nervousness. "The pleasure is all mine, Senator," her voice feigned a confidence that was building slowly.

The conversation flowed almost as quickly as the champagne, shifting from lighthearted banter about the gala to more serious discussions about local politics and community initiatives. Sofia found herself drawn into the exchange, probably helped by her now third glass of champagne, her own opinions and insights being welcomed and valued. She was surprised by the genuine interest these powerful individuals showed in her work as well as her perspective.

As the conversation drew to a close, Sofia couldn't help but feel a sense of accomplishment. She had navigated the social intricacies of the gala, held her own in conversations with influential figures, and even sparked a genuine connection with a few.

With a renewed air of confidence, fueled by the glittering atmosphere and another glass of champagne, Sofia playfully bounced on the balls of her feet, her eyes sparkling. "So," she tilted her head with a playful curiosity, "when do I get to meet your parents?"

Josh's gaze darted around the room, a flicker of hesitation crossing his features. "I'm sure they'll show up somewhere soon. They're famous for making a grand entrance... fashionably late to their own parties."

Sofia giggled, the champagne loosening her inhibitions and amplifying the magical atmosphere. The room seemed to shimmer around her, the music a vibrant pulse, the laughter a symphony of merriment.

Josh let out a short laugh as Sofia stumbled slightly, his hand instinctively reaching out to steady her. "Whoa there, Sof," he teased gently, taking her champagne flute. "How many of those have you had?"

"I'm really not sure," she admitted with a playful grin, "but I plan on having a couple more!"

"In that case," Josh declared, his pace quickening as he playfully escorted her out of the ballroom, "we'd better get you somewhere quieter!"

Sofia laughed, trying to keep up with Josh as she navigated the flowing fabric of her gown. Suddenly, she felt a tug that pulled her to a stop, and a ripping sound pierced the air. "Oh no!" she gasped, her voice laced with alarm.

Josh stopped, turning to face her with concern. "What? What happened?"

"I think my heel got stuck on my dress and ripped it!" she exclaimed, her voice filled with dismay. She bent down, her fingers carefully lifting the hem of the gown to inspect the damage.

As she searched for the tear, Josh's voice suddenly shifted, adopting a formal tone, a hint of tension in his voice. "Hello, Father."

"Hello, Josh," a deep, sophisticated voice replied, its coldness sending a shiver down Sofia's spine.

She looked up, her eyes widening as she met the gaze of a handsome man in his mid-fifties. His impeccably tailored suit exuded an air of authority. He stood there, his expression unreadable, his salt-and-pepper hair gleaming in the dim light of the hallway.

"Oh, Dad," he regained his composure, "this is Sofia, my friend I've told you about. Sofia, this is my dad, Thomas McCoy." He moved to stand beside Sofia, a subtle gesture of protectiveness.

"It's nice to meet you, Sofia," Thomas said formally, his voice lacking any warmth. "I hope you are enjoying our home so far."

"Your home is absolutely beautiful, Mr. McCoy." Sofia mustered a friendly smile despite the intimidation she felt. "Thank you so much for letting me attend. It's been magical."

Thomas nodded curtly. "Any friend of Josh's is welcome anytime. Enjoy your evening."

Josh and Sofia watched as Thomas passed them, continuing down the hall and disappearing into the ballroom, his presence leaving a lingering chill in the air. Sofia turned to Josh, her eyes wide with uncertainty. "I'm not sure he liked me," she whispered, her voice laced with doubt.

"He liked you," Josh reassured her, his arm wrapping around her waist in a gesture that was both comforting and possessive. "You'd know if he didn't."

Sofia looked at him, confused. "How can you tell?"

"You'd know, believe me." His voice was serious, a hint of warning in his tone.

They continued down the long hallway, its walls adorned with expensive portraits illuminated by soft display lights. The hallway twisted and turned, eventually opening into a smaller, more intimate parlor area. A mahogany bar, fully stocked with gleaming bottles, stretched along one wall, while the rest of the space was encased in floor-to-ceiling windows that soared twenty feet high, offering a breathtaking view of the moonlit gardens. Victorian-style couches and chairs were scattered throughout, creating cozy conversation nooks.

Josh approached the bar, returning with two glasses filled with a golden liquid and a pretty bottle filled with the same glowing liquid. "Try this," he handed Sofia one of the glasses. "It's straight honey whiskey, a favorite of mine."

Sofia, intrigued, took a sip, the warmth of the whiskey spreading through her chest like a small fire. Her eyes caught sight of what seemed to be another room on the other side of the windows. Josh, sensing her curiosity, led her towards a set of large French doors that opened into a magnificent conservatory.

The greenhouse was expansive, bathed in the occasional soft hanging light. Every space was taken, a haven of lush greenery and vibrant blooms. Every imaginable color of rose, delicate peonies, and exotic flowers Sofia couldn't name filled the space, their fragrances mingling in a heady symphony. Ivy and other hanging plants cascaded from above, their tendrils weaving a tapestry of green against the glass panes, and throughout the many aisles, creating a secretive, dreamlike atmosphere. Small, winding paths led through the foliage, creating hidden nooks and intimate spaces.

"Josh! This is amazing!" Sofia exclaimed, her eyes sparkling with delight. She wandered through the greenhouse, her fingers gently brushing against the velvety petals, whispering words of admiration to the silent blooms.

She discovered a long, inviting window seat tucked away in a quiet, hidden corner, piled high with plush cushions and soft throws. It was the perfect hideaway, a secret haven where one could escape the world and get lost in a good book.

Sofia carefully arranged her dress and settled onto the window seat, accepting the newly filled glass of whiskey from Josh. She threw her head back and laughed, the sound echoing softly through the greenhouse. "I could sit here forever," she declared, her voice filled with contentment.

Josh chuckled, taking a long swig of his whiskey, savoring the burn as it went down. "It's one of my mom's favorite spots," he revealed. "She used to come down here when the noise of the house got too loud," Josh said softly, running a hand over a fern. "I'd find her curled up right there, hiding from the parties she was supposed to be hosting. It was the only place she felt real."

Sofia, gazing at the tranquil beauty surrounding them, nodded in understanding. "I can see why," she murmured.

They sat in comfortable silence for a while, sipping their

whiskey and enjoying the peaceful atmosphere. Josh, his voice low and intimate, began to share stories about the other guests at the gala, pointing out celebrities and influential figures Sofia hadn't recognized. As they talked, the tension from the encounter with his father seemed to dissipate, her body relaxing, enjoying the whiskey in her hand.

23

Chapter 23

The warmth of the greenhouse, the heavy scent of exotic flowers, and the mixture of numerous glasses of champagne and that potent honey whiskey were starting to take their toll on Sofia. A pleasant dizziness swirled through her, her vision blurring slightly at the edges, the world tilting at odd angles. She giggled at a joke Josh made, the sound echoing a little too loudly in the intimate space. She was undeniably and blissfully drunk.

Josh, too, was feeling the effects of the alcohol. His inhibitions were loosened, emboldening him and fueling the emotions he had been struggling to suppress. He reached for Sofia's hand, his fingers intertwining with hers. "Sofia," he began, his voice husky with a newfound intensity, "I have to tell you something."

Sofia, her senses pleasantly dulled, gazed at him with a soft smile. "Hmm?"

He hesitated, his gaze searching hers. "I… I have feelings for you, Sofia. More than just friends."

The smile remained on Sofia's face; she didn't want him

170

to feel bad for the way he felt. "Josh," she began, her hand resting gently on his cheek, "You are *so* amazing. But I… I don't feel the same way. I love you, but just as a friend. A *best* friend."

"I know," Josh interrupted, his voice edged with a desperate plea, "I know you aren't going to love me as more. But couldn't we just pretend, just for tonight? Let's forget about everything else and just… be together."

Sofia sat up and shook her head, her resolve firming despite the alcohol-induced haze. "No, Josh," her voice was gentle but unwavering. "I can't lie to you, and I can't lie to myself. I love Allie."

Josh's face hardened, his jaw clenching. "Why?" he demanded, his voice rising in frustration. "Why can't we just have this one night? Just one damn night."

"Because it wouldn't be fair to you, to Allie, or to me. I care about you, Josh, as a friend. I value your friendship, but that's all it can ever be."

Josh's grip on her hand tightened, his fingers digging into her skin, his voice thickening with anger. "Why? Why her? What does she have that I don't? I've done everything for you, I've offered you the world."

Sofia winced, a gasp escaping her lips as pain shot through her arm. "Josh, you're hurting me! Let go."

She tried to stand, but the alcohol betrayed her, her legs wobbling beneath her. She stumbled, her vision blurring, and reached out to steady herself, her hand grasping the edge of a tall plant stand. Josh, fueled by a mixture of alcohol and rejection, grabbed her upper arms, spinning her around to face him.

"Sofia," he growled, his voice thick with anger, "I've wanted you since the day I met you. I know you love me too, you just can't admit it because of Allie. Just admit it, damn it! Admit that you want me!"

Sofia stared into his eyes, fear replacing the earlier warmth. His gaze was wild and desperate; the playful charm she was accustomed to had disappeared. "Josh, I can't say that!" she cried, panic rising in her chest. "I don't love you! I don't want you like that! You're my friend, Josh. We can just be friends!"

Josh's grip tightened, his fingers digging into her upper arms, the pain intensifying. "No!" he shouted, his voice echoing through the greenhouse. "You're lying! You want me!"

Sofia screamed, "Josh! You're hurting me!"

His control snapped. He released one hand, his backhand connecting with Sofia's cheek with a sickening thud. The force of the blow sent her flying backwards, her head spinning, her forehead colliding with the edge of a wooden display table. She crumpled to the ground, her vision fading in and out. The last image on her mind was the fury-filled face of the man she had once called her friend.

A low moan escaped Sofia's lips as she lay on the ground, a wave of nausea washing over her. She felt a warm trickle on her face, and her fingers came away sticky with blood. "Josh, please don't," she whispered, her voice trembling with fear and confusion.

She pushed herself up onto her knees, her head pounding, blood dripping from the gash on her forehead. She stood, turning to face Josh, her eyes wide with disbelief and betrayal. "Josh," she pleaded, her voice cracking, "why?"

He stood frozen, his face a mask of rage and despair. His silence was more terrifying than any words he could have uttered.

Sofia scrambled backwards, fear lending her a burst of adrenaline. But as she tried to run, the room spun, and she stumbled, her hand catching on a nearby table laden with delicate orchids.

Josh lunged, his movements fueled by a desperate fury. He slammed her against the table, his powerful arms trapping her, his hand tangling in her hair, yanking her head back with brutal force. He clamped his other hand over her mouth, stifling her cries as she struggled against him, her weakened body no match for his rage.

He released her, and she stumbled back, tears streaming down her face, her neck and head throbbing with a searing pain. She turned to run, her legs heavy and uncoordinated, but Josh grabbed her hair, yanking her to the ground. He stood over her, his chest heaving, his eyes dark and wild, as if toying with his prey.

Sofia, her body wracked with pain and fear, had no idea who this man was anymore. Where was the Josh she knew, the friend who had brought her coffee every morning, the man she would laugh with? Where was the warmth in his eyes, the gentle touch of his hand? All she saw now was a stranger, a monster fueled by venom and a twisted sense of entitlement.

He grabbed her hair again, the intricate updo unravelling, the delicate headpiece he had gifted her falling to the floor with a soft clink. He hauled her to her feet, and as she looked at him, pleading for recognition, for mercy, he punched her with all his might.

The world exploded in a flash of white-hot pain. Sofia's consciousness wavered, her senses overwhelmed. She felt as if she were drowning, sinking into a dark abyss, her body a vessel adrift in a sea of pain. Then, with a gasp, she was back, the world rushing back in a dizzying blur. She tasted blood, thick and metallic, filling her mouth, choking her. She coughed, a spray of crimson staining the pristine white tiles of the greenhouse floor. Her nose throbbed with a sharp, piercing pain, and she knew it was broken.

A tug on her leg brought her back to the horrifying reality of her situation. Josh was dragging her across the floor, his grip relentless. She screamed, her voice raw and hoarse, the sound muffled by the blood in her throat. "Help me!" she cried, her nails digging into the unforgiving tiles, her knees scraping against the rough surface, leaving a bloody trail in their wake. But her cries were lost in the vastness of the greenhouse. Through the glass, the muffled, cheerful strains of a Christmas carol drifted in from the ballroom, a sickening, joyous soundtrack to her nightmare.

He dragged her to the secluded window seat and threw her onto the cushioned bench, the same spot where his mother used to hide from the world, the only place he had called sacred. Nothing was sacred anymore.

"Josh," her voice was broken, tears streaming down her face, "Josh, why?" She looked at him, desperately searching for a flicker of recognition in his eyes, but there was nothing there, only emptiness.

He loomed over her, his silence a heavy weight pressing down on her. She screamed again, her fists flailing weakly against his chest, but he grabbed her wrists, pinning them above her head.

"Please, Josh," she begged, her voice a desperate whisper, "don't do this."

But her pleas fell on deaf ears. He stared down at her, his eyes empty and cold, until they locked on her chest, her breasts heaving with fear and the struggle to breathe. His gaze fixated on the tiny glint of light sparkling from her chest, the two small diamonds of her precious necklace from Allie. It was a slap in the face, a constant reminder that Sofia belonged to someone else, that her heart did not belong to him. But for Sofia, that necklace was more than just a symbol of her love for Allie; it was a tangible representation of the love that she never dreamed possible.

The sight of it fueled Josh's rage, twisting it into a venomous jealousy. He tore the necklace from around her neck, watching her heart break further.

"It really is too bad she couldn't be here tonight," he sneered, a cruel smirk twisting his lips as he slowly watched her shatter beneath him.

He knew the significance of that necklace, the way it represented the deepest love she had ever known. And in that moment, fueled by a twisted desire for revenge, he saw it as a way to shatter not just her heart, but the very essence of her bond with Allie.

His free hand roamed over her body, violating her, claiming what was not his to take, his touch a cruel mockery of the love and tenderness she had shared with Allie. He tore at her dress, the expensive fabric ripping under his forceful grasp, exposing her to his hungry gaze, a violation that echoed the shattering of her trust, her sense of safety, her very soul. His hands and mouth roamed over her, leaving a trail of bruises, each one a mark of possession, a cruel declaration of his victory over both Sofia and the woman she loved.

In that moment, as Josh took what he so desperately

craved, he believed he had won. He had broken Sofia's body, shattered her spirit, and stolen the symbol of her love for Allie.

Sofia knew what was coming. Her friend, the man she had trusted, was about to betray her in the most horrific way imaginable. Tears streamed down her face, a mixture of fear, pain, and the crushing weight of betrayal. She closed her eyes, her heart shattering into a million pieces, the pain a physical manifestation of the emotional devastation consuming her.

She felt it end, the violation ceasing as abruptly as it had begun. Josh released her wrists, the blood rushing back into her numb hands, sending a fresh wave of agony through her. She kept her eyes closed, her head turned away, unable to bear the sight of him. The silence in the greenhouse was deafening, broken only by her ragged breaths and the distant echoes of the gala.

"Fuck," she heard him whisper, his voice hoarse with a mixture of shock and regret. "Fuck... Sofia."

The rage that had fueled him evaporated, leaving behind a cold, hollow pit of horror. Josh scrambled back, his breath hitching as he stared at the devastation he had wrought. He saw the blood smeared on her pale skin, the ripped fabric of her dress, the bruises already blooming like dark flowers. A wave of nausea crashed over him, a sickening realization of his own monstrosity.

"Shit. Shit. I'm sorry, Sofia, I... God, what did I do?" He raked a hand through his hair, his body shaking.

For a fleeting second, he was just a boy who had made a terrible, unforgivable mistake. But then, the weight of his legacy crashed down on him. He could hear his father's voice, stern and unforgiving, echoing in the cavernous silence of his mind: *McCoys don't make mistakes. A McCoy protects the name at all costs.*

He saw his life crumbling - law school, the firm, his inheritance, and the prestige he had been bred to defend. It would all be gone. Destroyed by this one night.

"What, Josh?" she finally spoke, her voice raw with pain and anger. She turned to look at him as he sat on top of her. Her right eye almost swollen shut, her left slowly crusting with dried blood. She forced her eyes open to meet his gaze with a defiance that belied her fear. "You raped me." The words were a quiet, bitter accusation that sliced through his panic. Her voice broke into a quiet sob. "You're a rapist."

The word hung in the air, heavy and final. *Rapist.*

It shattered his brief moment of remorse. That word was a death sentence. If she left this room, if she spoke that word to anyone, his life was over. The shame that had been building twisted instantly into a cold, terrifying calculation. He couldn't let that happen. He couldn't let her destroy everything his family had built.

Fix it, his father's voice seemed to hiss. *Clean up this mess.*

Josh's eyes widened, panic warring with the rage. He looked at the door, then back at her, a terrifying calculation taking place behind his eyes. He realized he couldn't undo what he'd done. He couldn't let her leave. He couldn't let her talk.

"I'm sorry, Sofia." his voice trembled as he moved towards her. "I'm so sorry." He lunged, his hands closing around her neck, his fingers tightening with a terrifying, desperate strength.

Sofia's hands flew to his chest; her nails scratching, clawing, fighting with a desperate strength she didn't know she possessed. Her eyes, wild with terror, searched his face, seeking a flicker of humanity, a glimmer of the friend she had once known. Her vision blurred, a white film creeping in from the edges. The pounding of her heart filled her ears, a frantic drumbeat that drowned out all other sounds. Then, darkness. The last image that flashed through her mind was Allie... her beautiful smile, a tiny flicker of light within the darkness pulling her down.

24

Chapter 24

The insistent ringing of her phone tore Allie from a deep sleep. She fumbled blindly for the device on her nightstand, her eyes squinting against the harsh glow of the screen. *Unknown number*. A flicker of annoyance crossed her features, but the late hour pricked at her instincts. She swiped to answer, voice rough with sleep.

"Hello?"

A sob, jagged and thick with panic, was the only immediate answer.

"Allie?"

The voice was distorted, but the cadence was familiar enough to send a jolt of adrenaline through Allie's veins. She sat up, the sleep vanishing instantly. "Isabella? What's wrong?"

"Sofia... it's Sofia..." Isabella's voice broke, dissolving into another sob.

Allie's heart lurched. "What about Sofia? Isabella, talk to me."

"She's... she's in the hospital. In San Antonio." The words

came out in a rush, trembling and fractured. "They found her unresponsive on the side of the road."

The words hit Allie like a punch, the air knocked from her lungs. "What? How? What happened?" Her voice rose in panic.

"We don't know," A sob choked Isabella's words. "Mom got a call from the hospital a few hours ago. They said someone found her and called 911. She's unconscious, Allie. They don't know if… if she's going to make it."

"Oh my god." The whisper scraped out of Allie's throat, choked with a sudden, suffocating fear. She was already moving, swinging her legs out of bed. "I'm coming. I'll be there as soon as I can."

"Please, Allie. Please hurry." Isabella's voice was desperate. "Mom's a mess and… and we need you."

The line went dead. Allie dropped the phone, the clatter echoing loudly in the silent room, but she barely heard it. A wave of dizziness washed over her, but she forced it down, her hands trembling violently as she tore off her pajamas. The soft cotton felt suddenly constricting, suffocating. Her mind was a chaotic jumble of images… Sofia's laughter, the depth of her hazel eyes, the warmth of her hand… flashing like a strobe light against the encroaching darkness.

Please, Sofia. Just hold on.

She pulled on the first clothes she touched. Jeans, a sweater, socks. Her fingers fumbling with buttons, breath coming in ragged gasps. She didn't bother checking a mirror; she just grabbed her keys and wallet and sprinted for the garage.

The drive was a blur of gray highway and rising terror. The early morning light began to paint the sky in cruel hues of lavender and orange, the world waking up beautiful and oblivious, while Allie's world threatened to end. She pushed the car to its limit, the speedometer needle climbing as she gripped the wheel until her knuckles turned white. Every mile felt like a marathon; every minute was an eternity of not knowing.

As the sun climbed higher, casting long shadows across the rolling hills, Allie's grip on the steering wheel tightened. It was only three days before Christmas, yet a dark cloud of fear had settled over her world. The image of Sofia, lying motionless in a hospital bed, haunted her thoughts.

By the time the sprawling San Antonio hospital complex came into view, the sun was fully up. Allie screeched into the parking lot, barely waiting for the engine to cut off before she was out the door. She dialed Isabella on the run, her fingers trembling.

"Isabella, I'm here." Her breath came in ragged gasps. "Where is she? What's the room number?"

Isabella, her voice rough with tears, gave her the information. Allie raced through the hospital corridors, her footsteps echoing in the sterile silence. Her eyes scanned the room numbers, her mind clinging to the digits like a lifeline: *ICU 101, 101, 101.*

She was buzzed into the ICU unit, her heart pounding in her chest. She pushed open the door to Sofia's room, and the scene inside stopped her dead.

The sterile silence of the room crashed against her, heavy and smelling of antiseptic and old blood. Sofia lay motionless in the bed, a pale figure amidst a tangle of tubes and wires.

Allie's legs turned to lead. She moved forward, drawn by a horrifying gravity. Cami was there, gently combing through Sofia's matted, blood-tangled hair. Blanca sat huddled by the bed, stroking Sofia's uninjured arm, her eyes swollen shut from crying. Isabella stood like a sentinel by the window, staring out at the bleak cityscape.

But Allie only had eyes for the bed.

She reached out, her fingers trembling as they brushed Sofia's hand. It was cold. Lifeless. A sob ripped its way out of Allie's chest, a raw, guttural sound that shattered the room's quiet.

"Sofia," her voice fractured into a thousand pieces. "Please wake up."

But Sofia remained motionless, lost in the silent abyss of unconsciousness. Allie sank into a chair beside the bed, her body trembling, her heart shattered. The world outside, with its Christmas cheer and festive decorations, seemed a cruel mockery. All that mattered now was Sofia, her life hanging in the balance, the future uncertain.

As the initial shock settled, Allie really *looked* at her, but as her gaze swept over Sofia's battered body, a disgusting realization hit her. This wasn't just an accident; this was violence, brutal and intentional.

Dark, angry bruises marred the smooth olive skin of Sofia's arms. Allie's own fingers instinctively traced the marks, her touch light as a feather, yet the phantom pain resonated deep within her. Her gaze traveled higher, her breath catching in her throat as she saw the constellation of bruises on Sofia's chest and neck, some so severe they were almost black. Bruises, dark and deep, encircled her neck like a cruel necklace. She choked back a sob as the nausea rose again.

Sofia's face was swollen and discolored, almost unrecognizable. Her left eye was so puffy it was almost shut, a grotesque purple bruise blooming across her cheekbone. Her nose, bandaged and clearly broken, was a testament to the force of the blow it had sustained. Dried blood crusted around her nostrils and on her lips, which were battered, split, and swollen.

Each bruise was a savage mark of possession and violence, a stark reminder of the violation Sofia had endured. Rage, cold and consuming, ignited in Allie's chest, warring with a sorrow so deep it felt like drowning. *Who did this? Who touched her?*

Allie's gaze lingered on Sofia's face, searching for a flicker of life, a sign that the woman she loved was still in there, fighting to return. But Sofia remained motionless, lost somewhere in a sea of unconsciousness, leaving Allie to grapple with the devastating reality and the agonizing uncertainty of the future.

She reached blindly across the sheets and found Blanca's hand amidst the tangle of sheets and tubes. Blanca's gaze met hers, her eyes red and swollen with tears, her face a mask of despair.

"Why would someone hurt her, Allie?" Her voice was raw, each word punctuated by a sob that tore at Allie's soul. "She's such a good girl, so kind, so loving..."

Allie's throat tightened, the words catching in her throat. She gripped Blanca's hand, her own tears threatening to spill over. "I don't know, Blanca," The words were rough with emotion. "She's everything good in the world. I don't understand how anyone could hurt her like this."

Blanca, overwhelmed by grief, broke down, her sobs echoing through the sterile room. She clutched Sofia's hand, her fingers intertwined with her daughter's, as if clinging to a life raft. "I just don't understand why."

Allie's lips trembled, silent tears tracing paths down her cheeks. She looked up at Isabella, who still stood by the window, her silhouette still against the morning sun. "Do they know what happened?"

Isabella slowly shook her head, tears streaming freely. "They found her on a country road near a country club. Someone called 911." She paused, her voice straining against the horror of the words. "They said… they said it looks like she was raped and strangled. Left for dead."

The words hit Allie, and the room spun. The image of Sofia, her beautiful, gentle Sofia, discarded and broken on a roadside, fueled a fury so deep and blinding that it made her vision blur.

But beneath the rage, there was sorrow, a gut-wrenching ache for the innocence that had been stolen.

She stumbled towards the bathroom, the sterile white tiles blurring as tears streamed down her face. She barely made it to the toilet before the contents of her stomach erupted, her body convulsing with the force of her grief. She sobbed uncontrollably, her cries echoing in the small, confined space. She screamed into the toilet bowl, a primal scream of rage, of despair, of a love that felt like it was being ripped from her grasp.

"Why, Sofia?" she gasped between heaving breaths, her voice a broken whisper. "Why my beautiful Sofia?"

25

Chapter 25

Hours crawled by, each one an eternity of agonizing uncertainty. The sterile silence of the hospital room pressed down on them like a heavy blanket of fear and grief. Blanca, her face etched with anguish, sat beside Sofia's bed, her hand resting lightly on her daughter's arm. Camilla, curled up in a chair in the corner, fought back tears, her gaze fixed on the rhythmic rise and fall of Sofia's chest driven by the ventilator. Isabella paced restlessly, her phone clutched in her hand, her brow furrowed with worry. And Allie, her heart a leaden weight in her chest, sat beside Sofia, her fingers tracing the outline of her hand, the coolness of her skin a constant reminder of just how fragile life is.

Suddenly, Allie sat up, a chilling realization piercing the fog of her grief. "Where's Josh?" Her tone was sharp with alarm. "Shouldn't he be here?"

The question hung in the air. Blanca's eyes were weary with her own unanswered questions, and Camilla's breath hitched in her throat. Isabella, her phone still clutched in her hand, shook her head slowly.

"I've called and texted him a few times." Her voice trembled, "but he hasn't answered. The texts haven't even been read."

A wave of dread washed over Allie. "Do you think... do you think something happened to him too?"

"I don't know," Isabella took out her phone, checking it for messages again. "We don't know who else to contact. The police have his information; they said they'd try to reach him and make sure he's okay. One of the officers was going to head to the McCoy mansion."

The silence returned, heavier now, laden with a new layer of fear and uncertainty. Where was Josh? Was he injured, lying unconscious somewhere, too? Or was he involved somehow in Sofia's attack? The questions swirled in Allie's mind, each one a terrifying possibility.

* * *

Only murmurs of prayer and the occasional question broke the hush of the room. Nurses bustled in and out, their voices low as they checked Sofia's vitals, adjusted IV drips, and made notes on their charts. Doctors, their faces etched with concern, conducted their examinations but offered little solace to anyone.

When a forensic specialist and her nurse arrived to conduct their examination, the family was asked to step back. The air in the waiting room stood still as the team meticulously documented the evidence of the assault on Sofia's broken body.

Detectives drifted in and out, their presence a constant, grim reminder of the crime committed. They spoke to each of them, their questions probing, their voices gentle yet insistent. Allie's heart pounded as she spoke to them; she wanted answers.

"Who did this to her?" Her voice trembled with barely suppressed rage. "Do you have any leads?"

The detectives offered little comfort. "We're still investigating, ma'am," one of them replied, his voice calm and measured. "We're following up on all leads, and we hope to have some answers soon."

"How soon?" Allie's voice was laced with desperation. "She's lying here, broken and unconscious, and you're telling us to wait?"

The detectives exchanged a look, a silent acknowledgment of the frustration and pain etched on Allie's face. "We understand your urgency, ma'am," the other detective said, "and we're doing everything we can to find the person responsible for this."

Their assurances offered little comfort as Allie sank back into her chair, the weight of their helplessness pressing down on her. Sofia's life hung in the balance, and there was little anyone could do to change that.

Allie felt the weight of isolation pressing down on her as she reached for her phone, her fingers instinctively dialing Dylann's number. The familiar voice on the other end offered a connection to a world that felt so different outside of her present one.

"Hey Dyl," she choked out, her voice trembling with emotion, "I'm in San Antonio. It's Sofia. She's hurt, dude."

Dylann's voice, usually filled with playful banter, instantly shifted, concern lacing her every word. "What!? What happened? Is she okay?"

Allie recounted the events of the past few hours, her voice

breaking as she described Sofia's injuries and the agonizing uncertainty of her condition. Dylann listened in stunned silence.

"Allie, I'm so sorry." Her voice filled with compassion. I'll give Danika a call, and we will be there as soon as we can. We'll swing by your place and grab some things for you, and we'll get a room near the hospital."

Allie choked back a sob. "Thank you, Dylann. I don't know what I'd do without you guys."

After hanging up, Allie forced herself to make another difficult call. She dialed her boss, her voice trembling as she explained the situation, the words catching in her throat. Her boss offered his condolences and assured her that her job was secure.

As she hung up the phone, despair crashed over her. It was only three days until Christmas, the time she was supposed to spend with Sofia and her family. They were supposed to be creating new traditions and memories. The thought of those plans, now shattered, sent a searing pain through her heart.

A nurse entered the room, her soft, caring gaze encompassing the small group huddled around Sofia's bed.

"I'm afraid that we're going to have to ask you all to wait in the ICU waiting room now. We normally don't allow visitors in here for so long, but due to the situation, we wanted to extend it for you all."

Allie's brow furrowed, her heart clenching at the thought of leaving Sofia alone. "We have to leave her?" The image of Sofia, lying vulnerable and unconscious, surrounded by the cold, impersonal machines, filled her with a profound sense of unease.

The nurse nodded softly, her eyes filled with understanding. "You can come back in a little while," she reassured them, "but the visitor rules in ICU are normally quite strict. We promise we will reach out to inform y'all if needed."

Blanca, who had been clinging to Sofia's hand in a silent vigil for hours, finally broke down, her tears flowing freely. "I don't want to leave her alone." Her gaze remained fixed on Sofia, her maternal instincts screaming against the forced separation.

Isabella, ever the pillar of strength, moved to her mother's side, her hands resting gently on Blanca's shoulders. "Come on, Mama." Her voice was soft and soothing. "They'll watch over her, and we could all probably use a break. We'll be back soon, sissy," she added, her voice cracking slightly as she addressed her unconscious sister.

Camilla joined Isabella as she helped her mother up, supporting her as she reluctantly moved away from Sofia's bedside.

Allie, her heart aching, approached Sofia, her fingers gently entwining with hers. "I love you, Sofia," she whispered, her voice thick with emotion. "I'll be right here. I'm not leaving."

She leaned down, pressing a soft kiss to Sofia's hand, her lips lingering on her cool skin. "Wake up, baby," she pleaded, her voice breaking. "Please, wake up."

With a final, lingering glance at Sofia's pale face, Allie reluctantly placed her hand back on the bed and turned away, following Blanca and the girls out of the room.

Soon after, Dylann and Danika arrived, carrying a small overnight bag for Allie. Their faces were etched with worry as they rushed to Allie's side, as Allie's composure broke seeing her best friends' faces. Danika, her eyes filled with tears, rushed into Allie's arms, embracing her fiercely. Dylann, not far behind, paused for a moment, allowing Danika her moment of raw emotion with Allie. Then, catching Allie's eye, she saw the deep pain reflected there and joined the embrace, her arms encircling both her friends.

Allie clung to them, soaking in the comfort of their compassion, the silent understanding that flowed between them palpable. In that moment, the walls of the cold, sterile hospital seemed to disappear, replaced by a reminder that she wasn't alone in this nightmare.

After a moment, Allie, with a lingering tremor in her voice, introduced Dylann and Danika to Blanca, Camilla and Isabella. They exchanged embraces, a silent extension of their love for Sofia, their collective hope for her recovery.

Allie sank into a hard, unforgiving chair, her heart aching. She explained what she knew of the events, her voice trembling as she described how Sofia had been found, the brutal details of the assault leaving silence in their wake.

Danika's eyes widened in horror, tears welling up, her voice choked with emotion. "What kind of monster..."

Dylann, her face pale and drawn, nodded grimly, her gaze fixed on the floor.

"They don't know where Josh is yet," Allie's voice was low, her gaze fixed on a stain in the floor. "No one has heard from him."

"Hello?" Isabella's voice broke the tense silence as she answered her phone. The voice on the other end was inaudible to the others.

"This is she. Oh, hello, Mr. McCoy." A cold dread washed over Allie as she listened, unsure of what they were about to hear.

"No, she's not okay." A pause, filled with the unspoken weight of the situation. "Yes, she was found on the side of a road, she's been assaulted." Another pause, the silence heavy with unspoken questions. "I'm glad he's okay. Tell him that we will let him know." Silence again, then a hesitant, "Oh. Okay." A final pause, then, "Okay, thank you."

Isabella hung up, her face etched with confusion. Allie was unable to contain her anxiety any longer. She stood up and walked over to Isabella, her friends and family watching and waiting to hear what was said.

"That was Josh's dad?"

Isabella nodded, the confusion in her eyes deepening. "Yes."

"Is Josh okay? What did he say?"

"He's okay." Isabella's voice was hesitant. "I guess the police woke him up when they showed up at the house. He said that they had no idea what happened, that Josh had been sleeping, he's been sick from drinking too much last night."

"He didn't know what happened to Sofia?" Allie's brow furrowed, a million questions filling her head.

Isabella shook her head. "He said they had no idea, that he just heard about it from the detectives. That he just wanted to call to see how Sofia is doing and that..." she hesitated, her gaze meeting Allie's, "that all communication needs to go through him for now."

Allie's body stiffened. "What? Why? That doesn't even make sense."

"It does if you're thinking like a lawyer protecting their client." Danika chimed in, her voice quiet but insightful. "It's exactly how my parents would react if it were me who was with someone that was assaulted."

A heavy silence fell over the group, the implications of Mr.

McCoy's words sinking in.

"He said that he would be checking in with the hospital," Isabella continued, "and would gladly have them move Sofia to the VIP room once she's stable enough if we'd like."

"What's the VIP room?" Camilla's brow furrowed in confusion.

"I think it's a private floor for wealthy patients," Allie answered absently, her mind racing. A VIP room. Secluded. Private. Controlled. It didn't feel like generosity; it felt like management.

"Oh." Camilla's brow scrunched, a hint of confusion lacing her voice. "Well, that was a nice offer, I guess."

But Allie couldn't shake the feeling that something was wrong. Josh's absence, his silence, the strange request from his father – it all felt off. The fact that Josh, Sofia's friend, hadn't even bothered to call and check on her himself, fueled a growing suspicion in Allie's heart. A suspicion that whispered a terrifying possibility, a possibility she desperately wanted to dismiss, but couldn't ignore.

26

Chapter 26

Christmas Eve arrived, an empty void of the festive cheer that usually filled the air. The stillness of the hospital room was a sad contrast to the carols and laughter that should have been echoing through the Flores family home. Days bled into nights, and Sofia remained trapped in the dark abyss of unconsciousness.

The doctors offered no answers to their questions. "Her body is healing, but it's a slow process. We can't say for sure when she'll wake up. It could be days, weeks, even months." And there was the unspoken risk that she wouldn't wake up at all.

Sofia's family, their faces etched with a mixture of hope and despair, kept a constant vigil at her bedside. Camilla and Isabella, torn between their responsibilities at home and their devotion to their sister, had eventually left to tend to life's necessities for a few days. They collected more clothes for their mother, paid any bills that needed attention, and took care of whatever needed to be done in their homes and their mother's.

Dylann and Danika had also departed that morning, their tearful goodbyes reflecting the grief and despair that hung heavy in the air. "We'll be back soon, Al," Dylann had promised, squeezing her hand. "Call if you need anything at all."

But Allie couldn't even fathom what she needed. Nothing seemed to matter in the face of Sofia's silent struggle. The world outside, with its twinkling lights, felt distant and irrelevant. All that mattered was the woman lying motionless in the hospital bed, her life hanging precariously in the balance.

With each passing day, Allie fought silently with the conflict between remaining positive and the overwhelming weight of dread that gnawed at the surface. How could she feel confident and outspoken when she was living in constant fear that the love of her life was slipping away, and she was powerless to stop it?

But amidst the despair, a flicker of defiance ignited within her. She couldn't give up, not now. Sofia needed her. Her family needed her. She had to find the strength to be their anchor and to see them all through this.

She took a deep breath, the cool air filling her lungs. There was still a chance, however small, that Sofia would wake up. She straightened her shoulders and gazed into Sofia's pale face, a silent vow forming in her heart. She would be strong, she would fight for their love, for their future, and for the chance to create those Christmas memories, even if it meant waiting a lifetime.

* * *

Most days, the ICU waiting room was a bunker of hush, broken only by the occasional muffled sobs and hushed whispers. It was a stillness that spoke of fear, uncertainty, and the agonizing wait for news. At times, it was a comforting quiet, a shared space of reflection and prayer. But there were heart-wrenching moments when the stillness was shattered by the cries of grief, the anguished sobs of families who had lost their loved ones, their battles fought and lost within the sterile walls of the hospital.

Allie and Sofia's family could do nothing but pray that those moments were never theirs to share. Each tearful goodbye, each hushed conversation filled with condolences, sent her into a spiral of anxiety, the image of Sofia's still body a constant reminder of the truth of what could happen.

She knew she needed to try to maintain some semblance of normalcy, to keep up with her work responsibilities. The thought of neglecting her duties, of allowing her department to fall behind, added another layer of stress to her already burdened shoulders. But the idea of leaving Sofia, even for the short time it would take to drive to Austin and back, filled her with terror. *What if something happened while she was gone? What if Sofia woke up and she wasn't there?*

Blanca, sensing Allie's internal struggle, gently encouraged her to take a break and attend to her responsibilities. "It's okay, Allie. Go and get what you need. Doing some work might be good for you, a distraction from all this worry. And you can always work from here while we wait."

Allie, though reluctant, recognized the wisdom in Blanca's words. She needed a change of scenery, a break from the suffocating atmosphere of the hospital. And perhaps, getting herself caught up in work would provide a temporary escape from the overwhelming thoughts that consumed her.

With a heavy heart, she kissed Sofia's forehead, whispering a promise to return soon, and set off for Austin.

The drive was a blur, the familiar scenery passing by unnoticed as her thoughts remained fixated on Sofia.

When she arrived at her empty townhome, she headed straight for the shower. The warm water cascaded over her skin as she closed her eyes. Finally, away from the chaos of the hospital, the nurses and Sofia's family, the dam broke.

A scream ripped from her throat, raw and guttural, echoing off the bathroom tiles. Her legs gave out, the weight of the last few days finally too heavy to bear, and she slid down the cold wall. She curled into herself, sobbing into her hands as the water rained down, masking her tears in its spray.

She allowed herself that break, the needed release. She allowed herself those few moments to feel the terror, the anger, and the crushing sadness.

Then, she forced herself to stand. She dressed quickly, packed a suitcase with essentials, and gathered her laptop and work files. Before leaving town, she stopped at a local store to pick up snacks and drinks for Sofia's family. She knew they had to be just as tired of the bland hospital food as she was.

As she drove back to San Antonio, the setting sun painting the sky in beautiful winter hues, a renewed sense of determination settled over her. She could do this. She *would* do this. She would balance work and life at the hospital, for however long it took. And she would not give up hope, not until Sofia opened her eyes and smiled at her again.

27

Chapter 27

It was Christmas, yet the spirit of the season seemed to have lost its way. There was no twinkling Christmas tree, no smell of fresh cookies in the air, no laughter or Christmas carols. The hospital halls were hushed. The only decoration was the tiny Christmas tree on the nurses' station, and the only carols were those softly playing through the radio, broken by the occasional cry from grieving families.

Allie, her heart heavy, sat beside Sofia's bed. Her fingers traced the delicate curve of Sofia's cheekbone, the skin cool to the touch. She leaned close, her forehead resting against the bed rail, and softly sang into the sterile air.

"Have yourself a merry little Christmas... let your heart be light..."

Her voice caught in her throat, tightening as the tears she had been holding back began to fall.

"Next year, all our troubles will be out of sight."

She closed her eyes and let the silence swallow the rest of the song. "Merry Christmas, beautiful." She whispered, her voice hoarse. "Please come back to me."

Later that day, a large bouquet arrived, a vibrant splash of color against the unforgiving backdrop. Red roses, white lilies, and delicate sprigs of baby's breath exploded from a pristine white vase, their sweet fragrance filling the room. Allie, her heart aching, picked out the card tucked among the blooms.

"Merry Christmas. I hope you get well soon. Love, Josh."

Allie's blood ran cold. Aside from the occasional, impersonal phone call from Mr. McCoy, they had heard nothing from Josh. The flowers, though a seemingly kind gesture, felt like a twisted attempt to maintain a facade of concern while Sofia lay unconscious. He was mocking them.

* * *

The day after Christmas, they sat in the waiting room, the room that had become their usual sanctuary. Isabella and Camilla had returned home to rest, their absence leaving a noticeable void in the small space.

Allie sat with her laptop open, staring blindly at a spreadsheet, her mind refusing to process the numbers. Across from her, Blanca sat with a rosary entangled in her fingers, her eyes red-rimmed and distant.

"Allie." Blanca's weary voice broke the heavy silence.

Allie looked up, blinking the grit from her eyes. "Yes, Blanca? Do you need something?"

Blanca shook her head slowly. She reached across the small gap between their chairs and covered Allie's hand with her own. Her palm was warm, despite the cold hospital air.

"You look like you are fading away, mija..." Blanca whispered. "You need to sleep. Go to the hotel for a few hours.

I'll stay here."

"I can't. I can't leave her. Every time I close my eyes, I see…" She trailed off, her breath shaking, unable to voice the horror of Sofia's injuries. "I promised I would keep her safe, Blanca. I promised."

Tears welled in Blanca's eyes, spilling over to track down her tired face. She squeezed Allie's hand, her grip surprisingly strong. "You didn't do this, Allie. Evil did this. Not you."

"But I wasn't there…" Allie sobbed quietly, the guilt that had been eating her alive finally spilling out. "I wasn't there when she needed me."

"Look at me," Blanca's command was gentle. Allie met her gaze. "My Sofia… she has always been soft. Gentle. But since she met you, she is stronger. She fought, Allie. The doctors said she fought."

Blanca's thumb brushed over Allie's knuckles. "She fought because she had something to come back to. She had you. You are her home now. You are her heart."

Allie crumbled, sliding off her chair to kneel on the floor in front of Blanca, burying her face in the older woman's lap. Blanca stroked her hair, murmuring soft prayers in Spanish as she cried with her. In that moment, they weren't just two women waiting for a patient; they were a mother and a daughter, bound together by the same terrifying love.

"Thank you," Allie whispered into the fabric of Blanca's skirt. "Thank you for sharing her with me."

"She was never just mine," Blanca replied softly, kissing the top of Allie's head. "She belongs to the world. And to you."

Allie moved back to her seat, feeling a tiny fraction lighter. They sat together for a long time, drawing strength from one another, until Blanca eventually dozed off in the chair, her head resting on Allie's shoulder as she tried, again, to work.

Suddenly, the quiet hum of the ICU was shattered.

Alarms blared - a sharp, rhythmic shrieking that sent ice through Allie's veins. Nurses rushed down the hallway, their shoes squeaking on the linoleum, their voices urgent and tense. Allie's head shot up, her heart leaping into her throat as she saw the red light above Sofia's room flashing.

Code Blue.

The nurses swarmed into Room 201, the glass door sliding shut behind them, sealing them in and shutting Allie out.

Allie scrambled to her feet, her laptop clattering to the floor. Her legs felt like jelly, her breath catching in a painful hitch. She ran toward the room, her mind a chaotic static of fear. But a grim-faced nurse intercepted her before she could reach the door, blocking her path.

"You can't come in here right now! Go and sit down. We'll let you know what's going on soon."

"Let me be with her," Allie's panic rose in her throat. "Please!"

"Let them work, honey." The nurse's voice was softer this time, but she didn't move.

Allie felt her body trembling violently as she watched helplessly through the glass. The nurses worked frantically around Sofia's bed, their movements a blur of terrifying efficiency. She strained to see through the gap in the curtain, her heart pounding a frantic rhythm against her ribs.

"Fight, Sofia," she whispered, her hands pressed against the cold glass, leaving foggy prints. "Fight, my love. Don't you dare leave me."

* * *

The agonizing wait stretched on, each tick of the wall clock a hammer blow against their frayed nerves. Blanca was awake now, standing beside Allie, clutching her rosary so tight her knuckles were white.

Then, the door opened. A figure emerged, Dr. Ramirez, Sofia's lead physician. He stepped into the waiting area, pulling his mask down. His gaze settled on Allie and Blanca, their faces desperate, pleading for news.

A flicker of a smile touched his lips, and a collective breath was held. "It's good news," his voice soothed the electric tension in the air. "She wasn't crashing. She was waking up."

The dam of emotions within Blanca finally broke. A sob, raw and powerful, erupted from her, her knees buckling beneath the weight of relief and gratitude. Allie, her own tears welling up, caught Blanca, her arms wrapping around her. She looked at Dr. Ramirez, her voice trembling with a mixture of disbelief and hope.

"She's waking up?" Allie's hands started to shake as her voice trembled with hope. "She's okay?"

Dr. Ramirez nodded, his expression a careful blend of optimism and caution. "She woke up fighting the ventilator. Her body was trying to breathe on its own, triggering the monitors. That's a very good sign. We've extubated her. She's groggy, but she is breathing room air."

He paused, his eyes kind. "She's not out of the woods yet, but this is a huge step in the right direction. We'll see how she does through the night without the ventilator. For now, we have her sedated to let her body rest and heal more. You can see her in a little while."

Allie, tears streaming down her face, could only nod, her voice choked with emotion. "Thank you, doctor."

She sank to her knees beside Blanca, their arms wrapped tightly around each other, as their tears fell and relief flooded through them like gentle rain. Sofia was going to be okay. The nightmare wasn't over; the road to recovery would be long and hard, but this moment, this glimmer of hope, was a precious gift.

"Merry Christmas, Mom," Allie whispered, her voice thick with emotion.

Blanca pulled back, cupped Allie's face, and smiled through her tears. "Merry Christmas, mija."

It was the day after Christmas, but the news of Sofia's awakening was the most precious gift they could have received.

28

Chapter 28

Sofia drifted back to consciousness, the world a hazy blur of muted colors and muffled sounds around her. A low groan broke through her lips, the suppressed sound of pain finally breaking through. She tried to open her eyes, but her right eyelid was so swollen it refused to cooperate. Her left eye flickered open, the harsh fluorescent lights of the hospital room momentarily blinding her.

Her mind was a cloud of confusion. Where was she? What had happened? Panic clawed at the edges of her consciousness, a terrifying sense of disorientation. She tried to speak, to yell out, but her voice was a dry croak, the words lost in the fog of her confusion.

"Mama?" she rasped, her voice barely audible.

Blanca, who had been dozing in the chair beside her bed, sprang to life, her eyes widening with relief and joy. "Sofia! Mija, you're awake!"

Sofia's gaze, unfocused and clouded with pain, searched for her mother's face. She saw a blurry figure with a familiar warmth; she knew it was her mom. She reached out, her hand trembling, her fingers finding her mother's.

"Mama."

"I'm here, mija," Blanca sobbed, her tears flowing freely now. "I'm right here."

Sofia's grip tightened on her mother's hand. She tried to focus, to piece together the fragments of memory that swirled in her mind, but the effort was too much. Exhaustion pulled at her, dragging her back towards the darkness.

This wasn't the first time she had come to. The initial awakening was a terrifying ordeal. She had thrashed against the tubes and wires, her screams echoing through the room, her fear palpable to those who witnessed it. They had to sedate her then, allowing her body and mind the rest they desperately needed.

But with each subsequent awakening, a little more of Sofia returned. Her voice grew stronger, her gaze clearer, her grip on reality firmer. She would wake, disoriented and confused, but the sight of her family, their voices filled with love and concern, would slowly ground her, reminding her of who she was and where she belonged.

They didn't talk to her about the attack, not yet. The focus was on her recovery, on reassuring her that she was safe, that she would be okay. And with each waking moment, Sofia clung to that hope, her hand reaching for her mother's, her eyes searching for Allie's familiar face.

"Allie?" She would whisper, her voice raspy but filled with a longing that transcended words.

And Allie would be there, her palm reaching out to meet Sofia's, their fingers intertwining in a silent promise of support and devotion.

The visits were often short, due to Sofia's exhaustion

and need for rest. But each time she woke, each time she recognized her loved ones, each time she squeezed their hands and whispered their names, was a victory, proof of her resilience. And they all knew that as she healed, she would learn more and hopefully remember what happened to put those who harmed her behind bars. They would be there for her, every step of the way, until she was strong enough to face the truth, to heal, and to reclaim her life.

* * *

Each day brought a glimmer of hope. Her voice got stronger, her laughter, though rare right now, was again filling with hints of her usual self. The swelling in her face was starting to heal, once again revealing the beautiful girl that was there before the brutal attack. Her right eye was still blurry, but showed signs of improvement, offering a promise of restored vision.

Physical therapy became a part of her daily routine, a challenging but necessary step towards regaining her strength and mobility. Her therapists guided her through exercises, gently pushing back against the frustration that often overwhelmed her. Doctors came and went. Their examinations were a constant reminder of the long road to recovery that lay ahead.

But a deeper wound remained. Sofia's memory was fragmented and hazy, even though it was slowly returning. She remembered flashes of the attack with distorted images. The identity of her attacker remained shrouded in a painful fog, lost in the persistent nightmares that woke her.

Counselors were brought in, their gentle voices and patient

questions aimed at helping Sofia to open up, to share the burden of her trauma. But Sofia, her eyes filled with a haunting fear, would retreat into silence, her gaze fixed on the sterile landscape outside the window, her heart a fortress guarding a secret too painful to reveal.

"She'll come around when she's ready," the counselors assured Allie and Blanca, their words offering a sliver of comfort. "It's important to give her space, to let her heal at her own pace."

But the police, driven by the urgency of their investigation, were less patient. They pressed Sofia for details, their questions a relentless assault on her fragile psyche. Allie, witnessing the distress in Sofia's eyes, the way her body would tense with fear at their approach, felt a surge of protective anger. She would gently intervene, her voice firm but calming, requesting that they give Sofia more time and more space to heal.

She understood the importance of their investigation, the need to bring those who did this to justice. But she couldn't bear to see Sofia retraumatized. She would be Sofia's shield, her advocate, her protector, until she was strong enough to face the truth and to speak her pain.

* * *

The pale blue hospital recliner cradled Sofia like a reluctant embrace. It faced the rain-streaked window, blurring the city lights into hazy smears. Allie sat on the hard wooden chair beside her.

"Allie?" Sofia's voice was a whisper against the rhythmic drumming of raindrops against the glass.

"Yes, Sof?" Allie's gaze was drawn to the delicate bruises beneath her eyes.

Sofia hesitated, a tremor running through her fingers. She inhaled deeply, the air catching in her throat. "Why hasn't Josh been here?"

The question, though expected, still landed like a physical blow. Allie's chest tightened, a knot of dread forming in her stomach. She took a slow, measured breath. "His dad's acting as his attorney and feels it's best he's not around right now while it's being investigated. He's called to check on you a few times but asked that all communication go through him for now."

She watched Sofia, searching for any flicker of reaction. But Sofia remained still, her gaze fixed on the rain-blurred town below. "Oh." The single syllable echoed the emptiness in the room.

Allie moved forward, her own chair scraping against the tiled floor. She took Sofia's hand, her fingers tracing the delicate bones beneath her cool skin. "Sof, you don't think Josh had anything to do with this, do you?"

Sofia's eyes drifted to the window as her brow furrowed, a flicker of pain crossing her face. "No, I don't think so." She raised a trembling hand to her temple, her fingers pressing against her skin as if trying to hold back the fragmented memories. "I don't remember, Allie. I can't remember it."

"It's okay," Allie gently stroked the back of Sofia's hand. "It's okay to not remember things right now. Let's talk about something else if you'd like."

Sofia nodded slowly, the movement barely perceptible. "I'd like that."

Allie gave Sofia's hand a gentle squeeze. She began to

speak, her voice low and soothing, recounting the latest viral TikToks that had made her laugh, anything to fill the silence and distract Sofia from whatever shadows might be lurking in her mind.

* * *

New Year's Eve arrived, leaving a bleak feeling on a night meant for celebration and new beginnings. Yet, Sofia's family, Allie, Dylann, and Danika were determined to bring a spark of joy to the somber space.

They gathered around Sofia's bed, their hearts filled with love as they shared stories, laughter, and tears. They toasted to the new year, their glasses clinking softly, all wishing for a year of healing, love, and joy. Their laughter was a welcome distraction from the worries that weighed heavily on their minds. And as the clock struck midnight, they all embraced, sharing a special bond of strength and love for Sofia.

* * *

January 3rd arrived, bringing with it a new wave of hope. Sofia's doctors entered the room, their faces etched with optimism.

"Sofia," Dr. Ramirez began, his voice gentle, "we've been monitoring your progress closely, and we're pleased with how far you've come. Your physical recovery has been remarkable, and we believe you're ready to take the next step."

Sofia, her gaze clear and focused, looked at him with a mix of anticipation and apprehension. "What does that mean, doctor?"

"It means we are discharging you." A smile graced his lips. "You'll continue your therapy locally, but you'll be able to recover in the comfort of your own home, surrounded by your loved ones."

A wave of relief washed over the room as everyone's eyes filled with tears of gratitude and happiness. Sofia looked at Allie, watching the tears form in her eyes as she reached for her hand.

"We're going home," she whispered, her voice filled with emotion.

"Yeah, we are, baby," Allie's eyes shone with tears. "We're going home."

29

Chapter 29

The door closed behind them as she heard the small click of the lock secure into place. It was a sound that used to mean safety, but now it echoed like a cage closing in on her. Sofia stood with her back to the door, staring into the open living space. Everything looked exactly the same as it had almost two weeks ago. The throw blanket was still draped over the arm of the beige sofa, holding the shape of a life she felt she no longer fit into. The air still smelled faintly of her favorite vanilla candle, but underneath it all she could smell was her own fear.

It was the same house, but she was a stranger in it.

Her skin felt too tight for her body. Every nerve ending was frayed, exposed, and screaming for her to run, but there was nowhere to run to. She took a step forward, and her legs trembled. The sheer exhaustion physically pressed down on her, dragging her toward the floor. She wasn't just tired. She felt hollow…. empty.

She walked into the kitchen, the floor cool beneath her socks. She rested her hands on the countertop and stared out the window above the sink. She used to love standing there doing dishes, seeing the town thrive below her. Now it felt... wrong. The sun was shining. It seemed cruel that the sun could still shine, that the birds could still fly, and that the world kept spinning when hers had stopped so violently.

She didn't hear Allie walking up behind her. The soft pad of footsteps was lost under the rushing sound of blood in Sofia's ears.

She closed her eyes and tried to breathe through the growing tightness in her chest, anxiety feeling like a wet blanket around her.

Then she felt it.

Arms wrapped around her waist from behind. A chest pressed against her back.

It was meant to be a comfort. It was meant to be love. It was Allie... she knew logically that it was Allie. But her body no longer knew logic. Her body only knew survival.

The sudden restriction of her movement sent a bolt of pure, white-hot lightning through her nervous system. The warmth on her back didn't feel like love. It felt like weight. It felt like suffocation... it felt like *him*.

The memory flashed, disjointed and terrifying. A heavy hand. The suffocating smell of dirt. The inability to move.

Sofia gasped, a strangled sound that tore from her throat. She violently threw her elbows back and twisted away, stumbling into the kitchen island. Her hip struck the edge of the counter hard enough to bruise.

"No!" She scrambled back until her spine hit the cabinets and slid down until she hit the floor. She pulled her knees to her chest and covered her head with her arms to hide. "Don't touch me. Don't touch me."

The room went silent.

Allie stood frozen in the center of the kitchen, her hands still raised in the empty air where Sofia had been standing a second ago. A complex storm washed over her face. First, the shock, followed instantly by a sharp pang of rejection that stung her heart like a physical slap.

Then came the anger. A searing rage directed at the invisible phantom who had done this. Whoever had touched Sofia, whoever had broken her down to this trembling mess on the kitchen floor, deserved to rot.

Allie stood there feeling helpless. She wanted to fix it. She wanted to scoop Sofia up and squeeze the pain out of her, tell her that she was ok, that she was there… but she realized in that moment that *her* touch was the enemy right now.

She took a deep, shaky breath to steady herself. She pushed aside the fleeting feeling of rejection. This wasn't about her feelings or her want to comfort the woman she loved. This was a primal response to the trauma that Sofia had endured.

Allie slowly lowered her hands. She took two deliberate steps backward to increase the distance between them.

"I'm sorry." Allie's voice cracked, but she forced it to remain steady. "I am so sorry, Sof. I shouldn't have done that without asking. I'm stepping back. See? I'm right here over by the table."

Sofia peeked out from behind her arms. Her eyes were wide, rimmed with red, and filled with a terror that broke Allie's heart.

"I'm sorry," her words were wet with tears. "I'm so sorry, Allie. I didn't mean to. I just… panicked." She gasped, raw grief gripping her. "I feel so broken, Allie."

"Hey," Allie said gently. "No. You do not apologize. Do you

hear me? You have nothing to apologize for. Not a single thing."

"I hurt you," Sofia sobbed. "I pushed you away. I'm so sorry."

"You protected yourself," Allie corrected. "And that is always okay."

Allie sank down to the floor slowly, but she stayed where she was on the other side of the kitchen. She sat with her feet planted on the ground and rested her hands on her own knees to show she wasn't reaching out yet.

"We are going to do this differently now," Allie said. "You get to lead this. I won't touch you unless you want me to. I won't crowd you. When you are okay with being held or touched, I will be here. Always. But only when *you* say so."

Sofia looked at her. The terror began to recede, replaced by a blinding grief. She looked at Allie sitting there, patient and solid. She wasn't asking for anything; she wasn't demanding affection or forcing normalcy. She was just existing in the space with her.

"I don't know how to be okay anymore." Sofia's body crumpled as she said the words. She felt lost, defeated, and alone even though she knew she wasn't.

"There isn't a time limit on this, Sof," Allie said. "We have all the time in the world. I'm not going anywhere. Regardless of how hard it gets, regardless of how long it takes, and regardless of how messy it is. I'm going to be right here."

Allie slowly extended her right hand across the wooden floor. She didn't reach all the way to Sofia. She just laid her hand flat on the floor, palm open. An invitation... a choice.

Sofia stared at the hand; it was her anchor in this storm. It was the same hand that had held hers during movies, the same hand that had cooked her dinner, and the same hand that held her, wrapped in safety, a thousand times before.

Slowly, painfully, Sofia uncurled from her defensive ball. She reached out, her fingers trembled as they brushed against Allie's. Allie didn't grab her… she waited until Sofia laced their fingers together and squeezed.

Only then did Allie grasp her hand back. She held it gently yet securely to let her know she was there, that she had her… in Sofia's time.

Sofia looked up and met Allie's eyes. There was no judgment there, there was no pity. There was only a fierce, unwavering truth. Allie *saw* her. She saw the pain and the dirt and the shame, and she loved her anyway.

The dam broke.

Sofia scrambled on her knees across the gap between them, desperate for the contact she had just rejected. She collided into Allie's chest.

"I've got you," Allie whispered, tears leaving wet traces down her face as they started to fall. "I've got you baby… always."

Allie wrapped her arms around Sofia, encompassing her in protection and comfort. She let Sofia press into her, sobbing against her skin until she had nothing left to cry.

For the first time since she woke up in the darkness, Sofia felt the cold begin to recede. She wasn't fixed…she wasn't healed… but she was held, she was safe, and she was loved.

30

Chapter 30

Two weeks had passed since Sofia's return home from the hospital. The bruises, cuts, and swelling had almost vanished, but the invisible scars, the ones etched deep within her mind and soul, continued to torment her.

Every night, the same nightmare replayed in her mind, her screams echoing through the quiet apartment. Sleep offered no escape, only a terrifying descent into the darkest recesses of her memory.

Camilla, being unable to shake her worry for her older sister, had moved in temporarily to provide comfort and support. She was a steady companion, helping with the everyday tasks that felt totally undoable to Sofia. She would help with cooking meals, tidying the apartment, but acting as a shoulder to cry on was her most important task. She also took on Sofia's business affairs, answering the phone, rescheduling clients, and fielding questions with a carefully crafted explanation of "an accident" and the need for time to heal.

Every morning, Camilla would walk down to the Peach

& Bean and order Sofia's favorite iced coffee, the Raspberry Cream Cold Brew, and a freshly baked scone, hoping to tempt her sister's appetite. But every day, the coffee and scone were barely touched.

Camilla watched as her beautiful sister became a shell of her former self. She was losing weight; her once-vibrant skin was now pale and drawn. Her hair, once thick and beautiful, was falling out in clumps. Her eyes, usually sparkling with life, were sunken and haunted by a darkness no one could touch.

Camilla felt a deep ache of helplessness. She wanted to fix things, to erase the pain, to bring back the compassionate and joyful sister she loved. But she knew there were no easy answers, no quick fixes for the trauma Sofia had endured. All she could do was be there, a constant presence, a steady support, offering love and understanding without judgment or expectation.

Allie, too, was a frequent visitor, her presence a source of comfort and strength for both Sofia and her family. She would often drive to Fredericksburg straight after work, arriving in the early evening, her exhaustion overshadowed by the need to be with Sofia. She would cook her dinner, trying hard to get her to eat something. She would sit silently with her, wrapped in her favorite cashmere throw. She would spend the night, holding Sofia close, whispering words of love and encouragement to soothe Sofia's troubled soul. Then, at the crack of dawn, she would slip away, returning to Austin and the demands of her job. She was so grateful for the flexibility that allowed her to work remotely part-time and to be present for Sofia as much as possible.

But despite the love and support that surrounded her, Sofia

remained trapped in a world of pain and fear. The trauma of the attack had left deep scars, invisible wounds that refused to heal. The nightmares continued, the flashbacks haunted her waking hours, and the fear of the unknown, the fear of the man who had violated her, lingered in the dark corners of her thoughts.

Going outside became a rarity as she struggled with the fear and anxiety of not remembering who had attacked her. Every corner, every dark crevice became a hiding place for the dark figure. Camilla or Allie would have to go around and check every corner, every dark place at night. They would check the windows and doors to make sure they were all secure. They did whatever it took to make Sofia as safe as possible. One of those items was a new baseball bat kept right beside Sofia's bed.

* * *

Allie arrived Thursday evening, her overnight bag bumping softly against her leg as she climbed the stairs to Sofia's apartment. She walked in, a warm smile gracing her lips as she greeted Camilla, who was curled up in the oversized pale yellow chair by the window, a steaming mug warming her hands. Allie raised her eyebrows, the question hanging in the air: *Where's Sofia?*

Cami took a sip of her tea and tilted her head towards the bed.

Allie nodded, her smile softening with a touch of concern. She moved towards the bed, her footsteps barely disturbing the quiet of the apartment. She found Sofia nestled under a soft white comforter with a grey cashmere throw draped over her.

Allie gently set her overnight bag at the foot of the bed. She sat beside Sofia, the bed dipping gently beneath her weight. "Sofia, love," her voice was a soothing whisper in the quiet room, "I'm here." She brushed a stray strand of hair from Sofia's forehead, her touch light and tender.

To Allie's surprise, Sofia's eyes fluttered open, a flicker of a smile gracing her lips. "Hi, babe," she murmured, her voice raspy with early sleep.

Allie felt a surge of hope warming within her. "Well, hey there," her smile widened. "How are you doing today?"

Sofia slowly pushed herself up, the covers falling away to reveal one of Allie's plain white t-shirts, a comforting reminder of Allie's presence even in her absence. Her hair was pulled back in a messy ponytail, the dark strands framing a face that was pale and drawn; the shadows under her eyes spoke of sleepless nights and lingering pain.

"I'm okay." Sofia's voice was weary, even though she tried to smile. "I tried to go down to the studio for a bit to answer some emails and stuff, but I didn't last that long." She sighed, her shoulders slumping with exhaustion. "I just… I just can't get the strength to do anything."

Allie reached out, her thumb gently caressing Sofia's cheek. "It's okay, babe. There's no rush. You'll do things when your body and mind are ready."

Sofia's gaze met Allie's, the vulnerability in her eyes mirroring the weariness in her voice. "That's what the therapist keeps telling me, but I need it to be now. This isn't me, this isn't who I am." Her voice cracked, the frustration and fear evident.

"Sofia, it isn't a contest. You were hurt, and it's okay to give yourself time to heal."

Camilla, drawn by the sound of their voices, entered the open bedroom area. She smiled at Sofia, her eyes filled with love. "Yeah," she chimed in, "and until then, you have us to help."

Sofia's gaze softened as she looked at them both, a glimmer of gratitude shining through the sadness. "I love you both for it." Her hands reached out to them. "Thank you."

Camilla stepped forward, taking Sofia's hand in hers, squeezing it gently. Allie followed suit, her lips pressing a soft kiss to Sofia's knuckles. "We love you."

They shared a moment of silent understanding, their love for Sofia a tangible presence in the quiet room.

"Alright," Allie broke the silence with a determined tone, "what are we having for dinner tonight? I'm starving." She hopped off the bed, planting a kiss on Sofia's forehead before heading towards the kitchen.

Dinner was a simple but comforting affair: chili and honey cornbread. Its sweetness a perfect complement to the savory dish. It was the perfect meal to chase away the winter chill, and to Allie's delight, Sofia even asked for seconds.

Afterwards, they gathered around the small, round dining table and played a game of Rotten Apples. Laughter gave life, once again, to Sofia's apartment.

Allie's heart swelled with joy as she listened to Sofia's laughter, a sound that had been a rare and precious commodity in recent weeks. Sofia was healing, slowly but surely, emerging from the darkness that had threatened to consume her.

The next morning, as Allie prepared breakfast, the enticing aroma of sizzling bacon, fluffy scrambled eggs, and sweet cream pancakes filled the air. Sofia, stirring from a restless sleep, slowly emerged from her comfortable bed, her footsteps dragging against the worn wooden floor as she made her way to the bathroom.

Suddenly, Sofia's voice, thick with confusion, echoed through the small apartment. "Allie? Can you come here for a minute?"

Allie, spatula in hand, approached the bathroom door, a concerned frown creasing her brow. "What's up, babe?" She gently pushed the door open a crack, peering in.

Sofia sat on the toilet, Allie's oversized white t-shirt pulled up over her legs and resting on her lap. Her brow was furrowed in deep thought, her fingers flicking in front of her, as if she was counting something. "Can you call Cami in here, please?"

Sofia's evident confusion and distress deepened Allie's concern. "Of course, babe," she turned towards the living room. "Hey, Cami, Sofia needs you."

Camilla appeared in the doorway, her usual bubbly demeanor replaced by a worried frown. "What's up, sissy? You okay?"

Sofia, her gaze fixed on her hands, finally spoke, her voice trembling slightly. "What day is it today?"

Camilla, confused, glanced at Allie before answering. "January 17th, why?"

"When did you last get your period?" Sofia's voice was tight with anxiety. "We usually get it around the same time… when was that?"

Camilla's brow furrowed as she exchanged a worried look with Allie. "Umm, I think I started around January 3rd," she racked her brain, trying to think back. "I was definitely off by last Wednesday when I went on that date with that talkative guy." She paused, her eyes searching Sofia's face. "Why? What's wrong?"

Sofia remained silent, her confusion deepening, her fingers twisting nervously in her lap.

"Baby," Allie broke the tense silence, "what's going on?"

Sofia finally looked up, her eyes filled with a mixture of fear and confusion. "I'm late."

"Shit." Cami breathed. The realization of what her sister was saying hit her.

Sofia's breathing quickened, her chest heaving as panic began to set in. Allie's mind raced, trying to process the implications of Sofia's words.

"Sissy, don't worry," Cami tried to keep her voice soothing, sensing her sister's distress. "Stress can cause girls to miss their periods. It's probably just that."

But the seed of doubt had been planted. Allie felt the blood drain from her face, the floor seeming to drop out from under her. A muffled gasp escaped Sofia's lips, snapping Allie back to the present. She rushed to Sofia's side, gently helping her off the toilet and leading her to the bed.

Sofia, her gaze fixed on the floor, remained silent, her breathing shallow and rapid.

"Baby, baby!" Allie tried to get Sofia's attention. "Look at me. It's probably nothing. Try to calm down, okay? Don't get yourself worked up. Your sister is probably right; it's probably just stress."

Allie's gaze met Camilla's, their eyes wide with a shared fear, the unspoken question hanging heavy in the air: *What if she's pregnant?*

<h1 style="text-align:center">31</h1>

Chapter 31

The aisles of the small pharmacy were empty. The store was silent outside of the generic music playing softly from above. Allie's shopping basket was filled with essentials for Sofia: Diet Coke, Peanut Butter M&M's, and a comforting assortment of herbal teas. She paused in the pharmacy aisle, her gaze drawn to a small box tucked discreetly on the shelf. A pregnancy test.

A cold dread settled in her stomach. She knew Sofia was terrified of the possibility; the thought of carrying a child conceived in violence was a major source of anxiety. But Allie also knew that the uncertainty was a heavy burden for her to carry, and the sooner Sofia knew, the better.

She reached for the box, her fingers tracing the smooth edges, a silent debate raging within her. Should she encourage Sofia to take the test? Would the knowledge, whatever the outcome, bring a sense of closure, a chance to move forward? Or would it shatter the small amount of progress Sofia had made recently?

Allie hesitated, her gaze flickering between the box in her

hand and the aisle stretching before her. She thought of Sofia, her pale face, the haunted look in her eyes. She thought of the trauma Sofia had endured, and she knew that the choice could have profound implications for their future.

With a deep breath, Allie placed the box in her basket. She would offer Sofia the choice and the power to confront the uncertainty of this one question. It wouldn't be easy, but Allie would be there every step of the way, regardless of the outcome.

The sky was darkening with rain clouds, the small patter of raindrops just beginning on the windshield as Allie pulled up to Sofia's apartment. She climbed the stairs, a growing sense of hesitation building within her. She had taken the pregnancy test out and put it in her bag until Sofia was ready… if that's the choice she made. But carrying it in her bag felt like a lead weight, weighing her down.

Allie opened the front door, her heart lifting at the sight of Sofia standing across the large, open space of the apartment. Sofia was dressed, a pair of comfortable jeans hugging her curves, a white t-shirt with a low scoop neckline revealing the delicate curve of her collarbone, and her favorite fuzzy slippers adorned her feet. Her hair, a cascade of loose waves, tumbled down her back, a sure sign that she hadn't used the blow dryer that morning.

As the door creaked open, Sofia turned around, a beautiful smile on her face when she saw that it was Allie. That smile would forever melt Allie's heart.

"Hey, beautiful," Allie's voice was filled with affection as she greeted her. "I got you some things. Hopefully, it's everything you'll need, at least for tonight."

Sofia crossed the room. She leaned up, pressing a soft kiss

to Allie's lips. "Thank you." Her voice still carrying a hint of fragility. She took the grocery bags from Allie's hands, her fingers brushing against Allie's, sending a shiver of warmth through her.

Sofia carried the bags to the kitchen island, her eyes scanning the contents. She pulled out a bag of Peanut Butter M&Ms and a frosty bottle of Diet Coke, a mischievous grin spreading across her face. She moved towards the oversized couch, sinking into its plush cushions, her body enveloped in its comforting embrace. She popped a few M&Ms into her mouth, savoring the sweet, chocolatey flavor. "Mmmm," she hummed contentedly, "thank you, babe. I needed these."

Allie smiled from behind the kitchen island as she pulled a cold bottle of her favorite beer from the fridge and poured it into an icy mug. "You're welcome," her gaze lingered on Sofia. "Did you want anything else to eat while I'm over here?"

Sofia shook her head, her eyes fixed on the TV screen, where the opening credits of a rom-com played. "No, I'm good right now. I snacked while you were gone."

Allie carried her beer into the living room and placed it on the coffee table coaster. She settled beside Sofia, gently lifting Sofia's legs and placing them on her lap, a small gesture of intimacy.

She watched Sofia, her heart fluttering as she took in the sight of her. Even in her casual attire, with her hair tousled and her face free of makeup, Sofia was breathtakingly beautiful. "You're so beautiful," Allie breathed, the words escaping her lips before she could stop them.

Sofia blushed, a delicate pink tingeing her cheeks. "You're making me blush."

They settled into the comfortable silence, the rom-com

playing on the screen a pleasant distraction. But Allie's mind kept returning to the pregnancy test hidden in her bag. Should she bring it up now? Would it be better to wait? The uncertainty gnawed at her.

Finally, unable to contain her concern any longer, Allie broke the silence. "Sof, have you thought any more about taking the test?"

Sofia's gaze remained fixed on the TV screen, her expression unreadable, her voice barely a whisper. "No, not really."

"I know it isn't an easy decision, babe," Allie's hand found Sofia's, "But I really think it's important to know."

Sofia abruptly pulled her feet away and sat up, her movements stiff and sudden. "I know."

Allie watched her, the silence stretching between them, heavy with unspoken worries.

"It's just…" Sofia's voice cracked, her eyes filling with tears. "I'm scared, Allie."

Allie's heart ached at the sight of Sofia's vulnerability. She moved closer, wrapping her arms around Sofia, pulling her close. "I know, babe." Her voice was a gentle murmur against Sofia's hair. "You have every right to be scared. I'm scared too. But being scared isn't going to change anything."

Sofia nodded silently, her head buried in Allie's chest, seeking the comfort of her embrace.

"If it's negative," Allie continued, her voice firm yet gentle, "then we take a huge breath and cry from relief. If it's positive, then…" she paused, her voice catching, "then we move forward in whatever direction you choose. There is no right or wrong answer here. And I'm going to be here, Sofia, regardless of the outcome, regardless of whatever choice you make. I'm here, and I'm going to love you through it."

Sofia pulled back, her red-rimmed eyes meeting Allie's. She nodded slowly, a tear tracing a path down her cheek. "I know," she whispered. "I know I need to know."

They found each other's hands, holding them tightly, as they looked into each other's eyes. Both looking for the strength they would need.

"I got a test at the store," Allie confessed, watching Sofia's reaction closely. "Just in case."

Sofia's eyes widened with a flicker of fear, "You did?"

Allie nodded, her thumb gently rubbing the back of Sofia's hand.

A heavy silence filled the room as Sofia's mind raced. She was scared to know. The thought of carrying the offspring of the monster who did this disgusted her. It made her feel like a monster could be growing inside her and sent a rage through her, a rage so deep that she wanted to tear at her stomach to somehow rid herself of this thing that might be inside her. But she knew she needed to know. She hadn't told anyone about these thoughts she was having. They were too dark to tell anyone, and she hated herself for even thinking them, let alone saying them out loud.

Sofia nodded, another tear escaping her eye. "Let's do it."

Allie, though relieved, was still surprised by Sofia's decisiveness. "Are you sure?" Do you want to wait for Cami to get back tomorrow?"

"No, I want it to just be us." She stood up, her movements purposeful, and walked towards the bathroom.

"Okay," Allie said, her own anxiety rising. "I'll get the test."

* * *

Three minutes. They had three minutes to wait. Three minutes that stretched into an eternity, each second a hammer blow against Sofia's fragile composure. She sat perched on the edge of the bathtub, her legs shaking nervously. Her hands gripped the cool edges of the tub, her knuckles white, her fingers trembling.

Allie stood in the doorway, her heart aching for Sofia, her mind a whirlwind of conflicting emotions. She watched Sofia's every move, her own anxiety mirroring the fear etched into Sofia's face. She longed to offer words of comfort, but what could she say that would truly help in this impossible moment?

The test sat on the counter, resting face down.

Each second ticked by with agonizing slowness, an eternity within a three-minute timeframe. Yet, a part of Sofia wished that time would stop, to freeze in this moment of agonizing suspense. If they never reached the three-minute mark, they wouldn't have to face the truth, the devastating reality that might lie hidden beneath the plastic casing.

"Sof," Allie's soft voice broke the silence. "It's time."

Sofia's breath hitched. She rose, her legs shaky, her movements hesitant as she approached the counter. Her arms wrapped tightly around herself, as if trying to protect herself with everything she had. She stared down at the test, her eyes wide with fear, her heart pounding against her ribs.

"I can't do it, Allie," she whispered, her voice barely audible, choked with emotion.

Allie moved closer, her hand resting gently on Sofia's back. "Do you want me to do it?"

"No," Sofia's voice trembled. "I'll do it. I just... need a minute."

Allie nodded, her gaze full of empathy. "I'm here."

Sofia took a deep, shuddering breath. Her shaking hand reached for the test. She picked it up, the smooth plastic cold against her skin.

Allie held her breath, her body tensing in anticipation. She stood beside Sofia, ready to offer whatever comfort she could.

Slowly, Sofia turned the test over, her eyes searching for the indicator lines. But she didn't have to search for long.

There, in the middle of the test stick, were two blazing pink lines, a stark and undeniable confirmation of her worst fears.

Sofia didn't just drop the test; she recoiled from it. She flung it away as if it had burned her, the plastic clattering loudly into the sink.

"No," she gasped, the word strangled. "No, no, no."

She backed away until she hit the wall, her hands flying to her stomach. She began to claw at her t-shirt, her fingers digging frantically into her own skin, scratching, pulling, desperate to tear the truth out of her body.

"Please, Allie," she pleaded, her voice jagged and broken. "Get it out, get it out of me!"

Allie lunged forward, grabbing Sofia's wrists, pulling her hands away from her stomach before she could hurt herself. "Sofia! Stop, baby, stop!"

Sofia's legs gave way, and they collapsed together onto the cold tile floor. Sofia fought against Allie's grip for a second longer like a wild, terrified animal before the fight drained out of her, replaced by a crushing despair.

She buried her face in Allie's chest, her body shaking with violent sobs, her cries echoing off the bathroom walls.

Sofia was pregnant.

Pregnant with the child of the man who had violated her. The monster was no longer just in her nightmares; it was growing inside her. And as she lay on the floor, held by the woman she loved, she felt completely, utterly shattered.

32

Chapter 32

The sterile gray walls of the police station seemed to close in on Sofia as she and Allie sat across from Detective Miller. Sofia, her hands clasped tightly in her lap, her gaze fixed on the worn surface of the detective's desk, felt a wave of nausea wash over her.

"There's some information we think y'all might need to know," Allie said as she held Sofia's hand, offering her as much comfort as she could in that moment.

Detective Miller stopped shuffling a mountain of papers on his desk and looked at them both. He leaned in as he adjusted his glasses, "What is it, Ms. Mackenzie?"

Sofia took a deep breath, steeling herself for the difficult conversation. "I… I'm pregnant," she said, the words catching in her throat.

Miller's brow furrowed. "Pregnant?" he echoed, his gaze shifting to Sofia. "And you believe this is related to the assault?"

Sofia nodded, tears welling up in her eyes. "Yes," she whispered, her voice barely audible. "It… it has to be."

Miller's gaze hardened, his professional demeanor momentarily cracking as a flicker of anger crossed his features. "Are you sure?" he pressed, his voice taking on a sharper edge. "Could it be anyone else?"

Allie bristled at the insinuation, her protective instincts flaring. "Sofia has only been with one man in her life, and that was years ago. Are you seriously suggesting—"

"I'm only trying to be thorough, Ms. Mackenzie," he said coldly as he looked at Allie.

He turned back to Sofia, his voice gentler now. "Sofia, I know this is a difficult time for you, but I need to ask you to be absolutely certain. Can you definitively say that the only possible father of this child is the man who attacked you?"

Sofia, her heart aching, nodded slowly. "Yes," she whispered, her voice filled with a quiet certainty. "It's him."

Allie squeezed Sofia's hand reassuringly.

A couple of papers slipped off Detective Miller's desk as he found his writing pad and started writing notes down. "What are you going to do about the pregnancy?" he asked, his voice detached and businesslike.

The question hit Sofia like a punch to the gut. She hadn't allowed herself to think that far ahead, her mind consumed by the trauma of the attack. The thought of carrying this child, a constant reminder of the violence she had endured, filled her with a visceral dread.

"I… I don't know," she stammered, her voice trembling. "I just want to be rid of it."

Miller looked up at her briefly, giving her a quick nod before looking back down at his notepad and continuing to write. "You know the laws in Texas have changed and abortion isn't an option here anymore, even for rape victims.

There's a DNA test that can be done a little further along in the pregnancy, or after the child is born. We can talk about the logistics of that down the line."

Allie's heart clenched at the sight of Sofia's distress. Her eyes, wide and filled with a raw panic, stared at the detective. One hand still clung to Allie's, the other cradled her stomach.

"I have to *carry* this baby?" she choked out, her voice a broken whisper, the words echoing disbelief and horror.

Detective Miller, his pen poised over his notepad, paused, his gaze catching Sofia's. "As long as you remain living in the state of Texas," he confirmed, his voice heavy with the weight of the law, "yes."

A sob tore from Sofia's throat, her body folding over itself as she sat in the chair. Allie's arms instinctively wrapped around her, offering a haven of comfort and support. She glared at Miller, her eyes blazing with a protective fervor.

"Do you still need us, or can I take her now?" she demanded, her voice laced with a barely suppressed indignation.

"No, you're fine to go, I'll call if I need anything else." He said flatly, picking his pen back up and starting to write again.

Allie gently helped Sofia to her feet, her arm a steady support as they navigated the police station. As they stepped out of the imposing red stone building, the sunlight, filtering through a cloudy sky, offered a fleeting warmth, but it did little to penetrate the chill inside them both.

Allie helped Sofia into the car before sliding into the driver's side. Sofia sat silently, her arms wrapped around herself tightly as if trying to hold herself and her world together.

Allie remained silent, her heart aching for Sofia. Words seemed inadequate in that moment; she simply sat beside

Sofia, silently offering her all of her love and support.

The silence was finally broken by a choked sob escaping Sofia's lips. "I can't have this baby, Allie," she whispered, her voice raw with anguish. "I can't do it." The dam of her emotions finally broke, and she dissolved into sobs, her body trembling with the force of her grief.

Allie reached out, pulling Sofia into her arms. She held her close, her embrace a desperate attempt to mend the shattered pieces of the woman she loved. Sofia clung to her, her tears soaking Allie's shirt, her sobs a heart-wrenching symphony of despair. Allie's heart shattered with Sofia's. She felt so helpless, wanting to do anything and everything to take this all away, but she knew there was little she could do.

An hour later, they pulled up to Sofia's home, and Allie helped her from the car. She hadn't said anything else after breaking down; she just allowed Allie to hold her until she silently pulled away and looked out the window at the rain that had just begun.

Allie guided her up the stairs and into her apartment, where her sisters and mother awaited. She had called Sofia's family that morning, her voice trembling as she relayed the news of the pregnancy test. Blanca had broken down, her sobs echoing through the phone. Camilla and Isabella had responded with quiet strength, promising to be there for Sofia and to offer their unwavering support.

As they entered the apartment, Sofia's eyes met her mother's, the raw pain and empathy reflected in Blanca's gaze mirroring her own. "Mama," she sobbed, her voice breaking, and Blanca ran to her, holding her close.

"Oh, mija," her mother cried, her voice thick with emotion, "I'm so sorry, my love. I'm so, so sorry."

Camilla and Isabella joined the embrace, their arms forming a protective circle around Sofia and their mother, holding onto Sofia as if trying to breathe strength and love into her.

Allie, witnessing the raw emotion of the scene, quietly set Sofia's purse down and retreated to the kitchen. She wanted to offer something, anything, to ease their pain. The thought of warm chai tea, one of Sofia's favorites, came to mind. As she reached for the teapot, her hand trembled, and a wave of grief crashed over her. She set the teapot down, her sobs finally escaping, muffled by the running water as she leaned against the sink, her body shuddering with the force of her emotions.

Her heart broke for Sofia, the most gentle, loving soul she had ever met, destroyed by some devious, hateful person. And for what? And now she had to carry the baby of this evil person? Then what? She had to give birth, go through all that pain, and give it to someone else to raise? She didn't deserve this. She didn't deserve ANY of this.

The rest of the evening unfolded in a tapestry of quiet moments and unspoken understanding. Sofia's family and Allie rallied around her, their hearts heavy with the burden she carried.

They sat in comfortable silence, the gentle ticking of the clock a soothing rhythm. Their presence was a comforting weight, a reminder that Sofia was not alone. They watched movies, their eyes flickering between the screen and Sofia's face, searching for any flicker of emotion, any sign that she was engaged, that she was present in the moment. They shared stories, their voices soft and gentle, a temporary escape from the harsh reality that awaited her.

At times, a spark of laughter would break through the

somber atmosphere, a welcome reminder of the joy that still existed in their world, a fragile hope that one day, laughter would once again fill Sofia's eyes. But even in those moments of levity, a deep undercurrent of sadness remained, a silent acknowledgment of the pain that lingered beneath the surface, one that wouldn't end any time soon.

Sofia never mentioned the pregnancy, the word hanging unspoken in the air. They all respected her silence and followed her lead. They knew that when Sofia was ready, she would speak, she would share her burden, and she would decide her path forward. And until then, they would be there, in whatever form she needed, whenever she needed.

33

Chapter 33

The rain tapped against the bedroom windowpane, a soft and weeping rhythm that matched the ache inside Sofia's chest. The house was quiet, in a painful, silent slumber. Her sisters and her mom had left a few hours ago, leaving an exhausted Allie to collide with the bed shortly after.

Sofia couldn't turn her mind off, especially at night. All of the questions, the thoughts, the fears. Medication helped to cradle her into oblivion for the night, but she hated the way she felt the day after.

She lay there, wrapped in the blankets she used to love, listening to Allie's breathing, the lullaby of it being enough to ease her into sleep just weeks ago. But now… sleep didn't come easily, and when it did, it was filled with monsters.

Sofia slid her hand slowly under her pillow, not wanting to disturb Allie. She found her phone and pulled it out, trying her best to shield Allie from its glow.

She turned the brightness down until the screen was a ghost of blue light. Her fingers trembled as she typed. She didn't want to know… but she had to know.

She typed in keywords regarding Texas abortion laws, aiding and abetting, and penalties for crossing state lines.

The words on the screen blurred through her tears. She read about Senate Bill 8, the cold, sharp legal terms that turned mercy into a crime.

Civil liability.
Ten thousand dollars.
Felony charges.
Human trafficking.

The air left the room.

Sofia pulled up a legal analysis that explained how a driver could be prosecuted. How a person who simply paid for a hotel room or helped cover gas could be sued by a stranger they had never met. The law wasn't just a wall, it was a weapon. If she let Allie or anyone else drive her, if she let them help to save her from this, the weapon would turn on the people she loved most in the world.

A sob caught in her throat.

The mattress shifted as Allie turned to Sofia. The slightest sound from her woke her immediately.

"Sof?" Allie's voice was rough with sleep and worry. "Are you okay? What's wrong?"

Sofia took a deep breath. She couldn't hide this from her. She turned over, the ghostly light illuminating the tears that were sliding silently down her cheeks.

"We can't go," Sofia whispered. Her voice was cracked, fragile. "We can't go to New Mexico, Allie. We can't go anywhere."

Allie sat up, wiping the sleep from her eyes. "Babe, we

talked about this. I don't care about the risk, I'll drive you to the moon if I have to."

"It isn't just a risk." Tears soaked her face as she held the phone out, her hand shaking. "I'm trapped, Allie. Look! They can call it trafficking. Even you just driving me… trafficking. They can put you in prison. They can take your entire life apart just for holding my hand while we cross a line on a map."

Allie took the phone into her hand as she looked at the screen. The harsh reality of the text stared back at her. She went quiet, the weight of the new laws settling over them like a suffocating cloud.

"I won't let you," Sofia whispered as she raised her head to look into Allie's eyes. Her tears sparkled as they fell down her beautiful cheeks. "I won't let you or anyone else go to prison for me. This man has already destroyed me… I won't let him destroy those that I love, too."

Allie pulled Sofia into her arms. Sofia didn't fight it. She melted into her embrace like a bird seeking shelter in a hurricane.

"I wanted this." Sofia's voice broke with the ghost of a dream. "Not this… not like this. I wanted to be a mom… my whole life, I dreamt of it. I even have a list of baby names I wanted to name them. Sweet, gentle, unique names. Winter, Sage, Amadeo, River."

Allie smiled as she gently rubbed Sofia's back. "Those do sound like names you would like. Perfect names."

Sofia nodded against her chest as another sob caught in her throat. "I wanted to be able to choose a donor with the person I chose to spend my life with, to become a mother with. I wanted to create a life out of love. I wanted to be able to look down at my child and see me… see love."

She placed a hand gently over her flat stomach. It wasn't protective… it was mourning.

"But he violated me and planted this pain inside of me. And now? Now men who have never had to feel the fear of footsteps behind them in the dark, who have never had to fear walking to their car alone… have decided what choice I get to make."

Allie felt Sofia's tears drip from her eyes and onto her chest.

"They stole my choice," she sobbed. "The man who did this took my safety… and now the law has taken my voice. Where is the justice in that? They talk about life, but what about mine? Does my life not matter because I'm now a vessel?"

Allie's jaw tensed as she listened to her words. "You are not just a vessel. You are the most amazingly strong person I've ever met."

"I don't feel strong." Her voice was but a whisper, broken and lost. "I don't feel human either. I feel occupied. I feel like my body is a house that someone broke into, and now… the police… the ones that are meant to protect us… are telling me I have to let the intruder live in my home with me."

She looked at Allie with a gaze so full of hurt that it broke Allie's heart into a million pieces.

"I wanted to be a mother on my terms. I wanted to cry happy tears. I wanted to be scared because I loved that child so much, not because I was forced into it. It isn't fair, Allie. I'm serving a life sentence for a crime I didn't commit."

Allie had no good answer for this. No words that would make this better. It was the truth… the painful, life-shattering truth. She knew she couldn't fix this for her; she could just hold on. She wrapped Sofia in her arms and held her tightly.

"I'm here," Allie whispered into Sofia's hair. "This is a fucked up cage that you're in. But I'm in here with you, Sof. I see the bars… but I'm sitting right here on the floor with you. I'm not leaving. I'm going to hold your hand through the fire, through the rain… through all of it."

Sofia closed her eyes, the ink of the laws dark and permanent in front of her. She was a prisoner in her own body, forced to carry this heavy burden that she never asked for. She let herself weep as Allie held her. For the dream she had lost and for the nightmare that had replaced it.

34

Chapter 34

A brisk wind, carrying the sharp, clean scent of approaching spring, whipped through Fredericksburg as Allie and Sofia strolled down the cobblestone street hand in hand. It was Valentine's Day, February 14th, and the early morning air hinted at the promise of the Texas sun.

The morning light was just beginning to climb above the horizon, casting long, dancing shadows and painting the cottage storefronts with a soft, warm glow.

The Peach & Bean was already humming with activity. A queue snaked out the door, the crowd waiting on their special Valentine's Day scones and donuts.

Allie pulled out a wrought-iron chair for Sofia on the small patio, then headed inside to navigate the crowd and collect their online order from the designated To-Go area.

She returned, carrying two tall iced coffees and a small, brown paper bag that exuded the irresistible scent of warm pastries. The sugary, buttery aroma made her stomach rumble.

Sofia smiled, a genuine, beautiful smile, as Allie handed

her the iced coffee and scones. She took a nibble of the soft scone, letting its flavors mingle in her mouth. "Can I talk to you about something?"

"Anything." Allie sank into the cold iron chair beside her.

"I've been thinking about Josh lately." Sofia looked past Allie's shoulder and into the cafe as she watched the people inside.

"Oh?"

"Yeah, I mean I know I've brought it up before…" Silence. The heart-shaped scone crumbled softly in Sofia's hand as she stared out at the street, a frown creasing her brow. "It's not just that he's not *here*," her voice was quiet, barely audible above the street noise. "It's… I miss him, Allie. I miss our friendship."

Allie's gaze softened. She reached across the small table and gently squeezed Sofia's hand. "I know, Sof."

"It feels wrong." Sofia continued, her voice gaining a slight edge. "Like he's abandoned me. And I keep thinking… maybe I should reach out. Maybe I should just call him, tell him what's happening. Ask him…" she trailed off, her eyes clouding with a mix of confusion and unrest. "Ask him about that night. About everything. I need to know what happened, Allie. I need to… remember."

She looked at Allie, her hazel eyes pleading. "I want to ask him where I went, *why* I went. I need to know if he knows anything that could help."

Allie's heart ached for her. "I understand, Sof. I really do." She hesitated, then confessed, "I've been wanting to talk to him too. There's just so many questions. But… I've tried. I've called, I've texted. Nothing."

Sofia's frown deepened. "Nothing?"

"Not a word. I get the feeling his dad has him completely cut off from communicating with us."

Sofia's gaze drifted back to the street, a sense of isolation settling over her. "It's like he's disappeared," she whispered. "And I feel like… like I'm being punished for something I don't even remember."

"You're not being punished, Sof." Allie's voice was firm, filled with reassurance. "This whole thing sucks, babe." She reached for Sofia's other hand, holding both gently. "We will figure things out. We'll do it together."

Sofia managed a weak smile. "Thank you, Allie. I don't know what I'd do without you."

"You don't have to. I'm not going anywhere."

The sun broke through the oak tree, casting a tapestry of light and shade across them as Allie took another bite of her scone and leaned back. She never felt at ease with the Josh thing; something about the defensiveness his dad had displayed nagged at her, but maybe that's just the way that attorneys act in situations like this. She didn't know, but she knew that she needed some answers, more than what the detectives were giving them and she wanted those answers today.

After they finished their coffee, they set back for Sofia's apartment. Sofia had a busy day of couples sessions, and Allie had to start her daily remote work routine.

As she started her day, she sat at the small desk in Sofia's apartment. Her laptop was open, and the work waited as she stared blankly at the screen. She pulled out her phone and dialed Detective Miller's number. She hesitated for a moment, took a deep breath, and put the phone to her ear.

The phone rang endlessly before it was answered.

"Detective Miller," said a rushed male voice.

"Hey, Detective, it's Allie Mackenzie. Any updates on Sofia's case?"

"It's ongoing, Ms. Mackenzie." Miller's voice was flat, professional. "We're still pursuing leads on the man or men Sofia left the party with, and we're looking into a report from the couple who called 911 on the man they saw not far from where Sofia was found."

"What about DNA?" Allie pressed. "Surely you found something on her body."

"Her body was wiped down well, Ms. Mackenzie," Miller replied. "We found no DNA from anyone we'd label a suspect."

Allie took a deep breath, "Well, what about camera footage? I'm sure the McCoys' mansion has a hundred of them."

"None. The McCoys had their entire camera system down for the weekend due to the high-profile guests staying there for the gala. Mr. McCoy said it's a regular thing they do for privacy."

Allie paused, a knot of frustration tightening in her chest. "Has Josh been looked at as a suspect? I mean, Sofia went there with *him*."

"No." Miller's voice was flat and firm, almost as if annoyed by the question. "Multiple witnesses place him at the gala all evening. His alibi is airtight."

"Well, what else can we do here?" Allie demanded, her voice rising. "This is ridiculous!"

"For now, it's a waiting game. We'll keep the investigation open, but frankly, our best bet might be after the baby is born."

Allie took another pause, "There has to be some DNA from

the rape kit. She's pregnant for Christ's sake!!"

Miller hesitated, a subtle shift in his tone. "Normally, yes. But… we just got word that multiple test kits at the lab were labeled as contaminated or improperly handled. Sofia's was one of them."

"What?" Allie's voice was a harsh whisper. "Why hasn't Sofia been notified about this?"

Miller paused, and for the first time, his professional mask slipped. He sounded tired. "It happens, Ms. Mackenzie. Items get misplaced. Labels get smudged. I was going to get around to speaking with y'all sometime this week."

Allie ended the call and slammed her phone down. She was furious, a white-hot rage burning in her chest. Contaminated? Improperly handled? This had to be a sick joke.

She stood abruptly, the small office chair scraping against the wood floor. She needed to move, to burn off this anger. She started pacing the apartment, but the small space started feeling suffocating. Then she grabbed her coat and headed out for a walk; the cool February air hitting her face was welcome against the burning she felt inside.

She needed to calm down. She needed to think. She couldn't tell Sofia this, not yet. Not like this. She would call Isabella later, find out the best way to break the news, and then they would do it together.

* * *

The call to Isabella didn't go well. She was just as upset as Allie was and scared for her sister. Though Sofia was healing and doing better, she was still fragile, and they were afraid this news would break her. How do you tell someone you love that the evidence they clung to… the hope to answer the question of who assaulted them and left them for dead, and whose child they were unwillingly carrying… is now destroyed?

How do you shelter someone you deeply love from being hurt, yet again? Their decision was to talk to Sofia's therapist and see about telling her together; the extra support being there might help with breaking the news.

35

Chapter 35

The quietness of the morning was broken by a wide-awake Camilla, already on her second latte, bursting through the door to Sofia's apartment, a drink carrier in hand.

"Good morning!" She almost sang into the still apartment. She set the drinks down on the kitchen counter and bounded over to the bed where Sofia and Allie were still nestled, attempting to steal a few more precious moments of sleep.

She pounced onto the bed and into Sofia's lap, "Sissy! WAKE UP!" she playfully yelled, "You too, Allie! It's morning time!"

Sofia's laughter echoed through the lofty apartment, the sound washing over Allie with a comforting warmth. "Good morning, hermanita." Her voice was still thick with sleep as she ruffled her little sister's long, dark hair. "Why are you here so early? What time is it anyway?"

A soft groan came from Allie as she turned over onto her back, blinking against the sudden intrusion of daylight. She raised her head to look at Cami, a playful smirk on her face, "Too damn early, is what time it is."

"Oh, hush, grumpypants," Cami teased. "It's 8:30, plenty late enough for both of y'all to wake up and get dressed. Mom and Izzy will be here in an hour."

Sofia groaned as she lifted her little sister off her and sat up, pushing the sleep-mussed hair from her eyes. "Fiiinnneee. Did you bring my coffee?"

"Duh," Cami rolled her eyes with a dramatic flair as she walked towards the lattes on the counter. "Of course I did, sissy! I always come with drinks in hand… or I make them." She chuckled as she carried the carrier over to the bed, the mild sweetness of the lattes filling the air.

As the drinks were handed out, Sofia chirped, "So, Heather is coming over here for the family counseling session today?"

Allie nodded, the cool smoothness of her iced coffee a welcome contrast to the lingering warmth of sleep. "Yep. She'll be here at 10:00 a.m. How are you feeling about it?"

Sofia shrugged and took a sip of her iced coffee. "Fine, I guess. Not really sure exactly what to expect, but y'all are wonderful, so how hard could it be?"

A genuine smile played across Allie's face as she ran her hand down Sofia's back. "We think *you* are the amazing one, beautiful."

Cami nodded in agreement, a rare moment of seriousness softening her features as she smiled at her big sister. Cami was a pro at being the annoying little sister, but the admiration she had for Sofia was beautifully evident.

Allie and Sofia quickly changed into comfortable clothes while Cami settled on the couch, completely engrossed in some raunchy reality series about people on an island being tempted to cheat on each other. Allie fake gagged as she walked up and sat next to Cami, throwing her arm playfully around her. "Gross, Cami, I can feel my brain cells rotting already."

Cami rolled her eyes and elbowed Allie in the ribs. "Maybe *yours* are, but *I* like it. Therefore, we are watching it."

The sound of Allie and Cami's laughter made Sofia's heart melt. Allie was the perfect addition to her family and to her life. She couldn't have ever dreamed of more. Smiling, she walked over to the couch and squished in between the woman she was in love with and her little sister. "Welp, guess we are just waiting on mom and Isabella," she said just as the door creaked open.

Isabella and Blanca walked in together, each holding a cold cup of soda.

"Hey there," Izzy smiled at everyone as she took off her sweater and hung it on the coat rack by the door.

Blanca looked over at everyone and waved, her smile bright and warm. "Hello, my loves!" Blanca had already fully embraced Allie as one of her own and had now become "mija" as well, a term of endearment she had come to cherish.

They all shared hugs before settling into their seats, the apartment buzzing with a comfortable, familial energy as they awaited Sofia's therapist, Heather, to arrive. As planned, Isabella and Allie were the only ones who knew the devastating news that needed to be broken to Sofia. Patiently waiting for the two weeks to pass to tell Sofia and the family had felt like an eternity; each day dragged by under the weight of their secret. But now, here they were, lingering to tell Sofia something that could shatter her world, once again.

A soft knock sounded through the apartment, and Allie jumped up to answer it, the sound of her new family's chatter spilling into the hallway as she opened the old wooden door.

Heather, Sofia's therapist, stood in the doorway, a warm smile on her face. She wore a light-brown, loose-knit sweater and casual denim jeans, her notepad hugged against her chest, and her trusty, antique-pink Stanley tumbler in hand.

"Hi there, Allie." Her voice was calm and soothing as ever as she adjusted her wide-rimmed black glasses.

Allie smiled back, ushering her inside. A nervous flutter danced in her stomach, a knot of apprehension tightening as she realized the moment of truth was fast approaching.

Heather walked in, her gaze sweeping over everyone with a warm smile. "Good morning, do we have everyone here?"

"Yep!" "Mhm." "Yes," came the chorus of confirmations as Heather moved gracefully to the window seat in the living room. It was the perfect vantage point, centered in front of the others, allowing her to observe and connect with each person.

Heather looked around at everyone slowly as she smiled, "How is everyone this morning?" Her voice was almost melodic, smooth and empathetic, the perfect voice of a therapist.

Everyone answered with the usual "goods" and "fines" as they waited for the family meeting to begin.

Heather's friendly green eyes settled on Sofia, nestled comfortably on the couch with Allie's arm resting protectively behind her. "Sofia, how have you been this week?"

Sofia shifted slightly, a thoughtful expression crossing her face. "I've been good. Pretty much the same, nothing really significant has happened." She paused, reflecting on the past few days. "I think working again has really helped. It keeps my mind busy, and I can tap into my creative side, which always makes me happy."

Heather nodded, her pen gliding smoothly across her notepad. "That's good! It's always encouraging when we can re-engage with aspects of our old lives. It's an important part of healing." She smiled warmly at Sofia. "Anything else?"

Sofia shook her head. "No, not that I can think of."

"Well, there is something that the family needs to discuss," Heather began, her voice gentle yet firm, "and I wanted to be here to offer my support in any way needed."

Sofia, Cami, and Blanca exchanged confused glances.

"There is?" A tremor of anxiety laced Sofia's voice.

Allie reached for Sofia's hand, giving it a reassuring squeeze, offering courage to both Sofia and herself.

Heather nodded, acknowledging Sofia's nervousness. She paused, allowing a moment for the weight of her words to sink in. "A few weeks ago, some information came to light that Allie and Isabella felt was important for you to know. They wanted the family present to provide love and support."

Sofia's eyes darted between Allie and Isabella, wide with apprehension. Allie's heart clenched in her chest as she tightened her grip on Sofia's hand, fighting to keep her own breathing steady.

"Sofia?" Heather said softly, drawing her attention back.

"Hmm?" Sofia's voice was flat, betraying the effort it took to maintain her composure.

"Sofia," Heather's voice was low and steady, her focus remaining on Sofia. "There's been some recent news from Detective Miller that may be upsetting." Sofia remained silent, her gaze fixed on the rug beneath her feet. Heather's voice remained calm and soothing as she delivered the news. "There was an issue with the evidence processing at the lab. Your rape kit was compromised. They won't be able to extract any DNA from it, which means it won't be able to help identify your attacker."

Sofia's hand started shaking as Allie held it, her breathing became rapid and shallow. Allie squeezed her hand and wrapped the arm that was already around her even tighter, as if trying to hold her pieces together.

A small cry escaped Sofia's lips. Heather moved closer, her hand reaching out to take Sofia's. "Sofia," she said, her voice filled with empathy, "I am so, so sorry. I know this news is devastating, and everything you're feeling right now is valid. Your family is here to support you, however you need. For now, we're just going to rally around you and love you." She glanced at Isabella's stoic face, Blanca's silent tears, and Camilla's shocked and angry expression. "Come, everyone," she urged, calling them closer.

Sofia's family rose and moved towards her. Blanca and Camilla knelt in front of her, their hands joining the growing circle of support. Isabella moved behind the couch, resting a comforting hand on Sofia's shoulder.

Sofia began to weep, her body shaking with sobs. Her family and Heather remained steadfast, a circle of complete love and support surrounding her. Tears flowed freely as her family and Allie cried alongside Sofia.

Heather stayed for another hour, talking softly with each of them, supporting Sofia as she moved through the deep ache of feeling powerless. The police had failed her. The lab had failed her. The system that was supposed to protect her had simply shrugged.

Sofia sat in the center of her weeping family, her gaze drifting down to her stomach.

For days, she had looked at her own body with revulsion.

She had viewed the life growing inside her as a parasite, a monster, a continuation of the violence. But as the tears dried on her cheeks, a cold clarity washed over her.

They lost the DNA, Heather had said.

No, Sofia thought, her pulse quickening. *They lost the kit. They didn't lose the DNA.*

Slowly, deliberately, Sofia uncurled her fist. She pressed her palm flat against her lower stomach.

The room seemed to quiet around her. The compromised test kit no longer mattered. The growing cells within her held the undeniable truth. This baby, the strongest testimony to the horrific violation she had endured, was no longer just a burden. It was her proof.

She would have to wait. She would have to endure the pregnancy. But she would do it.

Her hand tightened against her stomach, a silent vow made in the quiet of her soul. This baby would be the key to his downfall. Justice would be hers.

36

Chapter 36

The crinkling of the thin paper beneath her was almost the only sound heard in the quiet ultrasound room. The lights were already dim as she lay on the exam table waiting for the technician. Allie was, of course, by her side. Sitting quietly, letting Sofia breathe silently, struggling with the internal turmoil.

Twenty weeks. Twenty weeks since that night, twenty weeks of carrying the unwanted consequence, the living evidence. She still couldn't bring herself to think of it as a baby, a child. It was a burden, a means to an end.

The ultrasound tech finally entered. She was a woman with kind eyes and a gentle smile. She took a seat and then squeezed warm gel onto Sofia's abdomen. "Alright, honey, let's take a peek and see how things are progressing."

The wand pressed against her skin, cool and slick, and the image flickered to life on the screen. Sofia averted her gaze, a wave of nausea rising in her throat. Every movement, every flicker on the screen, was a jarring reminder of what had been done to her.

The room was suddenly filled with a rhythmic, rapid *whoosh-whoosh-whoosh.* It sounded like galloping horses, frantic and loud. To anyone else, it was the pulse of life. To Sofia, it was the echo of panic. It felt like the adrenaline rushing in her ears that night in the greenhouse. She squeezed her eyes shut, wishing she could plug her ears against the invasive hum of the stranger living inside her.

"Everything looks good so far." The tech chirped after about 30 minutes of the exam. "Heartbeat is strong, growth is right on track, and it looks like we are still at a September 13th due date." She paused, then added softly, "Would you like to know the sex?"

"No," Sofia's voice was sharp. Laced with a bitterness she couldn't disguise. "I don't want to know anything about it."

The tech's smile faltered, giving way to a look of under-standing. She glanced at Allie, offering a sympathetic nod.

Allie shifted in her chair, leaning closer to Sofia as she held her hand. "What if we just have them write it down?" Her voice was soft and soothing. "Just in case, you know, you decide you want to know later on."

Sofia hesitated, the internal conflict raging within her. A flicker of maternal instinct was struggling to break through the wall of resentment she had erected. With a sigh, she relented, the weight of the world carried in that single movement.

"Fine." Her voice was barely a whisper. "But I don't want to know now."

The tech nodded, her smile returning. "No problem, honey. We'll just pop it in an envelope for you." She finished the scan with a mix of medical jargon that washed over Sofia, barely registering.

Allie squeezed her hand, her eyes warm and reassuring. Sofia closed her eyes, willing herself to detach, to see this as just another step in the process, another hurdle to overcome on the path to justice. But the fluttering movement beneath the tech's wand, the undeniable reality of the life growing within her, made it impossible to ignore the emotional turmoil brewing beneath the surface.

Back at the apartment, Sofia settled onto one of the stools at the kitchen island while Allie poured them both a drink.

"So, it looks like I'll be leaving pretty early for Austin tomorrow," Allie said as she set the cold Diet Coke in front of Sofia. "I have meetings pretty late, so I'll probably just stay there. Are you okay with that?"

Sofia nodded, taking a sip. "Of course, babe. Do what you need to do. I'm okay here."

Allie studied Sofia's face, trying to gauge her true feelings. "Are you sure? You had a pretty intense experience today, and I don't want to leave if…"

"I'm okay, promise," Sofia looked up at Allie with a smile. Her smile seemed genuine, but Allie was hesitant to take it at face value these days.

Allie nodded, taking a quick drink. "Okay then. Do you want me to ask Cami to come over and stay?"

Sofia chuckled. "I love my baby sis, but please, no. I need a little space. A night to myself will be good, I think. I *promise* I can survive without you for a few hours."

Allie darted around the island, scooping Sofia into a playful embrace. "Oh yeah?" she teased, poking Sofia in the ribs. "You can survive without me, huh?"

Sofia let out a playful squeal, snuggling into Allie's comforting warmth. "I love you, you know?" she murmured, leaning her head back against Allie's shoulder.

"I know," Allie lovingly tightened her hold on Sofia's waist. "I love you too."

After dinner, Sofia loaded the dishwasher and wiped down the kitchen island. As she moved, the small white envelope from the ultrasound tech slipped from the counter and drifted to the floor. She picked it up, her fingers tracing the familiar shape, and hesitated.

A conflict surged within her, anger competing with curiosity. Did she want to know? *Could* she know? Every day, she fought to see this baby as nothing more than a means to an end, the living DNA of the man who had used her body and left her for dead. But a part of her, a part she desperately tried to ignore, struggled against that cold detachment.

Allie approached quietly, noticing the envelope in Sofia's hand, the tension radiating from her. She knew the struggle raging within, a battle with no clear victor.

"Want to talk about it?"

Sofia turned the envelope over and over in her hands, shaking her head. "No?" Her voice was small, uncertain. "I don't know. I don't know what to do, Allie."

She looked up, meeting Allie's gaze. Sadness and empathy reflected back at her. "I hate this," she whispered, a tear tracing a lonely path down her cheek.

"I know." Her heart ached for Sofia. "Let's sit, okay?"

They settled on the couch, Allie's arm a comforting weight around Sofia's shoulders as she stared at the envelope.

"Sofia," Allie began gently, "all of your anger and hurt and hate for what happened are valid. It's okay to be angry, you *should* be. But..." she hesitated, choosing her words carefully. "I can't help but think that this baby is as much *you* as it is anything else, regardless of how it happened. And all those feelings you're battling, the love and the hate… it's okay to feel love, too."

Allie's words, spoken with such soothing sincerity, were the words Sofia had longed to hear but been too afraid to acknowledge.

Tears welled in Sofia's eyes as she met Allie's gaze. "How can I let myself love something that was made from hate?"

Allie searched her eyes. "I don't know, Sof. All I know is that all those feelings are okay, including the love. It's okay to say 'baby,' it's okay to feel something other than hate. It's just… all okay. There's no right answer here."

Tears streamed down Sofia's face as she sobbed. "I don't want to hate it, I don't," she cried. "I want to be better than that, to allow myself to feel… but I'm so angry!"

Allie pulled her close, stroking her hair as she wept. "I wish I could take this all away, my love," she murmured, her voice low and earnest. "But you need to know that whatever choice you make is okay. Whether you decide to let someone else raise it, or you decide to raise it yourself. Your family will be here, and I'll be here. We're all going to walk this journey together, you just lead the way."

Sofia nodded against Allie's chest, her shirt damp with tears.

Allie held her silently until her sobs subsided. Sofia took a long, shuddering breath, her body relaxing into Allie's embrace. "I'm scared to know, Al. But I want to know."

They held each other tightly, as if they were trying to squeeze strength into one another. "Are you sure?"

Sofia sat up, meeting Allie's gaze with newfound resolve. "I think so. I don't know if it'll change anything, but I think I want to know."

She looked down at the envelope that had remained clutched in her hand. Her fingers trembled as she turned it over, the flap tucked neatly in.

As she stared at the white paper, a desperate prayer formed in the quiet of her mind.

Please, she pleaded silently, her heart hammering against her ribs. *Please let it be a girl.*

She could do a girl. A girl was safe. A girl would be soft, a reflection of herself, of her mother, of her sisters. A girl she could protect. But a boy? The thought sent a spike of ice through her veins. A boy would grow up to have his hands. His strength. A boy would grow up to be a man, and right now, men were the monsters in her nightmares. She didn't know if she could look into the face of a son and not see the shadow of the father who had forced him into existence.

Taking a deep breath, steadied by Allie's presence beside her, she pulled the flap open and drew out the folded paper.

Her hands shook as she held it, bracing herself for the answer. It wasn't about the sex of the baby, not really. It was about making it real, acknowledging the life growing inside her. It would solidify the fact that this wasn't just about justice; it was about a baby. A baby that was half her rapist and half her, and she wasn't sure how she was going to see past that, or if she ever would.

Holding her breath, she slowly unfolded the paper and read the single sentence scrawled across it:

It's a Boy.

37

Chapter 37

The darkness clung to Sofia, the familiar nightmare unfolding before her once again. A dark figure, its face blank and horrifying, loomed over her. But this time, the shadows shifted and contorted. The figure didn't just growl or strike; it leaned in close, intimate and terrifying.

"I've got you, Sof," a familiar voice whispered.

The faceless man morphed. The blur sharpened into blond hair, a charming jawline, and baby blue eyes that usually sparkled with warmth.

Josh.

He wasn't grimacing. He was smiling. It was the same friendly, confident smile he gave her when they laughed together. The same smile he gave her mother and sisters… but his hands were pinning her wrists above her.

"*I love you,*" Josh whispered, his friendly face drifting closer as he shattered her world. "*I know you want me too.*"

A scream tore through her as she awoke, dread radiating

through her body. Her heart raced inside her chest, her breathing felt constricted as she gasped for air.

Josh. It was Josh! The pieces of the puzzle clicked into place, not just with clarity, but with a sickening thud.

Josh.

She laughed with him. She trusted him. She loved him.

Her mouth filled with bile as she scrambled out of bed, barely making it to the bathroom before she retched into the sink. Her body convulsed, trying to purge the sickness of the realization.

Trembling, she wiped her mouth and fumbled for her phone, her fingers clumsily dialing Allie's number. The phone seemed to ring for an eternity before Allie's sleepy voice answered.

"Sofia? What's wrong? Is everything okay?"

"Allie," Sofia sobbed, her voice barely recognizable. "It was him. It was Josh."

"Sofia, slow down. I can't understand you. What about Josh?"

"Josh," she choked out, the words catching in her throat. "It was *him*, Allie! He attacked me!"

A stunned silence filled the line. Then, Allie's voice, sharp and urgent, cut through Sofia's growing panic. "Sofia, listen to me. I'm coming home right now. I'm going to call Cami and have her come over to stay with you. Just breathe, okay? I'm on my way."

"I can't breathe," Sofia gasped, her chest constricting, the walls of the apartment closing in on her. "I can't—"

"Sofia, focus on my voice. Can you hear me? I'm calling Cami now. Just stay on the line with me, okay?"

Allie's voice switched to a three-way call, Cami's sleepy

confusion filtering through the speaker.

"Cami, it's Allie. I need you to go to Sofia's apartment right now. She's having a panic attack. I'm on my way back from Austin, but I need you there now."

"Oh my god, is she okay? I'm on my way!"

Sofia clung to the sound of Allie's voice, a lifeline in the swirling chaos of her fear. Her breaths came in ragged gasps, her body trembling uncontrollably. Josh. The man she had trusted, the friend she had grown to love. He was the monster who had violated her, who had left her broken and bleeding. The realization bore down on her, a crushing weight.

"Sofia, babe, Cami's on her way. Just hang in there, okay? I'm coming as fast as I can."

Sofia could only nod, her voice lost in the storm raging within her.

* * *

Allie arrived just over an hour later, thankful that she hadn't been pulled over for speeding. She ran into Sofia's apartment to a scene that nearly brought her to her knees.

Sofia lay curled on the living room floor, the only light emanating from a small lamp on the side table. Cami sat beside her, cradling her sister in her arms as Sofia sobbed. Sofia's growing belly peeked from beneath the white pajama shirt she wore.

Rage suddenly surged through Allie. Josh was the one responsible for everything Sofia was going through. Josh was the one responsible for the child she was now forced to carry. She clenched her fists, concentrating on her breathing to quell the indignation burning inside her. Then, she moved toward Sofia, sinking to her knees. Sofia threw herself into Allie's arms, both of them collapsing against the couch as Sofia sobbed.

Allie held her close, absorbing the tremors of her grief, fighting back the whirlwind of emotions.

Then, a memory flashed in Allie's mind. The bouquet of flowers at the hospital. The red roses and white lilies. The card that read, *"Get well soon. Love, Josh."*

Her blood ran cold. He had sent flowers. He had sent *love* to the woman he had left for dead. He had walked around free, playing the concerned friend, mocking them with his "kindness" while Sofia lay in a coma.

The fury that surged through Allie was blinding. He wasn't just a rapist... he was a sociopath.

"How could he do this to me?" Sofia's voice was raw with pain. "I trusted him, I loved him."

Allie's voice was thick with emotion as she answered, "I don't know, baby. I don't know."

Cami and Allie remained by Sofia's side until dawn, offering unwavering support and love. As the first rays of sunlight filtered through the windows, Allie knew they couldn't delay the inevitable any longer. They needed to call Detective Miller, a task that would undoubtedly reopen barely healed wounds.

"Sof, we need to call Detective Miller."

Sofia's gaze lifted slowly, her eyes red-rimmed and filled with a weariness that mirrored Allie's own. "I know," she whispered, her voice hoarse from crying.

Allie gently helped her into a sitting position, then pulled out her phone. Her heart ached for Sofia, for the ordeal she had endured, and the difficult conversation that lay ahead.

"Are you ready?"

Sofia nodded, taking a deep breath to steady herself. "I'm ready."

Allie punched in Detective Miller's number, her finger hovering over the call button for a moment before she pressed it. The phone rang, and to her surprise, it was answered almost immediately.

"Detective Miller," the gruff voice barked.

Allie swallowed, her throat tight with apprehension. "Detective, it's Allie MacKenzie and Sofia Flores. We… we need to talk. Sofia remembers who attacked her."

A brief silence hung in the air, heavy with anticipation. "Oh?" Miller's voice was suddenly alert, the weariness replaced by a sharp focus. "We definitely need to talk then. I can be there this morning. Will you be at Sofia's?"

"Yes. We'll be here."

"Alright, I'll be there soon, probably around nine or ten. Depends on how the morning shapes up."

"Okay, Detective. We'll be here," Allie ended the call with a shaky exhale. She looked at Sofia, whose face was pale, a mixture of fear and determination etched into her features. Allie reached out, taking Sofia's hand in hers, "Remember, Sof, we're in this together."

Sofia nodded as Cami took her other hand, a gentle wave of appreciation flowing through her for these two humans and their love and support, which guided her through the depths of this ongoing nightmare.

38

Chapter 38

A heavy silence fell over the apartment as Detective Miller entered. He glanced around briefly before approaching Sofia, who sat at the dining table, her shoulders slumped with the weight of the revelation.

"Hello, Sofia," Detective Miller nodded his head as he sat down across from her. He pulled out a notepad and flipped it open. "So, you remember who attacked you?"

"Yes," Sofia's hands trembled in her lap. "It was Josh McCoy."

Miller looked at her, unblinking, "And what makes you say that it was Josh McCoy?"

Sofia kept her gaze fixed on the table. "I don't really know. I had the same dream about the attack that I always do, but I saw Josh's face this time."

Miller set his pen down. "So, you just had a dream that it was Josh?"

"Well, yes," Sofia admitted, her tone wavering. "But I *know* it was him. I know it inside."

"Do you recall any details of the attack or what happened?"

Sofia shook her head hesitantly. "Not really. I remember small things. I remember being at the gala, dancing. I remember being hit hard, but I can't see a face. I remember falling… the smell of dirt… seeing plants? I remember…" her voice trailed off.

Detective Miller waited patiently. "You remember what, Ms. Flores?"

"I remember the weight of someone on top of me, choking me. Then… nothing." Her body sagged as the memory overwhelmed her.

"But you don't recall any faces? Just in this dream?"

"I know it was him, Detective. I don't want it to be him, but it was." Her voice shook as she wrapped her arms around herself, seeking a comfort she couldn't find.

Miller leaned back, tapping his pen. "Josh McCoy? He's a friend of yours, isn't he? Sometimes trauma makes the brain replace a scary stranger with a familiar face. It's a coping mechanism, Sofia. You're likely projecting."

Detective Miller closed his notepad with a sigh, turning his attention to Allie. "I'll put it in the file, Ms. MacKenzie, but as I said, there isn't much we can do about dreams."

Sofia, unable to bear the dismissal, pushed her chair back and fled the room, the sound of a door clicking shut echoing moments later.

Allie nodded silently, understanding the limitations of the situation, though frustration gnawed at her. They needed more.

"I'll see myself out," Detective Miller said, rising to leave. "Give me a call if she remembers anything real."

"We will," Allie assured him, locking the door behind him. She then made her way to the bathroom and knocked softly.

"Sof, he's gone now. Do you want to come out, or want me to come in?"

A moment of silence stretched between them before Sofia's quiet voice reached her. "No," her voice was heavy with despair. "I just need some time alone."

"Okay," Allie sighed, taking a deep breath. "I'm going to run to the Peach & Bean. I need some coffee, and I'll grab us some breakfast. I love you."

As Allie turned to leave, she heard Sofia's muffled sobs and a faint, "I love you too. Thank you."

* * *

Detective Miller slid into the seat of his police car and reached for his phone as he closed the door. Punching in a number, he pulled away from Sofia's apartment, the dial tone a steady pulse in the heavy quiet.

It rang a few times before a voice, sharp with privilege and arrogance, cut through the tension. "Thomas McCoy speaking. What can I do for you, Detective Miller?"

Miller took a deep breath, the weight of his next words settling heavily in his gut. "Mr. McCoy," he said, "she's starting to remember."

39

Chapter 39

The air in Thomas McCoy's home office hung thick and heavy, a cloying mix of expensive leather and the faint scent of his overly priced Parisian cologne. The dark oak walls, polished to a deep, reflective sheen, seemed to absorb the meager light filtering through the semi-sheer curtains of the oversized window, casting the room in a perpetual twilight. The smooth surface of the mahogany desk felt slick beneath Thomas's fingertips as he picked up the heavy, brass-trimmed phone, an antique that had remained in his father's office until his passing.

"Hello, Father," Josh answered, his voice a thin, reedy tremor.

"Josh, what the fuck were you thinking!" The words hissed through Thomas's teeth, low and menacing. "Do you have any idea what a fucking mess you've made?"

Josh was speechless. He wasn't sure exactly what this was about, but he didn't want to throw around any guesses either.

"I'm not sure what you are referring to, Father."

Thomas scoffed into the phone. His hot, angry breath was

almost palpable through the receiver. "Well, let me fill you in, *son*." His condescending tone was thick, like cold, viscous honey. "The little accident we had to clean up for you, the one who is somehow still walking around town? She's pregnant."

Josh's voice hitched in his throat, "She's…"

"Yes, you fucking dumbass," Thomas interrupted, the sharp edge of his voice cutting through the hush. "But she's not only pregnant, she's starting to remember, and she brought your name to Detective Miller."

"Shit," his hands started to shake. "Dad, what am…"

"Don't you *dare* 'Dad' me right now, you fucking idiot." Thomas' voice was low and angry, a dangerous growl. "You have no idea what all this family had to put on the line to clean up this mess."

A small sound from the doorway, a soft, almost inaudible creak of the heavy oak, caught Thomas' attention. "Hold on," he put the phone down and walked to the half-open door of his expansive home office. He opened the door and looked down the marble-floored hallway to see his wife, Eleanor, walking briskly away.

"Eleanor," Thomas called after her, his voice edged with annoyance.

Eleanor stopped, her breath catching in her throat, a shallow, panicked gasp. A shiver of terror radiated through her body. She turned slowly, a carefully constructed smile on her face. "Yes, dear?"

Thomas' eyes pierced through hers, his expression a tense, hard, unyielding gaze. "Did you need something?"

Eleanor carefully cleared her throat, hoping to disguise any apprehension or knowledge she possessed. "No, darling. I heard you on the phone and didn't want to interrupt.

I'll come again later." She smiled again, a forced, brittle expression, her back straightening as she did.

Thomas paused, watching her, his eyes narrowed. "You can talk to me when you bring me lunch. Don't bother me for now."

Eleanor nodded her head in understanding, "I'll see you at lunch then, darling."

Thomas stepped back into his office, closing the door so it remained open only a crack, and returned to the phone lying on his desk.

"That was your mother; you'd better hope she never finds out what a failure her precious son is."

Josh sighed into the phone, "How do we know this baby is mine, though?"

Thomas sat back in his expensive leather office chair. "Are you implying your precious Sofia was sleeping around? I thought she was a lesbian?"

"She is." Josh took a deep breath, the faint, metallic tang of dread now a constant, almost physical presence. "What do we do? How the hell do I get out of this now?" His voice became tenser with every word, the realization hitting him.

"I don't know," Thomas said, his voice dropping into a cold, predatory rhythm. "But we can work with that. You're going to have to admit to the sex, Josh. But we don't just admit it. We weaponize it."

"Weaponize it? How?"

"You tell them the truth… or at least, the version of the truth that destroys her credibility." His voice dripped with malice. "You tell them that she has been secretly obsessed with you. That this whole 'lesbian' thing is just a façade, a cry for attention. Tell them that night, she finally dropped the act. She wanted you. She begged for it. It was consensual, it was passionate, and it was entirely her idea."

Josh's voice trembled, a mix of hope and fear. "I… I thought she did love me, Dad. I told her I loved her that night."

"Exactly." Thomas snapped, seizing on his son's delusion. "Stick to that. You were lovers. But then? The regret set in. She panicked. She felt ashamed of betraying her little girlfriend, of betraying her 'lifestyle.' She became hysterical, unstable. She ran."

Thomas leaned forward in his chair, a cruel smile touching his lips. "And this is where we bury her, Josh. You tell them she ran off the property in a blind panic. You stayed at the party; we have witnesses for that. She left the safety of the estate, walking alone in the dark, emotionally unhinged."

Silence. "Why do you think I had my associates dispose of her across town that night?" His voice was low and terrifyingly calm. "Do you think I called in a favor just to scrape a problem off my floor? No."

He paused, letting the weight of his cruelty sink in.

Thomas took a deep breath, annoyance coloring his tone. "I had them dump her miles away to build your defense, Josh. While she was bleeding in the back of that van, I was already winning your case. That distance is your alibi. It proves she left. It proves she met the *real* monster somewhere else."

"So… I'm just the secret lover? Is that even going to work, Dad? What the fuck am I going to do?" Josh's hands were shaking even more now, the tremor spreading through his entire body.

A loud bang echoed as Thomas slammed his fist down on the wood, the resounding thud rattling the glass container holding his pens. "You are going to shut your ass up and do exactly as I tell you to, that's what you are going to do. I'll get with Detective Miller on how exactly we need to play this out, but you are going to do everything you are told, and you are going to continue to stay out of Fredericksburg for as long as this takes."

Josh's voice was shaky, a trembling whisper. "Yes, Father. I'll do whatever it takes."

"We already have Judge Thompson, Senator Davis, and multiple other congressmen who have said you were at the gala all evening and that they saw her drunk and leaving with someone else, no one is going to want to question them, so I don't think it will be too difficult to sway anyone if it comes to that, but the pregnancy…" His voice trailed off as rage filled his face and voice, a hot, burning sensation. "How could you be so *careless?*"

"I'm sorry, Dad. I—"

His father's angry voice interrupted quickly, "I don't want to hear it. You fucked up, and I have to clean up after you, again." He paused, his fingers quickly tapping his pen on his desk as he thought. "This is going to have to get ugly, Josh. We are going to have to scare her into silence. I can't see any other way to get around this now."

Josh paused, his heart racing in his chest. "What… what do you mean, dad?"

"I mean," Thomas snapped, "that we are going to have to put some fear into Sofia's life. Real fear. The kind that keeps her awake at night. The kind that makes her look over her shoulder every time she leaves her house."

The ice in his glass clinked together as he emptied it of its Scotch. "A terrified woman makes a terrible witness," Thomas was cold and calculated. He paused, his voice dropping to a whisper that was somehow louder than a shout. "And there is the matter of her condition. High-risk pregnancies are notoriously fragile, Josh. Stress is dangerous. Panic is dangerous. And accidents… accidents always happen. Do not confuse biology with legacy, boy. Until that child is gone, you are vulnerable. So we apply pressure. We make her world unsafe. And if she loses the baby in the process? We call it a tragedy, and we move on."

"Dad, I—"

"You nothing, Josh. This is all on *you*. Whatever happens to her from here is on *you*. Remember that." His voice was a tangle of rage and disappointment as he slammed the phone down.

The loud bang made Eleanor jump as she stood still against the wall outside the office, listening. Tears silently fell as she covered her mouth with her shaking hands. She closed her eyes, trying to shut out the conversation she had just heard. The nightmare from months ago wasn't over; it had just begun.

Chapter 40

The soft satin of her black Dolce & Gabbana midi dress rustled as she fled the hallway. Her carefully manicured nails dug crescents into the palms of her soft hands, a desperate, hushed scream against the suffocating elegance of her life and the fakeness of it all. The vision of polished grace and gentle smiles was a facade crumbling at the edges, revealing the wounded woman beneath. She reached her dressing room, a sanctuary of meticulously arranged dresses and sparkling jewelry, and with trembling hands, she knelt before a locked drawer in her closet's central island. The small lock clicked open. Inside, nestled in one of the many velvet jewelry boxes, lay a delicate gold necklace. Two simple diamonds, one pear shape, the other a marquise, caught the light, their brilliance a cruel mockery of the darkness they now represented. It was Sofia's necklace.

Eleanor's breath hitched as she lifted it. The gold chain felt heavy in her palm, colder than the room around her. It didn't feel like jewelry. It felt like a shackle. A golden chain that bound her to the crime, to the silence, and to the girl whose life they had stolen. The diamonds seemed to shimmer, blurring as tears welled in her eyes. The memory of the Christmas Gala, the night that was supposed to be a glittering highlight of the social calendar, flooded back to her.

* * *

Eleanor stood in front of the beautifully ornate mirror in her private sanctuary, steadying herself to face the night, to play her part. Her hands trembled as she pulled up the folded straps of her crimson Oscar de la Renta off-the-shoulder peasant dress. She reached behind her, pulling up the zipper as she looked up and caught her reflection. A stranger in a familiar face stared back at her.

Her light brown hair looked sophisticated in its elegant updo. The sides were swept low to create perfectly pinned waves that ended in a full, low bun at the nape of her neck.

The beautiful curves of her slim face were bronzed and contoured with an almost professional flair. Eleanor always did her own make-up; she knew precisely how Thomas demanded it. Every other time, Thomas had made her wash it off and redo it.

A subtle rosy blush lay across her cheeks, the swell under her left eye almost unnoticeable, hidden expertly beneath layers of expensive concealer and powder.

Her fingers traced the outline of the deep bruise, a silent, painful reminder of the violence that lurked behind closed doors, and she stopped a silent tear from falling. She was already so late to the party, forced to redo her hair and make-up after the violent disagreement that had marred the start of the evening. This was nothing new, of course. Her entire married life had been a carefully curated prison of control and abuse, but as Thomas religiously reminded her, "This was the price to live such a life of privilege."

She reapplied her matte velvet lipstick, a perfect match to her matching floor-length satin gown. She smoothed the dress down her sides, a gesture of practiced composure, and took one last look. Her breath was deep and slow, a familiar sadness settling over her.

She exited her expansive closet and made her way down the long marble hallway towards the main stairs, the tapping of her scarlet heels muted by the thick, plush rug that ran the hall's length.

Suddenly, she heard her son Josh's voice. It sounded urgent, broken, as if he were crying. She quickened her pace to outside Thomas's office, the source of the sound.

She slowly and cautiously made her way outside the wooden doors so she could hear, afraid to enter without warning. Thomas didn't like her entering without permission. She quieted her breathing so she could listen.

"Dad, I didn't mean to..." Josh's voice was broken, a sob caught in his throat. "She...she just wouldn't stop. She called me a rapist and... and I lost it. It was an accident."

"An accident?" Thomas' voice was a low, dangerous growl. "You accidentally killed her? You really are a fool."

Eleanor froze. The tone, the deflection, the blame... it wasn't just Josh speaking. It was Thomas. Her son hadn't just inherited his father's eyes; he had inherited his father's violence.

"Please, Dad, you have to help me. I didn't mean to, I swear. I didn't mean to do any of this." Josh pleaded, his voice thick with tears.

"Shut up. We don't have time for this. We need to move, and we need to move now. Thompson, get in touch with whoever we can trust. Make sure they understand that discretion is paramount. They will take her off the property, somewhere... remote."

A short, tense silence followed before Judge Thompson's nervous voice broke in. "I, I don't know about this Thomas. Maybe we should..."

"Maybe we should, what, Dean?" Thomas' voice growled through his teeth, a low, menacing threat. "You remember just who made your family. You owe my family everything you have. One word, and your whole existence could crumble. Do you understand me, Judge?"

Judge Thompson's voice shook. "Yes, Thomas. I, I understand you. I'll make the calls now."

"And the conservatory?" a gruff voice, unfamiliar to Eleanor, asked.

"Clean it. Every surface. Every trace. Scrub it until it gleams," Thomas commanded. "Josh, you'll go to the gala. Immediately. Mingle with everyone. Smile. Act as if nothing happened. We will all say you were there all evening. We all saw her, drunk and stumbling. We saw her leave with someone, someone we don't know. Am I understood?"

"Yes, Father." Josh choked out, his voice barely a whisper.

"Understood." Said another unfamiliar voice, a chilling echo.

"Good. Now move. We don't have a moment to waste. Miller is five minutes out."

The heavy wooden doors opened, and Eleanor ducked into the shadows of an alcove, her heart hammering against her ribs as Thomas and Josh swept past her, heading toward the front entrance to meet their "fixer."

Silence settled over the hallway, heavy and suffocating. Eleanor knew she should run. She should go back to her room, fix her face, and pretend she heard nothing. But a morbid, terrifying pull drew her feet toward the conservatory. She needed to know. She needed to see what her son had done.

She pushed the glass door open.

The scent hit her first. It was the damp, earthy smell of potting soil mixed with the sharp, metallic tang of copper.

She made her way through the large conservatory until she neared her beloved hiding space.

It was a crushing scene before her.

A large ceramic planter was overturned, and dirt spilled across the pristine white tiles. But it was the other marks that made Eleanor's stomach turn. Two long, crimson smudged trails cut through the spilled soil on the marble floor... drag marks. Someone had been pulled, dead weight, across the room.

Her eyes followed the trail to the far corner, and a gasp tore from her throat.

Blood.

It wasn't just a drop; it was a scene of violence. A spray of crimson speckled the white petals of a nearby orchid, a gruesome contrast to the delicate flower.

A trail of large drops and small pools was scattered near the hidden window seat she had once called her safe space. It was no longer safe. It was no longer hers.

Eleanor trembled, her hand flying to her mouth to hold back a scream. My son, she thought, the realization shattering her soul. My sweet boy did this.

And then, amidst the horror, a glint caught the moonlight.

Lying near the edge of the blood pool, half-buried in a smear of blood-stained dirt, was gold.

Eleanor stepped forward, her red heels stepping gingerly over the drag marks. She knelt, her expensive gown pooling on the dirty floor, and reached out. Her fingers brushed the cold metal. It was a delicate necklace with two diamonds. The clasp was snapped, broken by force in the struggle.

This was proof. Proof of the struggle. Proof that a girl had been here. Proof that Josh hadn't just made a mistake... he had destroyed someone.

The sound of tires crunching on gravel outside snapped her back to reality. Car doors slammed. Heavy footsteps echoed on the walkway.

"Miller, bring the bleach. I want this floor stripped," she heard Thomas bark. "And be quick, I don't want any of our other guests knowing about this."

"Already on it, Mr. McCoy."

Eleanor's blood ran cold. That wasn't a cleaner. That was Detective Miller. The police weren't coming to investigate; they were coming to erase the truth.

Panic seized her. She didn't weigh the morality. She was a mother, and her son was in danger. With a trembling hand, she snatched the blood-speckled necklace from the floor and shoved it deep into the hidden pocket of her gown.

She scrambled backward, fleeing the room just as the back door to the conservatory opened. She ran back to the shadows, her heart breaking and bleeding, the weight of the gold in her pocket pulling her down like chains and bricks.

She had saved the evidence. But in doing so, she had damned herself.

* * *

Eleanor gave the necklace one last, lingering look and stored it back in its velvet box, tucking it away from the world, like she tucked away the fractured memories of that horrific evening. Every day, she lived a lie, a carefully constructed illusion she desperately wished would simply vanish, leaving her in the quiet solitude of truth. She had always known her husband was a monster, a predator cloaked in wealth and power, but now, the chilling realization settled upon her like a suffocating shroud: the son she loved more than anything, the boy she had nurtured and cherished, was a monster as well.

Her eyes flew open, a sudden, desperate urgency seizing her. She needed to see Sofia. She needed to see if the horrifying claim was true, to witness the tangible proof of her son's monstrous act. And somehow, impossibly, she needed to warn her, to shield her from the storm that was about to break. But how? How was she supposed to help this girl, this victim of her own son's violence, carrying a life conceived in darkness, when she couldn't even summon the courage to help herself? How could she protect anyone when she was trapped in her own prison made of platinum and diamonds?

A wave of despair threatened to drown her, but a flicker of defiance ignited within her. She wasn't sure how, but she knew, with a chilling certainty, that somehow, someway, she was going to make this right. She had to. The weight of her complicity and the years of silent submission pressed down on her. She would not, could not, allow another life to be destroyed, not if she had any breath left in her body. The carefully constructed walls of her perfect life were crumbling, and in their destruction, a terrifying, fragile hope bloomed.

41

Chapter 41

Sofia sat nestled in the new grey glider chair, positioned to catch the soft afternoon light streaming through the living room window. Her hands rested protectively on her rounding stomach as Allie sat across from her, silently watching her slow, rhythmic rocking.

"Sof, I wanted to talk to you about something." Allie's tone was a warm caress in the quietness of the room.

Sofia's eyes flicked up to meet Allie's. "Hmm?"

"How would you feel about me moving here? We could find a place together, and I'd be able to be here full-time, aside from my weekly business trips." She watched as Sofia's gaze shifted fully to her, her eyes searching, questioning.

"You would want to live here full-time? With me?" Sofia's voice was a whisper... a tremor of disbelief and hope. She could feel her heart begin to race.

A small, tender chuckle escaped Allie's lips. "Well, yeah. I wouldn't want to move here to live with anyone else. I'm here almost all the time anyway, and I could be here to help more."

Sofia paused, her eyes scrutinizing Allie's, seeking the truth within their depths. "Allie, I would love nothing more than to have you with me all the time," her voice thick with emotion, "but I want it to be something you want to do, not something you feel like you need to do."

The couch creaked as Allie sat up and leaned forward, bridging the space between them, her eyes filled with an unwavering sincerity. "I want nothing more." Her voice was a low, fervent promise. "You are my home now, Sofia."

Sofia felt a strange flutter in her stomach, a delicate dance of nerves and anticipation, but she wasn't sure if it was her own pulse or the now very active baby within her. Her hand moved instinctively to where she felt the flutter, a small, unconscious smile blooming on her lips.

"I think he flipped or something." She looked down at her stomach with soft wonder.

"Oh?" Allie moved to sit in front of Sofia, her fingers pressing gently against the spot where Sofia's hand rested.

Sofia smiled, her hand covering Allie's, the warmth of their touch a comforting anchor. "Yeah, he's been moving so much lately, and it's getting stronger. Maybe he's telling us he likes the idea."

Both of them beamed at the thought, a shared moment of tender connection, as another small bump rippled beneath their hands.

"I think he definitely agrees." She looked up at Sofia, her heart brimming with affection as she saw Sofia genuinely smiling down at her stomach.

Sofia looked up, her eyes catching Allie's, her heart pounding as she looked into their beautiful depths. These last six months had been so trying and difficult, but Allie hadn't left her side once. She was always there, waiting with open arms, with love and compassion. If she had the choice, she would spend the rest of her life showing Allie the love and dedication that she had shown her through these months. She knew, without a doubt, that she wanted to build a home with Allie. Just her, Allie, and… a baby?

Suddenly, the thought crashed through her, a jolt of realization that sent a shiver through her entire being. This entire time, she had viewed the baby as a means to an end, a tool for justice, a symbol of her pain. But now, gazing into Allie's loving eyes, she saw a future she hadn't allowed herself to envision. A future that included a child. A beautiful little boy, running through their home, filling it with laughter and life. The little boy she carried now, a tiny, fragile life that was becoming inextricably intertwined with her own. A future that held more than just justice, but also, perhaps, a chance at love and a chance at family.

"What about your house in Austin, though?" Sofia questioned, her voice laced with gentle curiosity.

Allie shrugged softly. "I'll probably just rent it out. That'll cover my mortgage and leave some extra money as well. Any idea on what you'd want to do with the apartment?"

"Oh gosh, that's easy," Sofia chuckled, "Cami has wanted this place since I bought it. I'll just rent it to her and make it affordable. She'll be in heaven."

Allie nodded, a genuine smile gracing her lips. "She will totally love that. Maybe we can take a look at a couple of places tomorrow? The sooner we get moved in, the better, since the baby will be…"

She caught herself mid-sentence, her eyes widening slightly as she looked up at Sofia, a flicker of apprehension crossing her face. "I'm so sorry, Sof. I didn't mean to… it just came out."

Sofia shook her head, but she didn't speak immediately. She looked down at her stomach, her thumb tracing the curve.

"I was so scared," she whispered, the confession hanging heavy in the air. "For months, I was terrified that if I looked at him, I'd see Josh… I was scared that… that bad blood creates bad men."

She looked up at Allie, tears swimming in her eyes. "But you were right. He isn't just *his*. He's mine. And if we raise him… if *you* help me raise him… he won't be a monster. He'll be good. Because we'll make sure he's good."

She leaned forward, capturing Allie's hand and pressing it firmly against the spot where the baby was kicking, a strong, rhythmic thud against their palms.

Allie nodded, her hand a gentle caress on Sofia's stomach. "He *will* be good, Sof. He's half you. We will teach him to see beauty in every small thing, just like you do. We will teach him to be gentle. We will teach him to love, because that's all he will ever know."

"I think I love him, Allie," she choked out, the dam finally breaking. "I think I'm finally ready to be his mom."

Allie placed her hand over Sofia's, intertwining their fingers. "Or ours, if you'd be okay with that. We could be a family."

A soft sob escaped Sofia, a release of pent-up emotion, as she smiled into Allie's eyes, her spirit overflowing with a fragile hope. "I'd really like that."

Allie rose and sat on the arm of the chair, wrapping her arm around Sofia, pulling her close. They were going to be happy, regardless of anything. They were going to be a family, a haven built on love, resilience and compassion.

Sofia closed her eyes, breathing in Allie's scent. For the first time in months, the world didn't feel dangerous. She felt untouchable. She felt safe.

42

Chapter 42

Two weeks later, a moving truck, filled with the combined belongings of Sofia and Allie, rumbled to a stop in front of their new rental home. Twelve Cottage Avenue was an adorable two-story cottage, a relic of the 1930s, lovingly remodeled to embrace modern amenities without sacrificing its original charm.

Sofia's family began unloading furniture and boxes, their laughter and chatter filling the air, as Allie's best friends, Danika and Dylann, pulled into the long, paved driveway.

Danika, a force of exuberant energy, rushed to Sofia and wrapped her in a tight, affectionate embrace. "Oh my goodness! The house is gorgeous, and so are you, girl!"

Sofia hugged Danika back with a playful scoff. "I feel like a parade float, but thank you! I love this house so much already."

Allie walked up and draped an arm around Danika's shoulders, giving them a gentle squeeze. "Thanks for showing up this weekend. We really appreciate the help."

Danika returned the gesture, looping an arm around Allie's

waist. "You know we wouldn't be anywhere else! I still can't believe you're moving away from us, but if it had to be for anything, Sofia is the best reason there could be."

Sofia smiled genuinely at Danika and took her hand. "Thanks, girl. We love you, and we're holding you to those weekend visits."

"Honey," Danika's smile widened, her eyes sparkling with mischief, "You are going to get sick of us; we will be here so much."

"Yeah," echoed Dylann as she passed by, hauling a massive white rug toward the porch. She stopped next to Isabella, giving her a playful nudge with her elbow. "I've already blocked off every weekend for the next seven months to be right here, reclaiming my righteous title as Game King from Isabella."

Isabella rolled her eyes but couldn't hide her grin. "If you drop that rug, Dylann, I'm telling Camilla that you cheated at Werewolf last time."

"I did no such thing." Dylann laughed, dragging the rug behind her as the two of them headed inside, bickering like old friends.

Watching them, Allie felt a surge of contentment. This was the family that she would choose over and over again.

The group of three erupted in laughter as Sofia's sisters passed by, carrying a couple of boxes.

"Why don't you girls go inside and start putting things away and let the rest of us handle the heavy lifting?" Allie suggested, stepping to the side.

"Deal!" Danika exclaimed, pulling Sofia along. "These nails cannot handle manual labor anyway."

Sofia chuckled, turning to look at Allie, blowing her a

playful kiss. Allie pretended to catch it in mid-air, tucking it into her pocket, and mouthed, *"I love you."*

Danika and Sofia made their way up the path, passing the delicate flowers that lined both sides, their sweet fragrance filling the air. The house was a quaint home with light beige siding and white shutters framing each window. The light-burnt-orange door, with its small picture window, radiated a cozy glow, and the covered porch, spanning the length of the house, promised lazy mornings filled with coffee and conversation.

They stepped through the open door into the blue-gray living room, where three large picture windows let sunlight flood the space, creating a homey, airy atmosphere. The rooms, though not large, were perfectly adequate for their small family of two, soon to be three. The upstairs boasted a primary bedroom, a guest room, which Danika had already declared the 'Official Auntie Suite,' and a future nursery. Both Sofia and Allie had fallen in love with the house the moment they saw it, knowing that, for now, this was the place they would call home.

* * *

As the day waned and evening descended, they finished unloading the moving truck and arranged as much furniture as their weary bodies would allow. Sofia and Danika had ventured out to pick up pizza, beer, and sodas, a feast for their hardworking helpers, and now, they all gathered around the large kitchen island, eating and laughing.

The scene was a beautiful, noisy chaos. Dylann was trying to convince Camilla that pineapple belonged on pizza, while Isabella and Danika were already planning the housewarming party. Sofia leaned against Allie, her face glowing in the kitchen light. She looked happy… truly happy. Allie wrapped an arm around her, pulling her close. The sound of their family's laughter was a symphony.

Allie knew they would need this foundation. They weren't just moving furniture; they were building a fortress of love around this child. *Their* child.

* * *

That evening, as they settled into the soft comfort of their new bed, their eyelids heavy with exhaustion, Allie pulled Sofia close, wrapping her arms around Sofia in a comforting, protective embrace. Sofia rested her head on Allie's chest, the steady thrum of Allie's heartbeat acting as her favorite soundtrack.

"Allie?" Sofia's soft voice, a whisper of exhaustion, barely disturbed the quiet of the room.

Allie kept her eyes shut as she answered her, her voice low and tired, "Yes, love?"

"Thank you."

The pillow gently rustled as Allie lifted her head and looked down at her, "For what, babe?"

Sofia shrugged softly. "For being you. For choosing me every day, even when you didn't have to. I know that there have been some really rough days since everything happened. Some days I wasn't able to be who you needed, but I want you to know that every single day I was so thankful that I had you. Every single day I still am. I love you so much."

Allie was silent for a moment before she placed her fingers

under Sofia's chin and lifted it to look her in her beautiful hazel eyes. "I wouldn't have chosen to be anywhere else, Sofia. Even on your hardest days, loving you is the easiest thing I've ever done. This, right here, is exactly where I want to be."

Sofia leaned up and kissed Allie tenderly on the lips. "I love you."

Allie brushed a gentle kiss against Sofia's lips, her voice a sleepy murmur, thick with affection. "I love you more."

43

Chapter 43

The July heat shimmered in the air as Sofia made her way to her car, heavy grocery bags digging into her arms. She popped the trunk with a click and carefully arranged the bags, ensuring they wouldn't spill on the drive home. As she reached for the trunk lid, a sleek black sedan rolled up nearby, bringing with it a wave of unease. She turned, her brow furrowing, and saw a man with dark sunglasses, his face an impassive mask, staring straight at her. There was no smile, no friendly nod, only a cold, unwavering gaze.

Despite the prickle of unease, her ingrained Texan politeness compelled her to smile and offer a small wave before sliding her rounded belly behind the wheel. She placed her purse on the passenger seat and prepared to reverse, only to discover the same black car had pulled right behind her, blocking her exit.

Sofia looked around, hoping he was waiting for someone to leave a parking space, but she saw no one. As she continued to scan, she caught the man's gaze again. He was positioned perfectly for direct eye contact, his stare sending a chilling wave down her spine, quickening her breath.

She looked away and tried to shake the rising feeling that something was off. "He's just waiting for someone," she muttered to herself, a flimsy attempt at self-reassurance. She glanced in her side mirror, only to find the man still staring, unmoving.

A surge of anger, fueled by fear, propelled her hand to the horn. Its blare startled a couple of elderly ladies walking past. They glared at her, a mixture of anger and curiosity on their faces, as she mouthed "Sorry," and offered a meek wave.

She looked again in her side mirror, her breath catching in her throat, but he was gone. A wave of relief washed over her, and she slumped slightly, putting the car in reverse and slowly navigating through the parking lot. She flipped her turn signal on to turn left, waiting for a break in traffic, when she saw him again, immediately behind her, the dark sunglasses concealing the eyes she knew were fixed on her in the rearview mirror.

A jolt of pure terror shot through her. She floored it, seizing a small gap in traffic to make the turn. She sped up a little, hoping to create enough distance between them that he could go his way and she could go hers. But the traffic light turned red, forcing her to an abrupt halt. She watched in her mirrors, her heart thundering against her ribs, as the midnight black sedan weaved through the cars and parked two vehicles behind her.

Her heart dropped in her chest, fear rising as she tried to talk it down. "Sofia, calm down," she whispered, her voice trembling. "It's just a coincidence. He isn't following you."

The light turned green, and she resumed driving, a little faster than she normally would, her intuition screaming at her to run. The turn onto their street was approaching. She flipped on her blinker, only to see him mirror her move. She snapped off her signal and continued driving.

"Siri, call Allie." She commanded with a strained voice, waiting for the phone to connect.

The phone rang through her car as she waited for Allie to answer. "Pick up, pick up," she begged as she glanced in the mirror, the vehicle still following her.

"Damn it!" She hissed, her voice laced with fear, as the call went to Allie's voicemail.

"Siri, call Mom," she said again, her voice tight with panic, knowing her mother would answer.

"Hi, Mija!" Blanca's cheery voice rang over the phone.

"Mom, I'm pretty sure someone's following me, a man." Sofia blurted out, her words tumbling over each other.

"What?" Blanca's tone shifted, the cheer vanishing, replaced by alarm. "What man? What's happening, Mija?"

"I'm not sure, Mom, but I'm pretty sure he's following me. I'm heading to the police station, but I'm still about 8 minutes away from it. Can you try calling Allie for me? Tell her to meet me there?"

"Of course, Mija! I'm going to call you back as soon as I reach her." Blanca's voice trembled with worry. "Don't stop for him, ok? Go straight to the police station and keep honking outside the doors until someone comes out."

"I will, Mama, I love you." The phone disconnected, and Sofia glanced in the mirror again. The car was locked onto her, the man's face a mask of cold, unwavering intent.

She accelerated, her small car straining against the sudden surge of power, knowing even a traffic stop was preferable to being alone with him. She made erratic turns through neighborhoods, desperate to confirm she wasn't crazy and he was, in fact, following her.

She made a right and then a left through a quiet neighborhood, a sudden dead end forcing her to a screeching halt. A small park on the right and a house on the left.

"Shit!" She yelled as she looked behind her. The black sedan was pulling up, trapping her.

She could feel her heart pounding in her chest, fear flooding her senses. She scanned her surroundings, desperate for help, as the man opened his car door. Sofia slammed her foot on the gas. Her car leaped forward as the undercarriage scraped against the curb while she careened over it. She swerved through the park, a desperate, chaotic circle, as she flew past the man, now confirmed as her pursuer.

She raced through the streets and back out onto the main street, her tires screeching as she made a sharp right turn. Three minutes. The police station was three minutes away.

The phone suddenly rang; it was her mom. She reached her hand out to hit answer, the other gripping the steering wheel firmly as she sped down the street.

"Mom!" She yelled, her voice cracking with fear. "He's following me! He tried to trap me!"

"Mija!" Blanca screamed back as she started to panic. "Get to the police station! I couldn't reach Allie. I'm coming! I'm getting in my car now!"

Tears blurred Sofia's vision, fear threatening to overwhelm her. "I'm scared, Mom. I don't know what he wants."

"I'm here, my love. I'm not going to hang up until you get there. Take deep breaths. You're going to be ok."

Sofia took a shaky breath, fighting the sobs that wanted to escape. "There's no license plates on his car. It's a black sedan, he's an older white guy, maybe 50? I don't know. Wearing a black shirt and black sunglasses. Just in case something happens, Mama."

"Nothing's going to happen, Mija. You're going to lead him right to the station."

"I'm almost there." Sofia glanced in her mirrors. The sedan was gone, replaced by a large red truck. She sighed in relief, focusing on the upcoming police station.

She saw it approaching on her left. She sped up, weaving through traffic as she saw an opening, and she took it, racing into the parking lot. An officer walking towards his car turned sharply to look at her.

She pulled up to the building and blared the horn, drawing the officers' attention.

She turned towards the road, and there, slowing down, was the black sedan. The man's gaze fixed on her. He took his hand out, his fingers making the sign of a gun, and pretended to pull the trigger. Her heart dropped in her chest as he drove off, an officer approaching her door.

"Do you need help, ma'am?" An officer said as he walked up, a puzzled expression on his face.

Minutes later, her mother's car screeched to a halt, and Blanca rushed to Sofia, wrapping her in a tight embrace. "Are you okay? What happened? Who was he?"

Sofia hugged her mother back, her body still trembling. "I'm okay, Mom. I don't know who he was. I don't know why he was following me. I didn't recognize him at all."

She recounted the event to her mother as she finished talking with the officers.

"Ma'am, we will follow you over to your place and have an officer drive by a few times tonight. As we discussed before, there's nothing we can really do about someone just following you, but we will patrol as a safety measure." The officer's rough voice matched his weathered Texas appearance.

Sofia nodded as her mother chimed in. "I'm following you home too, and I'm staying the night. I don't care what you say. Cami is bringing my stuff, and we're camping on the couch."

Sofia chuckled as she leaned forward and kissed her mom on the forehead. "You don't have to do that, Mom, but thank you, I'll never say no to you camping on my couch, even if you do live fifteen minutes away."

* * *

Allie leaned back, stretching her arms above her head, a groan of relief escaping her lips. Thankful that the grueling three-hour virtual meeting had finally drawn to a close, she swiveled in her office chair as the leather creaked softly beneath her.

A sudden commotion outside her window snagged her attention. She peered through the glass to see Sofia standing near her car with Blanca, both of them speaking with a uniformed police officer.

A jolt of pure adrenaline shot through Allie. She flew out of her chair, the wheels spinning wildly before it slammed with a sharp crack against the dresser.

The front door burst open, hitting the wall with a thud as Allie sprinted toward them. "Sofia, what's going on? What happened? Are you okay?" She reached Sofia, her hands framing her face, her eyes frantically scanning her for any sign of injury.

Sofia nodded, her voice slightly shaky. "I'm okay. Someone was following me. The officer escorted me home, and Mom insisted on coming as well."

"Followed you? What do you mean? What happened?" Allie's voice was strained.

"Let's go inside so I can sit down, and I'll tell you. It's hot, and my back is hurting." Sofia stretched her back, a soft groan escaping her lips, her belly a prominent curve beneath her shirt, as she reached for Allie's hand.

Allie's grip tightened around Sofia's as she led her inside, the cool air rushing from the open door. Blanca followed behind, carrying the grocery bags. They made their way into the living room, Allie gently placing a pillow behind Sofia's back as she settled onto the large couch, her eyes fixed on Sofia, waiting with bated breath to hear what had transpired.

Sofia sighed, the weight of the afternoon settling upon her, as she propped her swollen feet up on the small ottoman. The quiet hum of the air conditioning filled the brief silence before she began to recount the terrifying events of her grocery run.

44

Chapter 44

The glow of the TV flickered across Sofia and Allie as they snuggled together on the plush couch, a half-eaten bowl of popcorn resting between them. Their favorite rom-com, usually a source of lighthearted comfort, offered only a temporary distraction from the unease that had settled around them the past few weeks.

Just as Sofia started to relax into the familiar storyline, her phone buzzed on the coffee table. They exchanged a glance before Sofia picked up the phone and released an annoyed sigh. The caller ID displayed the dreaded words "Unknown Number." The silent invasion of these creepy calls was a daily occurrence, leaving Sofia flustered and increasingly on edge.

She answered, holding the cool glass of the phone slightly away from her ear, already bracing herself. And there it was , the soft, steady rhythm of a man breathing. Close. Invasive. Unseen.

A wave of annoyance washed over her. Without saying a word, she ended the call and tossed the phone back onto the table with a frustrated thud.

"Another one?"

Sofia nodded, pulling the soft throw blanket tighter around herself. "Yep. Same as always." Her voice was tight with irritation and a deeper, underlying fear. "It's so exhausting already. I don't understand why this shit is happening, and the fact that the police say they can't do anything makes it even worse."

"I know, Sof," Allie murmured, pulling her closer. "It's beyond frustrating. The calls, the tires… and now the back door. It's escalating."

"Exactly!" Her voice rose in frustration and fear. "I don't even know if they broke in or if they were just trying to scare us. I just don't get how it isn't enough for them to do something!" She shook her head, a bitter laugh escaping. "It's like they are waiting for one of us to die before they help, and then it's too damn late."

Allie's brow furrowed. "Don't say that."

"But it feels like that's where this is heading!" Sofia's voice cracked. "I can't sleep. Every creak of the house, every passing car… I think it's someone coming to get me. It's terrifying."

Allie held Sofia closely for a moment. "I know, babe. You have every right to feel that fear." She paused and got up from the couch. "One minute, I'll be right back."

Sofia watched her go, a flicker of curiosity mixed with her anxiety. A few minutes later, Allie returned, carrying a medium-sized box.

"What's this?" Sofia watched as Allie placed the box on the coffee table.

Allie knelt down and opened it, revealing a couple of small, sleek security cameras, cords, magnetic sensors, and a compact central control panel. "I picked this up on my way home yesterday. I'm hoping that if something else happens, it'll help us catch who it is, and we can give it to the police. The security sensors won't hurt to have either."

Sofia picked up the thin instruction booklet and opened it. "Oh, babe, this is such a good idea! Why didn't we think about this earlier?"

Allie shrugged as she lined up the various components on the coffee table. "I've actually questioned that myself. It'll make me feel better as well because I'll be able to get notifications and pull up the feed when I'm in Austin this week, and the control panel has an emergency button if it's ever needed."

"Oh, yeah?" A small, playful grin appeared on Sofia's face.

Allie chuckled, the sound a brief moment of lightness in the tense atmosphere. "Yeah, so feel free to walk around naked when I'm gone."

"Oh my god," Sofia rolled her eyes, her hand now resting on top of her round stomach. "No one wants to see *this* naked right now."

A gentle silence filled the room for a moment before Sofia looked up, finding Allie watching her with intense sincerity. Her voice was quiet and earnest, "Sofia, you might not realize this, but you are absolutely beautiful. Every part of you."

Sofia's voice started to interject, but she was silenced by Allie's firm, serious voice. "*Every…* part, Sofia." Her eyes never left Sofia's as she moved to position herself kneeling between Sofia's legs.

Sofia's breath hitched as she felt the warmth of Allie's hands slide up her shirt and slowly over her stomach. Allie leaned forward and tenderly kissed her skin, her lips tracing a sensual line up her smooth, round belly. The warmth of her lips settling between her breasts, and then finding her lips.

"I love you, Sofia." Allie's voice was a low, sensual murmur against her lips.

Sofia kissed Allie's soft lips again, a wave of affection washing over her. "I love you too, Allie."

Allie's lips curved into a gentle smile against Sofia's as she pulled slowly away. "Now let's get these things up. It'll make me feel better knowing you have access to quick help while I'm away."

* * *

Sofia opened the door as her little sister, Cami, came flying inside, a rush of the afternoon heat following her.

"Oh my God!" Cami gasped as she collapsed dramatically onto the soft cushions of the couch, the contents of her purse scattering slightly as it landed with a soft thump. "It is hot as balls out there!"

Allie looked up from the kitchen island, where she was packing a few lunches they had prepped, a confused smile on her lips. "Hot as balls? What does that even mean?" She laughed.

Cami shrugged, rolling over to look at them. "I don't know. It's just an expression, Al. Like me saying, 'Oh my God, sis, you look huge!'"

Sofia's mouth flew open in mock offense. "That's just rude! I am not huge." She gently rubbed her stomach, the cotton of her shirt riding up slightly to reveal her very pregnant belly.

Allie smirked and playfully tossed a cube of cheese at Cami, which landed softly on her shirt. "She is not huge. She's perfect." She bent down to press a tender kiss to Sofia's stomach while Cami rolled her eyes.

"Y'all are disgusting." Cami teased as she gathered the scattered belongings and tucked them back into her purse.

Allie kissed Sofia's lips, a lingering warmth passing between them as she finished packing her bags. She wanted to get on the road before traffic became a headache. She couldn't be late for their monthly manager meeting.

She grabbed her suit jacket from the back of the kitchen stool and walked over to Cami. "Hey, we aren't the ones talking about balls being hot, sicko."

"I can't with you." Cami rolled her eyes in mock exasperation as Allie pulled her into a tight hug.

Allie kissed the top of Cami's head, giving her a sisterly squeeze. "Take care of our girl, okay?"

"You know I will." Her voice was earnest despite the playful tone. Cami and Allie had grown close over the past couple of months. Allie had embraced her as the little sister she'd never had, and Cami only minded occasionally.

Allie grabbed her overnight bag and paused at the front door, her hand resting on the knob. "I'll be back early Saturday. Let me know if you want me to pick anything up in Austin. I can bring back Home Slice pizza. And call if *anything* happens. I want to be kept in the loop. Got it?"

She looked at both of them seriously as she waited for their answers. Cami nodded, her expression earnest, as Sofia smiled reassuringly. "Yes, love. We will let you know. Be safe and let me know when you get there. I love you."

"I love you more," Allie blew her a kiss before opening the door, a whoosh of warm air entering briefly before she closed and locked it behind her.

Even though Cami would be there with her and the security cameras were now in place, a knot of unease still tightened in her chest at the thought of leaving Sofia. She couldn't shake the feeling that something was wrong, and the need to uncover the reason behind their recent troubles was growing stronger with each passing day.

45

Chapter 45

The house felt noticeably quieter without Allie's grounded presence, the silence wrapping itself around the low hum of the refrigerator. Her car had only pulled out of the driveway an hour ago, yet the shift in the air was unmistakable. It wasn't a heavy quiet, though. It was a peaceful one, even with Cami there.

In the living room, the late afternoon sun streamed through the window, bathing the sofa in a soft, golden light. Sofia was reclined, propped up by pillows, a bowl of popcorn resting on her stomach. Cami was curled up sideways on the couch, her head resting in Sofia's lap. Cami stayed over regularly now, having practically moved in since the break-in attempt, a silent agreement to act as Sofia's protective deputy while Allie was away for work.

"I swear, Allie made us enough food for three days, then told me to call her every two hours, and triple-checked that I knew how to use the emergency button *and* that it was working," Sofia chuckled, gently twisting a strand of Cami's dark hair around her finger. "I'm pretty sure the security company is going to start ignoring her 'test' calls soon."

Cami sighed contentedly. "Classic Allie. She's going to have anxiety the entire trip, just worrying about you."

"She's worried," Sofia agreed, her voice soft. "She's trying to hold it together, but I know she hates leaving me right now. We both appreciate you putting aside your social life to come be a boring couch potato with me."

Cami scoffed, "I wish I knew what social life of mine you're talking about. Plus, you know I love hanging with you."

"I love hanging with you, too." Sofia smiled as she brushed her fingers through Cami's hair, the texture soft and familiar. "Plus, you're cheap labor. Who else is going to run to the kitchen for ice cream?"

Cami swatted playfully at Sofia's leg. "Hey! I am invaluable!"

A comfortable silence settled between them, broken only by the low drone of the television. Sofia loved these moments of easy intimacy with her little sister. Cami's breathing was deep and rhythmic against her thigh, and Sofia felt a wave of protective affection wash over her.

Then, a sharp, surprising pressure thumped against the back of Cami's head. Cami gasped, pulling away slightly, her eyes wide.

"Ow! What was that?"

Sofia laughed, her hand instinctively going to her swollen belly. "Someone was saying hello, I think. Either that or you're in his way."

Cami slowly lowered her head back down, positioning it directly over the spot where the kick had landed. She lay perfectly still, waiting. After a few seconds, she felt it again. A distinct, solid movement, this time a gentle roll followed by another tiny *thump*. Cami's hand flew to Sofia's stomach, touching the hard, round surface gently.

"Oh my God," Cami whispered, her voice choked with surprise and something deeply resonant. She looked up at Sofia, tears suddenly welling in her eyes.

For the first time, it hit her with a powerful, emotional force: she was going to be an Aunt... a *Tía*. She had been so focused on protecting Sofia and the uncertainty of the situation that she hadn't truly let herself connect with the baby. But this baby, growing under her sister's hands, was undeniably family. And family meant everything.

"I'm going to be a *Tía*." The Spanish word felt heavy and sacred on Cami's tongue. Her voice broke, and she buried her face in Sofia's neck, hugging her tightly. "I love him already, sissy, I do. I'm so sorry I haven't really... processed it."

Sofia held her sister fiercely. "Don't apologize. We've been living through a nightmare. But this right here?" She patted her stomach. "This is the good part. It took me a long time to see him as... good... but our family is getting bigger, Cami. No matter what."

They held each other for a long moment, the quiet, emotional weight of the future settling over them, a deep bond cemented by the tiny life kicking between them.

* * *

A couple of hours later, the comfortable bubble of shared intimacy had dissolved into heavy exhaustion, leaving both girls unable to keep their eyes open. They shut off the television, the dark screen reflecting their tired faces.

"I'm going to grab some more water and then crash," Cami

yawned, stretching luxuriously. "All that intense bonding is tiring."

Sofia chuckled, a tired rumble in her chest, as she ruffled Cami's hair. "Me too, being this huge is exhausting. I'm going to head upstairs. Don't forget to turn the alarm on before you head up."

Cami nodded, pulling her phone out as she shuffled toward the fridge. She flicked open TikTok to kill a few seconds while she waited for the ice dispenser. The sharpclinking of ice against metal echoed through the kitchen, but Cami was already deep in a rabbit hole of funny reels.

She laughed at a video, immediately opening the comments section as she started filling her bottle with cold water. The thought of the alarm had completely evaporated.

She walked out of the kitchen and up the stairs, eyes locked on her phone, leaving the house unsecured as she turned into the small guest bedroom directly to the left of the top of the stairs.

Sofia was already in her own room, the furthest one down the narrow hallway. She sank onto the bed and immediately video-called Allie to say goodnight. Their conversation was short, strained by shared exhaustion. They exchanged solemn *I love yous* before hanging up, Sofia drifting off to sleep almost instantly.

The house was cloaked in heavy, dense darkness broken only by the low light over the stove in the kitchen and the small, dim light on Sofia's nightstand that she now slept with.

Outside, the late-night silence was shattered by a nearly inaudible noise: the gentle, crunching whisper of boots on the gravel driveway.

A figure, dressed entirely in black with a dark ski mask

pulled taut over his face, moved with silent, predatory grace toward the back of the house. He paused at the single French door beside the kitchen, peering through the antique glass panes that offered a fragile view into the darkness.

With a muffled *crack*, he drove a small tool into the corner of one of the glass panels. The sharp, shattering crack was quickly absorbed by the night, leaving only a faint rain of broken glass on the floor inside. He reached through the opening, unlatched the door, and slipped inside.

The man stood motionless, a void of black against the kitchen's dim light. He didn't breathe; he waited. His focus was a cold, sharp blade, cutting through the shadows as he tracked the muffled sounds of life coming from upstairs. Zip ties hung ominously ready from a back pocket. He crept toward the stairs, his movements precise and utterly silent.

He paused at the top step, his body an unnerving shadow in the dark. A faint rustling sound, the soft *shift* of sheets, drifted from the room to his left… the guest room.

He moved toward the sound, his black boots making no sound on the wooden floor.

Cami was asleep, facing the door, defenseless. He lunged, his heavy, gloved hand clamped tightly over her mouth, pinning her with crushing weight against the mattress.

Cami's eyes snapped open in sheer terror. Unable to scream, her breath instantly stolen, primal panic seized her. She thrashed wildly, kicking out with desperate, blinding force and fighting against the solid, immovable weight pressing her down. Her fingers clawed wildly, trying to scratch at the ski-mask-covered face above her. Her leg slammed into the wooden dresser at the foot of the bed, sending the ceramic flower vase flying. It hit the floor with a deafening crash.

The crash jolted Sofia awake in the master bedroom. She sat bolt upright, recognizing the noise instantly, the unmistakable sound of something breaking near the stairs.

She scrambled off the mattress as quickly as her pregnant body would allow, her heart hammering a frantic rhythm against her ribs. She raced down the darkened hall, stopping abruptly at Cami's open door. Her eyes widened with cold terror as she saw the black-clad figure pinning her little sister.

She spun around, sprinting back into her room. Her hand gripped the smooth, familiar wood of the baseball bat she now kept beside the bed. Armed with raw adrenaline and the solid bat, she charged back down the hallway, bursting into Cami's room.

She swung hard, connecting with the man's broad back. The satisfying *thwack* of the impact made him grunt sharply and release Cami, staggering backward for a crucial moment.

"Run, Cami, run!" Sofia screamed, planting her feet between the attacker and her sister.

The man recovered instantly, turning his full, terrifying focus on Sofia. He flew at her, his hands closing around the bat as he brutally shoved her against the wall, trying to wrench the weapon from her grasp.

Cami hesitated for a paralyzed moment, her loyalty warring with her fear, before scrambling out of the room. She bolted, flying down the stairs toward the kitchen. She reached the security control console, her fingers frantically searching for the emergency button as a sickening realization hit her... she forgot to set the alarm.

She slammed her finger down on the emergency button, setting the alarm off in a deafening, piercing scream throughout the house as guilt and fear swarmed her body. This was her fault!

Sofia clung to the baseball bat with everything she had, the man's brutal strength overpowering her and pushing her backward. She knew with chilling certainty that if he got the bat, he would use it on her. Their brutal struggle carried them out of the room and into the narrow hallway. He slammed her against the wall again, and in the violent, twisting chaos of their fight, Sofia's body was thrown forcefully off balance.

She felt the terrifying loss of her footing on the top of the stairs, a sickening lurch as she was thrown backward. Her hand clawed at the air, desperately trying to find something to stop her.

The fall was a dizzying blur before her body struck the staircase with a brutal, jolting force, landing mid-stairs on her side. The impact was followed by a desperate, tumbling roll that ended with a heavy, crushing slam onto her stomach at the bottom of the stairs.

The breath was violently knocked out of her. A sharp, searing pain instantly flared across her abdomen. Her lungs burned, desperate and uselessly straining for air.

Through the deafening, piercing wail of the security alarm and the frantic pounding in her ears, her vision registered the quick flash of the man's black boots sprinting past her, followed by the jolting force of the front door slamming open. He was gone.

She heard Cami screaming her name, the sound raw and terrified above the alarm's blare, as her sister rushed to her side. The last thing Sofia saw was Cami's horrified face, kneeling inches away.

With a final, struggling whisper, choked with pain and the

battle for breath, Sofia managed one sound before losing consciousness:

"My baby."

46

Chapter 46

Eleanor's heels clicked against the marble, a sharp, rhythmic counterpoint to the frantic banging on the front door. "I'm coming," she called out, quickening her pace.

She gripped the cold, sleek handle and pulled the heavy door open. Detective Miller stood there, heaving, one hand braced against the frame. He looked wild, clothes disheveled, a black beanie crushed in a white-knuckled fist. When he looked up, his eyes were blown wide with panic.

"Where's Thomas?" He rasped. "I need to see him now."

He didn't wait for an invitation. Miller shoved past her, his shoulder checking hers hard enough to knock her off balance. Eleanor gripped the door to steady herself, frowning as she shut out the night air.

"I believe he's in his office," Eleanor said, smoothing her dress, trying to maintain composure in the face of his rudeness. "I can fetch him—"

"No." Miller cut her off. "I'll go myself."

He took a step toward the grand staircase and immediately recoiled, his hand flying to his lower back with a stifled groan.

Eleanor stepped forward instinctively, reaching out.

"Detective, you're hurt. Let me—"

"I said *no*," Miller snarled, pulling away. "I'm fine."

He forced himself upright and began to climb, his gait uneven and desperate. Eleanor watched him ascend, a cold knot forming in her stomach. Something was wrong. Deadly wrong.

She moved quickly to the kitchen, slipping into the narrow service staircase used by the staff. It was the only way to get upstairs unseen.

At the top of the landing, she stopped outside Thomas's office. She pressed her back against the wall, breath held in her throat, as she heard Miller knock once and then enter.

"Miller?" Thomas's voice came through the wood, gruff and confused. "What are you doing here?"

"It didn't go well," Miller groaned in pain as he tried to adjust himself. "She wasn't alone."

The office door clicked closed as Eleanor let out the breath she was holding. She had to know who they were talking about. She had her fears; she was sure it was Sofia, but she had to be certain.

She slid off her expensive heels, holding them in her hand, knowing she might need to have a quick and silent escape from the area. She tiptoed cautiously to the door and pressed her ear against it. The voices were muffled, but she could still make out what they were saying.

"What the fuck are you talking about?" Thomas growled. "This was supposed to be easy."

"Should have been," Miller retorted, his voice filled with pain. "But there was someone else there, and they had an alarm system installed since last time."

"Shit. So what happened? And why the fuck are you limping like an idiot?"

Miller groaned again. "She hit me in the back with a fucking bat. Pretty sure she messed something up. Pretty sure she's messed up, too."

"Is she dead?" Thomas asked. Flat. Unfeeling.

"Don't know," Miller responded. "She fell down the stairs… I had to run." He let out a pained hiss. "Pretty sure the kid won't make that fall though."

Eleanor's world stopped. The hallway seemed to tilt. *Sofia.*

The image of Sofia falling flashed in her mind, violent and visceral. All she could hear was the word "kid" echoing in her head. *Her grandson.* She pressed her forehead against the wall, her stomach turning. She clamped a hand over her mouth, trying to keep from retching loud enough for them to hear, and quietly retreated down the hall.

The reality of it settled onto her shoulders, heavier than any fear she had ever known. Thomas had ordered a hit on his own son's child. It was no longer just threats or cruel words. It was real blood.

For twenty-eight years, Eleanor had hidden behind expensive concealer and polite smiles. She had built a prison of crystal and platinum, convincing the world it was a castle. To everyone else, it was a life of luxury. To her, it had been a long, silent nightmare.

But that ended tonight.

She would not let Sofia, or that innocent baby, become another casualty of this house. She still loved her son, and despite everything, that baby was his blood. It deserved a chance. A life that wasn't stained by the hands of the McCoy men.

Eleanor gripped her shoes tighter, her resolve hardening like steel. She had been a victim for decades, but tonight, she would be a savior.

She didn't know the path forward, nor who she could trust. She only knew that she would secure their safety… if they were even still breathing… even if she had to trade her life for theirs.

She stood, leaving the red-soled Louboutins discarded on the carpet like shed skin. She didn't look back. She sprinted to her private quarters, hands trembling as she grabbed her ivory Prada linen duffle bag. She threw in the most basic clothes she could find in her drawers, a couple of shorts, and random t-shirts she had purchased for their upcoming lake vacation, her passport, a small velvet jewelry box hidden in the back of her safe, and a stack of cash she had been hiding for fifteen years. She had no idea how much it added up to, but it was her freedom. She knew Thomas would stop all of her cards as soon as he knew she was gone. The McCoy mansion would no longer be her home, nor her prison. Tonight, she would sever the chains she had worn for twenty-eight years. Tonight, she would find her strength again.

With the bag slung over her shoulder, she paused in the hallway. Her gaze drifted to the closed door at the end of the corridor; it was Josh's childhood room.

She pushed the door open and stepped into the silence. It felt like stepping into a mausoleum, a preserved museum of a boy who no longer existed. Moonlight filtered through the blinds, illuminating the trophies, the books, and the framed photos of a smiling boy with messy blond hair.

She walked to the bed where the Steiff mohair teddy bear

sat in the center of the navy duvet. It was the guardian of his dreams since the day he was born. It had been loved by him as he grew up, and still sat there even though it bore the wear of time.

Eleanor reached out, her fingers trembled as she picked it up. She brought the worn plush to her face and inhaled deeply. The scent of dust and old fabric filled her senses, unlocking a flood of memories. She saw the toddler taking his first steps into her arms. She felt the little hands that used to cling to her neck in fear of the dark. She heard the sweet voice that used to whisper *I love you, mommy* before he fell asleep.

Tears tracked hot paths down her cheeks as a sob tore through her chest. This was the moment. This was the funeral for the boy she had birthed, raised, and loved. She could no longer deny the truth that stared back at her from the shadows of this house. That innocent little boy was dead. He had been consumed by a man who made the choice of violence, hate, and privilege.

She couldn't save the man he had become, but she could save the innocence he had left behind. She tucked the bear into her bag as if she were tucking a child into bed. She didn't look back as she turned around. She walked out of the room and closed the door on the innocence of her son forever.

47

Chapter 47

Eleanor counted out the cash at the front desk of the Winchester Inn, a family-run relic on the outskirts of town. It was the kind of place that existed only in the periphery of Eleanor's world, usually only seen as a blur from the passenger window of one of their luxury cars. It was a dump, but it was the only place that accepted a flimsy lie about a lost wallet instead of a driver's license. Cash had a way of filling in the plot holes. The young girl didn't care enough to press as she popped her bubble gum, her blonde hair wild and unbrushed. Eleanor didn't plan on being around long enough for the lie to unravel anyway. She knew Thomas; his reach was long, and his goons would be hunting as soon as he realized she was gone.

Eleanor took the key to Room 5 and stepped out into the humid night air. She unlocked the door, pushing into the stagnant air that smelled heavily of mold and mothballs. She tossed her five plastic Walmart sacks onto the bed, and then, with a heavy sigh, set her ivory Prada bag down next to them. The contrast was jarring, the expensive ivory linen sitting against a maroon, seventies-era floral comforter that looked stained with decades of bad decisions. The room was depressing, but for tonight, it was a place to sleep and to figure out her next steps.

She sat at the small, old wooden table next to the window, the ancient, rickety chair creaking as she pulled out the burner phone she had picked up at Walmart earlier. Her hands trembled as she followed the instructions to get it activated, then she pulled out a piece of familiar stationery from her purse.

Three numbers. That was all that remained of her social circle.

Her personal phone had housed nearly three hundred contacts… CEOs, oil tycoons, charity directors. But in the cold light of survival, she knew she could rely on almost none of them.

She fingered the edge of the paper as her thoughts went back to her beloved convertible BMW she had abandoned at the Galleria, keys in the ignition to bait any trackers, and fled into the anonymity of the general public. She had used a stranger's cellphone in the ladies' bathroom, claiming to have lost hers, and called a cab to Walmart, where she picked up some essentials to get her through the next few days and her burner phone.

She smoothed the paper out onto the table, running her hands over it repeatedly as if it would help her know who to call. Her eyes kept being drawn back to *Marlene Davis*.

Senator Davis was a force of nature, a true Texas matriarch with a spine of steel and a heart that bled for the underdog. While Thomas McCoy spent his fortune building walls, Marlene spent hers tearing them down, advocating for women, children, and the LGBTQ+ community. Eleanor had helped her at many fundraisers and charity events over the years, and while they were not close, she knew that Senator Davis didn't care much for Thomas. She was everything Thomas would never align with, but she had a large following of supporters, and in the game of law, politics, and wealth, that's all that mattered.

Eleanor took a steadying breath and dialed.

"Senator Davis speaking," the voice answered, rich and languid as molasses.

"Marlene," Eleanor breathed, her voice threatening to crack. "It's Eleanor. Eleanor McCoy. Please, I beg you, don't say my name out loud."

There was a heavy pause on the line. The shift in Marlene's tone was subtle, a sharpening of attention. "Well, gracious darlin'. It has been an age."

"Marlene, is… is this call being recorded?" Eleanor stuttered.

"Why, yes, darling, of course. All my calls are." Marlene answered, her professional veneer firmly in place. "Matters of state and all that."

Eleanor squeezed her eyes shut, fear spiking. "But… Thomas… or anyone else. They can't just listen to them on a whim, can they?"

"Heavens no," Marlene scoffed, the warmth returning to her voice. "Only my senior staff have access, or a judge with a warrant. Sugar, what on earth is going on?"

"I'm in trouble, Marlene," Eleanor whispered, clutching the phone. "I need help, but discretion is… it is a matter of life and death. No one can know where I am. Not Thomas, not Detective Miller, not a soul in the police force. I want to trust you, Marlene. I *need* to believe you. You are the only one I can turn to. Can you give me your word?"

Marlene was silent for a long moment, the weight of the request hanging between them. When she spoke, the politician was gone, replaced by the woman. "You have my word, Eleanor. On my mother's Bible."

Eleanor expelled a breath she felt she'd been holding for twenty years. "Thank God. I need you, Marlene. This situation… it is vile. My entire family is going to be destroyed. If I am not careful, innocent lives will be lost. Including my own."

"You listen to me," Marlene said, her voice firm and grounded. "I have time for company tomorrow morning. I want you to come to the estate. Shall we say seven o'clock?"

"Yes, yes, I'd like that. I suppose I'd have to take a cab there."

"Don't you dare," Marlene cut in, her tone brooking no argument. "Do you trust me enough to tell me where you are? I will have Joel, my personal driver, come collect you."

"Can you trust him?" Eleanor asked with the skepticism of a hunted woman coloring her voice.

"With my life, sugar. And with yours."

"Okay," Eleanor felt herself relax slightly. "I'm at the Winchester Inn. It's just outside of Fredericksburg, off 87 North."

"The *Winchester*?" Marlene let out a sharp, scandalized breath. "Bless your heart. You pack your bags right this instant. I don't know the depths of this trouble, but you are not staying in that hovel a moment longer than necessary. You are coming to stay with me until we sort this mess out."

"I… I don't want to bring trouble to your doorstep, Marlene. I don't know if that's safe."

"Honey, I am a United States Senator," Marlene drawled, a hint of iron behind the velvet. "There is no place in Texas safer than my guest wing. You be ready."

"I will. Room 5."

"I'll see you in the morning, dear. Try to rest."

The line went dead. Eleanor sat there for a long time, staring at a cigarette burn marred into the cheap wood of the small table. Her heart hammered a frantic rhythm against her ribs. She was terrified of trusting anyone, but the relief of sharing the burden, even for a moment, was overwhelming.

She walked over to the bed, turning to sit on its edge, her hand running down the smooth material of her Prada bag before she reached in and took out the small mohair teddy bear. A sob, sharp and jagged, caught in her throat.

The gravity of what she had done finally crashed down on her. Her entire life, the carefully curated existence she had maintained for decades, was about to be incinerated. In doing this, she would lose everything. Her husband, her home, her immense wealth, her status in society. But the heaviest weight was the knowledge that her testimony would likely be the very thing that locked a cell door behind her own child. She was trading her role as his protector for the role of his accuser.

As the tears began to fall, hot and fast, she knew they weren't for the money. They weren't for the status.

Her tears were for her son.

She tried to tell herself it was for the best, but the thought of him in a cold, grey cell made her chest seize. She could no longer sit idly by in her ivory tower while he became a monster, twisted and molded by his father's cruel hands. She loved him, God, she loved him with a mother's fierce, blinding devotion, but she realized now that she would have to love him from a distance. To save his soul, she had to destroy his life.

Her chest heaved, the air in the room feeling too thin. Memories rushed her, not of the cold man he was today, but of the little boy who used to smell like grass and sunshine. She could almost feel the phantom weight of him sitting on her lap, his small hand tucked into hers as she read him stories. She had spent his whole life trying to shield him from his father's darkness, only to realize that the darkness had already swallowed him whole. To save the soul of that little boy, she had to destroy the man he'd become.

She collapsed onto the bed, burying her face into the old teddy bear to muffle her wails. She allowed herself to break, to mourn the living as if they were already dead. She knew she was doing what was right, but Lord, it was breaking her heart to do it.

48

Chapter 48

The world had narrowed down to the rhythmic, terrifying thump-thump-thump of the ambulance tires over asphalt. Outside the small windows, the night was pitch-black, the flashing red lights slicing through the darkness at 1:00 a.m. Sofia lay strapped to the narrow gurney, the vibrations traveling through her spine, but the throbbing ache in her sprained wrist and the sharp sting of her ankle were distant, muted signals. They belonged to a body she didn't care about right now.

The only sensation that mattered was the tightening in her abdomen, a cramping, unnatural vice grip that shouldn't be happening. Not yet.

He's too small, the thought looped in her mind. *He's six weeks early. He's not ready to breathe.*

"Ms. Flores, I need you to focus on your breathing." The paramedic's voice swam through the haze of her concussion.

Sofia stared up at the sterile ceiling of the ambulance, tears leaking from the corners of her eyes. "Is he… is he okay?" Her voice was a broken whisper, terrified of the answer.

"His heart rate is elevated, and it looks like you're having some contractions." The paramedic said with a clinical honesty that shattered her. "Labor and Delivery know we are on the way, and they'll do what is needed."

A cold, absolute dread washed over her, drowning out the pain. It wasn't just fear; it was an epiphany that hit her with the force of a physical blow. For months, she had been worried about how she would feel when he was born, if she would be able to truly feel deep love for him, about the future of their family, and her as a mother. But in this terrifying silence, knowing he was in distress, she realized with crystal clarity that she loved him more than her own life. He was hers. He was the only innocent, pure thing in a world that had turned violent over half a year ago. The thought of losing him felt like the air was being sucked out of the ambulance.

By the time they wheeled her into the trauma bay, which quickly transitioned to a transfer to Labor and Delivery, the room was a blur of frantic motion. The clock on the wall read 1:45 a.m.

"Sofia!"

The voice was familiar, laced with panic. Her mother rushed to the bedside, her face pale and streaked with tears. Isabella was right behind her, looking ready to fight God himself. They were touching her hair, holding her uninjured hand, whispering comforts in a mix of English and Spanish.

"We're here, mija. We're here," her mother sobbed, kissing her forehead.

"I hurt," Sofia whispered, the confession trembling on her lips. "Mom, they said… they said he's in distress."

"He's strong, like his mother," Isabella said fiercely, squeezing her fingers tight. "He's going to be fine. You hold on to that."

Sofia squeezed back, grateful for their warmth, but her eyes kept darting to the door. She loved them, but right now, surrounded by machines, strangers, and fear, she felt untethered. She was drifting in a storm, and she needed the only thing that could ground her.

"Allie," Sofia choked out. "Does she know? Is she coming?"

"Cami called her," Isabella brushed the hair off of Sofia's sweaty forehead. "She's coming, Sof. She's rushing."

"I need her." Sofia whimpered, a contraction seizing her belly, making her toes curl in agony. "I can't..."

Time became fluid, measured only by the beeping of the monitors and the waves of pain. It felt like hours, though it was likely barely past 2:00 a.m. when the door flew open with a crash.

Allie collided with the room.

She was breathless, chest heaving, still wearing soft cotton sleep shorts and a plain white t-shirt. Her feet were shoved into slip-on shoes, and her hair was a wild, tangled mess from being woken from a dead sleep. She looked frantic, disheveled, and completely petrified. To Sofia, she was the most beautiful thing she had ever seen.

"Sofia!" Allie gasped, ignoring the nurse who tried to intercept her. She rushed to the bedside, her hands hovering for a split second, afraid to touch where it might hurt, before settling gently on Sofia's shoulder and cheek.

"I'm here, I'm here." Allie breathed, her eyes scanning Sofia's battered face, the brace on her wrist, and the bruise blooming on her temple. Tears welled in Allie's eyes, spilling over. "Oh my god, Sof. I'm so sorry I wasn't here."

"You're here now," Sofia whispered, feeling the tension in

her shoulders finally break. She leaned into Allie's touch, grounding herself.

Allie spun toward Cami, who stood in the corner with her arms crossed tightly over her chest. "What happened? Tell me exactly what happened. Who was it?"

"I, I don't know Allie. I was asleep, and he attacked me." Cami's voice shook, the fear still evident through the anger. "We don't know who. He was masked. She tried to save me, Allie. She fought so hard, and she fell down the stairs fighting."

Allie turned back to Sofia, gripping her hand so tight her knuckles turned white. "I'm so sorry, my love. Did *you* see him?"

"Allie," Sofia whispered, the panic rising again as the monitor behind her let out a rapid, erratic trill. "The baby."

Allie's gaze snapped to the monitor, then to the doctor who had just entered the room.

"What's going on?" Allie demanded, her voice shaking with suppressed emotion. "What is that monitor saying? Why is it sounding like that?"

Dr. Evans, a stern but kind woman, stepped forward. "Sofia, the trauma has triggered preterm contractions, and the baby is experiencing some tachycardia. His heart rate is a little higher than we would like during those contractions. He could just be stressed from the shock or there could be an injury due to the fall; we won't know."

Sofia let out a broken sob. Allie leaned in immediately, pressing her forehead against Sofia's uninjured temple, murmuring soft reassurances. "It's okay, look at me. It's going to be ok." But Sofia could feel Allie trembling against her.

"We need to stop the labor, and we will see if that helps his heart rate calm down," Dr. Evans said firmly. "We're going to start you on Magnesium Sulfate to relax the uterus and stop the contractions. We're also administering a steroid to help his lungs mature rapidly, just in case."

Allie nodded, listening, her voice cracking as she spoke. "Whatever she needs, Doc. Just save them."

"I have to warn you, Sofia. The Magnesium… it's intense. You're going to feel very hot, flushed, and likely nauseous. It feels like the flu times ten. But it is the best chance we have to keep him inside."

"I don't care," Sofia gritted her teeth as another wave of pain hit her. "Give it to me. Make me feel terrible, I don't care. Just save my baby."

The next hour was a blur of misery. As the Magnesium hit her bloodstream, it felt like her veins were being filled with molten lead. She was burning from the inside out, her skin suddenly too tight for her bones. She tried to lift her hand to touch her face, but her arm felt like it belonged to someone else, a heavy, useless weight pinned to the bed. She dry-heaved into a plastic basin that Allie held for her, Allie's hand constantly rubbing her back, wiping her face with a cool cloth, whispering words of love that Sofia could barely hear over the roaring in her ears.

Through the haze of the drug, the heavy tread of boots on linoleum cut through the room. Two police officers stood in the doorway. It was nearly 3:30 a.m. now, and the hospital was quiet around them.

"Hello, Sofia, Camilla. We just need to finish up your statements with a few more questions," the officer said, clicking a pen.

"A statement?" Allie's voice rose, cracking with incredulity and exhaustion. "You want a statement *now*? Where were you *weeks* ago when we called about the car following her? Where were you when her tires were slashed in the driveway? Or the break-in?"

"Ma'am, we took reports—"

"You took reports and did nothing!" Allie shouted, the anger exploding out of her. It was the sound of a woman who had been frightened for months, helpless to stop what was happening. "We told you something was happening. We told you someone was escalating. And you did *nothing*. And now she's lying in a hospital bed *again*, praying that her baby doesn't die because of the assault you still haven't solved!"

"Allie," Cami touched her arm, but Allie shook her off, tears streaming down her face now.

"I want to know what you're going to do *now*," Allie demanded. "Who is investigating this? Who is protecting us? Why hasn't anything been *done??*"

A flicker of annoyance crossed the officer's face before he spoke. "We are looking at the security footage from your home system, ma'am. We are taking this seriously."

"Now. *Now* we are supposed to trust you when she could have *died*. Then what? Then you would have just pulled camera footage as well? This is a joke. Your department is a *joke*." Allie seethed. It took a lot to get her angry, for this side of her to show itself, but the thought of Sofia being attacked again, fighting for not only her life, but the baby's life and Cami's, drove her insane.

Eventually, the room cleared. The officers left. Her mother and Isabella, exhausted and tearful, were convinced to go get coffee and then go home to rest.

The deep, heavy silence of 4:00 a.m. settled over the

hospital room. The only light came from the glowing green lines of the fetal monitor, and the only sound was the steady, mechanical *thump-thump-thump* of his heart. It was a fragile rhythm, a tiny pulse of life that felt far too small to be fighting the weight of this room.

Cami was curled up in the uncomfortable visitor's chair, finally dozing off. Allie had pulled the small vinyl sofa as close to Sofia's bed as possible. She lay there, facing Sofia, her hand resting gently on top of the blankets covering Sofia's legs, her fingers twitching in her sleep.

But Sofia couldn't sleep.

The Magnesium made her body feel like it didn't belong to her, heavy and lethargic, dragging her down. But her mind was racing, spinning in circles that were becoming tighter and darker. Outside, the absolute black of night was just beginning to shift into a bruised purple, the very first hint that dawn was approaching.

Why?

The question tumbled through her mind. Slashed tires. Phone calls. The break-in where nothing was taken. And now this... a physical attack. The man hadn't tried to rob her. He hadn't asked for her purse. He attacked them. He had hurt her.

He had attacked Cami, but she now knew it was her he had come for.

It wasn't random. It was systematic. It was designed to terrorize. To silence.

The truth cut through the medication's fog like a blade. Sofia's breath hitched, a sob catching in her throat. She looked at Allie's sleeping form, realizing how much danger she had dragged this beautiful, fierce woman into.

They didn't want money. They didn't want her car.

"Josh." The whisper stuck in her throat, raw and painful.

The realization was ice cold. It was the McCoys. It had to be. Josh, with his political aspirations and his reputation to protect. She knew the truth about him; she was a liability.

This wasn't a warning anymore. Josh wasn't trying to scare her into silence… he was trying to delete the evidence. And the evidence was currently tethered to a monitor, fighting to breathe inside her. They didn't want her gone - they wanted her erased.

A hot tear slid down her cheek, landing on the pillow. She squeezed her eyes shut, her hand drifting protectively over the monitor strap on her belly, feeling the flutter of life beneath.

They tried to kill us, she realized, the horror of it settling deep in her bones as the first gray light of morning began to touch the windowsill. *And they aren't going to stop.*

49

Chapter 49

The morning light filtered through the threadbare curtains of Room 5, casting a sickly yellow hue over the dingy carpet. Eleanor sat on the edge of the sunken mattress, her bag packed and resting by her feet. She hadn't slept. Every creak of the motel settling, every car door slamming in the lot outside had sent a jolt of adrenaline through her veins.

When the knock came, it was precise. Two sharp raps.

She opened the door to find Joel, Marlene's assistant. He was a man of few words, dressed in a suit that cost more than this entire motel. "Mrs. McCoy," he said with a nod, reaching for her bag without waiting for a response.

Outside, a sleek black sedan idled, its engine a low purr. The windows were tinted so dark they seemed like oil slicks, impenetrable to the outside world. It was perfect. Inside that car, she was a ghost.

The drive to the estate outside of Austin was quiet. Joel was a professional; he didn't pry, didn't make small talk, and kept his eyes on the road. In the silence, Eleanor's mind drifted to dark, suffocating places. She stared at the back of the driver's seat, her imagination conjuring images of what Thomas would do when he realized she was truly gone. He wouldn't just be angry; he would be surgical in his dismantling of her life. He wasn't a man who lost things; he was a man who collected them, broke them, and kept the pieces.

And Josh. Her heart squeezed painfully as she pictured him sitting in a jail cell. Would he be cold? Would he feel alone? Would he hate her? The guilt settled in her stomach like a stone. A sob tried to crack through, a small sound escaping as it caught in her throat.

The scenery began to change as they entered the Texas Hill Country. The highways gave way to rolling green hills and ancient oaks. They slowed as they approached a massive iron gate, the Davis family crest wrought into the metal. A uniformed guard, young and handsome with a sharp jawline, stepped out of the booth.

He leaned down, peering into the driver's side. Joel lowered the window just an inch, enough to exchange a few quiet words. The guard's eyes flickered to the back seat, unreadable, before he nodded and hit the release button. The heavy gates swung open, granting them sanctuary.

The drive up to the house was a half-mile winding ribbon of pavement lined with white fences. Thoroughbred horses grazed in the paddocks on either side, their coats gleaming under the Texas sun. It was a picture of generational wealth and peace so far removed from the nightmare Eleanor had been living in that it felt like a hallucination.

The house itself rose from the landscape like a fortress of elegance. It was classic Texas architecture, built from blocks of local cream-colored limestone and accented with rustic wood slats. Modern black-framed windows punched through the stone, softening the look with sleek lines. An expansive front porch decked with beautiful classic rocking chairs on both sides lined the front of the home.

Joel brought the car to a smooth stop. He opened her door, offering a hand to help her out before retrieving her bag from the trunk.

At the massive double doors, a private security guard stood waiting. He wasn't wearing a police uniform, but the way he held himself suggested military training.

"Ma'am," he said politely, "I need to check for weapons. House policy."

Eleanor nodded numbly, raising her arms slightly as he did a quick, professional pat-down and checked her bag. It was a stark reminder that she was entering the home of a high-profile politician. Safety was a luxury here, but it came with conditions.

Once he was satisfied, he opened the door and escorted her inside.

The foyer opened into a Great Room that took Eleanor's breath away. The ceilings soared twenty feet high, and the far wall was made entirely of glass, offering a panoramic view of the ranch land that had been in Marlene's family for generations. The rolling hills seemed to go on forever, untouched and serene.

Click. Click. Click.

The sharp sound of heels on tile echoed from the foyer. Eleanor turned to see Senator Marlene Davis sweeping into the room. She was impeccable, as always, her hair perfectly coiffed, wearing a crisp linen blouse and slacks that looked effortless.

"Eleanor," Marlene's voice was warm and thick with her

drawl. She opened her arms wide and pulled Eleanor into a firm, formal Texan embrace, the kind that smelled of expensive perfume and hairspray, the kind that held you up when you couldn't stand on your own. She pulled back, holding Eleanor by the shoulders, her sharp eyes scanning Eleanor's face.

"Look at you, darlin'," Marlene said, her voice dropping to a concerned murmur. "You seem exhausted. Are you alright? Can I get you something? A sweet tea? Or maybe something stronger? You look like you could use a bourbon."

"I'm… I'm okay, Marlene. Thank you." Eleanor managed, her voice trembling. "Just tired."

Marlene nodded, her expression shifting from hostess to confidante. "I can see that. It's too open in here. Let's show you to your room. It's quieter in there for us to talk."

The guest room was a masterpiece of hill country elegance. High ceilings were crossed with thick, rough-hewn wooden beams that smelled of cedar. The walls were the same warm limestone as the exterior, softening the light that poured in. In the center of the room sat a massive bed made of reclaimed timber, piled high with crisp white pillows and covered in a delicate, lace-trimmed duvet.

A sitting area was arranged in front of a wall of windows, bathing the space in natural light. Two comfortable leather armchairs faced each other, a small table between them, resting on a luxurious white, long-haired fur rug.

"Sit," Marlene commanded gently.

They sank into the leather chairs. For a moment, the room was silent, save for the faint hum of the air conditioning. Marlene crossed her legs and leaned forward, resting her elbows on her knees. She studied Eleanor's face, stripping away the pleasantries.

"Eleanor, what on earth is going on, honey? Joel said you were shaking when he picked you up."

Eleanor felt the dam break. The stoic face she had worn for the drive, for the guards, crumbled.

"I didn't know where else to go," Eleanor confessed, her hands shaking as she clasped them in her lap. "I need help, Marlene. I need protection. I didn't know who else I could trust." She took a ragged breath. "Thomas… he's everywhere. He has the local police in his pocket. He has judges, he has the bank… everyone is under his spell or on his payroll. I couldn't go to the cops. I couldn't go home."

She choked back a sob. "He thinks he owns everything. He thinks he owns me."

Marlene reached across the small table and covered Eleanor's trembling hand with her own. Her skin was cool, her grip firm and unyielding.

"Well," Marlene said, her eyes flashing with a steeliness that reminded Eleanor exactly how this woman had survived decades in Texas politics. "He doesn't have me, Eleanor. I'm here, and I'm listening. Now tell me, what has happened?"

50

Chapter 50

Marlene sat in quiet contemplation, her eyes fixed on a meaningless spot on the expensive Alpaca rug, processing everything Eleanor had just spilled. The grandfather clock in the corner ticked loudly, filling the void where the air had been sucked out of the room.

Finally, Marlene leaned forward, her elbows resting heavily on her knees. Her voice was low, stripped of its usual bravado. "He raped her and left her for dead?"

Eleanor responded quietly, her voice barely a whisper. "Yes."

"And Thomas knew this... and tried to cover it up?"

Eleanor nodded, picking at a loose thread on the throw pillow she was clutching like a shield. "Yes."

"You know for a fact that Detective Miller and others are involved?" Marlene pressed, her eyes narrowing.

"I wasn't sure of his part in the aftermath until yesterday," Eleanor admitted, a shudder running through her. "But Detective Miller is definitely involved. He was there. He spoke to Thomas as if they were partners."

Marlene leaned back. Her body suddenly looked exhausted, as if the weight of the information was physically pressing her into the cushions. She rubbed her temples slowly. "This is bad, Eleanor. Truly bad."

The confirmation was the final straw. Eleanor cracked. The stoic mask she had worn since arriving crumbled, and a sob tore from her throat. "I know, Mar. I'm terrified. I don't know what to do."

Marlene didn't rush to comfort her with empty platitudes. She sat in silence, thinking, her sharp mind running through scenarios, calculating risks. After a long moment, she leaned forward again, her expression hardening into steel.

"This is what we are going to do."

Marlene's tone had shifted. It was no longer the voice of a friend; it was the planning of a strategist.

"I'm going to make a call," Marlene said. "I'm calling Chief Alex Dalton in Austin. We worked side by side for ten years before I retired to private practice. I trust him completely. He is a man of morals who lives by the law."

Eleanor wiped her eyes, listening intently.

"We need to move on this carefully," Marlene continued. "Until Dalton can get a team together that isn't on Thomas's payroll, you are staying right here. My security team is loyal and incredibly capable."

Marlene glanced toward the window before turning back to Eleanor. "Speaking of Joel, I'm going to have him drive you into Austin first thing this afternoon… to the bank. As an account holder with Thomas, you have every legal right to those funds. I want you to pull a large amount. Hell, pull all of it. Start a new life. There are no legal repercussions for taking marital assets, and it'll cripple his ability to move quickly."

Eleanor immediately shook her head. "No. I don't want any of that."

"Eleanor, you need resources—"

"I have resources," Eleanor interrupted, her voice trembling but firm. "I'm set for a while. I started saving years ago... skimming from my shopping budget, pocketing cash from events. I knew I'd need it when I was able to escape him." She took a shaky breath. "It's money he has no idea exists, so he won't miss it. If I drain the accounts, I'm just poking the bear. It'll piss him off even more, and right now, he'll be enraged enough."

Marlene looked at her, surprised, but a flicker of respect crossed her face.

"I have no idea what Thomas can ruin for my future," Eleanor continued, wringing her hands. "I have no doubt he will try and won't stop, even if he ends up behind bars. I can't give him any more ammunition."

Marlene held Eleanor's gaze for a long moment, assessing the woman in front of her. She saw the fear, but she also saw the spine of steel that had kept Eleanor alive this long.

Marlene's expression turned stern. "Eleanor, hun. You know that this is going to be a hard road, right? This isn't just about escaping. This ends with Thomas and Josh spending a long time in prison. Thomas will fight it the whole way through. His lawyers will try to make you out to be a liar, crazy or just in it for the money."

Marlene paused, letting the next words hang in the air. "And Josh... he may hate you. He may never speak to you again. You will be the main witness in all of this, Eleanor. You'll have to sit on a stand, face them in court, and say these things out loud to a jury. Are you prepared to do that?"

The room fell still again. Eleanor looked down at her hands. She thought of the years of silence. She thought of Josh, whom she had tried to protect, potentially looking at her with hatred. Then, she thought of the girl. The blood stain hidden on the conservatory floor. The roundness of her pregnant stomach when she saw her in public a few weeks ago.

Tears formed in Eleanor's eyes, hot and fast, falling onto her lap. She lifted her chin, meeting Marlene's gaze.

"Yes," she said quietly. "I have to. Sofia deserves better. And this baby… regardless of how it came about… deserves a good and happy life." Her voice cracked, but she pushed through. "I don't even know if she's okay. I just know that they deserve more. And I would never forgive myself if I sat back one more day and let this happen."

Marlene nodded slowly. It was the answer she needed to hear.

"Well then," she reached into her pants pocket and pulled out her phone. "It's time I call Chief Dalton."

She unlocked the screen, her thumb hovering over the contacts, before she looked up one last time.

"But first," Marlene added, "I'm going to have my assistant put in a call to the Fredericksburg hospital. We need to find that girl."

Marlene tapped the screen and held the phone to her ear, speaking in low, clipped tones to her assistant, Casey. Eleanor watched her, holding her breath. After a few instructions, Marlene hung up and set the phone on the reclaimed wood table.

"Now," she said softly, "we wait."

The hush that followed was agonizing. Eleanor stared at the phone as if it were a bomb waiting to detonate. Every second that ticked by on the grandfather clock felt like an hour. Eleanor's mind raced, images of Sofia, images of Josh, and the shadowy, terrifying concept of a baby that shared her son's blood but was born of such violence.

Ten minutes later, the phone buzzed against the wood, the sound making Eleanor jump in her skin.

Marlene snatched it up. "Casey? Talk to me."

Eleanor watched Marlene's face intently. She saw the seasoned attorney's brow furrow, her lips pressing into a thin line. Marlene's eyes flicked to Eleanor, then away, focusing on the floor.

"Okay," Marlene said, her voice lacking its usual punch. "Did you get a name?" A pause. "Camilla Flores. Good work."

Marlene listened for another moment, her expression darkening. "I understand. You did the right thing leaving your number. Let me know the second you hear anything else."

She ended the call and slowly lowered the phone. She didn't speak immediately, which terrified Eleanor more than anything else could have.

"Marlene?" Eleanor whispered.

Marlene sighed, a heavy, resigned sound. "Casey spoke to a sister of Sofia's; she's at the hospital with her now."

"And?" Eleanor leaned forward, gripping the armrests of her chair until her knuckles turned white.

"Sofia was just taken back for an emergency C-section," Marlene said gently. "There were complications with the fetal heart rate. The baby… the baby isn't doing well, El."

The blood drained from Eleanor's face. The reality of it

crashed into her chest. Eleanor had her moments of struggle with how to feel about this child. But now, hearing that its heart was struggling, that it was fighting for air, the abstraction vanished.

It was her grandchild.

"Oh god," Eleanor gasped, her hand flying to her mouth. "The baby… it might not…"

"We don't know yet," Marlene said quickly, reaching out to squeeze Eleanor's knee. "Casey told Camilla to call us the moment there is news. All we can do is hope."

Eleanor felt a fresh wave of tears for the tiny, innocent life that was currently fighting a battle it never asked for.

"I spent so many years worrying about reputation." Eleanor's voice was shaking but gaining strength with every word. She looked up at Marlene with fierce, wet eyes. "I worried about what people would say, about keeping the peace. But that baby is fighting for its life right now. A life my husband and son treated like trash."

She took a ragged breath, wiping her face with the back of her hand.

"That baby is the only innocent thing in this entire nightmare, Marlene. If it has the strength to fight to be here, then I have to find the strength to make sure there is a world safe enough for it to live in."

51

Chapter 51

The silence of the hospital room was a fragile thing, and when it shattered, it didn't break… it exploded.

The monitor, which had been offering a steady, rhythmic reassurance, suddenly screamed. The jagged line on the screen plummeted, a chilling red valley that refused to rise.

Before Allie could even stand, the door flew open. It wasn't just a nurse this time; it was a swarm. Dr. Evans was at the front, her face stripped of its earlier calm.

"We've lost the baseline," Evans barked, vaulting into action. "Heart rate is down to sixty. Fifty. It's stopping." She looked at Sofia, then to the team. "We are in life-or-death trouble here. We need to get to the OR *now* to save him."

The room dissolved into controlled chaos. Hands were everywhere… unhooking monitors from the wall, unlocking the wheels of the bed, shouting commands over one another.

"Prep OR One! Page Anesthesia! Let's move, let's move!"

Sofia's eyes were wide, saucers of sheer panic, scanning the room for Allie as the bed began to roll.

"Allie!" Sofia screamed, her hand reaching out.

Allie lunged forward, grabbing the metal rail of the bed as they shoved it toward the hallway. For a split second, the momentum slowed just enough for Allie to lean in, pressing a fierce, desperate kiss to Sofia's lips.

"I love you," Allie's voice cracked, but was loud enough to be heard over the shouting. "You are going to be alright. Both of you."

"Go!" Dr. Evans ordered.

The bed was ripped from Allie's grip. She stood frozen in the doorway, her hand still raised in the air, watching the woman she loved and their unborn son disappear down the sterile white hallway. The doors at the end swung shut, cutting off the view, leaving Allie standing in the sudden, deafening quiet.

Her body started to shake. It began in her hands and seized her knees. The fear wasn't a cold thing; it was hot and suffocating, overtaking her lungs.

"We didn't even get the nursery done." The words spilled into the empty room without her realizing it. It was such a stupid, small thing to worry about, but it felt like the only thing her brain could latch onto.

Suddenly, a warm hand slid into hers. Cami was there, squeezing tight.

"Don't worry, Allie. We will get it done."

Allie squeezed back, clinging to Cami like the only life preserver in a raging sea. She turned, her eyes wide and pleading. "They are going to be ok, right?"

Cami's heart broke. She looked at Allie, the woman who had been the stone wall, the protector, the stoic force that held everyone together through everything. To see her this petrified was more frightening than the alarm itself.

"They are going to be okay," Cami lied, praying to a God she hadn't spoken to in years that it was the truth. "I'm going to call Mom and Isabella."

Cami slipped out of the room, phone already to her ear, leaving Allie alone.

Allie turned to sit down, but stopped. She stared at the empty space where the bed had been just moments ago. The floor was littered with debris from the emergency: torn sterile wrappers, plastic caps, a discarded glove. It looked like a battlefield.

Her knees gave way.

Allie collapsed, hitting the linoleum hard, but she didn't feel the pain. A sob ripped through her chest, a guttural, animal sound that broke the silence, and she folded over herself, forehead touching the cold floor.

She cried silently, her shoulders heaving, begging the universe for mercy.

"Ma'am?"

The voice came from behind her. Allie scrambled to wipe her face, looking up to see a nurse in surgical greens standing in the doorway.

"The surgery is starting shortly," her tone was urgent but kind. "They are administering the spinal now. Sofia... she's asking for you. She won't stop asking. Do you want to be there?"

Allie was on her feet before the sentence was finished. "Yes... yes please bring me to her."

"Follow me. Quickly."

Allie ran, following the nurse to the scrub room, moving with mechanical efficiency... mask on, bunny suit over her clothes, shoe covers, hat. She scrubbed her hands until they were red, her heart hammering a frantic rhythm against her ribs.

"Let's go," Allie said with a nod.

The doors to the OR hissed open, and the cold hit her first. It was freezing, the air smelling of antiseptic. The lights were blindingly bright, focused on the center of the room.

Sofia was lying on a narrow metal table, a blue drape suspended in front of her chest like a curtain. Her arms were outstretched on boards, IVs taped into both wrists, making her look agonizingly vulnerable.

She was trembling violently. Her teeth chattered so hard that Allie could hear it from the door.

Allie rushed to the small stool by Sofia's head. Sofia's eyes rolled toward her, wet and terrified.

"I-I-I'm so c-c-cold," Sofia shivered, her words stuttering out.

"I know, baby, I know," Allie whispered, immediately smoothing the damp hair back from Sofia's forehead. She leaned in, kissing her temple, her cheek, and her ear. "I'm here. I've got you."

"Making the first incision." Dr. Evans announced from the other side of the drape.

"You're going to feel a lot of pressure, Sofia," the anesthesiologist said from behind them. "A lot of tugging. It's going to go fast. You shouldn't feel pain, but if you do, tell me immediately."

"O-ok," Sofia meekly replied. Tears leaked from the corners of her eyes, sliding down into her hairline.

Allie used her thumb to wipe them away, keeping her face close to Sofia's so she was the only thing Sofia could see. "Look at me, Sof. Just look at me. You're doing so good."

"I'm scared, Allie," Sofia's eyes searched Allie's.

"I know. Me too," Allie admitted, gripping Sofia's hand as tight as she dared. "But we're almost there. He's almost here."

Sofia gasped, her eyes widening. "Oh god... I feel it. I feel... everything moving."

Her head swam. It was a sickening sensation, as if her insides were being rearranged, pulled and stretched beyond capacity.

"Your baby is about to be born, Sofia," Dr. Evans said, her voice tight with focus. "You might not be able to hold him right away. We will have to see what condition he's in first."

Allie squeezed Sofia's hand, feeling the tremors running through Sofia's body. "Okay," they said in unison, their voices shaking.

Then, the tugging stopped. The pressure released.

"Baby is out," Dr. Evans said.

Time seemed to freeze. Allie waited. Sofia waited. They waited for the wail, the cry, the sound of life entering the world.

There was only the sound of suction and the hum of machines.

"Here," Evans said, passing the baby to the resuscitation team.

A rush of activity erupted to their right. Allie turned her head and watched as the team placed the baby on a warming table.

He was limp. His skin was a terrifying, dusky blue. It looked like there was no life left in him.

Allie's breath caught in her throat, a silent scream building in her chest. She squeezed Sofia's hand so hard her knuckles turned white, trying to anchor herself, trying not to let Sofia know what she was seeing.

"What's happening?" Sofia's voice started rising in panic. She tried to lift her head, but it felt like it weighed a million pounds. "Why isn't he crying? Allie?"

Allie couldn't answer. She watched a respiratory therapist place a mask over his tiny face, squeezing a bag. Another nurse was tapping a stopwatch.

"Someone talk to me!" Sofia cried out, struggling against the table. "What is happening with my baby? I don't hear him crying!"

Allie turned back to Sofia. She couldn't lie. Not now.

"He isn't breathing, Sof," Allie said, her voice shaking violently. "They... they are trying to get him to breathe."

She watched the team work on his tiny body, the light from the warming table making him look too bright, too exposed. He was so small he almost fit in the palm of a hand... and he was perfectly still.

The color drained from Sofia's face, leaving her gray. Her breathing hitched, hyperventilating. "No. No, no, no."

"Calm down, baby," Allie begged, pressing her forehead against Sofia's, mingling their tears. "You have to calm down. He's going to be okay. We just have to be positive. He's a fighter, like you. He's strong."

Sofia's breaths came in choked, jagged gasps. "What... if... Allie..."

"No, baby. Don't," Allie soothed, stroking her face frantically. "Don't go there. Just breathe."

"Still not breathing," Dr. Evans' voice cut through the room, sharp and commanding. "Heart rate is critical. We need to begin compressions."

The words stop their entire world from spinning.

Allie and Sofia broke. A simultaneous sob wrecked through them both.

Allie looked up just in time to see the doctor use two fingers on the center of his tiny, motionless chest. One, two, three…

The movement was so small. It was a rhythmic, artificial heartbeat provided by a stranger in a mask. Sofia squeezed her eyes shut, the chattering of her teeth finally stopping as a deep, hollow stillness took over. She didn't pray for a miracle; she just focused on the two fingers moving up and down, up and down, trying to push life into a heart that had every reason to stop.

"Fight, baby," Sofia whispered into the cold air, her voice a broken prayer. "Please… don't let them win."

52

Chapter 52

The morning sun was trying to break through the heavy hospital blinds, but inside the maternity ward, the air felt thick with the residue of a night that had lasted a lifetime.

Allie pushed the wheelchair slowly, her movements careful and deliberate, as if rolling over a crack in the linoleum might shatter the woman sitting in the seat. Sofia was a ghost of herself. The emergency surgery, the blood loss, and the heavy cocktail of pain medications had left her drifting in and out of consciousness.

Every few minutes, the motion would be too much. Sofia would groan, her hand flying to her mouth. Allie was ready every time. She would stop the chair, produce a plastic basin from her lap and hold Sofia's hair back while she retched, her body barely strong enough to even hold itself up.

"I've got you," Allie whispered, wiping Sofia's mouth with a cool, damp washcloth she'd kept ready. "I've got you, baby. Just breathe."

Sofia didn't want to see anyone else. Not yet. In the waiting room down the hall, Allie knew that Isabella, Camilla, and

349

their mother were sitting in a vigil of their own. They were waiting for news… good, bad, anything. They had come in briefly, kissing Sofia's forehead and whispering "I love yous," but they sensed the wall Sofia had built around herself. She needed space to process the trauma before she could accept the comfort.

They reached the double doors marked **NICU**. The sign warned of strict visiting hours and hand-washing protocols.

"Ready?" Allie asked softly.

Sofia nodded weakly, her eyes glazed but fixed on the doors. "Take me to him."

The baby still didn't have a name. Allie had asked gently in the recovery room, but Sofia had only looked away, her silence heavy and protective. To name him was to make him a person, a person with a future, a person who could leave a hole in the world if he didn't make it.

Allie stared at the clinical white card taped to the incubator: **BABY BOY FLORES**. It was so temporary, so fragile. She wanted to give him a name that acted like an anchor, something heavy enough to keep him from drifting away, but she understood. Sofia wasn't just waiting for the right name; she was waiting for a guarantee that the name would have someone to belong to. It was the only sliver of control Sofia had left in a world that had stripped her of everything else.

The doors swished open, and the atmosphere changed instantly.

It was alarming. The silence of the hallway was replaced by a symphony of small, high-pitched beeps and the hum of equipment. The lights were dimmed, creating a twilight effect. From the bays on either side, Allie heard the tiny, muffled cries of other infants, but as they rolled toward the far corner, their baby was silent.

"Here we are," Allie whispered, locking the wheels of the chair next to the large, clear plastic box.

The incubator hummed, a fortress of warmth keeping the world out.

Sofia leaned forward, groaning slightly as her incision pulled, but she didn't stop until her face was pressed against the plastic.

He was so small.

At four pounds and seven ounces, he looked lost among the technology keeping him alive. He was a landscape of wires and tubes. A relentless device puffed rhythmically beside him, a tube disappearing down his throat to breathe for him. His chest rose and fell, but it wasn't him doing the work. It was the machine forcing life into lungs that were far too tired to do it themselves.

Electrodes were plastered to his translucent skin, monitoring a heart that had almost stopped beating only hours ago.

"The doctors…" Sofia rasped, her voice rough from the vomiting. "What did they say?"

Allie pulled a stool close and sat knee-to-knee with Sofia. "They said there isn't much to tell yet, Sof. We just have to watch and wait. He… he isn't fully breathing on his own yet, but the doctor said he's 'over-breathing the vent' sometimes. It means he's trying. He's fighting the ventilator because he wants to do it himself."

Sofia stared at the boy, searching for a trace of herself in the curve of his cheek or the slope of his nose. He was a terrifying blend of her own blood and the nightmare she had survived. He was sedated, his eyes closed, his tiny body slack against the white bedding. It was agonizing to see him this way… so perfect, yet so fragile, like a glass bird that had been shattered before it ever had a chance to fly. He was the most beautiful thing she had ever seen, and the most painful thing she had ever been forced to look at.

Trembling, Sofia reached out. She unlatched the small, circular porthole on the incubator's side. The warm, humid air from inside rushed out to meet her hand.

She reached in, her hand looking massive next to his fragile frame. She didn't stroke his head or his back; he was too covered in wires. Instead, she slid her index finger gently into the palm of his hand.

For a moment, nothing happened.

Then, a reflex. The tiny, blue-tinged fingers curled inward. They wrapped around Sofia's finger and held on.

The breath caught in Sofia's throat, a sharp, ragged sound. A small sob escaped her lips, shattering the quiet of their corner. The tears that had been threatening to fall all morning finally broke loose, streaming down her pale cheeks.

She leaned her forehead against the cool plastic of the incubator, her finger still locked in his grip.

"Fight, baby boy," she whispered, her voice fierce and broken. "I know you are so strong. You can do this. Just fight. I love you."

"He knows you're there." A soft voice said from the other side of the incubator.

Allie and Sofia looked up to see a nurse standing there. She had kind eyes and moved with a practiced, gentle efficiency, checking the numbers on the monitor.

"I'm Sarah," she said quietly. "I'm his primary nurse today."

Sofia didn't pull her hand away from the baby, but her eyes searched Sarah's face desperately. "Is he… is he in pain?"

Sarah shook her head immediately. "No, sweetie. We have him on medication to keep him sedated and comfortable. He doesn't feel any pain. The ventilator looks scary, but right now, it's actually his best friend. It's doing all the hard work so his body can focus on resting and healing."

"He's so still," Sofia choked out.

"That's good for now," Sarah assured her, reaching into the other side of the incubator to adjust a small sensor on the baby's foot. "We want him still. We want him calm. His heart rate has been steady for the last hour, and his oxygen saturation has remained at 95%. That's a win."

She paused, looking from the baby to Sofia. "I've been doing this a long time. I can tell you, he's got a lot of fight in him. He gave us a scare last night, but he's holding his ground today. That's all we can ask for right now."

Sofia nodded, tears dripping off her chin. "Thank you."

"Take your time," Sarah whispered, stepping back into the shadows to give them privacy. "Talk to him. He knows your voice. That is one beautiful baby y'all have there."

Allie sat in the chair next to the incubator, watching the scene unfold. She looked at Sofia, the dark circles under her eyes, the hospital gown, and the raw, unfiltered grief. She wanted nothing more than to wipe that look away. She wanted Sofia's eyes to be filled with the joy of a new mother, with happiness, with the light that usually lived there.

She wanted this little boy to open his eyes. She wanted him to wake up and cry. She wanted him to feel the immense weight of the love that was already waiting for him… from Sofia, from her family and from their friends.

But for now, there was only the hum of the ventilator and the rhythmic beep of the monitor.

Allie leaned back into the uncomfortable hospital rocking chair next to them. She looked up at the analog clock on the wall. The second hand ticked relentlessly.

8:04 AM.

She looked down at her phone. **August 2nd.**

He was almost a day old. Twenty-four hours of fighting.

Allie closed her eyes, letting the rhythm of the rocking chair soothe her. She looked at Sofia's finger, still caught in that tiny, desperate grip, and realized the baby wasn't just fighting for his own life. He was anchoring Sofia to hers.

Happy Belated Birthday, Little Dude. I love you.

53

Chapter 53

The heavy cedar door of Marlene's estate swung open, releasing the rich, warm scent of wood into the cooling evening air. Standing there was a man who didn't just occupy the door frame; he seemed to own the space around him.

Chief Alex Dalton was striking, surprisingly young for a man with that much brass on his collar, and undeniably handsome in a way that usually disarmed people before they realized they were being interrogated. He had a sharp jawline, thick dark hair, and a lazy, confident smile that reached his eyes. He radiated a natural, easy charisma, the kind of Texas charm that could talk a jury into anything, but beneath it lay a current of steel.

He stepped inside, removing his hat with a fluid motion.

"Marlene," his voice was a smooth, deep drawl. "You look as dangerous as ever."

"Cut the charm, Alex," Marlene said, though her shoulders relaxed slightly. "We have work to do."

"With you? Always," he grinned but followed her immediately, his stride long and purposeful.

Marlene led him straight to the study where Eleanor was sitting, clutching a tall, cold glass of Sweet Tea. As they entered, Dalton's demeanor shifted. It was respectful and softer, yet still commanding the room.

"Chief Dalton," Marlene gestured to the woman in the chair. "This is Eleanor McCoy."

Dalton stopped. He looked at Eleanor, and for a split second, the calculation behind his eyes was visible before the charm slid back into place. He dipped his head politely.

"Mrs. McCoy, it's a pleasure. Though I wish it were under better circumstances."

"You know who I am?" Eleanor asked, her voice small.

Dalton offered a small, knowing smile. "Ma'am, it's hard to live in this part of Texas and not know the McCoys. Your reputation precedes you." He said it with enough warmth that it didn't feel like a threat, but the implication was clear. *I know exactly who you are, and I know exactly how much power your husband has.*

Marlene sat on the edge of her desk, looking down at him. "I'm going to be very clear with you, Alex. I called you because I trust you. You are the *only* person I am telling this to. So, if this leaks… if Thomas McCoy gets wind that his wife is talking before we are ready… I will know exactly where it stemmed from. And I will take immediate action."

Dalton didn't bristle. Instead, he leaned back, crossing an ankle over his knee, and offered Marlene a look of amused respect.

"Marlene, you wound me," he said smoothly. "But I get it. The stakes are high. You have my word. The leak won't come from me." Then, the smile vanished. His eyes, previously warm and engaging, turned to flint. The charm evaporated, replaced by the cold, hard focus of the law. "Now. Tell me why we're here."

"Do you have any loyalties to Thomas McCoy?" Marlene asked, testing him one last time.

"My loyalty is to the law," Dalton said, his voice dropping an octave, dead serious. "McCoy has deep pockets, I know that. But he doesn't own me."

"Are there others in your department that you know, beyond a shadow of a doubt, you can trust with a case of this magnitude?"

"Absolutely," Dalton replied, the confidence in his voice absolute. "McCoy may have a reach, Marlene, and I know he pads the pockets of a few uniforms, but that rot isn't within my direct department, and it sure as hell isn't on my team. My guys are solid."

Marlene studied him for a second longer, then nodded once. She turned to Eleanor. "Go ahead, El."

Eleanor took a shaky breath. She set the cup down, the glass rattling against the desk. She began her story. She spoke of the night of the gala. She spoke of her son, Josh, the golden boy with the dark soul, and the rape and attempted murder of Sofia. She detailed the cover-up led by her husband and Detective Miller. She spoke of the continued harassment, the attacks on Allie and Sofia and finally, the attempted murder of Sofia and the baby just yesterday.

Chief Dalton listened intently. He didn't interrupt, didn't charm and didn't smile. He sat like a statue, absorbing every word, his eyes dark with a simmering anger that he kept professionally checked. He pulled a small notebook from his pocket and took notes in a shorthand only he could read. When she finished, the room was silent.

"Thomas," Dalton tapped his pen against his notepad. "Is he friends with the District Attorney there? Any dealings?"

Marlene and Eleanor nodded in unison. "Very much so," Eleanor whispered. "They play golf every Sunday."

Dalton sighed, running a hand through his hair. He looked at Marlene, his expression grave. "Then we can't go through the DA. That well is poisoned. We need to contact Attorney General Powell right away. I'll make the call personally. We need to let him know the local investigation is compromised and have an official misconduct investigation opened."

He turned his gaze to Eleanor. The softness returned to his face, but it was protective now. "Mrs. McCoy, for your safety, it's best if we get you somewhere secure. A safe house. I can have a detail set up in an hour."

Marlene scoffed, the sound sharp. "Eleanor is not going anywhere. Do you really think somewhere is safer than here, with me? My security is top-tier, Alex. She stays."

Dalton looked at Marlene, a small smirk tugging at the corner of his mouth. "I figured you'd say that. Just wanted to offer the official option. She stays."

He turned back to look directly at Eleanor, his demeanor shifting back to the commander. "I am going to push this to move as quickly as possible, but there are going to be a lot of moving parts. We're looking at separate investigations here. One for Josh, for rape and attempted murder. That most likely will be assigned to my department to investigate alongside the State Police and the AG."

He flipped a page in his notebook. "Then, we have Detective Miller and Thomas for obstruction of justice and conspiracy to commit crimes. The Attorney General will handle that directly."

He leaned forward, his elbows on his knees, holding Eleanor's gaze. "Eleanor, you must not speak to anyone. No calls to family. No calls to friends. Nothing. This needs to be as silent as a tomb. We cannot afford a leak, even from someone you think you can trust with your life."

"How long will it take?" Eleanor asked, her voice small.

"I can't give you a timeline," Dalton admitted honestly. "It depends on the evidence. Corroborating your testimony is key."

Marlene scoffed again, crossing her arms. "We're going to have our hands full getting that. My team already pulled the official police reports from the night of the gala. The report claims there was no security footage. Thomas told the officers it was turned off due to 'high-profile clientele' being in attendance."

Eleanor's brow furrowed in confusion. "That's not true."

Marlene paused. "What isn't true?"

"Thomas always has the footage going," Eleanor said, sitting up straighter. "Even when he tells people he doesn't. He's far too possessive. He's terrified someone will steal from his ten-million-dollar art collection. He would *never* turn those cameras off." She shook her head. "He keeps *all* of the footage. In case he ever needs it for... anything. To use against people."

Dalton's eyebrows shot up. He exchanged a look with Marlene, a look of pure, adrenaline-fueled opportunity.

"Are you sure, Eleanor?" Marlene asked, her hands gripping the arms of her chair.

"Yes," Eleanor said firmly. "It's something we've argued about many times. He keeps them hidden in a safe in his home office. He transfers them to flash drives. Each drive has the month and year printed on it."

"Well, I'll be damned," Dalton murmured, a shark-like grin spreading across his face. "We need to get ahold of those ASAP. That footage… that is our Smoking Gun."

Eleanor stood up slowly, her shoulders suddenly sunken as if the weight of a thousand ships were on them. Her high heels clicked against the hardwood floor as she slowly paced a few steps away, then turned back to them.

"There's also a blood stain," she said quietly. "They tried to cover it up in the Conservatory. It was small, and the tiles were cleaned well, but I saw it one day while picking up some fallen leaves. It's a stain settled between the tiles. In the grout."

"I'll have a forensics team come in to look at the crime scene," Dalton said, writing furiously. "If it's in the grout, luminol will light it up like a Christmas tree."

Eleanor didn't sit back down. Instead, she walked silently toward the doorway leading to the guest quarters.

"Eleanor?" Marlene called out. "Where are you going?"

"I just need a moment," Eleanor said, her voice distant.

She disappeared into the guest room. Marlene and Dalton sat in silence, waiting. Five minutes later, Eleanor returned. She was holding a small object in her hands.

She stopped in the center of the room, looking down at the small velvet box in her hands, her thumbs tracing the seam.

To anyone else, it was just a box. But to Eleanor, it felt like she was holding the ashes of her life. She closed her eyes for a fleeting second, and in that still, dark moment, she didn't see the monster her son had become. She imagined the little boy with scraped knees running to her in the garden. The little boy who needed her, the little boy who loved her.

She loved him. She would *always* love him. It was a primal, biological ache that didn't care about logic or law. But then, the image shifted. She saw Sofia's broken body. She saw the brokenness in her eyes that her own son had put there. And she saw an innocent baby fighting for its life.

Her face crumpled, etched with a profound, shattering sadness. Her hands trembled violently as she walked toward Chief Dalton. She extended her arms, offering him the box.

"And there's this," she whispered, her voice fracturing.

"Mrs. McCoy?" Dalton asked gently, not reaching for it yet.

"I… I found this afterwards." Eleanor choked out. "It was hidden under one of the plant tables in the conservatory. It must have fallen off during the struggle."

Marlene slowly rose from her chair and walked over to look. She flipped the lid open.

Inside, two small diamonds sparkled under the study lights. But the sparkle was marred by a dark, rust colored crust dried on the chain and one of the diamonds. Dried blood.

Sofia's blood.

"I hid it," Eleanor confessed, tears spilling over her lashes. "For days, I just looked at it. I wanted to throw it in the river. I wanted to bury it. I wanted to protect him."

She looked up at Dalton, her eyes pleading for him to understand the impossible thing she was doing. She was a mother, and she was handing him the weapon that would end her son's life.

"But I can't." She sobbed softly. "I can't save him. Not this time. He has to pay. Even if it kills me, he has to pay."

She snapped the case closed, the sound echoing like a gunshot in the quiet room.

She wasn't just handing over evidence. She was handing over her son. She was choosing the girl he hurt over the boy she raised.

A single tear slid silently down her cheek, tracking through the powder on her face, as she placed the box into the Chief's hand.

Dalton took the box. He didn't handle it with the clinical detachment of a police officer; he held it with a heavy solemnity, feeling the weight of the mother's sacrifice in his palm.

He looked at the dark velvet box, then he looked up at Eleanor. The charm was gone. The smile was gone. In its place was a deep, quiet respect.

When he spoke, his voice was low, offering her the only comfort he could.

"I know what this cost you, Eleanor. I promise you, I'll carry it from here."

54

Chapter 54

The air in the hospital room felt heavy, a thick, sterile haze that seemed to press against Sofia's skin. It had been three days since the emergency C-section. Three days of a sharp, burning pull in her abdomen, of the rhythmic beeping of monitors, and of a world that had shrunk down to the size of a plexiglass box in the NICU.

Sofia spent every second she was allowed by the baby's side. When the nurses gently ushered her back to her room to rest, she lay in the dark, staring at the ceiling, her heart still tethered to that room down the hall. She talked to him through the glass. She hummed soft, broken melodies against the incubator. She whispered fierce, tear-filled commands for him to fight.

But he was still just "Baby Boy."

Every time Allie or a nurse asked about a name, a protective wall slammed down in Sofia's chest. It wasn't that she didn't love him. She did. The moment her finger had brushed his tiny palm, she had fallen in love with a terrifying, consuming intensity.

But then, the light would catch his face a certain way.

She would be sitting there, tracing the velvet softness of his ear or the delicate slope of his nose, and suddenly, the image would warp. She wouldn't see her son. She would see the shadow of the man who had raped her. She would recognize the jawline of the monster who had left her bleeding on the cold conservatory floor. The physical form of her trauma was no longer a memory she could push away; he was breathing right in front of her, tiny and innocent.

It was a war she fought in silence, a daily battle of the heart.

One minute, she was overwhelmed with a maternal adoration so pure it hurt. Next, a ball of suffocating heat would bubble up in her throat. She hated that he had Josh's nose. She hated that half of this beautiful, fragile creature belonged to a man who had tried to kill him.

How could she love him completely if she hated half of who he was?

The guilt of that thought ate her alive. She looked at his innocent, fighting body with wires taped to his translucent skin and felt like a monster for even thinking it. But the anger was there, festering like a wound that refused to close. She was furious at Josh. Not just for the violation of her body, but for this. For tainting this sacred experience. For forcing her to watch her son gasp for air. She loathed him. She despised the McCoys. She hated the unfairness of a universe that made her son fight for a life he hadn't even started living yet.

"Sof?" Allie's voice broke through the dark spiral of her thoughts.

Sofia blinked, turning her head on the pillow. The TV was murmuring in the background, casting a soft blue glow over the room. They only had two more days until discharge. The thought of walking out those automatic doors without him, of leaving her heart beating in a plastic box, felt like a physical amputation.

Allie was sitting on the edge of the bed, her presence warm and grounding. She reached out, tucking a stray lock of hair behind Sofia's ear.

"Do you have any ideas yet?" Allie asked softly, holding up a notebook.

"Maybe we could just look through a list together? See if something speaks to you?"

Sofia turned her head back to the TV, her jaw tightening as she fought back tears. "Not right now, Allie."

Allie sighed, shifting closer. Her voice was gentle, wrapped in patience, but there was a firmness to it. She could see the detachment warring with the love in Sofia's eyes, and she was desperate to bridge that gap.

"Sof, we are going home soon," Allie whispered, rubbing a soothing circle on Sofia's arm. "It would be nice for him to have a name before we leave. Just… something to call him. Something that's yours."

Sofia pulled the blanket higher, a shield against the conversation she wasn't strong enough to have. "Not right now, Allie. Please."

The room fell into a heavy, fragile silence.

Then, the speaker system in the ceiling crackled to life, shattering the quiet.

"Code Blue to the NICU. Code Blue to the NICU. Code Blue to the NICU."

The air left the room instantly. Both of their breaths stopped. For a heartbeat, the world suspended. Then, Sofia turned to look at Allie, her eyes wide, stripping away all the defenses, leaving only raw, naked terror.

"Could it?" Sofia whispered, her voice barely a breath. "Could it be him?"

She didn't wait for an answer. Sofia stood up, ignoring the sharp, tearing pain of her incision. Her feet were wobbly, the floor tilting dangerously.

"Sof, wait!" Allie scrambled up, throwing a strong arm around Sofia's waist just as her knees buckled.

"Take me to him!" Sofia cried, grabbing the front of Allie's shirt, her fingers digging in desperately. "I have to make sure he's okay! Go, Allie!"

Allie nodded, her face pale but her grip steady. "Okay. Let's go. I've got you."

She took the brunt of Sofia's weight, becoming her balance, and they moved as fast as Sofia's recovering body would allow... a frantic, shuffling run down the sterile hallway. The alarm was still dinging in the distance, a relentless heartbeat of disaster.

As they rounded the corner to the NICU double doors, Allie saw it through the glass.

The swarm.

A crowd of blue scrubs and white coats was gathered in the far corner. *Their* corner.

Allie's heart hammered. She stopped abruptly, planting her feet to stop them.

"It's him, Sof."

Sofia let out a strangled, wounded sound and tried to lunge forward. "Let me in! I need to go to him!"

Allie turned her body, blocking Sofia's path. She knew the protocol. They wouldn't buzz them in during a Code. If Sofia tried to pound on the glass, security would come. It would be chaos they couldn't afford.

"No, no, baby, stop," Allie begged, wrapping her arms around Sofia to restrain her.

"Let me go!" Sofia screamed, a sound of pure maternal agony that tore through the hallway. She scratched at Allie's arms, fighting with a strength born of panic. "That's my baby! Let me go to him!"

"I can't! They won't let us in!" Allie cried, pulling Sofia's head into the crook of her neck, cradling her as her body collapsed. "He's going to be okay, Sof. He's going to be okay."

But Allie felt her own voice breaking. Through the glass, she saw the doctor standing over the open incubator. She saw the tiny, motionless legs. She noticed the nurse squeezing the bag, breathing for him.

Sofia sobbed into Allie's shoulder, her fight draining away into despair. "I can't lose him, Allie. I can't..."

Allie slid her hand up into Sofia's hair, holding her head tight against her own chest, kissing her temple. Tears streamed down Allie's face, soaking into Sofia's hair. "I know, baby. I know. I can't either."

Sofia's chest heaved. She turned her head, pressing her tear-stained cheek against Allie's chest, watching the blurred flurry of activity through the glass.

"He's ours, Allie," Sofia choked out. "He's... he's our son."

Allie's sob caught in her throat. After days of "the baby" or silence, Sofia had claimed him. And she hadn't just claimed him for herself... she had claimed him for *them*.

Allie nodded, unable to speak, her throat too tight with emotion.

"I love him, Allie," Sofia wept, her body shaking in Allie's arms. "He can't die. Please don't let him die."

Allie couldn't promise. She could only hold on. They stood there, clung together, two women completely powerless against the tide of fate. They watched in terrified silence as the doctor stopped compressions to check the monitor. Stillness. The alarms were deafening, screaming that a life was fading.

Please, Allie silently begged the universe. *Please don't take him.*

Suddenly, the frantic activity stopped. The doctor looked up at the monitor, his shoulders dropping slightly.

"I got him!" A nurse shouted, her voice muffled through the glass but clear enough to hear. "We got him back! There's a pulse!"

Sofia's legs gave out completely. Allie didn't try to hold her up this time; she went down with her. They collapsed in a heap on the cold linoleum floor outside the NICU doors, sliding down the wall until they were a tangle of limbs and tears.

Sofia buried her face in her hands, sobbing uncontrollably. Not the screams of terror, but the deep, guttural release of someone who had been holding their breath for a lifetime.

Allie pulled Sofia into her lap, rocking her back and forth, crying into the curve of her neck. "He's back," Allie whispered, her voice shaking. "He's back, Sof. He's okay."

They sat there on the floor, ignoring the nurses passing by. He was back. He had fought, and he had won this round. But as Allie held Sofia, feeling the tremors running through her body, she knew the battle was far from over. They had a son. A son who was fighting to live every day. "Don't give up, little man," Allie whispered, praying the universe could hear.

55

Chapter 55

There is a specific kind of silence that falls over the world at 3:00 a.m. It is the hour between the death of yesterday and the birth of tomorrow. It is the hour when the veil is thinnest, when prayers are whispered, and when the debts of the soul come due.

On this night, across the sprawling darkness of Texas, justice did not arrive with a scream. It arrived with the heavy and inevitable weight of a gavel striking wood.

It was a reckoning. And it was simultaneous.

* * *

Dallas, Texas. 3:02 a.m.

High above the city, in a penthouse that Josh moved into days after he left Sofia for dead, the air was stagnant. The luxury apartment, usually a place of rest and beauty, was a place of filth and self-destruction.

Josh McCoy, the Golden Boy, the heir to the empire, lay

passed out on a leather sofa that cost more than a family's yearly income. He was a ruin of a man. His shirt was stained. His hair, usually perfectly coiffed, was greasy and matted against his forehead. On the glass coffee table, the remnants of a night spent trying to numb his own conscience sat in neat white lines next to a half-empty bottle.

He didn't hear the team move into the hallway. The breach wasn't an explosion; it was a shattering of the illusion.

"POLICE! SEARCH WARRANT!"

Flashlights cut through the gloom, blinding and unforgiving. Josh scrambled, slipping on the debris of his own unraveling life. He tried to stand, to summon the arrogance that had protected him since birth, but stripped of his father's money and his own false bravado, there was nothing left but a terrified boy.

"I'm a McCoy!" He wailed, shielding his eyes, his voice cracking. "You can't do this!"

But they could. An officer guided him to the floor... not with brutality, but with the firm and unyielding grip of consequence. The cold steel of the handcuffs clicked around his wrists, a sound that signaled the end of his reign.

"Joshua McCoy," the officer said, the words heavy in the room. "You are under arrest for rape and attempted murder."

He was hauled up, weeping, looking around his kingdom of filth. Realizing that for the first time in his life, no one was coming to save him.

The Golden Boy looked at his reflection in the dark window and saw nothing but a ghost. He was dragged from his tower, leaving the city lights behind. A boy who had broken a girl to feel powerful, now rendered completely powerless.

* * *

Fredericksburg, Texas. 3:02 a.m.

Detective Daniel Miller woke to the sound of his own karma coming home.

He didn't reach for his gun. He couldn't.

Sharp, piercing pain radiated up his spine as he tried to shift. The rigid back brace he wore, a souvenir from the night Sofia fought back, held him like a vice. He lay there in the dark, listening to the boots on his porch, and he felt a strange, terrifying sense of relief.

It's over, he thought. *The lie is finally over.*

When the bedroom door opened, revealing the grim faces of men he used to call brothers, Miller didn't speak. He raised his hands slowly, a surrender long overdue.

They pulled him from the sheets. He winced, his body stiff and broken, forced to walk without dignity in his boxers and his brace. As they led him out into the cool night air, he looked up at the stars and realized he would never see them from this side of a fence again. He had sold his badge for blood money, and tonight, the bill was paid.

* * *

The McCoy Estate. 3:02 a.m.

The silence of the Hill Country is profound, but tonight, it held a vibration. The ancient oaks lining the driveway stood as silent witnesses as the convoy of vehicles rolled in, lights off, like wolves closing in on prey.

Thomas McCoy slept in the center of his empire, believing himself to be untouchable. He believed his money was a fortress. He believed his influence was a shield.

But truth is the one thing money cannot bribe.

The crash of the front doors echoed through the marble halls like a thunderclap.

Thomas woke with a start, his heart hammering against his ribs. Before he could draw a breath, his sanctuary was violated. Flashlights swept over the silk drapes, the art collection, and the pristine floors.

"Thomas McCoy," a voice boomed, bouncing off the high ceilings. "Get on the ground."

He stood in his pajamas, disoriented, his face twisting from confusion into a deep, purple rage. "How dare you?" he hissed with entitlement dripping from his words. "Do you know who I am?"

"We know exactly who you are," the officer replied, his voice devoid of fear.

They didn't handle him with the reverence he demanded. They handled him like the criminal he was. He was forced to his knees, the cold marble biting into his skin, his hands bound behind his back. The King of Fredericksburg was dragged from his castle by the shuffling of feet and the heavy breathing of men he couldn't buy.

* * *

Outside the Estate. 3:50 a.m.

The night air was crisp, smelling of cedar and damp earth.

Marlene stood by the unmarked cruiser, her trench coat

pulled tight. She wasn't smiling; this moment was too heavy for joy. Beside her, Chief Dalton stood like a sentinel, his face carved from stone.

When the doors opened, and Thomas was marched out, the scene felt almost funereal.

Thomas saw them. He saw the woman who had been in his home many times, the woman who now outmaneuvered him, and the man who had refused to be bought. He stopped, digging his heels into the gravel, his eyes wild.

Thomas looked at them both, his lip sneering as he said, "I will bury you! I will burn your whole department to the ground!"

Dalton stepped forward. He moved slowly, deliberately. He didn't shout. He didn't posture. He simply leaned in, his voice a low rumble that cut through the night wind.

"Mr. McCoy," Dalton said, his eyes dark and serious. "The fire is already out. We have the flash drives from your safe. We have the footage you said didn't exist."

Thomas froze. His mouth opened, but no sound came out.

Dalton paused, letting the silence stretch, heavy and suffocating. "And we have Sofia's necklace, whoever you got to clean up the Conservatory must have missed it. It's ours now, McCoy."

The color drained from Thomas's face, leaving him gray and ghostly in the flashing lights. He looked at Marlene, then past her, realizing the betrayal had come from inside his own home. Eleanor.

"Take him," Dalton whispered.

The car door slammed shut, sealing Thomas inside a cage of wire and glass.

"It's quiet," Marlene whispered, looking at the house that

was now a crime scene.

"It's justice," Dalton replied softly. He turned his head toward the east. "Look."

Marlene turned.

Far in the distance, over the rolling hills, the sky was beginning to bruise with color. A deep, rich violet was bleeding into the black.

The sky was preparing for the sun, showing that even the longest night must eventually yield to the morning.

"I'll call Eleanor," Marlene said softly. "I know she'll be up waiting for word."

Dalton silently nodded, his gaze remaining on the horizon.

56

Chapter 56

The glass doors of the Mother and Baby wing reflected a woman Eleanor barely recognized. Her hair was perfectly sprayed, and her linen dress was crisp, but her eyes held a haunted depth that hadn't been there a week ago.

In her left hand, she clutched a vase of delicate pink peonies, their petals trembling slightly with the tremor in her wrist. In her right, she held a peace offering that felt impossibly heavy, a Bella Luna rabbit. It was floppy and soft, with long, dangling oatmeal-colored limbs and ears. A powder-blue bow sat neatly at its neck, and stitched into its little knit heart were the words *Welcome to the world.*

She took a deep, shuddering breath, filling her lungs with the sterile air of the entryway.

You can do this, she whispered to herself.

She stepped forward, and the automatic doors hissed open.

Eleanor was petrified. Every instinct in her body screamed at her to run, to hide back in the shadows where she had lived for thirty years. But a small, flickering flame of hope kept her feet moving. She hoped that maybe, just maybe, Sofia could see past the last name. Eleanor had torched her entire life, handing her husband and her only son over to the law, in the desperate hope that Sofia, Allie, and that innocent baby boy could have a life free of fear. She had sacrificed her family to save theirs.

She walked slowly toward the nurses' station. Marlene had handled the impossible logistics, speaking with Isabella that morning. It had taken convincing, but Isabella had agreed to play gatekeeper.

"I'm here to see Sofia in room 202," Eleanor said, her voice barely audible over the hum of the computers. "I believe they are expecting me."

The nurse glanced at a note, nodded, and pressed the buzzer.

Click.

The heavy security lock disengaged. Eleanor's heart slammed against her ribs in a rhythm of panic. Her feet wouldn't move. The door began to drift shut again, the opportunity closing. With a sudden surge of desperation, Eleanor reached out, catching the heavy door with her shoulder and pushing through into the postpartum wing.

Her heels clacked against the linoleum as she walked past open doors where tiny newborns were held, and mothers slept. She stopped at 202.

Her hands were shaking so violently that the water in the vase sloshed against the glass. She closed her eyes, forcing air into her lungs. *They have every right to hate you,* she reminded herself. *You are the mother of the monster. You are the villain in their story.*

But she needed to apologize. She needed to make amends, however inadequate they might be. She needed them to know, from her own lips, that the monsters were in cages, and she was the one who had locked them away.

From inside the room, she heard the laughter of a group of women. It was a soft, intimate sound that made bile rise in her throat. She was about to shatter that peace.

She knocked.

"I'll get it." Isabella's voice called, guarded and tight.

Isabella pulled the door open. She offered a curt nod, then turned to the bed.

"Someone is here to see you, Sof," Isabella said gently.

Sofia, looking pale but radiant against the white pillows, frowned slightly. "Who?"

Isabella sighed, her eyes meeting Eleanor's with a mixture of warning and pity. "Someone who would really like to speak with you. Just… let her talk, okay?"

Isabella opened the door wider, stepping past Eleanor. "We'll just be out here," she whispered as she looked at her mother and sister sitting by the window. She called to them, gesturing for them to leave with her as she pulled the door closed behind them.

Sofia looked at the woman standing in the doorway. She took in the expensive clothes, the nervous trembling, the floppy rabbit. Her brow furrowed in genuine confusion. She didn't know this woman.

"Hi there," Sofia's voice was a bit tentative as she tried to figure out who the woman standing in her hospital room was. "How can I help you?"

Eleanor took a single, terrified step forward. The room felt like it was spinning.

"Sofia, I'm…" Her voice failed. She swallowed hard, forcing the truth out. "I'm Eleanor. Eleanor… McCoy."

The air left the room.

Allie, who had been sitting by the bed, shot up like a rocket. Her face contorted into protective fury. She took a step toward Eleanor, shielding Sofia with her body.

"What the hell are you doing here?" Allie snarled, her hands balled into fists.

Eleanor flinched, but didn't retreat. She held her arms out slightly, the rabbit dangling from her hand. "Please. Please," she begged, her voice cracking. "I'm not here to harm. I promise. Please, just listen to what I have to say."

Sofia just stared, her hazel eyes wide, lost in the realization of whose mother stood before her.

Eleanor looked past Allie's anger, locking eyes with Sofia. "Please, Sofia. I need to say this."

Sofia reached out, placing a trembling hand on Allie's arm. "Let's let her say what she has to say."

Allie looked back, ready to argue, but Sofia shook her head. Sofia pointed a shaking finger toward the wooden chair next to her bed.

"Sit." She commanded firmly.

Allie glared at Eleanor one last time before retreating to sit on the edge of the bed, her arm wrapping protectively around Sofia's waist.

Eleanor released a shaky breath. She sank into the chair, placing the vase on the rolling bedside table next to her.

"These are for you," she whispered. Then, she leaned forward, her hands trembling as she placed the soft Bella Luna rabbit gently on the side of the bed.

"This... this is for..." Her breath hitched, tears instantly filling her eyes, blurring her vision. "This is for your son."

Sofia's eyes fluttered closed for a second. She took a deep

breath, opened them, and looked at Eleanor. Waiting.

"Sofia, I am so… I am so, so sorry." Eleanor began, the words tumbling out in a rush of grief. "I failed you. I failed to raise a man who respected life. I failed to see the darkness in my own home because I was too afraid to look. I know there is nothing I can ever do to fix this. I can't scrub the memory from your mind. I can't take back the pain. I would give my life if I could."

She looked at Sofia, pleading for understanding. "But I am taking steps to try and do as much as I can."

Allie flashed a look of sharp skepticism. "And how is that? What could you possibly do?"

Eleanor looked from Allie's fire to Sofia's sorrow. She straightened her spine.

"I came here because I wanted to personally let you know that Josh, Thomas, and Detective Miller have all been arrested."

Sofia let out a loud, strangled gasp. Her hands flew to her mouth. "What? When?"

Allie stiffened, her grip on Sofia tightening.

"This morning," Eleanor said softly. "Around three."

Sofia's face searched Eleanor's, tears beginning to spill over her lashes. "How did this happen? What changed? They told me I'd never be able to make a case against them."

Eleanor looked down at her manicured hands now resting limp in her lap. The silence stretched, heavy and profound.

"I turned them in." She whispered.

She looked up, meeting Sofia's gaze. "I gave the authorities the evidence that proved their guilt. The Attorney General executed the warrants this morning. They are investigating to see who else is involved."

She paused, fighting the sob rising in her throat. "I lived a life of abuse, Sofia. I was afraid to leave. I was afraid to breathe. I wanted to save Josh... I wanted to believe that my little boy wasn't capable of... of this. I wanted to hope that what I suspected wasn't true."

She choked out a sob, the dam finally breaking. "I'm so sorry he hurt you. I didn't want it to be true, but when I saw the proof... when I knew what he did to you..." She glanced at the rabbit. "And what he tried to do to the baby... I couldn't let them continue. You deserve so much better. So much more."

The tears fell freely now, splashing onto her clasped hands.

"I just lost my little boy," Eleanor wept, her voice barely a whisper. "But I'm hoping that it will somehow bring life to you and your beautiful family."

Sofia sat perfectly still. The room was silent aside from the hum of the hospital and Eleanor's quiet weeping.

Sofia wanted to be angry. She wanted to scream at this woman, to throw the flowers, to demand why she hadn't stopped it sooner. She wanted to hate the name McCoy. But as she looked at Eleanor, slumped in the hospital chair, she didn't see a monster. She didn't see an enemy.

She saw a mother who had just ripped her own heart out to save a stranger. She saw a woman who had broken her own chains to ensure Sofia wouldn't be bound by them.

Sofia looked at the rabbit, then at the woman who had brought it. The name 'McCoy' had been a bruise on her soul for months, a word that tasted like iron and fear. But looking at Eleanor, seeing the ruin of a mother's heart in her eyes, the weight suddenly shifted. Sofia reached out, her fingers brushing the soft oatmeal fur of the toy before settling over

Eleanor's trembling hand.

"I forgive you," Sofia said.

Her voice was soft, but the power of the words hit Eleanor like a physical wave. She looked up, her eyes swimming, searching Sofia's gaze for any trace of deception. She found only truth.

Eleanor broke. Her shoulders shook, her face crumbled into her hands, and she wept... not from grief, but from the overwhelming, purifying wash of grace. In those three words, the prison she had lived in for thirty years dissolved. In those three words, she found freedom. In those three words, she found life.

57

Chapter 57

Camilla had been a constant presence in the hospital room since the delivery, hovering in the corners like a worried shadow. She brought food and filled Sofia's water pitcher, but she moved with a quiet energy unlike her usual vibrant self. She was there, yet she felt miles away.

Sofia sat on the edge of the hospital bed and watched her sister organize the bedside table for the third time in an hour.

"Cami?" Sofia asked softly.

Camilla jumped slightly but turned with a forced smile. "Yeah, Sof? Do you need more water? I can run down the hall."

"No, I'm okay," She patted the spot on the mattress beside her. "I was just wondering if you have been down to see him yet."

Camilla froze. Her hand hovered over the plastic water pitcher. She didn't turn around. "Not yet. I've just been… busy helping you. Making sure you're good."

"I'm good. I'm going down there now. Do you want to come with me?"

Camilla glanced around while her feet walked a few steps towards the door. "I think I should stay here. In case Mom calls… or the nurse comes in."

Sofia frowned. She ignored the soreness in her body and stood up, moving slowly toward her little sister. "Cami, look at me. You're hesitating. Why don't you want to see him?"

"I do!" Camilla argued quickly, though her voice was high and tight. "Of course I do. He's my nephew. I just… I'm nervous. That's all."

Sofia stopped in front of her. She reached out and took Camilla's hands. They were trembling.

"Be honest with me," Sofia whispered as she searched Camilla's eyes. "Why don't you want to go?"

The question shattered the facade she wore. Camilla's face crumpled. Her shoulders shook, and a sob ripped through her chest that sounded like it had been trapped there for months.

"Because I put him there, sissy!" Cami wailed. She tried to pull her hands away, but Sofia held tight. "I did this to him and I did this to you!"

"What? Cami, what are you talking about?"

"The alarm!" Camilla choked out. "That night. You told me to set it, and I forgot. I forgot to set the alarm, Sof. It's my fault he got in. It's my fault you got hurt, and it's my fault that baby is fighting for his life now."

"I can't bear to face him," Cami sobbed. "I can't look at him and know he's hurting because of my mistake. I'll never forgive myself if he doesn't make it."

The room fell silent except for Cami's ragged breathing.

Sofia felt a fresh wave of heartbreak. Not for herself, but for her little sister who had been torturing herself in silence.

Sofia pulled Cami into her arms and held her tightly while she cried. She stroked her hair, waiting for the worst of the storm to pass.

"Forgive me," Cami whispered into Sofia's shoulder. "Please forgive me."

Sofia pulled back. She reached up and tilted her baby sister's face up to look at her. She wiped the tears away with her thumbs and smiled tenderly.

"I don't blame you for this, Hermanita," Sofia's voice left no room for doubt. "None of it. You didn't do this… a monster did. The only person responsible is the man who did it, and no one else."

Cami sniffled, searching Sofia's eyes for the truth.

"You are not to blame," Sofia repeated firmly. "Now, will you please come and say hi to your nephew with me?"

Cami let out a long, shaky breath. She nodded slowly.

They walked down the corridor together, hand in hand. The NICU was a different world that startled Cami. It was dim, filled with the rhythmic beeping of monitors and crying babies.

Sofia led Cami to the isolette in the corner.

Inside the glass case lay the baby. He was impossibly small, hooked up to wires that monitored his every breath. He looked fragile, but he was also beautiful. He had a tuft of dark hair and a perfect, tiny mouth.

Cami gasped softly. She brought her hand to her mouth. "Oh, Sof. He's so little."

"He's a fighter," Sofia whispered.

Sofia reached over and undid the latch on the incubator's side. She opened the small circular port.

"Put your hand in." She looked at her sister and smiled.

"Touch his hand."

Cami hesitated. Her hand hovered in the air, shaking. "I don't want to hurt him. He looks so breakable."

"You won't hurt him," Sofia promised. "He knows your voice from all those times you talked to him and sang to him. Now he needs to know your touch."

Slowly, gently, Cami reached through the opening. The air inside was warm and humid. She extended her index finger, moving with the agonizing slowness of someone touching a butterfly's wing.

She brushed the palm of his tiny hand with the tip of her finger.

Suddenly, his hand uncurled and his slender fingers wrapped around the tip of Cami's finger and squeezed.

It was a weak grip, but to Cami, it felt like the strongest thing in the world.

Her heart immediately melted. The guilt, the fear, and the shame seemed to evaporate in the warmth of the incubator, replaced by a rush of pure, overwhelming love. A smile graced her face, radiant and teary. A single tear slid down her cheek, but this one wasn't from pain or guilt.

"Hi there," Cami whispered, her voice thick with emotion. She leaned her forehead against the glass, never breaking the connection with his tiny hand. "I'm your Tia Cami... I love you so much already, baby boy. I can't wait to teach you about music, make you TikTok famous, and buy you every single toy you want... even... if your moms say no." She paused, looking down at him. "And... I'm sorry. I'll spend every day of the rest of my life making it up to you. I promise."

58

Chapter 58

The morning sun filtered through the hospital blinds, painting stripes of gold across the floor, but for Sofia, the light felt contradictory. It was a beautiful day, the day she was finally being discharged. But it felt like the hardest day of her life.

Leaving the hospital meant leaving him.

The thought was a physical ache, a hollow space in her chest that throbbed every time she imagined walking out those sliding glass doors without a car seat in her hand. How could she exist miles away from him? How could she sleep in a bed that wasn't next to his temporary bed? The biological pull to remain by his side was overwhelming, a primal tether that refused to stretch.

Yet amidst the heartache, a miracle was unfolding in the NICU.

He was winning.

Late last night, the rhythmic *whoosh-hiss* of the ventilator had been silenced. He had fought his way off the machine, his tiny lungs taking command. Now, he lay there with only a small nasal cannula, a thin, clear tube taped delicately under his nose, providing just enough supplemental oxygen to help him along.

Since Eleanor's visit… since the news that they were arrested and behind cold, hard bars… the air around them had shifted. It felt lighter. The suffocating dread was replaced by a tentative, blooming peace. It felt like life again.

Sofia sat in the rocking chair beside the incubator, her eyes tracing the rise and fall of his chest. He was awake, his dark, dewy eyes blinking slowly as he took in the blurred world around him. His little hand grasped her finger, his grip surprisingly strong.

Sarah, their lead nurse, approached with a soft smile. She checked the monitors, then looked down at Sofia.

"Would you like to hold him?"

Sofia's eyes grew large, swimming with sudden tears. "I can hold him?" Her voice was a whisper, filled with wonder and terror.

Sarah nodded. "You sure can. He's ready. Let's get you settled."

Sofia's heart pounded against her ribs. She was so nervous. He looked so fragile, a porcelain doll wired for sound. Her hands shook as she removed her shirt, wanting so badly to do skin-to-skin, sitting back deep into the rocking chair.

Allie pulled her stool closer, covering Sofia's trembling hand with her own warm one. "You are going to do great, babe," Allie whispered, her eyes shining. "You've got this."

Sarah and another nurse carefully lifted the tiny bundle. Wires trailed behind him like ribbons. Gently, reverently, they lowered him into Sofia's arms. They positioned his head against the skin of her chest, his tiny legs curling instinctively under his bum, the "frog" position he had known in the womb.

They covered him with a warm blanket, wrapping him tightly against her.

A soft gasp escaped Sofia's lips.

She closed her eyes, overwhelmed by the heat, the weight, the sheer *reality* of him. She placed her hand over his small back, feeling the rapid flutter of his heart beating against her own.

"Oh my gosh," she breathed, holding him as if she were holding the entire universe. She opened her eyes, looking down into his face, no longer separated by glass.

"Hello, my sweet boy," she cooed, her voice trembling with emotion. "I've been waiting a long time for this."

Allie watched them, her hand over her mouth to stifle a sob. The sight of Sofia, who had survived so much darkness, holding their precious, light-filled baby made her heart explode. It was a beauty so sharp it hurt. She leaned forward, kissing Sofia's temple, then kissing the baby's soft, fuzzy head.

"I love you both so much," Allie whispered, tears tracking down her cheeks. In that moment, she knew she had everything she had ever wanted. The most amazing woman by her side and now, a family to call her own.

Allie leaned back, giving them space. She let Sofia sink into the moment.

"You are so strong, my baby boy," Sofia rocked him gently. The movement was natural, ancient. "You have overcome so much already, and I'm so, so proud of you. I love you. I will always love you."

She kissed his forehead, inhaling the scent of him… milk and soap and miracles. She hummed a soft, wordless lullaby, the vibrations traveling from her chest to his.

Sofia closed her eyes, sinking into the bliss, when suddenly, a sound broke the quiet.

It was tiny. A little, squeaky protest.

Sofia's eyes flew open. It was him. It was his voice.

Somehow, hearing that first cry made her heart swell even larger, expanding beyond the boundaries of her ribs. The love grew deeper, wider, and more profound than she had ever imagined possible. She leaned her head down, cheek to cheek with him.

"Shhhh," she soothed, rocking him a little faster. "I've got you, sweet boy."

His little fingers grasped her pinky, holding on tight as he calmed down, comforted by her voice.

Quietly, Sofia whispered to him, sealing the bond.

"I love you, Phoenix." She tested the name, and it tasted like strength. "Phoenix Amadeo. You are a picture of resilience. Of strength. You are the tiniest little teacher of the purest form of love."

Allie's lips trembled as she heard the name. *Phoenix*, rising from the ashes. *Amadeo*, beloved of God.

"Welcome to the world, little Phoenix," Allie whispered.

* * *

The high of the morning crashed into the reality of the afternoon.

Allie finished packing the last of their toiletries into the bag. The room, which had been their sanctuary for a week, suddenly looked cold and sterile without their things scattered about. She piled the bags onto the rolling cart.

Sofia sat in the wheelchair near the door, staring at her lap.

"I think I have everything," Allie said, forcing a brightness into her voice she didn't feel.

Sofia was silent. She was battling a war inside herself. Every instinct screamed at her to get up, to go back to the NICU, to camp next to his plastic box. She wanted to be the one to feed him the tiny milliliters of milk. She wanted to change him. She wanted to be his mama, not a visitor.

Allie walked over and knelt in front of the wheelchair, blocking out the rest of the room.

"I'm not going to ask if you're okay," Allie said softly, her hands resting on Sofia's knees. "I know you're not. This is going to be really hard. But is there anything I can do or say in this moment to make it any easier for you?"

Sofia looked at Allie. Her beautiful ocean eyes were a lighter blue today... a sad, stormy blue. She reached out, placing her hand on the side of Allie's face, her thumb brushing Allie's cheek.

She shook her head slowly. "No. But I love you."

Allie smiled, a watery, sad smile. "I love you too."

She stood up as the nurse walked in with the discharge papers. "Are we ready?" the nurse asked kindly.

"Not at all," Allie admitted, squeezing Sofia's shoulder.

The nurse nodded knowingly. "It's never easy to have to leave your baby. But he is in the best hands he could be in, and we will take good care of him. I promise."

Sofia nodded, unable to speak. As the nurse unlocked the brakes and started rolling her toward the door, Sofia felt something inside her fracture. A sob built in her chest, hot and suffocating.

"He'll be home before you know it, sweetheart." The nurse patted her shoulder as they moved down the hallway. "Try to rest while you can."

Sofia didn't hear her. She only heard the distance growing between her and Phoenix. Every tile they rolled over was a step further away.

By the time they reached the curb outside, the fresh air felt like an assault. Cami was there, the car idling as she jumped out to help.

Sofia stood up from the wheelchair, but as she looked at the car, her feet refused to move.

She stopped, her body trembling. The dam broke.

"I can't do this," She cried as her voice cracked and she doubled over, clutching her stomach. "I can't leave him. I can't."

Cami looked at her sister with deep sadness, her own eyes filling with tears.

Allie dropped the bag she was holding and stepped in, wrapping her arm firmly around Sofia's waist, holding her up.

"I know, Sof." Allie soothed, pressing her lips to Sofia's temple. "I know. Listen to me. How about we just go home, get settled, and shower? I'll pack us some lunch, and we can come back for the rest of the evening. We'll be back in just a few hours."

She guided Sofia toward the open car door. Sofia's tears fell freely, dripping onto the pavement. She said nothing. She just nodded, broken.

She didn't have a choice. She let Allie slide her into the seat, leaving her heart behind in the building that towered above them.

59

Chapter 59

The tires crunched against the familiar pavement as Allie pulled the car up to the hospital entrance. It felt like they had made this drive a million times this month, a loop of anxiety, hope, exhaustion, and coffee. The sliding glass doors of the Mother and Baby unit greeted them like an old, demanding friend.

But today was different.

Today, the air didn't feel heavy with worry; it felt electric, vibrating with a joy they had almost forgotten how to feel. Today, they walked toward those doors not with trepidation, but with hearts so full they felt on the verge of bursting.

Phoenix was officially one month old.

Thirty days. Seven hundred and twenty hours of fighting. And he had won. He was gaining weight, his cheeks filling out with a delicious, milky chubbiness. He was holding his own temperature, and best of all, he was breathing entirely on his own. His cries, once weak and heartbreaking, were now strong, demanding, and utterly perfect. He was alert, his muddy blue eyes tracking them, soaking in the world with a

392

wisdom that seemed beyond his weeks.

For Allie, the last month had been life-changing in ways she hadn't expected. It wasn't just the baby; it was watching Sofia.

Every day, Allie watched her transform. She saw the fear slowly evaporate, replaced by a fierce, protective instinct. She watched Sofia let her guard down, stepping fully into the role of "Mama," allowing the overwhelming, biological flood of love to rush in. Seeing Sofia coo at him, seeing the way she melted when his tiny hand grabbed her finger—it was the most beautiful thing Allie had ever seen.

Allie had known for a long time that Sofia was her person. Her forever. But their lives had been a storm of survival for the past year. Between the assault, the trial prep, the pregnancy, the constant fear, and the premature birth, there had never been a moment to just *be*.

But even through the darkness, the light had found a way in. And for the last week, Allie had been preparing to catch it.

* * *

One Week Earlier

"Sarah, do you have a second?" Allie had whispered, pulling the lead nurse into the quiet alcove near the scrub sinks.

Sarah, who had become as much a friend as a nurse over the last month to both Mama and Mommy, nodded, sensing the nervous energy radiating off Allie. "Is everything okay? Is it Phoenix?"

"No, no, he's great," Allie assured her, her hands trembling slightly as she reached into her leather satchel, a new accessory

she'd sported since Phoenix arrived. "I actually need your help with something. For Sofia."

Sarah's face softened into a knowing smile. "Anything. You know I'd do anything for you two."

Allie took a deep breath and pulled out a small, light-washed wooden box. It was unassuming, rustic, and simple.

Sarah's eyes went wide.

Allie flipped the lid open.

Sarah gasped, her hands flying to her mouth. Nestled inside on a light ivory velvet cushion was a ring that was hauntingly beautiful. It wasn't a traditional diamond solitaire. The center stone was a two-carat, unheated blue oval Montana sapphire. It was breathtaking... the color of the ocean when the sunlight hits the waves just right. It shifted in the light, half sunlight, half deep water, holding a depth that felt endless.

On either side of the sapphire sat a single, one-carat marquise-shaped diamond, like leaves framing a flower. But the true magic was hidden.

"Look at the side," Allie whispered as she tilted the ring to show the gallery. Hidden from the top view, small round and marquise diamond buds were woven into the metalwork.

"It's called the 'Secret Garden' setting," Allie explained, her voice thick with emotion. "It's simple and elegant, but completely unique. Just like her."

A tear slid down Sarah's cheek. "Allie... this is... it's so perfect. You two deserve so much happiness." She threw her arms around Allie's neck, squeezing tight. "I'm so happy for you! I am SO on board! Tell me what I need to do!"

Allie grinned, the nerves settling into excitement. "Okay, so here is the plan..."

* * *

Sofia and Allie stood at the NICU entrance, buzzing the intercom. The lock clicked, and they pushed through the doors. The familiar hum of the unit surrounded them, but Sofia didn't look at the other babies. Her eyes went straight to their corner.

She stopped dead in her tracks, a gasp escaping her lips. A smile, bright and genuine, broke across her face like dawn.

Their corner of the NICU had been transformed.

Floating happily in the sterile air was a large cluster of balloons. There were white ones with bold blue print that read *"Happy Day!"* and *"I'm Going Home!"* Mixed in were pale blue balloons covered in tiny white hearts that simply said, *"I Love You."*

Sofia was giddy, the emotions of the day bubbling over. She half-laughed, half-cried, reading the balloons. "Oh my goodness," she whispered, looking back at Allie with shining eyes before turning back to the crib.

She tiptoed up to Phoenix's bed, Allie following close behind her, her pulse dancing in her veins.

"Hi, baby boy!" Sofia cooed, excitement trembling in her voice as she reached down. "You get to come home today, and mommy and I are so excited!"

Her hands gently touched his chest, preparing to pick him up. "Ohhh, what does your shirt say today?" She asked him, her eyes barely registering the white fabric at first.

Then, she froze.

Her eyes locked onto the pale blue lettering on the onesie. Her lips moved, whispering the words as she read them, her brain trying to catch up with her heart.

"Will... you... marry... my... mommy?"

Sofia's hand flew to her mouth. The air left her lungs. She spun around, turning toward Allie.

But Allie was no longer standing beside her. She was down on one knee on the hospital linoleum.

Sofia choked back a surprised sob. Allie looked up at her, holding the wooden box. Her beautiful, bright ocean eyes were brimming with tears, reflecting the sapphire in her hand.

"Sofia, my love," Allie began, her voice steady despite the emotion thickening the air. "For so long, the world tried to take things from you. They tried to take your voice, your safety, and your peace. But they couldn't take your heart. I chose this sapphire because it's like the sea; no matter how much rain falls or how hard the wind blows, it stays deep and constant. *You* are my constant. I don't want to just be the person who helped you survive the storm. I want to be the person you wake up to when the sun finally comes out."

Allie took a breath, holding Sofia's gaze, pouring every ounce of her soul into the words.

"I didn't know true love existed until you. And I never want to be a day without it again." Allie lifted the ring slightly. "Will you marry me?"

Sofia's tears broke free, spilling over her cheeks. Before she could even speak, a sound erupted from behind the curtained partition.

Applause.

Sofia whipped her head around to see the curtain pulled back. Standing there, crying and cheering, were the nurses, doctors, her mother, Isabella, Camilla, Danika, and Dylann. They had all been there, hiding, witnessing the moment their lives started over.

Sofia smiled at them all through her tears, her heart soaring, before turning back to the woman kneeling before her. Her smile was endearing, genuine, and glorious.

She nodded her head frantically, then dropped to her knees, disregarding the hard floor until she was eye-level with Allie.

"I would marry you a thousand times," Sofia whispered.

They crashed into each other, wrapping their arms around one another in an embrace like no other… a mix of relief, joy, and absolute certainty. They kissed excitedly, tasting the salt of their tears.

Allie pulled back, her hands sure as she took the ring out of the box. She slid it onto Sofia's finger. It fit perfectly.

Allie helped Sofia stand up. Sofia held out her hand, the sapphire catching the light, shimmering like deep water.

"Oh my gosh, Allie," she breathed. "This is the most beautiful ring I've ever seen."

Allie smiled, wiping a tear from Sofia's cheek. "Nothing compares to you, my love."

Their friends and family rushed over, a wave of warmth and congratulations. Arms wrapped around them as laughter filled the sterile room, and everyone took turns admiring the Secret Garden ring. They spoke of how happy they were, how much this was deserved, how glad they were that two souls who needed each other had finally found their way home.

Sofia and Allie thanked them all, their faces hurting from smiling, before turning to the most important task of the day.

Together, they packed up the most precious gift of all.

With Phoenix secure in his carrier, they made their way out of the NICU and toward the exit. Their entourage followed

behind them, a parade of love. The air outside felt different…
light, happy, and filled with a golden warmth, as if Heaven
itself had come down to walk them out.

They reached the car and watched as the nurse secured
Phoenix into his base. Before getting in, they paused. Allie
closed the back door and turned to Sofia.

The world fell away. It was just the two of them, standing
in the parking lot, but it felt like holy ground. Both of their
eyes filled with fresh tears, reflecting the magnitude of the
journey they had survived.

"I love you," Allie whispered. She took Sofia's hand, the
one now bearing the promise of forever, and raised it to her
lips, kissing the knuckles softly.

"I love you too." Sofia leaned in to kiss Allie softly on the
lips.

She pulled back, looking at her fiancé, then at the carseat
in the back.

"Let's get our little boy home."

60

Chapter 60

The phone felt heavy in Sofia's hand, a physical weight that matched the stone sitting in her stomach.

For months, the memory of Eleanor McCoy had haunted the edges of her new life. Sofia had seen her in passing at the court hearings, brief, painful glimpses of a woman who looked as if she were eroding from the inside out. Eleanor always presented herself with that trademark McCoy perfection, spine steel-straight, hair immovable, but her eyes were shattered glass. She would ask about Sofia, ask about Allie, and finally, with a voice barely rising above a whisper, she would ask about the baby.

Sofia had always kept her answers guarded, protective walls built high. "He's good." "He's growing." She never gave a name. She never offered a picture.

But as Phoenix grew and his personality began to bloom like a wildflower, something shifted in the marrow of Sofia's bones. She would look at her son, that overwhelming, terrifying tidal wave of love flooding her veins, and her thoughts would drift to the woman who had loved Josh just as fiercely once. Regardless of the monster Josh became, he had once been Eleanor's baby. He had been her innocent boy. And Eleanor had chosen to tear her own heart out, severing her connection to her child to save Sofia's.

It was a sacrifice that only a mother could truly understand, and the weight of it pressed on Sofia's heart.

Sofia took a deep breath, the air trembling in her lungs, and dialed the number Marlene had given to Isabella months ago.

It rang three times.

"Hello?" Eleanor's voice sounded thin and tired.

"Eleanor?" Sofia gripped the phone tighter to steady her hand. "It's Sofia."

Silence stretched on the line, thick and heavy with unsaid things. "Sofia… oh. Hello. Is… is everything okay?"

"Yes, everything is fine." Her voice softened. "I… I was calling to see if you might be free this Sunday? Maybe to meet for coffee?"

Another pause, this one filled with a quiet, audible shock. "I… yes. I would like that very much, Sofia."

"Okay. How about The Peach and Bean? Would noon work?"

"I will be there," Eleanor whispered. "Thank you, Sofia."

Sofia hung up and walked back into the living room from the porch. The air was crisp, but the scene in front of her was warm. Allie was sitting in the rocking chair with Phoenix on her lap. Allie was making a silly face, her nose scrunching up, when suddenly a sound erupted from the baby… a bubbling, joyous belly laugh that rose into the air like a song.

It was the most beautiful sound in the world to both of them.

"She agreed," Sofia said quietly, leaning against the door frame, watching her family.

Allie looked up, her smile softening as she saw the complicated look on Sofia's face. "How are you feeling about that?"

Sofia shrugged, wrapping her arms around herself as if to hold the conflicting emotions together. "Confused. I feel in my heart that it's the right thing... but there's still that little war inside of me, you know? Part of me wants to protect him from anything connected to that name. But the other part... the mother part... knows she needs this. And maybe I do too."

Allie nodded, her eyes full of infinite understanding. "That's valid, babe. It's okay to feel the war. But I only want you to do this if you will truly be okay with it."

Sofia walked over and sat on the bench beside the rocker. She reached out, grasping Phoenix's tiny, warm hand. He squeezed her finger, anchoring her to the present, to the safety they had built.

"I know it's right," she whispered.

* * *

Sunday arrived carrying the crisp, biting chill of the first day of Winter.

Eleanor wrapped herself in her thick charcoal cashmere sweater, pulling it tight like armor as she stepped out of her front door. She was terrified. Her hands shook as she unlocked her car, the keys jingling. She didn't know what Sofia wanted. Did she want to scream at her? Did she need closure? Did she want to tell her to never speak to them again? Eleanor wanted desperately to tell Sofia that she thought of them daily, that she prayed for their happiness every night before she cried herself to sleep, but she didn't want to overstep. She knew her place was on the periphery, an exile of her own making.

She entered The Peach and Bean, the bell above the door jingling cheerfully.

She scanned the room, her heart hammering a frantic beat against her ribs.

She saw Allie first. Allie raised a hand, waving her over with a small, encouraging smile. Sofia's back was to the door, her dark hair cascading over her shoulders, shielding her from view.

Eleanor walked slowly, taking a deep, steadying breath with every step, trying to compose herself. *Just be grateful she called,* Eleanor told herself. *Just listen. Take whatever she gives you.*

She reached the table and opened her mouth to offer a greeting, but the words died in her throat.

Sofia turned in her chair, and there, sitting contentedly in her lap, was the baby.

Eleanor hadn't expected him. She hadn't dared to hope she would ever see him this close, let alone be in the same room with him. Her hand flew to her mouth, stifling a gasp as she choked back instant, hot tears.

He was… magnificent. He had dark curls and eyes that held the universe, gazing around with innocent wonder.

Eleanor sank slowly into the empty chair, unable to tear her gaze away from him, feeling as though she were in the presence of something holy.

"Well, hi there, handsome." She smiled as her voice

trembled with raw, unfiltered emotion. She looked up at Sofia, her eyes shining with unshed tears. "He's beautiful, Sofia. He really is."

Sofia smiled, a genuine, soft expression that reached her eyes. "And he's such a happy baby. Even through everything."

Eleanor nodded, unable to look away from the miracle before her. "I can see that."

"Are you a happy baby?" She cooed to him, unable to help herself.

In return, Phoenix let out a wet, happy coo, kicking his legs in excitement. He raised his hand from under the table, bringing it to his mouth to chew on something with intense focus.

Eleanor froze.

Clutched in his tiny fist was a wad of oatmeal-colored fur... a long, floppy rabbit ear.

Eleanor's lip trembled. It was the Bella Luna rabbit. The peace offering she had left on the hospital bed, terrified it would be thrown in the trash. Instead, he was chewing on it like it was his best friend.

Sofia watched the realization wash over Eleanor's face. She smiled gently, a look of mercy. "It's his favorite thing. He won't sleep without it."

Eleanor felt a hot tear escape as it fell down her cheek. She wiped it away quickly, sitting up straighter, trying to pull herself together. "Thank you," she said earnestly, her voice thick. "Thank you for letting me see him. I know I had no right to hope for it, but... I pray for it all the time."

"That's kind of why I wanted to see you today, Eleanor."

She adjusted Phoenix on her lap, taking a deep breath to steady her own nerves. "I think of you a lot. I think of the sacrifice you made for me… well… for us. I don't want you to ever think that I don't realize what a massive thing that was. You gave up your son to save mine. You didn't have to do what you did."

Sofia paused, looking down at Phoenix, then lifting her gaze back to Eleanor with a profound sincerity.

"I don't even know how this would work, exactly. But… maybe we can form some type of relationship. One where you could be involved in our lives somehow. In *his* life."

Eleanor took a shaky breath, her heart expanding in her chest until it physically hurt. It was an olive branch she didn't feel she deserved, extended by hands she had failed to protect.

"I would really, really like that," Eleanor whispered, her voice cracking.

They smiled at each other, a genuine, heartfelt connection forged in the fire of shared trauma and incredible grace.

Eleanor leaned forward, drawn to the child like a magnet. "What is his name?"

"Phoenix," Sofia replied.

Phoenix, Eleanor thought. *Rising from the ashes.* It was perfect.

"Would you like to hold him?"

Eleanor stopped breathing for a second. She nodded, her eyes wide with disbelief. "I would like nothing more."

Sofia stood up gently and transferred the warm weight of the baby into Eleanor's waiting arms.

Eleanor adjusted him, cradling him against her chest. He looked up at her, cooing softly, waving the damp rabbit ear in the air.

"Hi there, sweetheart," Eleanor murmured, tears blurring her vision completely now. "It is *so* nice to meet you."

She leaned down, pressing a soft, lingering kiss to the top of his head. "Oh my goodness, sweet boy," she whispered, the words barely audible. A tear slipped from her lash and landed in his dark hair, a silent baptism of love and regret.

She looked up at Allie, and then at Sofia, mouthing the words, *Thank you.*

Eleanor wasn't sure what this relationship would look like. It would be a slow cruise in a rocky ocean, navigating the wreckage of the past to find safe harbor. But she would take it. She would take whatever crumbs of connection they were willing to give.

The past few months had been soul-crushing, a lonely existence in a silent house filled with ghosts. But this day… this moment… holding the future in her arms? It was a gift of hope she never imagined she would receive.

She looked at Sofia, a woman of incredible resilience and mercy, and Eleanor made a silent vow to the universe. She would spend every single day of the rest of her life earning this grace.

61

Chapter 61

The early April morning arrived like a promise kept.

The sky was a deep, impossible blue, brushed with scattered, fluffy clouds that drifted lazily, casting soft shadows over the Hill Country. Below, the world was waking up. The trees were heavy with blossoms. Dogwoods and redbuds exploding in shades of white and pink. Every breeze carried the sweet, heady scent of jasmine and earth. It was the season of new life, the perfect backdrop for a day that was entirely about a new beginning.

Inside the bridal suite, the air was light, effervescent with joy and the clinking of crystal champagne flutes.

Sofia sat in a velvet chair, a flute of champagne resting on the vanity as the stylist worked the final touches into her hair. It cascaded down her back in loose, glossy waves, the dark strands catching the light. One side was swept back, pinned securely with a delicate lace barrette that looked like spun sugar against her hair.

Around her, the most important women in her life were a vision in white satin. Her mother, Blanca, and her sisters,

Isabella and Camilla, wore matching robes embroidered with the words *"Mother of the Bride"* and *"Bridesmaid"* in gold thread.

Blanca and Isabella sat on the plush cream couch, their hair and makeup already flawless.

"I still can't believe it's here." Isabella's eyes were misty as she looked at Sofia. "After everything… watching you sit there, looking this happy? It's the only thing I've wanted for over a year."

"It's not just happy," Blanca added softly, crossing her legs. "It's peace. That's what I see. And I couldn't have asked God for a better person to give that to you than Allie. She doesn't just love you, mija. She cherishes you."

Sofia met her mother's eyes in the mirror, her heart swelling. "She really does, Mama. I'm the lucky one."

"Okay, okay, before we all cry off our mascara," Cami announced, jumping up from her chair with infectious energy. "It's gown time!"

She bounded to the large walk-in closet, the white satin of her robe fluttering, and carefully brought out the bridesmaids' dresses. They were elegant in their simplicity, satin floor-length A-line gowns in a soft light champagne hue. The bodices were fitted, leading into romantic, soft-draped shoulders that promised to move beautifully in the wind.

"These are going to look so good!" Cami swooned, holding one up against herself. "Seriously, Sof, thank you for picking a dress we actually look hot in."

The room erupted in laughter, but it was cut short by a rhythmic knock at the heavy double doors.

"I got it!" Cami chirped, running barefoot to answer.

She pulled the door open and gasped playfully. Standing

there was Dylann.

Dylann stood out in a custom-tailored suit that perfectly matched the bridesmaids' dresses' champagne color. The fit was impeccable, hugging her frame with a sharpness that was both feminine and refined. Her light brown hair, usually tossed up or messy, was straightened to perfection, falling like a sheet of silk down her back. She appeared stylish, handsome, and undeniably sexy.

Dylann flashed a charming grin at Cami before stepping into the room.

"Room service," Dylann joked, though her eyes immediately found Sofia. She walked over, her demeanor softening. "You look incredible, Sof. And you aren't even in the dress yet."

"You clean up nice yourself, Dylann." Sofia teased.

Dylann handed a small white gift bag to Cami, who passed it eagerly to Sofia.

"This is for you. From Allie. She told me to tell you that Phoenix is good. He's currently keeping the entire wedding party entertained over there. He has us all wrapped around his little finger."

Sofia laughed, the image settling her nerves. Then she looked at the bag in her lap. "Allie sent me something?"

Her mouth flew open. "We told each other we weren't going to do gifts until the honeymoon! That sneak!"

"Just open it, sissy." Cami rolled her eyes affectionately, leaning over the back of the chair.

Sofia chuckled, her hands trembling slightly as she undid the perfect white bow tying the handles together. She reached into the tissue paper and pulled out a sleek, black velvet jewelry box.

The room went quiet.

Sofia opened the lid slowly.

Her breath hitched, and her lip began to tremble instantly. Nestled against the black velvet was a delicate gold chain holding a pendant that made her heart stop. It was a perfect replica of the necklace Allie had given her before the nightmare began. The necklace that had been the physical weight of their love in those early times.

But there was one small difference.

Where there had once been two stones, there was now a third, smaller stone. They sparkled fiercely under the vanity lights as Sofia took them in.

A small, rolled-up note was tucked into the lid. Sofia pulled it out, her fingers shaking as she unrolled the paper. Allie's familiar, strong handwriting filled the page.

For the woman who is my entire world,

They say diamonds are forever, but they have nothing on us. I wanted to replace the necklace you lost, but I couldn't just give you back the past. We are so much more than we were then.

These three stones now tell our whole story.

One for the woman who has shown me the impossible. One for the love that grew between us. And the smallest one, for the beautiful boy who made us a family.

I look at you, and I look at him, and I know that I have already won at life. I can't wait to meet you at the altar.

-Allie

A tear escaped Sofia's long lashes, splashing onto the paper. She pressed the note to her chest, closing her eyes as the wave of love crashed over her. It wasn't just jewelry. It was a reclaiming. It was Allie saying, *We survived, and look what we built.*

Sofia looked up to see her mother, Isabella and Camilla huddled together, all of them silently crying. They moved in as one unit, gathering around Sofia in a collective embrace of white satin and unconditional love. They blotted her tears and their own, laughing through the emotional release.

"Okay," the wedding coordinator stepped out from the shadows of the room, holding a large white garment bag. "It's time."

The mood shifted from sentimental to sacred.

Blanca stood up, wiping her eyes. "Okay. Let's get you dressed."

She took Sofia's hand and led her into the privacy of the bedroom. The coordinator unzipped the bag, revealing the masterpiece inside.

Blanca helped Sofia step into the gown, her hands steady and reverent. She pulled the fabric up, the zipper gliding smoothly up Sofia's back. Blanca took in her beautiful daughter, resting her hands gently on Sofia's bare arms.

For a moment, neither spoke. They just looked at the reflection… the mother who had prayed for this day and the daughter who had fought to reach it.

"You are so beautiful, mija," Blanca spoke around the lump in her throat. "I am so, so proud of you. And I am so happy for you both. As a mother, I could ask for nothing better than the love Allie has for you. You two are lucky, mija. That kind of love is rare. Always love one another and be true to one another, even on the bad days."

Sofia placed her hand over her mother's, squeezing tight.

She met Blanca's gaze in the mirror, seeing the history of strength passed down through generations.

"I will, Mama," Sofia promised. "I love you."

Sofia looked stunning. The dress was custom-made, a vision of ethereal romance that seemed to float around her. It was a light ivory A-line gown with a pleated sweetheart neckline that highlighted her decolletage. The bodice was a work of art, featuring romantic white flowers softly embroidered into the fabric, trickling down past the waist.

The sides of the bodice were semi-sheer, adding a touch of modern delicacy, with sheer chiffon that draped lazily off her shoulders, framing her collarbones. The skirt was made of soft, flowing chiffon that pooled on the floor like a cloud, extending into a breathtaking chapel-length train. Scattered across the skirt, the embroidered flowers reappeared, pooling toward the bottom hem like falling petals.

It was the most romantic dress they had ever seen. It wasn't just a dress, it was Sofia... soft, resilient, and blooming.

Sofia took a deep breath, watching her chest rise and fall in the mirror. She felt the weight of the new necklace against her skin as she lifted her hand to it, pressing it against her body. She thought of Phoenix laughing with Allie's chosen family. She thought of Allie waiting for her.

Blanca picked up the bouquet, a beautiful, delicate mix of white peonies, ivory lisianthus, Queen Anne's lace, and small white spray roses tied with a champagne ribbon, and handed it to her daughter.

Sofia took one last look at herself. The girl who had been shattered was gone. The woman in the mirror was whole and truly happy.

She turned to Blanca, her eyes clear and bright.

"I'm ready, Mama."

62

Chapter 62

The golden hour in the Texas Hill Country is not just a time of day; it is a feeling. It is the moment when the harshness of the world softens into amber and gold, when the light catches the dust motes dancing in the air and turns them into magic.

Under the canopy of ancient, sprawling oaks, the world had been transformed into a living fairytale.

Thousands of twinkling string lights were wrapped tight around the rough bark of the trees, climbing high into the branches where white lanterns hung suspended, glowing like captured stars. The air was sweet with the scent of blooming jasmine. It was a sensory overload of romance, a cathedral built of nature and light.

Allie stood at the end of the aisle, her heartbeat a steady clock, counting down every second until she was able to say *I do, I will, Forever, Completely.*

She looked perfect. Her hand-stitched, light ivory three-piece suit was tailored to within an inch of its life, hugging her frame. The five-button vest sat smoothly against her tan skin, the deep V of it adding a sharp, modern edge. The open jacket fit her shape flawlessly, and her slim trousers were rolled just above the ankle, revealing trendy alligator dress shoes that grounded her stance.

For the first time in years, her hair was down. Her beautiful dark blonde curls cascaded over one shoulder, softening the sharp lines of her suit. A single white rose was pinned to her lapel, resting right over her heart.

She looked out at the aisle before her. It was a tunnel of dreams. A canopy of white, ivory, and blush-pink flowers hung from the posts overhead, creating a cascade of blooms that shielded the path from the rest of the world. The guest chairs, antique gold with plush white seats, glowed in the late afternoon sun.

Behind her, the altar was a masterpiece. A massive archway overflowed with white and ivory hydrangeas, roses, and light colored wildflowers, dripping with crystals that caught the golden sunbeams, scattering rainbows across the grass.

Allie took a deep breath, her eyes scanning the eighty guests, the intimacy of the gathering wrapping around her, soft and warm. But then, her gaze snagged on the front row. Two chairs sat empty.

A pang of old grief, sharp and familiar, pierced her chest. They should have been here. Her parents should have been seeing this.

Suddenly, a warm hand squeezed her shoulder.

Allie looked to her right. Dylann stood there, flanked by Danika, both looking striking in their champagne suits. Dylann didn't say a word; she just squeezed harder, a silent reminder. *We are here. You are not alone.*

Allie covered Dylann's hand with her own for a fleeting second, grounding herself. That hole in her heart would always exist, but as she looked at the faces in the crowd, Sofia's family, their friends, and the community they had built from the ashes, she knew she was rich in love. This was her chosen family. And it was enough.

The low hum of conversation died down as the first notes of an acoustic guitar floated on the breeze.

A talented friend stood to the side, her voice rising clear and soulful as she sang a stripped-down, haunting rendition of *Latch.*

"You lift my heart up, when the rest of me is down... You, you enchant me even when you're not around..."

Isabella and Cami stepped onto the aisle, their smiles bright enough to rival the sun. They walked with a lightness, a joy that set the tone, taking their places on the opposite side of the altar.

Then, the breath caught in Allie's throat.

Eleanor stepped into the floral canopy.

She looked regal, softer than Allie had ever seen her, her face glowing with a peace that had been hard-won. And in her arms, wearing a tiny ivory suit that perfectly matched Allie's, was Phoenix.

Tears sprang to Allie's eyes instantly.

Seeing Eleanor holding him... the grandmother who had chosen justice over blood, the woman who had walked through fire to be here... it was overwhelming. Their bond had grown deep roots over the past few months. Eleanor wasn't a guest; she was family.

For Eleanor, the walk down the aisle felt like redemption. She held her beautiful grandson close, his little hand gripping the strap to her dress. She looked ahead at Allie, and past her to where Sofia would soon be, and felt a profound sense of belonging. She was walking toward the healthy, kind, loving family she had always dreamed of but never possessed. Until now.

Eleanor reached the altar. She kissed Allie's cheek, a lingering, maternal press of affection, and then passed Phoenix into Allie's arms.

Allie buried her face in the baby's neck for a second, inhaling his scent, before handing him back to Eleanor, who took her seat in the front row, holding the future in her lap.

The music shifted. The guitar slowed, deepening into a melody that tugged at the soul. The singer's voice dropped to a whispery, emotional timbre as *Feels Like Home* began to play.

"Something in your eyes makes me wanna lose myself..."

The guests stood. Allie turned her eyes to the start of the aisle.

And then, the world stopped.

Sofia appeared.

Beside her mother, Sofia stood framed by the flowers. The golden hour light hit her from behind, turning the edges of her silhouette into pure radiance. The wind picked up softly, catching the chiffon layers of her dress, making the fabric dance and float around her. The embroidered flowers on her gown seemed to cascade like a waterfall as she stood there.

She was ethereal. She was a vision of grace and survival.

"Makes me wanna lose myself in your arms..."

Allie's breath hitched, a sob trapping itself in her chest. The tears fell freely now, unashamed. She watched Sofia's face… the gentle smile, her beautiful hazel eyes locked solely on her.

Sofia saw Allie waiting. She saw the tears, the love, the open vulnerability. She tightened her grip on her mother's arm for a moment before stepping forward.

Every step down that aisle was a step away from the pain of the past. Every step was a declaration. She wasn't walking toward a wedding… she was walking toward her life. She was walking toward the safety, the passion, and the peace she had fought so hard to keep.

"There's something in your voice, makes my heart beat fast... Hope this feeling lasts, the rest of my life..."

Sofia reached the altar. Blanca kissed her daughter, placing Sofia's hand into Allie's.

When their skin touched, the circuit closed. The trembling stopped.

They stood under the arch of crystals and flowers, surrounded by the twinkling lights of the ancient oaks, two women who had been broken by the world and had rebuilt themselves with pieces of each other.

Allie looked deep into Sofia's eyes, seeing the reflection of her own soul. There were no words needed for what passed between them in that silence. It was a profound, heavy, beautiful truth.

They had not just survived the storm. They had become the shelter.

As the sun dipped below the horizon, casting the world in a twilight glow, they stood together… Allie, Sofia, and the little boy watching from the front row. The darkness had tried to take them, but love…fierce, unyielding, and patient… had proven to be the only thing that truly mattered.

They were finally, perfectly, home.

Epilogue

Final Justice: The State of Texas vs. McCoy & Miller

The Austin Chronicle – Judicial Briefs April 12, 2025

In a landmark case that has shaken the Texas Hill Country, Judge Sarah H. Vance has handed down the final sentencing in the McCoy conspiracy.

- **Joshua McCoy:** Found guilty on all counts of Aggravated Sexual Assault and Attempted Murder. Due to the high-profile nature of the case and the severity of the victim's injuries, he has been sentenced to **life in prison with no possibility of parole.**
- **Thomas McCoy:** Found guilty of Obstruction of Justice, Conspiracy to Commit Murder, and multiple counts of Bribery. The "King of Fredericksburg" saw his empire dismantled as the court seized assets totaling over **$40 million** to be placed into a trust for victims of sexual violence. He has been sentenced to **35 years** in a maximum-security facility.
- **Daniel Miller:** Forfeited his badge and pension. He received a 20-year sentence for Official Misconduct and Evidence Tampering.

Reports indicate that **Eleanor McCoy**, the primary whistle-blower in the case, has officially dropped the McCoy name and reverted to her maiden name, Eleanor Powell. She has moved out of the Hill Country estate, which is currently slated for auction.

* * *

The Shelter

The house was quiet aside from the low hum of the baby monitor.

Sofia stood in the doorway of the nursery, her wedding ring catching the dim glow of the nightlight. She was no longer wearing the white chiffon gown; she was in a soft, worn-out t-shirt and shorts, the "bride" replaced by the "mother." Inside the crib, Phoenix was a small, warm bundle of dreams, his chest rising and falling in perfect peace.

A pair of strong arms wrapped around her waist from behind. Allie leaned her chin on Sofia's shoulder, her breath warm against her neck.

"He's finally out," Allie whispered, her voice thick with the exhaustion of a beautiful day.

Sofia leaned back into her wife, closing her eyes. "He fought the sleep as long as he could. Just like his Mom."

Allie chuckled, a low, vibrating sound. She reached out and took Sofia's hand, lacing their fingers together. "The news came through today. It's official. The sentencing is done. It's over, Sof. They're never coming back."

Sofia took a deep breath, expecting to feel a surge of anger or a tremor of fear. But there was nothing. No fire, no ice.

Just a calm, flat emptiness where the McCoys used to live. They had become small. Irrelevant.

"I know," Sofia said, turning in Allie's arms to face her. She looked at the woman who had stood between her and the world, the woman who had helped her build a cathedral out of ashes. "But they've been gone for a long time. They didn't even cross my mind during the vows."

Allie smiled, her ocean eyes soft. "Good. Because they don't get a single second of our 'forever.'"

They stood there for a long moment, watching their son… the living proof that love… does in fact… win. Then, Allie led Sofia away from the nursery, toward their own bed, their own life, and the first night of a future they had fought like hell to earn.

Behind them, the little oatmeal-colored rabbit sat tucked in the corner of the crib, a silent witness to a war that was finally, truly, over.

THE END

About the Author

Hi. I'm Crystal Lopez, a wandering soul raised by the Texas heat, now settled among the peaceful lakes of Minnesota. As a Native American, lesbian, and trauma survivor, my stories are born from the fragments of truth I've gathered along this journey called life. I write about surviving the things meant to break us and finally discovering the kind of love that truly heals. *Silencing Sofia* is my debut novel and the first book in the *Of Shadows and Silence* trilogy, written for the heart that isn't afraid of the dark, and for the soul that's still searching for the light. I am currently hard at work on book two. When I'm not writing, I'm usually spending time with my wife, Savannah, and our son, Aspen.

You can connect with me on:

- https://www.authorcrystallopez.com
- https://x.com/CLopezBooks
- https://www.facebook.com/authorcrystallopez